Alice beyond Wonderland

ALICE *beyond* WONDERLAND

essays for the twenty-first century

edited by Cristopher Hollingsworth

foreword by Karoline Leach

UNIVERSITY OF IOWA PRESS IOWA CITY

University of Iowa Press, Iowa City 52242

www.uipress.uiowa.edu
Printed in the United States of America
Design by Sara T. Sauers

The University of Iowa Press is a member of Green Press Initiative and is committed to preserving natural resources.

Printed on acid-free paper

Library of Congress Cataloging-in-Publication Data
Alice beyond wonderland: essays for the twenty-first century / edited by Cristopher Hollingsworth; foreword by Karoline Leach.
p. cm.
Includes bibliographical references and index.
ISBN 978-1-58729-819-6 (cloth)
ISBN 978-1-60938-513-2 (paperback)
1. Carroll, Lewis, 1832–1898. Alice's adventures in Wonderland. 2. Children's stories, English—History and criticism. 3. Fantasy fiction, English—History and criticism. I. Hollingsworth, Cristopher, 1961–
PR4611.A73A37 2009 2009012913
823'.8—dc22

To Debra

Contents

Foreword

This collection of essays is one of the first to emerge since Carroll scholarship was "galvanized" by the emergence of what we now call the Carroll Myth. As such, it is an interesting way marker. Until recently, an almost perfect consensus reigned in Carroll scholarship; Carroll/Dodgson was considered explained, diagnosed, his strange life an open book with little about it that was either deep or mysterious. He was the shy and virginal clergyman who stumbled into genius through intense love of a child; the man with no life, whose transparent, barely registered existence held only one story: that of his tragic but ultimately innocent deviancy, his ultimate failure to engage with adulthood. The belief amounted to an axiom, an unquestioned truth all adhered to; and as a result biographical and literary investigation was almost nil. In contrast to other comparable literary disciplines, debate was sparse and the spectrum of opinion extraordinarily narrow. There was no perceived need to look for new answers, since all was presumed known and understood.

The biographical image of "Carroll" was developed from and inhabited the world of intuition and legend, *sans* hard evidence, because hard evidence was for a long time unavailable and afterward considered of secondary importance to known truths. For a century, Charles Dodgson was viewed and described within an isolation field that separated him from his contemporaries, the past, the future, and even most of his own life, and was defined by "strangeness." Everything he did or said was regarded as essentially quaint, prim, or deviant simply because *he* said or did it. And in place of analysis, the Myth itself began a process of evolution, and intuition, guesswork, or even individual imagination became—however much we strenuously deny it—acceptable tools for developing understanding. Alice Liddell was, for example, routinely cited as synonymous with "Alice" the dreamchild, and this was then used as biographical evidence that Dodgson was obsessed with the girl, even though Dodgson himself repeatedly stated that his "Alice" and

Alice Liddell were entirely separate entities ("my dreamchild, named after a real Alice but nonetheless a dreamchild"; Carroll, "Marriage"). In similar vein, his child photography was—for many still is—seen as a substitute for the sexual act, and not as a product of the artistic age in which he lived; no more—or less—a "pursuit of innocents" than Rejlander's or Cameron's. He was routinely presented as a man who avoided adult relationships, even though his women friends dominated large sections of his life and were a primary source of pleasure for him and sometimes a scandal for his society. Sometimes the prism of this mythic image could truly turn light back upon itself and make black into white. One biographer confronted by the reality of Dodgson's own words on the subject of remarriage after divorce or widowhood metamorphosed them into their diametrical opposite. This is what Dodgson actually said: "those who object to all remarriage, even after the death of a husband or wife, take a view that seems to me at variance with scripture as well as with common sense" (Carroll, "Marriage"); but this is what appeared in the biography: "Dodgson's personal code of conduct was so strict, that, while sympathetic to those who felt otherwise, he himself considered widowers were wrong to remarry" (Clark 147).

More suitable to the image of "Carroll" undoubtedly. But an entire reversal of anything Dodgson ever actually said. In an only slightly less dramatic example, his reaction to Ellen Terry's scandalous elopement[1] was presented as a symptom of his unrelenting primness, as if he alone had chosen to stop associating with her, even though it is quite evident from even casual reading that Terry was rejected by Society en masse, and even her own sister kept her at a distance until she became a "decent" married woman again. When Dodgson refused to see her socially, he was only doing what his class and social milieu dictated, not—as we were constantly told—expressing his overwhelming prudishness, and Dodgson's subsequent comments on Terry's conduct make it clear that he did not condemn her anywhere near as much as his society expected him to do. "I do not allow that her case resembled at all that of those poor women who, without any pretence of love, sell themselves to the first comer. It much more resembles the case of those many women who are living as faithfully and devotedly as lawful wives without having gone through any ceremony and who are, I believe, married in God's sight, though not in man's," he told Mrs. Baird in 1894 (Carroll, *Letters* 1015–6). This is not the prim and nervous "Carroll," but it *is* Dodgson. But this easily obtainable truth had no impact on the mythic presentation of the incident in his biography.

In the same vein of unconscious reinvention, the well-respected Martin Gardner, in his preface to the Dover edition of *Sylvie and Bruno*, makes the assumption that the beautiful heroine of the novel, Lady Muriel Orme, is modeled on (who else?) Alice Liddell, and bolsters this claim by observing: "In a letter to Furniss [Dodgson's illustrator], Carroll says he [Arthur, the hero of the novel] is 'forty at least' . . . Lady Muriel Orme . . . is about 21, almost exactly as much younger than Arthur as Alice Liddell was younger than Carroll" (xii). Nothing wrong with that you might think—until you look at what Dodgson actually wrote to Furniss, which was a complaint about Furniss's illustration of Arthur making the hero look "too old: Arthur won't do at all! . . . He is forty at least. I want him to be about twenty five . . . capable of being a passionate lover" (Collingwood 260). It's entirely obvious from this—and indeed is stated clearly in the body of the novel—that Muriel is not intended by Dodgson to be "almost exactly as much younger than Arthur as Alice Liddell was younger than Carroll." In fact she and Arthur were intended to be contemporaries of near the same age. How do we explain Gardner's total misconception other than by assuming that for Gardner, as for most commentators before the emergence of awareness of the Myth, the "Carroll" of legend and biography, in whom all things lead to Alice Liddell, was simply more real than the real words that Dodgson himself wrote down? Gardner, arch opponent of all things belief-driven and antirational, was himself in the grip of a deep and highly nonrational belief system: the faith in "Carroll." We can assume Dodgson would have approved the irony.

Not only biographers have engaged in this reinvention. Even those who knew Dodgson seem to have been drawn into the need to remake him as "Carroll," even to the extent of entirely reinventing their own personal experience. Examples are legion, and I cite several in the latest edition of *In the Shadow of the Dreamchild*. Here let's look at the curious case of John Martin-Harvey.

Martin-Harvey was an actor-manager of the 1890s. In 1889 he married Nellie DaSilva, an actress who had at one time been a "child friend" of Dodgson. A few years later he met Dodgson himself in Eastbourne. His story is interesting. Writing in 1933, just after the centenary of Dodgson's birth, Martin-Harvey told a vivid tale of his wife's childhood involvement with Lewis Carroll, and followed this up with a description of a later visit made by himself and grown-up Nellie to Dodgson's lodgings in Eastbourne, where Dodgson showed them photos, and—says Martin-Harvey—confided his "intense aversion" to the theater. "We could not induce him to visit the theatre . . . he was strange, and I thought quite unreasonable on this subject" (Cohen, *Lewis Carroll* 185–6). This is truly bizarre. As anyone who has studied Dodgson's life could tell, Dodgson was devoted to the stage throughout his entire adult life, was constantly visiting theaters and seeing plays, and counted some very celebrated actresses among his child and woman friends. And Martin-Harvey must have known this perfectly well, because his first encounter with Dodgson had been *at* the Lyceum Theatre, where Dodgson had just been to see a show and was going backstage to visit his friend the famous actress Ellen Terry. Not only this, but the very day before Martin-Harvey and his wife visited him for a second time in Eastbourne, Dodgson had attended the Devonshire Park theater to see Martin-Harvey's own company playing a triple bill, and the day following, Dodgson actually wrote to Martin-Harvey and asked him to come visit again and bring another actress from the company with him.

It's clear from this that Martin-Harvey cannot have believed—in 1894—that Dodgson had an aversion to the theater. Yet by 1933, when he wrote his memoir, he had apparently come to believe it completely, and even "remembered" how "strange" he had thought it all was. Presumably he unconsciously reconstructed his own experience because extreme austerity was more in keeping with the "truth" of the Carroll Myth. And he was far from being alone. As I have shown in my book, many, many cases can be cited of people who knew Dodgson well radically realigning their own personal experience away from documented reality and toward the expectation of the burgeoning "Carroll."

Now, ten years on from the first discussion of the Myth as a concept, the elderly and specious image of the nervous clergyman, afraid of adulthood and adult experience, spending his nonlife in lonely unrequited love for a succession of small girls, has begun to give way to the historical reality on which proper analysis can begin. I'm hopeful that in the future Dodgson will start to take precedence over "Carroll," and we'll begin to explore the mature, secretive man, the friend of Maurice and Rossetti, the lover of Swinburne's erotic poetry, the frequenter of theaters; the man whose friendships with women brought him joy and scandal, who believed in the supremacy of love and beauty, whose life was riven by religious questions and a brief intense guilt that came near to unhinging him. His anomalous relationship with the female, from angel child to mature seductress, his guilt, his religious questings, his apparent inward dichotomies, his manifold contradictions—these are the realities that underpin his genius, his mystery, and any study of his life and work that wants to be taken seriously must henceforth begin to recognize them, deal with them, explore and explain them. Unlike the lives of Thackeray, Dickens, Trollope, and Rossetti, Dodgson's life is still a largely unworked seam. In a sense, after 110 years, his biography is still waiting to be written. And, beyond that, the social and psychological processes at work in the comprehensive readjustment of memory into myth have as much to tell psychologists and behaviorists as biographers and historians. It's of course not an isolated phenomenon, but it is an extreme and therefore illuminating example.

Not only is a radical revision of the accepted biography essential, but study of the myth-making process itself can tell us so much—perhaps more than we are comfortable knowing—about the way we construct our societal and individual realities.

—*Karoline Leach*

NOTE

1. Ellen Terry (1847–1928) was, as child and adult, one of Britain's most popular female actors. She was especially admired for her Shakespeare roles and famous for her complicated love life. While married to James Frederick Watts, her first husband, Terry took up with Edward William Godwin, eventually bearing him two children out of wedlock. —Ed.

WORKS CITED

Carroll, Lewis. Ed. Morton N. Cohen, *The Letters of Lewis Carroll.* Vol. 2. London: Macmillan, 1979.

——. "Marriage Service." Unpublished essay, 1877. Harcourt Amory Collection, Harvard University.

——. *Sylvie and Bruno.* New York: Dover, 1988.

Clark, Anne. *Lewis Carroll.* London: J. M. Dent, 1979.

Cohen, Morton N., ed. *Lewis Carroll: Interviews and Recollections.* Iowa City: University of Iowa Press, 1989.

Collingwood, Stuart Dodgson. *The Life and Letters of Lewis Carroll.* London: T. Fisher Unwin, 1898.

Leach, Karoline. *In the Shadow of the Dreamchild: A New Understanding of Lewis Carroll.* London: Peter Owen, 1999.

Acknowledgments

I wish to thank Debra Roy and Ronald Christ for their generous counsel, sharp minds and pencils, and belief in this book and the Wonderland project. Without the support and patience of Holly Carver, Joseph Parsons, and Charlotte Wright of the University of Iowa Press, this collection would not have seen print. I am grateful for the comments that helped me to shape such a protean subject, and I deeply appreciate Karoline Leach's and Rudy Rucker's interest in this collection. T. M. and F. M. Face, thank you.

Cristopher Hollingsworth

Introduction

> I had of course always known *Alice in Wonderland*, but to me Alice and the White Rabbit and the Red Queen—and the Dormouse and the Mad Hatter and the Cheshire Cat—were endowed with all the vitality and reality and being of an age-old myth; and how they had managed to get into a book was really neither here nor there.
> —ETHEL M. ROWELL, "To Me He Was Mr. Dodgson"

> The present epoch will perhaps be above all the epoch of space. We are in the epoch of simultaneity: we are in the epoch of juxtaposition, the epoch of the near and far, of the side-by-side, of the dispersed. We are at a moment, I believe, when our experience of the world is less that of a long life developing through time than that of a network that connects points and intersects with its own skein. . . .
>
> The space in which we live, which draws us out of ourselves, in which the erosion of our lives, our time and our history occurs, the space that claws and gnaws at us, is also, in itself, a heterogeneous space.
> —MICHEL FOUCAULT, "Of Other Spaces"

The World as Wonderland: A Spatial Perspective on Lewis Carroll's *Alice* Books

It is fitting that Karoline Leach's voice leads this collection of new essays on Lewis Carroll, his *Alice* books, and Wonderland. Leach is the author of the groundbreaking and, to some, heretical *In the Shadow of the Dreamchild: A New Understanding of Lewis Carroll*. This 1999 study, recently updated and reissued, identifies and challenges the "Carroll Myth," a view of Lewis Carroll/Charles Lutwidge Dodgson as, in Leach's words, "the shy and virginal clergyman who stumbled into genius through intense love of a child." Carroll and his admirers together cultivated the myth of Saint Carroll, which to this day remains good for business and ornaments many a sunny garden of children's literature. After Freudians publicized the garden's abundant fruit (even better for business), our Saint, sexualized to fit a hipper, corset-and-riding-crop view of the Victorians, acquired his scandalous doppelganger.

The collective imagination loves twins and to tweedle: it happily engenders and vigorously employs antitheses of every stripe. Contraries mean conflict; doubles disturb and delight with their uncanny implications of the Other and other worlds. Sister universes: In classic Wonderland, Alice enjoys perfect weather, creatures, and conversations; meets the royals; and even becomes a queen. In the long shadows of gothic Wonderland, observed by a grinning cat's head, the Saint's dark twin trolls for little girls.

Despite the continued growth of Carroll studies, including scrupulously documented investigations of Carroll's photographic oeuvre and his lifelong interest in the theater, the Carroll Myth continues its largely unexamined reign as the convenient truth of one Victorian professor's soul and the key to his life and works. And on the conference circuit, the appetite for evidence of Victorian perversion is about the same this century as in the last. Subtly here, stridently there, the Myth colors interpretation, channeling thought, shaping argument.

A figure like Shakespeare or Milton generates a cultural and intellectual industry so large and complex that no one myth may dominate for very long, if at all. This is not the case with Carroll studies, which is a new and limited field. As a scholar and teacher of Carroll's books, his influence, and aspects of the cultural system that I call the "Carroll complex," I have come to the opinion that the debate over about whether Charles Lutwidge Dodgson was nasty or nice is a distraction from his most consequential creation, Wonderland—not the storybook place posited by Carroll's Victorian texts but, rather, what we have made of and with this space. The future of Carroll studies, if it is to have a future that is relevant and interesting to persons outside a cadre of area specialists, acknowledges but is not centered on Carroll's life, texts, or milieu. Yes, of course, Carroll's *Alice* books are important subjects of study, both as texts and products (and, if need be, symptoms) of a specific moment in Victorian culture. It is commonly observed and easily verified that these texts are widely quoted and translated. However, as Michael Hancher observes, Alice no longer "needs books [and their readers] to survive. She has escaped her narration and her narrator" (202). Hancher continues:

> The dreamlike, episodic structure of both books, the heavily charged psychological subtext, and the explicit privileging of pictorial illustra-

> tion, have from the start led her [Alice's] audiences to register her story in terms of character, scene, myth, and image, rather than of plot, narrative voice, or (save for some memorable phrases) diction. . . . *Alice* is a happily overdetermined and polymorphous text. It thrives in an indefinite number of forms, which amalgamate differently in the experience of each viewer, hearer, and reader, old or young. The threatened disintegration of Alice's personal identity in Wonderland prefigures her actual dispersal, and renewal, among her audiences. (202)

Although Hancher grants individual readers too much interpretative autonomy and undercuts some of his argument's most powerful implications by exaggerating Alice's textual and extratextual importance, he helpfully identifies a significant relationship between the form of Carroll's Victorian texts, their audiences' responses, and a subtending and evolving cultural complex of episodes and images, fragments and echoes, allusions and retellings and commentary. Whatever was "in" Carroll's books has been free and busy in the wider world for some time.

The *Alice* books, the Carroll Myth, and indeed Alice herself and her story—the narrative of Alice's adventures that has become in the collective imagination a "large controlling image that gives philosophical meaning to the facts of ordinary life" (Watt 232), as well as the fruits of popularization in various media and academic scholarship—constitute the Wonderland complex. I mean the word "complex" much as *Webster's Third New International Dictionary* does: "an association of related things . . . in intricate combination." Such an association can be cultural (a group of focused traits, activities, processes, or artifacts, including architectural structures). The word also has psychological implications: "a system of repressed or suppressed desires and memories that exerts a dominating influence on the personality"; moreover, it connotes intellectual mystery: "a group of obviously related units . . . of which the degree and the nature of the relationship is imperfectly known." The Wonderland complex may be defined, then, as an intricate and imperfectly known cultural system, having important psychological and expressive implications, and organized around the "story space" of Wonderland.

Differences in conceptual magnitude and density necessitate a distinction between the larger, distributed, and abstract Wonderland complex and the story space of Wonderland, the complex's more stable, composite "core" that is made of Alice's narrative of adventures and the unique, heterogeneous space of Wonderland. From a (Kenneth) Burkean perspective, Alice's narrative is a series of iterations of the same *act* (unexpected contact with a narratively inconsequential and minor [antisublime] wonder). Alice's *act*ion of falling into, inadvertently confronting, a wonder is "consubstantial" (sharing the same substance) with the *scene* in which it occurs:[1] Wonderland. Because it is simultaneously both unknown and abstract (a space) and familiar and homely (a place) (Tuan 3–6), this uniquely unpredictable and heterogeneous imaginary world is widely understood and used as a theory and practical element of thinking and expression.

Wonderland may be used in argument, as when a proposition or institutional logic is described as "Alice-in-Wonderland thinking." This common redaction of Wonderland is not, however, simply a way of saying "X = nonsense": it is a literary relative of the Aristotelian common topoi, building blocks of reasoning such as "argument by degree" and "cause and effect." Both of these common topoi require imaginative staging, visualization in the mind's eye. In contrast, the literary topos Wonderland, since it invokes a specific imaginary space (and has the potential to function as a world metaphor) defined by variety, surprise, nonsense, surrealism, and/or inversion and reversal, more powerfully arouses and involves *both* the imagination's spatial and reasoning faculties.[2] No simple allusion to a popular Victorian children's book, the use of Wonderland in argument, as in the example above, or as a structural or world-building schema in imaginative literature, to one degree or another involves a text and its audience with Wonderland spaces.

What other story space is quite like this one, unfolding with an elusive, improvisational necessity—punctuated, mind you, by disjunctive movements from one discrete space to another? To illustrate: (1) Alice sees and follows a clothed, talking rabbit that consults a watch [episode 1, space 1]. (2) She follows the rabbit down a hole, falling in slow motion down a commodious and furnished shaft [episode 2, space 2]. (3) She has size-altering adventures in a large hallway complete with a miniature doorway into a garden, a glass table, and a magic key and consumables [episode 3, space 3]. (4) She must swim in a deep pool of her own tears, along with a crowd of large, sentient animals [episode 4]. (5) Alice converses and plays a game with the animals [episode 5]. (6) After the animals leave, Alice hears footsteps. It's the White Rabbit searching for his fan and gloves. To be helpful, she starts looking for them herself and notices that "everything seemed to have changed since her swim in the pool; and the great hall with the glass table and the little door, had vanished completely" (Carroll, *Alice's Adventures* 27) [episode 6, space 4]. As befits a story composed with no plan and "made up almost wholly of bits and scraps" (Carroll, "*Alice* on the Stage" 281), the local narrative relationships between these five episodes are sketchy and whimsical; the same goes for the rest of the book. Moreover, the narrative and spatial vagaries and disjunctions of the Looking-Glass World of *Through the Looking-Glass* are even more extreme, despite the chess-game plot.

Because the differences between a realistic story space and Carroll's are stark, and thus simplifying, Wonderland's uniqueness is better gauged by comparing it with other frankly imaginative worlds that foreground the category of space. In *Gulliver's Travels*, specific creatures and aspects of Lilliput, England, and Brobdingnag form an exponential series of magnitude: 1, 10, 100. Though the dimensions of people and things in Gulliver's narrative may vary, space and time are consistently Newtonian, as unchanging as Swift's view of human nature. Stranger than any land visited by Gulliver is that described by Edwin A. Abbott in his novel *Flatland*. Yet, though this universe radically differs from our own (it has no dimension of height/thickness), this difference is presented as a consistent principle, an "axiom" whose implications profoundly and predictably shape the narrative and serve several didactic purposes. When Rudy Rucker, in the science fiction novel *Postsingular*, describes different dimensions, radical alterity is systematic. For example, our familiar "Lobrane" universe is six times smaller, denser, and faster than the "Hibrane" universe, a difference that may be computed and understood with the help of the "orphidnet" (a super Internet) and its self-generating and organizing artificial intelligences (65–92). Of these four story spaces—and despite the fact that, like Abbott and Rucker, Carroll was a mathematician—Carroll's is the least predictable, the most spatially and ontologically variegated.

The tension at the heart of Carroll's *Alices*, in Marshall McLuhan's view, involves the elemental stuff of space and time. Wonderland is where universes of the human imagination grapple, merge and mutate, and are born. Into the

> uniform Euclidean world of continuous space-and-time, Carroll drove a fantasia of discontinuous space-and-time that anticipated Kafka, Joyce, and Eliot. Carroll, the mathematical contemporary of Clerk Maxwell, was quite *avant-garde* enough to know about the non-Euclidean geometries coming into vogue in his time. He gave the confident Victorians a playful foretaste of Einsteinian time-and-space in *Alice in Wonderland*. Bosch had provided his era a foretaste of the

> new continuous time-and-space of uniform perspective. Bosch looked ahead to the modern world with horror, as Shakespeare did in *King Lear*, and as Pope did in *The Dunciad*. But Lewis Carroll greeted the electronic age of space-time with a cheer. (McLuhan 162)

The texts of the *Alice* books are incompatible with—indeed, actively oppositional to—reason, consistency, and, therefore, a singular and unifying perspective, such as that offered by the Carroll Myth. In this light, if we are to understand a cultural construction on the order of the Wonderland complex, our approach must be bold, inclusive, and experimental.

The Path to Wonderland

Alice's story is the proper fable for this "epoch of space," for our space-and-time rich, technologically involved lives. I therefore have organized this collection of new essays on Carroll, Wonderland, and space to accord with the opening arc of *Alice's Adventures*, a defining movement from the mundane to the wonderful that is known to nearly everyone. This arc is the type for (post)modernity's headlong and surprising evolution from a culture in many ways built on print and the printed book, thus worshiping the literary *objet d'art*, to the image- and movement-saturated matrix of the present.

Alice looks into her older sister's book and finds it boring. She asks herself (and us readers, as we are listening—listening with twenty-first-century ears), "What is the use of a book . . . without pictures [visual and spatial copia] or conversations [vocal and verbal interconnection and simultaneity]?" (*Alice's Adventures* 7). Then she sees and hears the White Rabbit, who just so happens to be in a thoroughly modern pickle, complete with the appropriate gesture involving a complex, portable machine: he is late, so he consults his timepiece. Therefore, however one chooses to interpret Alice's defining movement from A to B, from boring book to Wonderland, or from waking to sleeping, or from innocence to knowledge, this arc of action involves the passing of time and the consequences of this passing: preparation for a shift from one space-time to another, the first of a cascade of such movements.

As I have mentioned, the three topics of this collection—literature, image, and culture—are arranged to suggest a trajectory from the known into the unknown, from the relatively stable pastness of a storybook place to the dynamism of a cultural complex. This schema should not, however, be construed as defining the texts that I have grouped under each heading.

What follows is a sketch of each section that suggests how I see its contents fitting together. As editor, I have balanced thematic emphasis with a desire to see what is out there: I have kept my net wide and my mind open, asking for—and receiving—a fascinating range of original thinking about the spaces of Wonderland.

Literature

Though my "path to Wonderland" treats narrative literature as old-fashioned, the five texts gathered under this rubric are anything but. They are unified by a refreshing conceptual hybridity that bears critical fruit: each is rooted in the familiar ground of literary production and criticism, while at the same time engaged with Wonderland in the context of one or more ideas of space. Rachel Falconer, an experienced traveler in literary spaces, in "Underworld Portmanteaux: Dante's Hell and Carroll's Wonderland in Women's Memoirs of Mental Illness" investigates the pairing of Dantean and Carrollian underworlds in women's autopathographies, such as Marya Hornbacher's *Wasted*, Susanna Kaysen's *Girl, Interrupted*, and several semi-fictional memoirs. In these narratives of young women searching for meaning and survival, Dante's highly structured space is predominantly masculine and institutional; Carroll's offers a feminine and more psychologically responsive alternative order and symbol system.

Christine Roth investigates another social, literary, and spatial dyad, adulthood/childhood. In "Looking through the Spyglass: Lewis Carroll, James Barrie, and the Empire of Childhood," Roth argues that, increasingly through the Victorian era, adulthood and childhood became separate, even as British culture became progressively burdened by the conduct and consequences of colonialism and empire. This new historical context in turn stimulated and shaped the "golden age" of British children's literature. Writers like Lewis Carroll and J. M. Barrie "conceived of children as mediators between the spaces of childhood and adulthood, creating . . . child characters who are not as much natives as double agents, of sorts," in untamed invented lands. Like the exotic scenes described in nineteenth-century travel narratives pouring in from around the empire, Carroll's and Barrie's fictions blend nostalgic visions of "long ago" and "far away." As a result, writes Roth, "the looking glasses and windows of the children's stories take on the imperialistic, voyeuristic, and objectifying underpinnings of the spyglass."

The idea that classic children's literature uses ideas of space to articulate a confluence of and a conflict between spatially articulated discourses also informs Elizabeth Throesch's "Nonsense in the Fourth Dimension of Literature: Hyperspace Philosophy, the 'New' Mathematics, and the *Alice* Books." Foundational aspects of Carroll's nonsense and Wonderland itself, Throesch argues, are the product of Carroll's critical engagement with new developments in geometry and algebra, including "hyperspace philosophy," which posits and explores the existence and nature of the fourth dimension. Throesch argues that Carroll and the nineteenth-century philosopher Charles Howard Hinton share common ground through the trope of hypostatization, the "literalization of abstractions." Beyond confirming McLuhan's principle that spatial hypertrophy in art signifies a struggle between worldviews, Throesch's investigation places Carroll and his best-known books in a new context, enriching our understanding of Carrollian poetic and motive.

In nonfiction works such as *Mind Tools* and novels including *Spaceland* and *Postsingular*, Rudy Rucker, too, amplifies and challenges our thinking about Carroll and space. Responding to questions asked by Steve Hooley and me, Rucker discusses his early exposure to the *Alice* books, their presence in popular culture, and their influence on his thought and art. Most interesting to me is what Rucker's answers reveal about the way his mind works: the precision, quickness, and creative boldness of his thinking suggest parallels to the power and quality of Carroll's imagination. When asked by Hooley if he plans how he will use Carroll in a given work, Rucker replies, "I think that Carroll's images have permanently infested my mind, and that they pop out unexpectedly." In this sense we are all like Rucker, happily infested by Carroll and his Wonderland, a story space that, in Rucker's words, "continue[s] to celebrate the gnarliness and unpredictability of the individual mind."[3]

Though I doubt Carol Mavor would think of herself as a "gnarly" thinker, her essay's knotty complexity and improvisational qualities suggest this same Carrollian capacity to astonish. "Alicious Objects: Believing in Six Impossible Things before Breakfast, or Reading *Alice* Nostologically" is an act of literary criticism, an academically valuable interpretation of Carroll's *Alice* books from the perspective of age instead of youth. Through Mavor's lens, the White Queen and her memory problems are shown to be as important as Alice's youthful struggle with identity. The essay is also frankly creative, in some respects the application of Carroll's mixed-media, scrapbook poetic to the form of the essay and the space of memory. Mavor's voice is a prominent character in this particular Wonderland; its wonders are memories and original associations, such as the recollection of Disney's colorful singing flowers and the constellation of Carroll's use of the term "white stone" in his journals with stones and the remembered past in Ruskin, Proust, and Woolf.

Image

Carroll's photographs and Carroll the photographer are increasingly common topics among scholars, as the products and practices of the Victorian "black art" help situate Carroll in his milieu and suggest connections between Carroll's perspective and our own. My essay, "Improvising Spaces: Victorian Photography, Carrollian Narrative, and Modern Collage," treats Carroll's *Alices* as an outgrowth of, on the one hand, his youthful experiments with scrapbook magazines and, on the other, his actual photographic practice as an adult, which involved telling and illustrating improvised stories to children and mastering the intrinsically episodic and performative art of the Victorian photo album. I explore the possibility that the unique structure of his *Alice* books anticipates the expressive logic of what Hannah Höch calls "photomatter," a thoroughly modern aesthetic of surprise and insight arising from the juxtaposition of disparate photographic images and spaces.

Stephen Monteiro, author of "Lovely Gardens and Dark Rooms: Alice, the Queen, and the Spaces of Photography," approaches Carroll as an amateur art photographer, who worked against and yet imbibed the conventional social gestures and meanings of the *carte-de-visite*. Wonderland and the Looking-Glass World feature numerous situations that, Monteiro argues, recall and satirize aspects of the *carte-de-visite* style. Moreover, Monteiro discovers in the way Carroll photographed children a tension between technologically enabled reality and theatrical fantasy that sheds light on Carroll's written poetic and the space of Wonderland. More radical still is Monteiro's suggestion that the *Alices* may be read as an album of images that chronicles the progress of the protomodernist subject.

In "Photographic Wonderland: Intermediality and Identity in Lewis Carroll's *Alice* Books," Franz Meier also discovers and details a connection between Carroll's moment and our own. Meier does so, however, through a close analysis of the latent influence of photography on the illustrated text of the *Alice* books. Through attending to "'implicit' intermedial connections," Meier exposes an "intricate subtext referring to photography." Even more significant is the argument that this subtext creates a "photographic space" capable of staging "surprisingly modern experiences . . . and questions of identity." The uniqueness and indeed the survival and astounding popularity of *Alice's Adventures* and *Through the Looking-Glass*, Meier argues, may all be seen as issuing from Carroll challenging and enriching a conventional, linear narrative with an intrinsically atemporal photographic aesthetic and perspective. The product is a space that makes a special appeal to our media-drenched subjectivities.

Mou-Lan Wong, too, emphasizes the role of images in the reader's experience. But where Meier tracks Wonderland's photographic subtext, Wong's "Generations of Re-generation: Re-creating Wonderland through Text, Illustrations, and the Reader's Hands" focuses on John Tenniel's illustrations and their studied placement in and interdependence with Carroll's text. Wong's analysis both illuminates the *Alice* books in their Victorian contexts and helps explain their survival and amazing popularity. But the uniqueness of Wong's argument lies in its attention to "how Carroll assembles layers of visual and verbal interplay around the imagery of hands"; this is a technique that stimulates and involves the reader's mind and (implicitly) his or her hands—the entire organism—in a highly spatial story-telling experience. Wong's investigation urges us to reexamine what we mean by reading and to number reader-text interactivity among Carroll's many artistic accomplishments.

Culture

These three essays suggest farther (but by no means the farthest) reaches of Wonderland, which continues to expand as translations, adaptations, and mutations of the *Alices* spread through popular and world culture. Anne Witchard's work on Carroll's child photography and late Victorian chinoiserie demonstrates that we still have much to learn about reading Wonderland as an aspect of Carroll's full and marvelously varied life and his own cultural milieu. In "Chinoiserie Wonderlands of the Fin de Siècle: Twinkletoes in Chinatown," Witchard argues that Carroll's children's fiction and especially his photographs of children are informed by the theatrical space of London's East End orientalist theater. Of special note are Witchard's careful historical linkages between several of Carroll's most famous child photographs and chinoiserie props. In this light, the eroticism that the Carroll Myth simplifies and erroneously transforms into Carroll's private obsession is more accurately treated as a matter of public display and debate.

In "Body as Wonderland: Alice's Graphic Iteration in *Lost Girls*," Helen Pilinovsky investigates the twentieth century's increasing sexualization of Alice and Wonderland. Pilinovsky discusses what she calls Alice's "maturation" narrative (the third of three types of Alice retellings), which "is based in an uneasy fascination with the circumstances surrounding the composition of her [Alice's] original story and the myth of her relationship with Lewis Carroll." Part survey of cultural history and part lesson in how the Carroll Myth has become a generative fact of contemporary Wonderland, Pilinovsky's argument culminates in an analysis of Alan Moore and Melinda Gebbie's controversial *Lost Girls* that features the graphic novel's cultural context.

The principle that culture is key to understanding Wonderland is further and richly demonstrated by Sean Somers's "Arisu in Harajuku: Yagawa Sumiko's Wonderland as Translation, Theory, and Performance." There have been many translations of Carroll's *Alice* books into Japanese, Somers observes, but of them Yagawa Sumiko's exerts the most influence over the performed identity of the *Gosu-Rori*, the Gothic-Lolita "subculture of neo-Victorian enthusiasts." Yagawa's Wonderland is a realm of *fushigi*, a word that, among other things, signifies mystery, wonder, and enchantment. The *fushigi* of Wonderland transforms Alice, reasons the *Gosu-Rori*, and therefore this story space has the power to transform us. It is through following Alice, reenacting her fearless journey through an unknown land, and using symbols of Wonderland to "refine oneself," that one meets other *Gosu-Rori*. In (by American lights) hierarchical and traditional Japanese society, Wonderland, loosed from its European origins and thereby transformed, has become a locus of community and a template for self and social reform. Indeed, as the essays in this collection demonstrate, far from being of the past and a passive subject of study, Wonderland is part of a shared cognitive and cultural horizon, an unfolding complex of spaces that has much to teach us about ourselves, our moment, and the *Lebenswelt* of the future.

NOTES

1. See the excerpts from Burke's *A Grammar of Motives* that appear in *The Rhetorical Tradition*, edited by Patricia Bizzell and Bruce Herzberg. Of particular relevance are "Introduction: The Five Key Terms of Dramatism" (Burke 992–1006) and "Scene: The Featuring of the Terms" (Burke 1016–18).
2. Edward P. J. Corbett's analysis of the topoi is a model of clarity. See his *Classical Rhetoric for the Modern Student*, 94–132. For a definition of the literary topos and its involvement with different types of literary/ideated space, see my *Poetics of the Hive*, 55–60.
3. In his essay "Seek the Gnarl," Rucker defines "gnarl" as a "level of complexity that lies in the zone between predictability and randomness" (2). He gives examples of gnarliness: "Clouds, fire, and water are gnarly in the sense of being beautifully intricate, with purposeful-looking but not quite comprehensible patterns. And of course all living things are gnarly, in that they inevitably do

things that are much more complex than one might have expected. The shapes of tree branches are the standard example of gnarl. The life cycle of a jellyfish is way gnarly. The wild three-dimensional paths that a humming-bird sweeps out are kind of gnarly too, and, if the truth be told, your ears are gnarly as well" (3).

WORKS CITED

Abbott, Edwin A. *Flatland: A Romance of Many Dimensions*. 5th ed., rev. New York: Harper and Row, 1983.

Burke, Kenneth. Excerpts from *A Grammar of Motives*. *The Rhetorical Tradition: Readings from Classical Traditions to the Present*. Ed. Patricia Bizzell and Bruce Herzberg. Boston: Bedford/St. Martin's Press, 1990. 992–1018.

Carroll, Lewis. *Alice's Adventures in Wonderland* and *Through the Looking-Glass and What Alice Found There*. *Alice in Wonderland*. Ed. Donald J. Gray. 2nd ed. New York: Norton, 1992. 1–209.

——. Excerpts from "*Alice* on the Stage." *Alice in Wonderland*. Ed. Donald J. Gray. 2nd ed. New York: Norton, 1992. 280–2.

Corbett, Edward P. J. *Classical Rhetoric for the Modern Student*. 3rd ed. New York: Oxford University Press, 1990.

Foucault, Michel. "Of Other Spaces." Trans. Jay Miskowiec. *Foucault.info*, n.d. Accessed 12 Dec. 2008.

Hancher, Michael. "Alice's Audiences." *Romanticism and Children's Literature in Nineteenth-Century England*. Ed. James Holt McGavran, Jr. Athens: University of Georgia Press, 1991. 190–207.

Hollingsworth, Cristopher. *Poetics of the Hive: The Insect Metaphor in Literature*. Iowa City: University of Iowa Press, 2001.

Leach, Karoline. *In the Shadow of the Dreamchild: A New Understanding of Lewis Carroll*. London: Peter Owen, 1999.

McLuhan, Marshall. *Understanding Media: The Extensions of Man*. New York: McGraw-Hill, 1965.

Rowell, Ethel M. "To Me He Was Mr. Dodgson." *Alice in Wonderland*. Ed. Donald J. Gray. 2nd ed. New York: Norton, 1992. 307–9.

Rucker, Rudy. *Mind Tools: The Five Levels of Mathematical Reality*. Boston: Houghton Mifflin, 1987.

——. *Postsingular*. New York: Tor Books, 2007.

——. "Seek the Gnarl," 4/2/2005. Rudyrucker.com, 2 Apr. 2005. Accessed 29 Nov. 2008. http://www.rudyrucker.com/pdf/icfatalk2005.pdf.

——. *Spaceland: A Novel of the Fourth Dimension*. New York: Tor Books, 2002.

Swift, Jonathan. *Gulliver's Travels*. Gulliver's Travels *and Other Writings by Jonathan Swift*. Ed. Miriam Kosh Starkman. New York: Bantam Books, 1981. 21–277.

Tuan, Yi-Fu. *Space and Place: The Perspective of Experience*. Minneapolis: University of Minnesota Press, 1977.

Watt, Ian. *Myths of Modern Individualism: Faust, Don Quixote, Don Juan, Robinson Crusoe*. New York: Cambridge University Press, 1996.

Literature

Rachel Falconer

Underworld Portmanteaux

Dante's Hell and Carroll's Wonderland in Women's Memoirs of Mental Illness

Explicating the elision of "lithe" and "slimy" into the neologism "slithy" in Carroll's poem "Jabberwocky," Humpty Dumpty famously coined the term "portmanteau" for words that pack together two meanings. In this essay, I argue that in contemporary women's memoirs of mental illness, two types of imaginary underworlds are "portmanteau-ed" together to convey how a patient experiences the journey through an often frightening and bewildering period of mental ill health. The memoirists, or autopathographers, very often retrospectively construct this period of time spent outside "normal" consciousness as a temporally arrested space or underworld in which they have become temporarily entrapped, a world that implicitly remains there, even when they have escaped and returned to normal life. Unsurprisingly, the dominant metaphor for this underworld has been a kind of hell, visualized in memory and mapped out as a graded series of ever-constricting circles, often consciously modeled on the spatialized hell of Dante's *Inferno*. Much more unexpected, though, is the sense of the remembering narrator's ambiguous attitude to this remembered space; in retrospect, it is not simply hell but also, at the same time, a Wonderland in which unlooked-for discoveries are made, and in which these shattered and fragmented subjects discover unanticipated spaces for play as they descend ever lower. My argument is that, while these memoirs allude to a range of different imaginary hells (the hell of Milton's *Paradise Lost*, for example), the underworlds of Dante and Lewis Carroll are yoked together and hybridized in particular ways to produce a complex underworld space that is at once authorizing and radicalizing, punishing and (potentially) ludic.

The shift from Dantean to Carrollian register becomes an important narratorial strategy for resisting entrapment in a preexisting patriarchal discourse about women's mental health. Drawing upon Carroll's ludic texts, these narrators open up more intimate "wonderlands" within the medically recognizable framing categories, or named "circles" of their illness. Thus the hybridization of references to underworld spaces, Dante's hell on one hand and Carroll's Wonderland on the other, creates a doubled and doubling kind of memoir, at once serious and frivolous, public and intimate, rational and "disorderly." This chapter will focus on the use of such hybridization strategies in Marya Hornbacher's memoir of anorexia, *Wasted*. To substantiate the argument, there will be additional reference to a wider range of autopathographical texts: three memoirs (Susanna Kaysen's *Girl, Interrupted*, Carol North's *Welcome, Silence*, and Linda Hart's *Phone at Nine Just to Say You're Alive*) and two semifictional memoirs (Lauren Slater's *Spasm* and Angela Carter's "Flesh and the Mirror"). Like Dante's poem, these contemporary memoirs function as apotropaic texts, warning the fascinated/horrified reader of our propinquity to shipwreck and disaster, despite the apparent securities—economic, social, political, and personal—that many Western, middle-class readers enjoy. At the same time, though, these texts invite us winningly to cross the border into a fantastical experience, to view the world from inside out and upside down, to experience Alice's moment of free fall and her awakening into an enriched reality.

Many contemporary women's memoirs of mental illness represent the experience of a threshold crossing from the everyday to the Real, or alternatively an eruption of the Real into the everyday, thus conveying a sense of the porousness of everyday reality and ordinary "rational" consciousness. Even when the illness materializes gradually, such memoirs often record a single moment of rupture, a caesural break dividing the ordinary from the "disordered" self. Thus Susanna Kaysen, writing about her two-year-long "personality disorder," compares herself to the girl in Vermeer's painting, "interrupted at her music: as my life had been, interrupted in the music of being seventeen" (*Girl* 167). And Marya Hornbacher, describing a much more protracted (fourteen-year) struggle with an eating disorder, recalls, "one minute I was your average nine-year-old. . . . The next minute I was walking, in a surreal haze . . . into the bathroom . . . sticking my first two fingers down my throat, and throwing up until I spat blood" (*Wasted* 9). Representing the onset of illness as a caesural rupture, such memoirs often draw upon the image of Dante's pilgrim, who famously found himself lost "in the middle of the journey of our life" ("nel mezzo del cammin di nostra vita"; *Inferno* 1.1).[1] This exiled wanderer, at once an individual and an epic everyman ("I" and "our life"), has become an important signifier for Western, secular subjectivity as it is precipitously exposed to invisible psychic, historical, and/or sociopolitical forces.[2] But in contemporary women's illness memoirs, the "right path" connotes stable mental health, while the "dark wood" is the spatialized image of the remembered illness. The caesural rupture to mental health precipitates the remembered, former self onto a journey through an infernal space: "on a perilous journey from which he or she may never return" (*Girl* 15); "ever so easy to go. Harder to find your way back" (*Wasted* 10). Both these passages recall Dante's wayfaring pilgrim, who in turn recalls Virgil's epic hero Aeneas.[3]

But in contrast to Dante's *Inferno*, the life-severing break occurs in both *Wasted* and *Girl, Interrupted* when the protagonist is quite young, rather than in her "middle" years. Her descent journey, when contrasted with that of the older, iconic pilgrim, lacks a certain gravitas, a Dantean weight of authority. Another model for the descent thus emerges, shadowing the Dantean allusion; this is Alice's unheroic, accidental tumble into Wonderland. I would argue that the sense of difference from Dante—a difference in gender, age, authority—precipitates the narrator of the illness memoir to turn to Carroll's Alice. Here, in this ostensibly child-centered text, the narrator can remember and speak out without fear of being contradicted or silenced. In *Girl, Interrupted*, Susanna Kaysen actually takes some care to distance herself from Alice: "I wasn't simply going nuts, tumbling down a shaft into Wonderland. It was my misfortune—or salvation—to be at all times perfectly conscious of my misperceptions of reality" (*Girl* 41). But I would argue that the allusion in fact underlines her closeness to Alice, who is similarly conscious of the differences between ordinary and Wonderland realities. In Hornbacher's *Wasted*, allusions to a Dantean journey are playfully "portmanteau-ed" together with references to Carroll's two *Alice* texts: "and so I went through the looking glass, stepped into the netherworld, where up is down and food is greed, where convex mirrors cover the walls" (*Wasted* 10).

These hybrid, doubled memoirs bear close relation to the *écriture féminine* celebrated by Hélène Cixous and other poststructuralist French feminist theorists. The contiguity is unsurprising, given that *Through the Looking-Glass* was a seminal text for both Cixous and Luce Irigaray, in their exploration of how female subjectivity might be created outside the structures of Symbolic, patriarchal discourse.[4] For Irigaray in *This Sex Which Is Not One*, the looking glass seems to be exclusively an instrument of the male gaze. Either a woman *is* the mirror, the surface that reflects the male gaze and gives the subject his sense of identity, or the woman internalizes the male gaze and uses the mirror to see herself through his eyes (as a nonsubject). Female subjectivity thus remains fragmentary, cut off from its sense of self (which, according to Irigaray, would be a plurality if it were allowed to apprehend itself without distortion). Either she is trapped as a nonsubject within the economy of patriarchy on *this* side of the glass, or she is trapped on the *other* side of the glass, which, in *This Sex Which Is Not One*, is synonymous with Wonderland, the underworld, and the unconscious, a state of nonsubjectivity.[5] Hornbacher's memoir certainly records just such a relationship with the mirror at the start of her illness. Feeling betrayed by her growing body (in retrospect, "just a typical little girl body, round and healthy, given to climbing, nakedness, the hungers of the flesh" [*Wasted* 14]), Marya stares in the mirror until "suddenly I felt a split in my brain: I didn't recognize her. I divided into two: the self in my head and the girl in the mirror" (15).[6] Thus far the reflection in the mirror is what the internalized patriarchal subject sees, with disapproval and horror at bodily excess. "Wonderland" is where girls get suppressed, trapped by the patriarchal tyranny of the mirror.

When Marya decides to "step through the glass," however, the nature of the mirror changes, and Wonderland becomes a realm in which female subjectivity, albeit of an upside-down and back-to-front kind, becomes possible. References to Carroll's *Through the Looking-Glass* and *Alice's Adventures* begin to fill out or shadow the allusions to Dante's *Inferno*, producing an image of a doubled world: a surface reality of apparently continuing normality and a "depth" reality in which Marya undertakes a quest to discover a different kind of selfhood. The idea of a quest to regain one's lost self is, of course, quintessentially Dantean; but in this memoir, the quest is also undertaken as a flight from—and at the same time, a flight toward—an unacknowledged, impossible female subjectivity:

> The colors of this time are deep and pervasive, blood reds and shadows, dark rooms, dark halls, a very dark desire. (59)

> I was carefully constructing my own private hell . . . two plots circling each other. . . . There was self by day and self by night. (59)

Thus the first steps downward are taken willingly, playfully, as a kind of experiment in trying out forbidden subjectivities. Doubling her narration by directly quoting Carroll's Alice, Hornbacher depicts her former self descending into illness, yet resisting the descent:

> And it is so very seductive. It is so reassuring, so all-consuming, so entertaining.
>
> At first.
>
> *"Well!" thought Alice to herself. "After such a fall as this, I shall think nothing of tumbling down-stairs! How brave they'll all think me at home!"* (64–5)

Marya passes the point of no return before she has even consciously consented to embark on the descent journey. Her journey is a "tumble"—both accidental and a product of her "willfulness," like Alice's fall but certainly unlike Dante's divinely sanctioned threshold crossing.

Dante experiences the underworld as an unambiguously evil space, or at least, theologically speaking, its goodness consists of its capacity to deliver souls, like his, from a state of sinfulness. Alice's underworld can be harsh and punishing, but it is, of course, a "wonder" land. Alice undergoes an underworldly metamorphosis, but not only through a *via negativa*; she and the reader are also changed through delight and divertissement. Similarly, while Marya's self-inflicted journey into the underworld is retrospectively understood by her older self to have been almost fatally dangerous, and she warns her readers in no uncertain terms not to try it themselves, it is also an experience from which she patently benefits. Somewhere in this alternative, "depth" reality, as she terms it, Marya discovers a subjectivity that bears close relation to the subject that Cixous described, existing on the "wrong" side of the looking glass. But if Cixous makes a clear distinction between Carroll's two Alices, the one in Wonderland lacking the assurance and power of the girl on the other side of the mirror, Hornbacher fails to note these distinctions, in part because her Alice, Marya, is only intermittently assured and powerful.[7] In Cixous's reading of *Through the Looking-Glass*, Alice escapes Dodgson's desire to "fix" her in his fantasy world. In Hornbacher's memoir, Marya's relation to authority is more ambiguous. Like Dante, she desires to be "saved" by an authoritative figure, in her case, a medical doctor who would recognize the sources of her illness and magically cure her; she also wants to be "fixed" in the fantasy worlds of bulimia and anorexia; but there is a third aspect of Marya that wishes to remain unfixed by either of these discourses of power. Thus she slides between references to Dante and Carroll, and between Wonderland and the other side of the looking glass. For example, quotations from *Through the Looking-Glass* are sometimes cited incorrectly as being from *Alice's Adventures* (e.g., *Wasted* 9).

Thus in its allusions to Dante and Dodgson, a certain dodginess (if you will excuse the pun) pervades Hornbacher's memoir. The references to Dante create expectations of a redemptive infernal journey, in which a "lost" former self finds grace in hell and emerges to become the text's supernaturally "saved," authoritative, epic-voiced narrator. But allusions to the *Alice* books subvert these expectations, as the narrator lapses from speaking with a consciously public, ambitiously epic voice into addressing her reader in a guilty, intimate, confessional tone. At the same time, as her assimilation of *Through the Looking-Glass* intimates, the narrator refuses to class her experience as fantastical, wonderful, or even moderately positive. Thus she resists knitting up her memories into a graceful, symmetrically balanced, cathedral-like text space, but instead revels in creating an immoderate, contradictory, disordered, ludic memoir. Of course, she wants to chart the journey that restores her mental health and "sanity," but at the same time she will not translate "health" into a Dantean sense of being "saved" because she maintains an ambiguous relation to patriarchal, medical discourse even after she has emerged from the "underworld" of ill health.

Contemporary women's autopathographies like *Wasted* thus combine Dantean and Carrollian motifs and narrative strategies in (at least) four distinct but interdependent modes. First, the topography of the actual, material world into which their mental illness projects them is presented as an infernal landscape, arrested in time, like Dante's *Inferno*. The experience of illness is constructed as a funnel shape, with graded tiers in which each stage of the illness feels more constricting and painful than the last. At the same time, drawing on the example of the two *Alice* texts, Hornbacher represents this underworld as a space that radicalizes the protagonist, empowering her to resist the demons she meets along the way.

Second, the history and development of the illness is presented as a journey into the underworld, beginning with an infernal threshold crossing into a mythic world, which is also an ill-fated (or self-destructive) tumble "down the rabbit hole."

Third, the narrator of the illness memoir represents her former self as a subject on a quest for secret knowledge; generally, the secret she seeks is the cause and/or source of her mental illness. Like her former self, the recovered self or narrator faces challenges on the journey of her narration, the greatest of which is to find for her text a language and a form together capable of articulating her forbidden knowledge and conveying it to the reader. This narratorial quest should not be understood as something supplementary, or secondary, to the protagonist's quest. In accordance with Jonathan Culler's analysis of the double logic of narration (in which story implicitly precedes discourse, but is also a product of that discourse), Marya's history of anorexia obviously precedes her later self's relation of the experience, but at the same time, the lack of an appropriate language to "tell the self" might well be understood as one of the factors triggering the self-harming illness described in her narration.[8] The logic of narration in this case suggests that the protagonist's "fatal tumble" has occurred as a consequence of the lack of a language in which to express a sense of psychic disorder. In this situation, Carroll's slippery "nonsense" wordplay becomes an important supplement to Dante's language—his controlled *terza rima*, his universalizing middle style, his confident epic voice.

Finally, from her "underworldly" perspective in the underworld, the narrator proffers a satirical view of "overworldly" values and cultural norms. Dante's hell is a space from which the poet observes contemporary culture from a defamiliarized perspective, and from which he launches his most scathing political critiques. But his hell is also a place where divine, rational justice is expressed, where every punishment is a *contrapasso* perfectly suited to (the appropriate response to, the expression of) a particular sin. But illness memoirs often invoke the more modern, secular sense of hell, as a place or historical event that expresses human *in*justice and *un*reason. Thus Alice's Looking-Glass World, where things appear inverted, and Wonderland, which is governed by absurdist logic, come closer to reflecting these writers' experience of a stretch of life lived outside (or beneath) the normal spaces of social interchange.

In contemporary illness memoirs, the world of mental ill health, when spatialized as a region of eternal suffering, is often shown to lack the gravitas and solidity of Dante's hell. The allusions to Dante serve to emphasize the provisionality, or absurdity, of institutions dedicated to curing and managing mental ill health. Moreover, the removal of the patient from a normal social context into a mythically extratemporal space has the double-edged effect of divesting her of free will while at the same time radicalizing her consciousness. Thus the relation of the patient to this underworld space is Dantean and Carrollian, submissive and ludic at the same time.

In Western culture, the diagnosis and treatment of mental disorder happens largely behind closed doors, and recovered patients often describe passing beyond public consciousness in this way as a kind of threshold crossing into another world. Patients are also often treated at a series of different institutions, each for successively more "desperate" or "hopeless" cases. So in illness memoirs, the various medical institutions are frequently recalled as a graded sequence of underworlds, the one layered above or below the next. In Hornbacher's *Wasted*, for example, there are three institutions graded according to degrees of patients' illness and the amount of restraint under which they are placed: Methodist House, Lowe House, and Willmar, the last of these constituting lowest hell for Marya (184). While *Wasted* provides a particularly pronounced example of a spatially tiered experience, other illness memoirs create similar gradations and implicit moral hierarchies. In *Phone at Nine Just to Say You're Alive*, a journal recording an eleven-month struggle with schizophrenia, suicidal depression, and psychosis, Linda Hart represents the asylum and psychiatric ward in which she was hospitalized as a Dantean underworld divided into upper and lower realms. Her journal begins in the lower hell of Brendon Ward, a secure unit for dangerous patients, where Linda has been detained after attempting suicide. She is later moved to a psychiatric ward in a general hospital, which she characterizes as an upper hell presided over by a Charon/Minos figure, the unempathetic consultant psychiatrist, Graham Drake, who administers drug dosages and issues orders for transfer to Brendon Ward. And in her memoir of schizophrenia, *Welcome, Silence*, Carol North likewise represents the psychiatric ward of her hospital as a hell ("some medieval mistake"; 88) that induces "an overwhelming sense of despondency bordering on despair" (20). Crossing the threshold for the first time, she feels she is leaving the material world: "a set of double doors swallowed me head first. *Is this the entrance to Infinity? Here goes . . .*" (89, italics in the original). The representation of the medical institution as a hierarchically tiered space, lying somewhere outside of ordinary historical time, recalls the claustrophobic spaces of Dante's funnel-shaped inferno. Likewise, the sense of despair the patient feels when being admitted to the institution echoes the message that Dante's pilgrim reads over the entrance gate to hell: "abandon hope, all you who enter."

A further reference to medieval and classical underworld space occurs in Susanna Kaysen's *Girl, Interrupted*, which relates the author's experience of a two-year stay at McLean's Psychiatric Hospital in Boston, Massachusetts, while being treated for a condition diagnosed as "character or personality disorder." Quoting Virgil's sibyl in *Aeneid* 6, Kaysen anticipates her reader's query, "how did you get in there? . . . All I can tell them is, It's easy" (5).[9] For Kaysen, mental institutions constitute one of the many parallel worlds inhabited by the socially powerless: "worlds of the insane, the criminal, the crippled, the dying, perhaps of the dead as well" (5). In a common room at McLean's (the year is 1967), the patients watch news coverage of the Vietnam War, identifying with war victims who seem to be falling into a parallel world like theirs, "tiny bodies [who] fell to the ground on our TV screen: black people, young people, Vietnamese people, poor people" (92).

In all the examples above, the medical institution resembles a hellish underworld that recalls Dante's *Inferno* and, in some cases, Virgil's Hades. But at the same time, in women's illness memoirs, this space has a radicalizing influence on its patients that can be likened to the effect of Wonderland on the young Alice. One reason for the female patient's radicalization is that she often finds herself in (perceived) opposition to a series of male antagonists. Another reason is that, unlike Dante's pilgrim, she does not descend into the underworld by conscious choice. She "tumbles down" through accident or misfortune; ill health and hospitalization are things that happen *to* her, not paths she actively chooses for her soul's salvation. Grouped together with other female patients in a hospital, the patient (more like a Dantean damned soul than pilgrim in this respect) discovers a sorority that becomes increasingly vociferous in its resistance to medical procedures, and increasingly cohesive as a militant group, as a result of its very isolation from social responsibility or recognition from the outside world. In narrating her experience, the recovered patient retains this sense of opposition and distance from (perceived) patriarchal control, even if, paradoxically, her temporary incarceration contributes to restoring her mental health. In these memoirs, male psychiatrists, doctors, and nurses are frequently caricatured and their authority diminished by comparisons to figures from Wonderland. For example, Hornbacher quotes the Tweedle twins telling Alice she is not real (9) and the Caterpillar telling her that being different sizes isn't confusing (76–7); both allusions make a mockery of the medical advice Marya is given during the course of her illness. In Carroll's Wonderland, Alice receives an overabundance of advice, but she freely rejects any direction that seems to her too arbitrary or absurd. She never entirely forgets that hers is the only living voice in a country of invented, fantastical creatures. Similarly, for the protagonist in these illness memoirs, the more infernally absurd her surroundings become, the more sane she appears to herself. Incarceration increases her defiance and produces a new speaking voice—a gallows humor whose power derives, paradoxically, from a recognition of powerlessness: "'Keep your temper,' said the Caterpillar. 'Is that all?' said Alice" (*Wasted* 77). Like Alice, the mental patient travels through her underworld without the authority of a heavenly patron; hence her power is not derived from heaven, but must be stolen, surreptitiously and daringly, from the "mad" underworld itself.

The representation of mental illness as a journey taken downward through space is by no means a "natural" or universal narrative strategy. In other places and other historical periods, mental illness has been narrativized as an aerial flight to the heavens, for example.[10] It is in part due to Dante's widespread influence, as well as the popularization of the Freudian concept of a psyche tiered into two or three layers (superego over ego over id and/or conscious over unconscious mind), that autopathographers in Western culture so often represent mental illness as a descent journey into a dark, subterraneous realm, followed by a reascent to light and health. This is the case with Lauren Slater's *Spasm*, subtitled "a memoir with lies," which describes epileptic illness and/or Münchausen syndrome as a journey through the four stages of a classic grand mal epileptic seizure: "onset," "rigid stage," "convulsion," and "recovery." These four stages are represented as corresponding to Dante's katabatic narrative structure,[11] with its four distinctive narrative cruces: threshold crossing, descent, inversion, and reascent. At the same time, the Dantean narrative structure of *Spasm* is hybridized with allusions to texts by writers with epilepsy such as Jean-Paul Sartre and, it has been speculated, Lewis Carroll.[12] With Slater's "epileptic" models, the katabatic hinge movement is less clearly visible; and in particular, the reascent from the underworld is less final. *Spasm* celebrates not so much the art of homecoming (which both *Inferno* and *Aeneid* derive from Homer's *Odyssey*) as the art of falling safely; the primary role model for the artful tumbler in her text is not Dante's pilgrim but Carroll's Alice. The book concludes with Lauren accepting her psychically unstable condition (although whether this is Münchausen's or epilepsy remains unclear) in terms that recall Alice's fall down the rabbit hole: "You give up the ground, which you never really had to begin with, . . . the one fact I will ever and only have. I have the fact of falling . . . I will miss my mark, and fall . . . straight into the hole. Alice is there. The queen is there. My mother is there" (*Spasm* 216). The underground space where the narrator finally decides to take up permanent residence is also a markedly feminized space. Having had a difficult relationship with a very demanding, unpredictable mother, Lauren makes space for her presence in this underworld, both in fantasized form as Wonderland's "queen" and as herself, Lauren's real mother.

The katabatic structure of Marya's journey in *Wasted* is even more explicitly delineated. The development of Marya's eating disorder from bulimia to the more life-threatening condition of anorexia is mapped out as a descent journey from upper to lower hell. The condition of bulimia allegorically corresponds to Dante's upper hell, the circles where the violent are punished, because bulimia "acknowledges the body explicitly, violently" (*Wasted* 93). Marya not only moves bodily through hell; her body *becomes* her hell: it contracts the further "down" she descends into her eating disorder, just as the circles of hell become smaller the further Dante descends. At the same time, in her bulimic phase, Marya's body is an amorphous, malleable shape closer to Alice's than Dante's: "my weight has ranged . . . from 135 pounds to 52, inching up and then plummeting back down. I have gotten 'well,' then 'sick,' then 'well'" (2–3). Marya compares herself repeatedly to Alice, remembering how the heroine burgeoned to a height of nine feet then shrank to the size of a mouse (*Wasted* 20 and elsewhere). And in contrast to Dante, the protagonist of Hornbacher's memoir is both damned soul and devil, because she herself inflicts the punishment on her own mind and body. Like Alice, Marya is the inventor of the underworld of her adventures. This is a crucial point, because as she eventually discovers, Marya has the power to exit hell as soon as she decides it is a dream of her own making.

But before this moment of recognition arrives, Marya travels through a lower hell, a more serious phase of eating disorder. Her relation to her body changes as she enters what appears to be a different kind of space. Allegorically, this is represented as a kind of frozen Cocytian lake: "Past the border of a fiery life lies the netherworld. I can trace this road, which took me through places so hot the very air burned the lungs. I did not turn back. I pressed on, and eventually passed over the border, beyond which lies a place that is wordless and cold, so cold that it, like mercury, burns a freezing blue flame" (95). At this stage of the journey, bodily pain is no longer experienced as self-inflicted punishment but rather as "a strange state of grace" (6), a blissful "removal of the bearer from the material realm" (153). In the upper circles of illness, allusions to Alice had served to lighten and carnivalize the infernal atmosphere. "How did your eating disorder start?" Marya has her implied reader ask. "Hell if I know, I say. I just wanted to see what would happen. Curiosity, of course, killed the cat" (9). The jocular tone suggests a Cheshire Cat–like narrator who, if reduced to a ghost, nevertheless carries on grinning.

But once she reaches lower hell, the narrator's tone darkens, and the references to Dante introduce a dangerous note to the Carrollian adventure. Thus the narrator implicitly distances herself from her former, Alice-like confidence: "women fling themselves down the rabbit hole, everyone else is going, it can't be dangerous" (129). But the tumble down the rabbit hole shades into a fatal, irreversible fall, as Marya's body descends numerically down the weighing scales, toward a vanishing point:

> and then I hit bottom and thought:
> I think I'm dead.
> Finally.
> Fifty-two.
> Then everything goes white. (271)[13]

"Fifty-two" is the lightest weight Marya is able to "achieve" before she collapses and is hospitalized. The "lightness" of being able to manipulate her body image, like "Alice on 'shrooms" (39), fades here into the "lightness" of the body near death, and the moral as well as physical lightness of souls in the underworld.[14] In *Inferno*, the pilgrim does reach a point where the pull of gravity is reversed, and he is able to ascend from hell with much less effort than it took to go down. The material reason for this is that he has passed through the center of the Earth, as Virgil explains: "tu passasti 'l punto / al qual si traggon d'ogne parte i pesi" ("you passed the point to which all weights are drawn from every part"; *Inferno* 34.110–1). The theological reason for his "lightness" is that the pilgrim has been spiritually reborn and is now ready for the second leg of the journey, through purgatory.

In the absence of the Dantean possibility of spiritual transformation, the war on weight becomes a religion in itself. As Hornbacher writes, "[W]e expect, in this world, that human beings will bear a human weight and force—there is a fascination with all human rebellions against material limits, with that small step into the supernatural. . . . I am not saying that the act of erasing the body *is* magic, but it *feels* magical" (129). Throughout her memoir, Hornbacher invokes religious language and imagery to convey the intensity of her experience. She compares her self-inflicted torture, for example, to the sufferings of Saint Margaret of Cortona, who starved herself to death in 1297 (125–6), although presumably Margaret died for her faith rather than an ideal of thinness. By comparing her experience to these medieval journeys of extreme faith, Marya implicitly exposes a moral hollowness at the core of her narrative. There is no salvific principle driving her narrative, and no otherworldly vision of hell (or paradise) to convey to her reader. This being the case, a more humanistic motive has to emerge before the reascent can take place. And once again, Carroll's ludic dream space provides the key for a reversal of the downward spiral toward anorexia. Marya's "ground zero" conversion consists of a "leap of faith" toward a "basic ethical principle: if I was alive, then I had a responsibility to stay alive and do something with the life I had been given" (280). In the final trial scene in *Alice in Wonderland* (Carroll 97), Alice listens to the ludicrous charges brought against the Jack of Hearts, then hears the Queen's arbitrary sentence passed against herself ("off with her head!"). This causes Alice to leap indignantly to her feet and sweep away her fears along with the entire underworld space and its inhabitants ("why, you're nothing but a pack of cards!").

The "ground zero" of Marya's descent journey is the "whiteout" she experiences once she reaches "fifty-two" on her scales. But the return journey (which in *Inferno* takes only seven lines to narrate) is far from smooth for Marya. For the anorectic, Hornbacher writes, "there is never a sudden revelation" (279). More mutedly, she concludes that her anorexia "was not cured. It will not be cured. But it has changed. So have I" (277). While the text's allusions to Dante create expectations of an absolute conversion and cure, the parallels drawn with *Alice* suggest, on the contrary, that there will be no caesural break dividing past and present selves:

> It's never over. Not really. Not when you stay down there as long as I did, not when you've lived in the netherworld longer than you've lived this material one. . . . You never come all the way out of the mirror; you stand, for the rest of your life, with one foot in this world and one in another, where everything is upside down and backward and sad. (285)

Rather than escaping the mirror or Wonderland altogether, Marya straddles the two realities. Being a subject has become "an interesting balancing act. . . . It's a glass-half-empty-or-half-full sort of place, I could tip either way. It's a place where one can either hope or despair" (278). This image of Marya corresponds to that of Alice learning to control her magical size swings by trial and error, and eventually creating the shape she wants by alternating careful nibbles of cake with sips from the bottle. Hornbacher here gives a tragic cast to the condition of living on, still half in the looking glass ("where everything is upside down and backward and sad"). But at the same time, the bifocal perspective, living half in the underworld and half in the "normal" world, is empowering for Hornbacher as a writer. Her uniquely bifocal perspective, at once orderly and *dis*orderly, becomes the basis for her claim to authority for writing (reflecting, reasoning, signifying) about Dis, or hell. Like Alice, then, she steals a form of authority from the underworld itself, despite the harsh judgment she encounters there (the Queen's cry of "off with her head" or, in Marya's case, her own self-willed annihilation).

One of the unresolved questions of Hornbacher's memoir is what caused her eating disorder in the first place, and in narrative terms, what provided the impetus for her descent into the underworld of mental ill health. The contrasting models of Dante and Alice implicitly provide two possible causalities; either it was a chosen path or it was a chance tumble, either a necessary journey into self-awakening or a fortuitous adventure leading to unlooked-for discoveries. Angela Carter's semiautobiographical memoir, "Flesh and the Mirror," in *Burning Your Boats*, presents an illuminating contrast to Hornbacher's *Wasted* on the question of causality in an underworld journey. Carter represents the protagonist of her memoir, a semifictional, younger self, stumbling into an underworld during her stay in Tokyo. When her lover fails to meet her boat at the harbor, she wanders disillusioned and directionless through the city. Her aimless journey becomes a descent of a Carrollian, rather than Dantean, kind:

> I had fallen through one of those holes life leaves in it; these peculiar holes are the entrances to the counters at which you pay the price of the way you live.
>
> Random chance operates in relation to these existential lacunae; one tumbles down them when . . . one is lost. One is at the mercy of events. (72)

Like Dante's pilgrim, this protagonist is paying a price for her choice of relationship (implicitly, one in which she has consented to play a traditional, passive role). But her metamorphosis is more Carrollian than Dantean, as she tumbles, apparently randomly, into a fantastical, unreal adventure. Carter goes on to recount how she met a stranger in the city, went home with him to his flat, and had sex on a bed beneath a giant mirror mounted on the ceiling. Having metaphorically tumbled down a rabbit hole, she thus discovers herself on Alice's second adventure, transformed by a looking glass: "the magic mirror presented me with a hitherto unconsidered notion of myself as I. Without any intention of mine, I had been defined by the action reflected in the mirror. I beset me. I was the subject of the sentence written on the mirror" (70). Unlike Dante, she does not need to will her own metamorphosis; indeed, the epic sense of heroic will is precisely what she leaves behind. For her, the mirror is "magic," transformative, because it refuses to conspire with her in the way Carter maintains that women and mirrors generally conspire: to "evade the action I/she performs" (70). She does not *will* her transformation, but is surprised by seeing herself act out of character (having sex with the stranger). Confronted with the image of this other, bolder self, she has no choice but to acknowledge the "she" in the mirror as "I." The underworld space transforms her, not by teaching her obedience to a prescripted destiny, but by showing her an unscripted self. Her descent journey ends with an affirmation of identity on both a psychic and a textual level ("I was the subject of the sentence"). Thus by sidestepping the Dantean model of the epic, divinely sanctioned descent journey, Carter discovers a mode of performing a self that is both "I" and "she." Carter returns to this theme in her short story "Wolf-Alice," in which a prelapsarian couple (wolf-bred Alice and a vampiric Duke) invent nonpatriarchal subjectivities for each other, in the reflection of a magic mirror.[15] Once again, it is Carroll's looking glass, rather than the Dantean threshold crossing, that provides the space in which prescripted gender roles can be cast aside and alternative subjectivities forged.

Hornbacher's protagonist is more ambivalent about her underworldly experience than Carter's, and she draws more fluidly from Carroll and Dante both to give spatial form to her memories, as we have seen, and to provide a sense of causation, or alternatively a lack of causation, to her narrative. Marya is unable to pinpoint the reasons why she embarked on her fourteen-year journey through "the hell of eating disorders" (2). At the end of the narrative, she rejects the idea that she was ever fully transformed or cured of her illness, so there is no retrospective plot logic that might provide cause and meaning to her experience; there is none of the hindsight that allows the Dantean poet to perceive his former self on a journey leading to a present state of grace, or an autobiographer to reflect that "illness made me the person I am today." Since she maintains that she is not fully cured, the path she has traveled is not automatically justified by the end point she has attained. And yet, on the other hand, Marya resists retrospectively reshaping her experience as a magic, fortuitous adventure. So she hesitates between Dante and Carroll, creating a ludic text haunted by epic shadows, and an epic text enlivened by a sense of the ridiculous and the unscripted or unscriptable.

The uncertain shape of Hornbacher's memoir reflects both the constant flux of Marya's body weight as well as the fluctuating and precarious subjectivity of the narrator. On the one hand, the narrator (like Dante's pilgrim in the first circle of hell) aspires to high literary status; she begins each chapter with an extract from Nietzsche or Beckett, Anne Sexton or Sylvia Plath, or Carroll's two *Alice* books, and midchapter she quotes liberally from Robert Frost, Theodore Roethke, and other well-known writers on mental torment or despair. She also intends to be taken seriously as an authority on eating disorders; the memoir begins by recounting in scathing tones an encounter with a doctor who refuses to acknowledge her expertise. She cites medical journals in support of her observations about her former self, footnotes references to psychiatric studies, and includes a copious bibliography of medical sources.

On the other hand, the very extent of these citations tends to work against the narrator's claims to authority on a medical or high literary basis. Rather, these various textual excesses mimetically enact the behaviors of people with eating disorders, as Hornbacher characterizes them: "extreme," "highly competitive," "perfectionistic," "tending toward excess" (6). Other signs of textual excess include the fact that *Wasted* has two different subtitles (on the cover, paradoxically, the more private and confessional "coming back from an addiction to starvation" and on the title page, the more formal "A Memoir of Anorexia and Bulimia"); two beginnings ("Introduction: Notes on the Netherworld" and "Chapter 1: Childhood"); two endings ("Afterword: The Wreck: Now" and "Present Day"); and numerous climactic peripeteiae instead of a single, dramatic one ("There. My life split in half"; 64 and elsewhere). In fact, the form of the narrative imitates Marya's personality, for whom "everything is terribly grand and crashing, very Sturm and Drang" (281). Just as anorexia is an attempt to experience "a *real* drama, not a sitcom but a GRAND EPIC" (281), so the narrator aims to take the reader on a "*real* epic" journey to hell and back. Hornbacher characterizes anorexia as a condition to which the bulimic aspires (153), and the text mirrors this aspirational condition. *Wasted* is full of grand gestures, pronouncements, jeremiads; but their very iteration tends to undermine the memoir's claims to Dantean authority.

Whether we will "gain" (in any sense) from reading *Wasted* when to varying degrees, we are participants with Marya in a culture that Hornbacher metaphorically figures as bulimic is a question left undecided in this doubling memoir. Hornbacher's persistent use of the second person both suggests a tendency to mask or evade herself as an "I" ("I'd lost the sense of first-person"; 261) and invites the reader to identify closely with her experiences of eating disorder (as well as her narratorial evasions). Because it lacks a definitive break between past and narrating self, *Wasted* does not work straightforwardly in the manner of a conversion narrative like Dante's. At first glance, the aesthetic is rather that of Carroll's *Wonderland* texts, in which the adult narrator retrospectively constructs the underworld as a space seductively distanced from the constraints of the adult world—an underworld not of punishment but of play.

But in fact, *Wasted* consists of a curious blend of these differing aesthetics. Although Hornbacher and the implied reader collude with Marya to an extent, finding bulimic metamorphoses more fascinating a condition than reasonably good health, there *is* a Dantean reach toward judgment in this memoir. What Hornbacher wishes to condemn is not the individual lost soul aspiring to the condition of anorexia, but rather the obsessive contemporary culture that produces such lost souls. "Culturally, we would be diagnosed as bulimic," Marya says, because "we seesaw madly, hair flying and eyes alight, between crazed and constant consumption" and a "fanatical belief in the moral superiority of self-denial and self-control" (154). Marya's experience is therefore just one instance of an entire culture's acceleration toward telescoped adulthood, induced by a diet of insubstantial pop culture, like Alice's magically induced size.

Hornbacher is clear that whatever her individual reasons for developing anorexia, her illness is expressive of a more wide-scale cultural yearning for something more than Carrollian metamorphosis, for something more closely akin to Dantean salvation. As Marya comments dryly, "had I lived in a culture where 'thinness' was not regarded as a strange state of grace, I might have sought out other means of attaining that grace" (6–7). If "bulimia hearkens back to the hedonistic Roman days of pleasure and feast," anorexia, by contrast, can provide the postmodern subject with a sense of connection to "the medieval age of bodily mortification" (153). In this contrast, there seems to be a hidden critique of Wonderland, which permits the "I" to choose any shape because no shape is binding and final. In the absence of traditional religious faith, anorexia provides the secular subject with a *via negativa* to a quasi-spiritual revelation, in which the (always disorderly, excessive) body is inverted, measured and judged by its empty spaces: "I could see . . . a little oval space from knee to crotch. I stared at the space where my torso had been, the space between the bones" (252). Again, Marya's fascination with hollowed body parts reflects a wider cultural desire for spiritual metamorphosis through negation.

As we have seen, the possibility of a Dantean revelation and conversion is displaced to the margins of this unstable, shape-shifting text. At the text's center is the doubled perspective of an under/overworldly narrator, an Alice figure half inside, half escaped from the looking glass. A description of two relationships frame the memoir proper. In the introduction, two recovering anorectics, the narrator and a young female friend, exchange confidences over an uneasy lunch, "playing normal" (1). In the afterword, the narrator refers to her anonymous husband, and to a marriage that remains sketchy, unfleshed out, one might say, on the issue of physical relationships and eating disorders. Such relationships are clearly crucial to Marya's recovery. While Hornbacher questions and challenges the authority of doctors, psychiatrists, and even her literary predecessors, she rarely subjects her friends' discourses to the same scathing cross-examination. Thus her memoir suggests that one of the ways out of hell or, alternatively, of surviving half in and half out of Wonderland, is by sustaining friendships with other "underworlders." If, as Bakhtin argues of all autobiographical writing, *Wasted* lacks a sense of outsideness, its strength lies in its depiction of a subject (protagonist, narrator) in balance: neither sick nor well, close to disaster but toughly resistant, solitary but sociable. Flanked by twinned underworld guides, Tweedle-Dante and Tweedle-Alice, Hornbacher creates a narrative of disaster that resists revelatory consolation while it says much about the arts of survival.

NOTES

1. All translations are mine, unless otherwise specified.
2. See Falconer, and for modernist precursors, Pike.
3. Compare Virgil, "the descent to Avernus [hell] is easy, but to retrace your steps, this is the task, this the difficulty" ("facilis descensus Averno . . . sed revocare gradum . . . hoc opus, hic labor est"; *Aeneid* 6.126–29; Fairclough translation).
4. On the Real, the Imaginary, and the Symbolic, see Lacan 62–87. For a reexamination of Lacan's notion of the subject from a feminist psychoanalytic perspective, see Mitchell and Rose.
5. See Irigaray, chapters 1 and 2.
6. To avoid confusion, I refer to the protagonist in the text by first name (in this case, Marya) and the memoir's author by last name (Hornbacher).
7. Cixous 233. For Cixous's original French text, see the introduction to Jean Gattégno and Henri Parisot's translation of Carroll's *Through the Looking-Glass* and *The Hunting of the Snark*. For a discussion of Cixous's reading of Alice, see Royle.
8. Culler 169–87.

9. Dante repeatedly alludes to this Virgilian passage, for example, *Inferno* 16.78–108.
10. On aerial journeys into the afterlife, see Zaleski 45–60.
11. *Katabasis* literally means "a going down." Metaphorically, *katabasis* (or in Latin, *descensus ad inferos*) was used by the Greeks more particularly to refer to a story about a living person who visits the land of the dead and returns more or less unscathed. See Clark 32.
12. Controversy still persists as to whether Lewis Carroll suffered from temporal lobe epilepsy or not. For a brief review of the debate and a refutation of the latest claims that he had epilepsy, see Burstein. Whatever the medical facts, the belief that he *was* epileptic is certainly still widespread. He is cited as such, for example, on the Epilepsy Therapy Development Project Web site. This site draws supporting evidence from descriptions of falls and other "seizure" experiences in *Alice*: "the very sensation initiating Alice's adventures—that of falling down a hole—is a familiar one to many people with seizures. Alice often feels that her own body (or the objects around her) is shrinking or growing before her eyes, another seizure symptom." Carroll is included among the epileptic writers and artists named in *Spasm*, although Lauren is a self-avowedly unreliable narrator who is clearly capable of treating popular myth as a biographical probability.
13. Cristopher Hollingsworth plausibly suggests that there may be a visual reference here to the Mouse's tale in *Alice's Adventures*.
14. Lightness is mentioned as a sign of a damned soul in many katabatic narratives. See, for example, *Aeneid* 6.411–4, and Milton's *Paradise Lost* 4.1011–2, where Satan is told, "read thy lot in yon celestial sign / Where thou art weighed, and shown how light, how weak." The trope recurs in contemporary katabatic testimonies such as Millu's *Smoke over Birkenau*, in which the weightless exit via the chimney is universally feared as the worst death, and Levi's *The Truce*, where as a free man, Levi is surprised to feel his bed sink under his weight (379).
15. The mirror motif is ubiquitous in Angela Carter's writing, but see especially "Reflections" in Carter, *Burning* 81–95.

WORKS CITED

Burstein, Sandor. Letter. "Lewis Carroll's Neurologic Symptoms." *The Carrollian* 1 (Spring 1998): 55.

Carroll, Lewis. *Alice's Adventures in Wonderland* and *Through the Looking-Glass and What Alice Found There*. *Alice in Wonderland*. Ed. Donald J. Gray. 2nd ed. London: Norton, 1992. 1–209.

———. *De l'autre côté du miroir et ce qu'Alice y trouva / Through the Looking-Glass and What Alice Found There; La chasse au snark / The Hunting of the Snark*. Trans. Jean Gattégno and Henri Parisot. Bilingue Aubier-Flammarion 42. [Paris]: Aubier-Flammarion, 1971.

Carter, Angela. *Burning Your Boats: Collected Short Stories*. London: Vintage, 1996.

———. *Nights at the Circus*. London: Pan Books, 1985.
———. *The Passion of New Eve*. London: Virago, 1982.
Cixous, Hélène. "Introduction to Lewis Carroll's *Through the Looking-Glass* and *The Hunting of the Snark*." *New Literary History* 13.2 (1982): 231–51.
Clark, Raymond. *Catabasis: Vergil and the Wisdom Tradition*. Amsterdam: B. R. Gruner, 1979.
Culler, Jonathan. *The Pursuit of Signs: Semiotics, Literature, Deconstruction*. London: Routledge, 1981.
Dante Alighieri. *The Divine Comedy*. Trans. Charles Singleton. 6 vols. Princeton: Princeton University Press, 1989.
Epilepsy Therapy Development Project. Accessed 19 June 2006. http://www.epilepsy.com/epilepsy/famous_writers.html.
Falconer, Rachel. *Hell in Contemporary Literature: Western Descent Narratives since 1945*. Edinburgh: Edinburgh University Press, 2005.
Hart, Linda. *Phone at Nine Just to Say You're Alive*. London: Macmillan, 1997.
Hornbacher, Marya. *Wasted: A Memoir of Anorexia and Bulimia*. London: HarperCollins, 1999.
Irigaray, Luce. *This Sex Which Is Not One*. Trans. Catherine Porter. Ithaca: Cornell University Press, 1977.
Kaysen, Susanna. *Girl, Interrupted*. London: Virago, 2000.
Lacan, Jacques. "The Insistence of the Letter in the Unconscious." *Modern Criticism and Theory*. Ed. David Lodge. 2nd ed. Harlow: Longman, 2000. 62–87.
Levi, Primo. *If This Is a Man* and *The Truce*. Trans. Stuart Woolf. London: Abacus, 1995.
Millu, Liana. *Smoke over Birkenau*. Jerusalem: Jewish Publication Society, 1991.
Milton, John. *Milton: Paradise Lost*. Ed. Alastair Fowler. 2nd ed. Harlow: Longman, 1998.
Mitchell, Juliet, and Jacqueline Rose, eds. *Feminine Sexuality: Jacques Lacan and the École Freudienne*. Trans. Jacqueline Rose. New York: Norton, 1985.
North, Carol. *Welcome, Silence: My Triumph over Schizophrenia*. London: Arrow Books, 1990.
Pike, David. *Passage through Hell: Modernist Descents, Medieval Underworlds*. Ithaca: Cornell University Press, 1997.
Royle, Nicholas. "Portmanteau." *New Literary History* 37.1 (2006): 237–47.
Schachter, Steven C., ed. "Classical Writers with Epilepsy." 28 Dec. 2006. http://www.epilepsy.com/epilepsy/famous_writers.
Slater, Lauren. *Spasm: A Memoir with Lies*. London: Methuen, 2000.
Virgil. *Aeneid*. Trans. H. Rushton Fairclough. Vol. 2. London: William Heinemann, 1978.
Zaleski, Carol. *Otherworld Journeys: Accounts of Near-Death Experience in Medieval and Modern Times*. Oxford: Oxford University Press, 1987.

Christine Roth

Looking through the Spyglass

Lewis Carroll, James Barrie, and the Empire of Childhood

As the eighteenth century came to a close, Romantic writers such as Blake and Wordsworth pursued their desire for connection with a "natural" and "innocent" self by imagining childhood as distinctly separate from the dark materiality and corruption of adult life. Throughout the nineteenth century, writers celebrated the "essential autonomy of an innocent or mythic child"; yet this natural and innocent childhood was a "retrospective phenomenon," one from which adults "felt sadly distant" (Austin 76). So, as the Victorians increasingly sequestered a much-needed and protected/protective nostalgic space of wild childhood, they also closed off that space to adult desires and experience. Between the mid-nineteenth century and its turn into the twentieth, when fantasies for and of children flourished in what has been called the golden age of children's literature, writers such as Lewis Carroll and James Barrie attempted to reconnect with that sequestered world by using child subjects as mediators between the spaces of childhood and adulthood, creating fictional(ized) child characters who are not as much natives as double agents, of sorts, in the untamed Wonderland or wild territories of Neverland.

Because any physical or mental movement away from adult Victorian society tended to be constructed as regressive—"the traveling subject discovering not a new land so much as a new location for old, nostalgic fictions about places lost in the distant past[1], not found in the distant present" (Rennie 1)—young characters such as Alice and Peter function as what Edward Said would describe as a "median category," which the story's nostalgic narrative voices both observe and calibrate in response to adult longing and desire (Said 54).[2] Like the exotic scenes described in nineteenth-century travel narratives pouring in from around the empire, the fictional spaces of Wonderland and Neverland mingle "long ago" and "far away," and the narrative spyglass that reaches into such fictional childhood spaces provides a participatory voyeuristic experience. By imagining both the space's native Others and child Others as negations (bodies that lack a story of their own), Carroll, Barrie, and their adult readers perform a kind of erasure, clearing a space for the expansion of an adult imagination and for the pursuit of adult desires within such a fantasy space; however, the adult presence comes through the child's perspective and experience, passively commenting on what the child sees and feels.[3]

The narrator of the *Through the Looking-Glass* frame poem, for example, experiences the dream world only through Alice's "nest of gladness" and is able to tell her, as if he is a thought in her head, that "we are but older children, dear / Who fret to find our bedtime near" (lines 28, 23–4)—the "we" referring to the adult presence traveling vicariously through the girl. Indeed, as U. C. Knoepflmacher suggests, Alice herself "is soon led to grasp what Carroll has come to understand, namely, that forward progress may be meaningless without a capacity for regress: to meet the Red Queen whose 'adult' power she covets Alice must 'try the plan' of walking backward, 'in the opposite direction,' a strategy that 'beautifully' succeeds for her as well as for her creator" (499). In this way, travel to the faraway elusive gardens and forests of Wonderland stands in for travel to the long-ago childhood of the narrator—a conflation of space and time that Barrie reiterates in the spatial and temporal directions to Neverland: "Second to the right and straight on till morning" (*Peter Pan* 40).

Expanding the imaginative territory even further, children themselves came to symbolize nostalgic spaces suspended between past and present. This move comes, in some part, from adult men's consideration of their own childhoods as specifically feminine, making the physical body of a girl herself into a nostalgic space. Because the first six years of male life in the nineteenth century carried a "clear stamp of femininity, especially in retrospect," little girls provided the logical intermediary for relived childhood experiences for adult men (Robson 4). Indeed, many stories about children in idealized or fantastical situations cannot be considered without reference to a "pervasive fantasy of male development in which men become masculine only after an initial feminine stage" (Robson 3). Hence, little girls in Victorian art and literature exist within a sanctified space of childhood, not for their own pleasure or purposes, but as a service to nostalgic adults. In this way, the mere presence of idealized girl figures offered male writers an opportunity to visit a remote, imaginary past, a fantasy space that stands in for their own idyllic childhoods, thereby enabling them to escape a masculine-gendered sphere. A girl, furthermore, radically distant from an adult male by virtue of her physical difference, "more perfectly represent[ed] the safe, feminized, time of the nursery from which [the adult male] has been irrevocably banished" (135).[4]

This imaginative overlap between a geographically distant present and a temporally distant past can be traced back to Wordsworth's longing for a childlike communion with nature that is both geographically and temporally remote, most famously illustrated in his vision of his own child self "sport[ing] upon the shore" of an "immortal sea," though "inland far [he] be," and an association between the purity and freedom of the Noble Savage with that of child (Wordsworth lines 169, 166, 165). Such a celebration of the "natural" but remote innocence and freedom of both the child and the colonial native paved a way for escapist literature, both travel narratives and children's literature, that places readers in imaginative "contact zones," to use Mary Louise Pratt's term (Pratt 33). So, only through the eyes and body of a child—childhood's "native"—could an adult return, if only fleetingly, to a prelapsarian space from which he or she had been banished.

In her influential study *The Case of Peter Pan, or the Impossibility of Children's Fiction*, Jacqueline Rose defines children's literature as an aggressive act of colonization in which the adult author manipulates the child into identifying with an image of childhood that satisfies the adult's own needs and desires (26). Just as Perry Nodelman claims that adults writing for children are always and inevitably taking part in an oppressive and imperialist activity, Rose claims that authors depict childhood as a stable, separate category, thus forcing the child to function as the adult's opposite or Other—a primitive, innocent, and transparent being. Carroll and Barrie create juvenile characters who bridge the chaotic, unconstrained world of childhood and the safe, enclosed world of adult domestic culture, enabling adult authors/readers to look out on a world of childhood fantasy through the eyes of figures who have access to experiences and perspectives that would otherwise be inaccessible to them. In doing so, the adult authors maintain a certain distance from the children themselves. Because of this distance and detachment, the looking glass and windows of the children's stories take on the imperialistic, "voyeuristic and objectifying underpinnings of the spyglass as an investigative instrument"—an image that "evokes not just the penetrating male gaze of science" behind the lenses but "the imperial white gaze of colonialism" through which Carroll and Barrie viewed the "distant shores" of childhood (Jacobs 24).

Alice through the Spyglass

> If Wonderland really represents the underground of [Alice's] own psyche, it is a psyche not entirely her own. . . . As Alice encounters the creatures of Wonderland and the Looking-Glass world, Carroll creates not a quest for identity, or a solitary journey into the self, but rather a sequence of spectacles for childhood voyeurism.
>
> —SUSAN SHERER, "Secrecy and Autonomy in Lewis Carroll"

As psychoanalytic critic Susan Sherer points out, "to read a text as an exposition of a subject's inner world is to assume that it is through the lens of that subject's psyche that we identify symbols and organize meaning" (2); however, the psychological distance and occasional resistance between Alice and her imaginary world suggests that the child's "inner world" and psychic "lens" are not her own. Instead, she responds to situations and characters with a nostalgic longing and sense of loss that seem out of place in a child, and the *Alice* stories "articulate a double message"(7): on the one hand, they create the illusion that adult readers are watching Alice voyeuristically as she travels through a childhood space, enticing us with soliloquies and descriptions that focus on her isolation and vulnerability; on the other hand, they reveal an adult perspective and focus every time Alice fails to recognize or react to the natives sympathetically. It is as if the stories draw us into a childhood fantasy space and then teasingly insist on a certain distance (7).

Nowhere is this "psychological dissociation" more evident than in the *Wonderland* and *Looking-Glass* frame poems—poems that may be said to frame the psychological subtexts of the stories by inviting an adult nostalgic reading of the children's stories (2). In the prefatory poem to *Alice's Adventures in Wonderland* (1865), Carroll sets up childhood as a sanctified spiritual and temporal space—a charmed miniature lifetime that leads inevitably to a figurative death and adulthood. The poem begins "in a golden afternoon . . . under dreamy weather" and follows a "dream-child moving through a land / Of wonders wild and new" (lines 1–8, 21–2).[5] It is a "golden" and "dreamy" childhood landscape, shrouded in "wonder." When "the tale is done," however, the girl and her crew must travel home, "beneath the setting sun" (line 36). The end of the day suggests the end of her childhood—a figurative death that is made explicit in the final stanza, when the story becomes a funerary wreath on childhood's grave: "Alice! a childish story take, / And with a gentle hand / Lay it where Childhood's dreams are twined / In Memory's mystic band, / Like pilgrim's withered wreath of flowers / Plucked in a far-off land" (lines 37–42). By laying the wreath at the grave of her lost childhood, Alice, whom Carroll addresses anxiously from his vicarious position outside the poem's action, must surrender her place as a child/native in a dream(ing) world that is now "far-off" and inaccessible. In fact, by the time we reach the concluding poem to *Through the Looking-Glass, and What Alice Found There* (1871), Alice is an eerie specter of her former self. As predicted in the preface, "Long has paled that sunny sky; / Echoes fade and memories die; / Autumn frosts have slain July" (lines 7–9). Still, the children seem to be able to remain in a dreamscape while the real world withers and dies: "In a Wonderland they lie, / Dreaming as the days go by, / Dreaming as the summers die; / . . . Life, what is it but a dream?" (lines 16–8, 21). The children sit passively at a distance from the narrator, "their desires carefully edited to correspond to those of the adult speaker, who creates the poem unilaterally" (Geer 19). Just as Carroll's "pure and simple spright" in an untitled acrostic poem for Gertrude Chataway conjures "bright memories of that sunlit shore / Yet haunt[s] [his] dreaming gaze" (lines 6, 15–6), Alice seems tied to her role in enabling an adult to "gaze" nostalgically onto that Wordsworthian "sunlit shore."[6] And as she becomes more and more abstract, eventually "haunting" Carroll "phantomwise" and "moving under skies / Never seen by waking eyes" in the *Looking-Glass* epilogue (lines 10–2), we can begin to see the little girl in Carroll's stories as a spectral, intermediary spyglass for the author's own nostalgic gaze.

In both *Alice's Adventures* and *Through the Looking-Glass*, Carroll sustains such an intermediary perspective through the figure of Alice herself, who seems to embody the telescopic link between adult/outsider and child/native. Indeed, just as Alice observes that she "must be shutting up like a telescope" in "Down the Rabbit-Hole," she is later alarmed in "Advice from a Caterpillar" to find her neck telescoping into "an immense length of neck, which seemed to rise like a stalk out of a sea of green leaves that lay far below her," dramatically changing her own perspective on Wonderland (60). In this scene, as in many others, the narrator of the *Alice* stories is not disengaged from the actions and does not merely record the events happening to Alice. Instead, he focuses on Alice herself, regarding her as a vehicle for nostalgic travel as well as a nostalgic destination in herself.[7] The Wonderland story, for example, opens with Alice's private thoughts, and we immediately experience the action *through* her, not from outside her. *Looking-Glass*, however, begins with Alice's actions, and the narrator establishes an outside perspective that encourages us to look at Alice as a curiosity all her own, through asides like "I wish I could tell you half the things Alice used to say," and corrections like "But this is taking us away from Alice's speech to the kitten" (145). Only after Alice has crossed into the Looking-Glass World does the narrator have access to her thoughts.

In this way, the language of the *Alice* stories establishes the child/native as a sort of double agent; and, as the narrator vicariously adopts different identities, positions, and perspectives, the telescopic narrative reaches into the nostalgic spaces of both childhood and the child. As James Kincaid observes, "Peter [Pan], the child, is lodged in the world of play and the adult is stuck in the world of power; Alice, the apparent child (actually the adult) is firmly in the world of power and the apparent adult (actually the child) is in the world of play" (276). Alice is what Kincaid refers to as a "false child," a child who wants only to resist the nonsensical world of Wonderland. As a result, Wonderland and Alice occasionally reveal the "grown-up" desires driving the narrative and, as a result, undergo dramatic size changes. Alice constantly responds to the childish world of play and nonsense with logic and manners, she is generally willing to take on adult responsibility (the pig baby, for example), she resists intimidation, and she is eventually expelled from Wonderland amid accusations of breaking "Rule Forty-two" by being too grown-up (124).[8] In this final scene, after a story full of such adult behavior, her size actually shoots up out of control, eventually growing to her "full size" in the courtroom as she seems to lose her childlike sense of play once and for all and observes, "You're nothing but a pack of cards" (129).

Indeed, throughout the stories, Alice's awkward position as a child possessed by an adult consciousness is continually exaggerated by barely governable growth spurts, and, given Alice's shape-shifting in so many scenes, we begin to see her as both a prelapsarian child and a postlapsarian (or "fallen") adult. Like the ghostly specter-girl, "dreaming as the summers die" as "autumn frosts [slay] July" in *Looking-Glass*'s concluding poem, Alice finds herself strangely ill-fitted for the world of childhood fantasy. As soon as she walks away from the dead leaves, she comes across a door that leads to an

Edenic garden. It is "the loveliest garden you ever saw. How she longed to get out of that dark hall and wander about among those beds of bright flowers and those cool fountains, but she could not even get her head through the doorway" (21). Alice, as a vehicle or lens for Carroll's own longing gaze, yearns for this Eden, but she is too "grown" to enter it. The door leading to this prelapsarian golden afternoon, opened only with a golden key (recalling the golden colors of childhood in the story's prefatory poem), is designed for creatures much smaller than she. Furthermore, once Alice is aware of her large size, she speaks of the potential dangers in sipping from the bottle marked "DRINK ME" as if she were an adult speaking about children's unique vulnerabilities:

> 'No, *I'll look first,*' she said, '*and see whether it's marked "poison" or not*'; for she had read several nice little histories about children who had got burnt, and eaten up by wild beasts and other unpleasant things, all because they WOULD not remember the simple rules their friends had taught them: such as, that a red-hot poker will burn you if you hold it too long; and that if you cut your finger VERY deeply with a knife, it usually bleeds; and she had never forgotten that, if you drink much from a bottle marked '*poison,*' it is almost certain to disagree with you, sooner or later. (22)

The voice behind these musings plays with the girl's malleable identity until she reaches her breaking point. But, when Alice does begin to cry, she scolds herself for her behavior, though she sounds more like Lewis Carroll and is, in fact, interrupted by Carroll's authorial voice: "'You ought to be ashamed of yourself,' said Alice, 'a great girl like you' (she might as well say this), 'to go crying this way!'" (27).

Perhaps the clearest clue we receive about Alice's role as intermediary comes through her meeting with a creature who traditionally symbolizes transformation and growth, a caterpillar (or imminent butterfly). When Alice and the Caterpillar meet, their conversation immediately focuses on shape-shifting and ambiguous identity:

> The Caterpillar and Alice looked at each other for some time in silence: at last the Caterpillar took the hookah out of its mouth, and addressed her in a languid, sleepy voice.
>
> "Who are *you*?" said the Caterpillar.
>
> This was not an encouraging opening for a conversation. Alice re-

> plied, rather shyly, "I—I hardly know, sir, just at present—at least I know who I *was* when I got up this morning, but I think I must have been changed several times since then." (53)

Since her arrival in Wonderland, Alice has begun to recognize that she is neither child nor adult, and she cannot say who or what she is at any moment: "I don't keep the same size for ten minutes together!" she laments (55).

In a particularly revealing scene, Alice responds to the Caterpillar's request for a recitation by changing the poem "You are old, Father William" into a boy's inquiries about an aging father's ability to remain youthful. Yet, Father William seems anything but geriatric: he stands on his head, turns back-somersaults, devours food with a ravenous appetite, and balances an eel on the end of his nose. We learn through the poem that he is able to perform all of these acts because of skills and strengths from his youth. As in so many scenes in the *Alice* stories, Carroll emphasizes the aging adult behind seemingly whimsical, youthful behavior.

In *Looking-Glass*, Alice again grapples explicitly with the idea that she is merely the imaginative extension of an adult man when she, along with Tweedledee and Tweedledum, come across the Red King sleeping in the woods:

> "He's dreaming now," said Tweedledee: "and what do you think he's dreaming about?"
>
> Alice said, "Nobody can guess that."
>
> "Why about *you*!" Tweedledee exclaimed, clapping his hands triumphantly. "And if he left off dreaming about you, where do you suppose you'd be?"
>
> "Where I am now of course," said Alice.
>
> "Not you!" Tweedledee retorted contemptuously. "You'd be nowhere. Why you're only a sort of thing in his dream!"
>
> "If that there King was to wake," added Tweedledum, "you'd go out—bang!—just like a candle!" (189)

Later, when Alice returns home, her individual existence is still called into question. She wonders, "No, Kitty, let's consider who it was that dreamed at all. . . . it *must* have been either me or the Red King. He was part of my dream, of course—but I was part of his dream, too!" (271). Alice becomes literally spectral and intermediate—a man's vision of a child who is telescoped into an arcadian space of nostalgic play.

Going Native in Neverland

> Children remain the most colonized persons on the globe.
> —RODERICK MCGILLIS, "Postcolonial/Postindependence Perspective"

Like *Alice's Adventures* and *Looking-Glass*, the Peter Pan stories also imagine a sort of imperialistic occupation of not only a child's fantasy but a child's mind as well. In fact, the first view of Neverland, which admirably serves to orient the action and to introduce the principal themes, is possible only by occupying the children's fantasies, and the flamingos, lagoons, and wigwams have significant imperial implications, as do their subsequent relationship with pirates, Native American and Caribbean cultures, and African animals.

In this way, like the Wonderland located in Alice's dreams, Neverland exists not only exclusively for children but also exclusively in children. And, once again, children themselves symbolize nostalgic spaces. Mrs. Darling, for example, discovers Neverland only by "rummag[ing]" in the minds of her children: "Mrs. Darling first heard of Peter when she was tidying up her children's minds. It is the nightly custom of every good mother after her children are asleep to rummage in their minds and put things straight for next morning, repacking into their proper places the many articles that have wandered during the day" (2). So, again, because the island is, in fact, so inaccessible to adults, the Darling children act as the spyglass for adults who learn about Peter Pan and Neverland surreptitiously:

> I don't know whether you have ever seen a map of a person's mind. Doctors sometimes draw maps of other parts of you, and your own map can become intensely interesting, but catch them trying to draw a map of a child's mind. . . . There are zigzag lines on it, just like your temperature on a card, and these are probably roads in the island, for the Neverland is always more or less an island, with astonishing splashes of colour here and there, and coral reefs and rakish-looking craft in the offing, and savages and lonely lairs, and gnomes who are mostly tailors, and caves through which a river runs, and princes with six elder brothers, and a hut fast going to decay, and one very small old lady with a hooked nose. (Barrie, *Peter Pan* 6)

For Barrie, the child's mind is a Conradian playground: a blank space on a map that seems to transport the imperialistic adult (the Doctor) back in time, back to his own earliest beginnings as a child. By peering into the children's minds, the adult can watch from outside and report back the Neverland adventures that he spies: "Will they reach the nursery in time? If so, how delightful for them, and we shall breathe a sigh of relief, but there will be no story. On the other hand, if they are not there in time, I solemnly promise that it will all come right in the end" (39).

So the adult narrator watches with bated breath as he relays accounts of mermaids, pirates, exotic beasts, supernatural creatures (fairies), life-threatening conflicts, and primitive communities. Like nineteenth-century travel narratives, the stories telescope readers into an imaginatively stimulating foreign setting in which narrators attempt to mediate their own cultural presuppositions and desires between those they voyeuristically observe in these foreign cultures. And, throughout the texts, the narrators' perspectives maintain a constant awareness of both cultures (English/non-English, adult/child) and their differences, for, even though the Peter Pan stories began as pantomimes, the written versions undoubtedly assume an adult audience raised on Wordsworthian notions of childhood and its distant shores. As the narrator commiserates, "On these magic shores children at play are for ever beaching their coracles. We too have been there; we can still hear the sound of the surf, though we shall land no more" (7).

Yet, while adults can no longer land on the "magic shores" themselves, by establishing channels between wild child in Neverland and domestic observer in Britain, Barrie secures a way for adults to escape the real world and regain their ability to play, to feel, and to fly—to break the social, psychological, and physical laws of Victorian society. Like Carroll, he uses his juvenile characters as a vehicle for his own longing gaze. Neverland—Barrie's own Wonderland garden of delights—is too small for adults; however, the sight of child characters in the distance gives the adult voyeur passage through an imaginary window into a realm of innocent adventure.

Given that Barrie gives adult readers this access to Neverland through a sort of spyglass, it is not surprising that the narrator describes the island's "natives" with the methodical thoroughness of a scientist. He moves from descriptions of the layout of the communities and the construction of dwellings to comments about the physique of the natives, their clothing, ornaments, tools, and utensils, and on to observations about their language, myths, kinship systems, social and family relations, and gender roles. When the narrator invites readers to "pretend to lie here among the sugar-cane and watch them," and then describes the "chief forces of the island" as they proceed by him

(52–3), his descriptive style directly echoes that of Charles Kingsley in *At Last: Christmas in the West Indies* as he describes the "Port of Spain":

> The straight and level street, swarming with dogs, vultures, chickens, and goats, passes now out of the old into the newer part of the city. . . . But what would—or at least ought to—strike the newcomer's eye with most pleasurable surprise, and make him realize into what a new world he has been suddenly translated—even more than the Negroes, and the black vultures sitting on roof-ridges, or stalking about in mid-street—are the flowers. (95–6)

The present-tense verbs, the "translation" of the reader into a new world, and the sense of wonder in Kingsley's narrative seem to provide a model for the way in which Barrie's narrator reports what he sees in Neverland. After taking inventory of the boys as they pass, the narrator in *Peter Pan* describes the dark pirates, moving from the "Italian Cecco" to the "gigantic black behind him" to the completely tattooed Bill Jukes to Cookson, "said to be Black Murphy's brother (but this was never proved)," and Gentleman Starkey, then to Skylights, "the Irish bo'sun Smee," Noodler, "whose hands were fixed on backwards; and Robt. Mullins and Alf Mason and many another ruffian long known and feared on the Spanish Main" (55). Finally, the narrator focuses on Captain Hook and the "redskins" who follow him:

> In the midst of them, the blackest and largest jewel in that dark setting, reclined James Hook. . . . In person he was cadaverous and black-avized, and his hair was dressed in long curls, which at a little distance looked like black candles, and gave a singularly threatening expression to his handsome countenance. . . . On the trail of the pirates, stealing noiselessly down the war-path, which is not visible to inexperienced eyes, come the redskins, every one of them with his eyes peeled. They carry tomahawks and knives, and their naked bodies gleam with paint and oil. Strung around them are scalps, of boys as well as of pirates, for these are the Piccaninny tribe, and not to be confused with the softer-hearted Delawares or the Hurons. (55–7)

As a pirate, Hook recalls vivid, exotic descriptions coming to England from the Caribbean—descriptions that rely on the wonder and titillation behind a vicarious and clandestine experience of Neverland as an arcadian childhood space.

Because of this adult presence both in the fantasy spaces of Wonderland and Neverland and in the fantasy bodies of the children themselves, children's identities exist in a constant state of flux. For instance, in *Alice's Adventures in Wonderland*, readers find themselves dropped into what U. C. Knoepflmacher calls a "childland"; yet we find no child there, for the desires and anxieties behind her eyes belong to a middle-aged male subject. And Barrie's stage instruction in the dramatic version of *Peter Pan or The Boy Who Would Not Grow Up* that "all the characters, whether grown-ups or babes, must wear a child's outlook on life as their only important adornment" ultimately makes child and adult almost indistinguishable in Neverland (*Plays* 22). In each text, however, "primitive" and exotic childhood spaces are telescopically and vicariously experienced by an adult narrator/writer/reader longing to connect with an idyllic past that is imagined as both geographically and temporally remote. In this way, adults can repeatedly return to Wonderland and Neverland, and the elements of the texts can be located, specified, classified, with the assurance that these nostalgic spaces are not susceptible to historical contingencies.

NOTES

1. See Spurr.
2. According to Edward Said, a "median category" emerges as one of the key features of orientalist writing in all genres: a conceptual category that exists between the completely novel and the well-known, "a category that allows one to see new things, things seen for the first time, as versions of a previously known thing" (58–9).
3. Clearly I am relying here on James Kincaid's *Child-Loving: The Erotic Child and Victorian Culture*, in which Kincaid argues that childhood is a hollow category and that children are blank spaces defined only by the adult desires projected onto them.
4. Such a fascination with the little-girl figure can also be explained by what nineteenth-century writers and artists referred to as the cult of the little girl, a cultural phenomenon in which English female children were constructed and obsessively worshipped as *amie-enfants* between 1860 and 1911.
5. All the Lewis Carroll poetry quoted in this essay can be found in *The Complete Stories and Poems of Lewis Carroll*.
6. This line again refers to William Wordsworth's famous passage in "Ode. Intimations of Immortality from Recollections of Early Childhood": Though inland far we be, / Our Souls have sight of that immortal sea / Which brought us hither, / Can in a moment travel thither, / And see the Children sport upon the shore, / And hear the mighty waters rolling evermore" (lines 162–7).

7. I am using the masculine pronoun "he" to refer to Carroll's narrator.
8. "Rule Forty-two. *All persons more than a mile high to leave the court.* . . . It's the oldest rule in the book" (Carroll 124–5).

WORKS CITED

Austin, Linda M. "Children of Childhood: Nostalgia and the Romantic Legacy." *Studies in Romanticism* 42.1 (2003): 75–76.

Barrie, J. M. *Peter Pan*. New York: New American Library, 1987.

———. *Peter Pan and Other Plays*. Oxford: Clarendon, 1995.

Carroll, Lewis. *The Complete Stories and Poems of Lewis Carroll*. New York: Gramercy Books, 2002.

Geer, Jennifer. "'All sorts of pitfalls and surprises': Competing Views of Idealized Girlhood in Lewis Carroll's Alice Books." *Children's Literature* 31 (2003): 1–24.

Jacobs, Karen. "From 'Spy Glass' to 'Horizon': Tracking the Anthropological Gaze in Zora Neal Hurston." *Postcolonial Perspectives on Women Writers from Africa, the Caribbean, and the U.S.* Ed. Martin Japtok. Trenton, NJ: Africa World Press, 2003.

Kincaid, James R. *Child-Loving: The Erotic Child and Victorian Culture*. New York: Routledge, 1992.

Kingsley, Charles. *At Last: Christmas in the West Indies*. 2 vols. London: Macmillan, 1871.

Knoepflmacher, U. C. "The Balancing of Child and Adult: An Approach to Victorian Fantasies for Children." *Nineteenth-Century Fiction* 37.4 (1983): 497–530.

McGillis, Roderick. Introduction. "Postcolonial/Postindependence Perspective: Children's and Young Adult Literature." Ed. Meena Khorana and Roderick McGillis. Special issue of *Ariel* 28.1 (1997): 7.

Nodelman, Perry. "The Other: Orientalism, Colonialism, and Children's Literature." *Children's Literature Association Quarterly* 17 (1992): 29–35.

Pratt, Mary Louise. "Arts of the Contact Zone." *Profession* (1991): 33–40.

Rennie, Neil. *Far-Fetched Facts: The Literature of Travel and the Idea of the South Seas*. Oxford: Clarendon, 1998.

Robson, Catherine. *Men in Wonderland: The Lost Girlhood of the Victorian Gentleman*. Princeton: Princeton University Press, 2001.

Rose, Jacqueline. *The Case of Peter Pan, or the Impossibility of Children's Fiction*. Philadelphia: University of Pennsylvania Press, 1992.

Said, Edward. *Orientalism*. New York: Vintage, 1978.

Sherer, Susan. "Secrecy and Autonomy in Lewis Carroll." *Philosophy and Literature* 20.1 (1996): 1–19.

Spurr, David. *The Rhetoric of Empire: Colonial Discourse in Journalism, Travel Writing, and Imperial Administration*. Durham: Duke University Press, 1993.

Wordsworth, William. "Ode: Intimations of Immortality from Recollections of Early Childhood." *Romantic Poetry: An Annotated Anthology*. Ed. Michael O'Neill and Charles Mahoney. Malden: Blackwell, 2008. 162–8.

Elizabeth Throesch ◎

Nonsense in the Fourth Dimension of Literature

Hyperspace Philosophy, the "New" Mathematics, and the *Alice* Books

The Victorian conception of the fourth dimension of space, as popularized by Charles Howard Hinton and others, was often conflated with the new non-Euclidean geometries that were becoming increasingly popular in the second half of the nineteenth century. More appropriately classified under "*n* dimensional" or "*p* dimensional" geometries, the fourth dimension was considered by many proponents, whom Linda Dalrymple Henderson (*Fourth Dimension*) describes as "hyperspace philosophers," to be a higher dimension of space that encompasses the familiar three dimensions. The most popular device used in hyperspace philosophy to explain the fourth dimension to popular audiences was the dimensional analogy, where the reader is asked to imagine his or her relationship to a fantastic scenario of a two-dimensional world, and then analogically work out the relation of the third dimension to the fourth dimension of space. A German psychologist and mathematician, Gustav Theodor Fechner, offered the first known dimensional analogy in print, in an 1846 essay titled "Der Raum hat Vier Dimensionen" (Space Has Four Dimensions). Although the dimensional analogy reached its pinnacle as a fictional device in 1884 with the publication of Edwin Abbott's novel *Flatland: A Romance of Many Dimensions*, it continued to be used into the twentieth century. According to Henderson, it was not until the 1940s that the discourse of the *spatial* fourth dimension had been occluded by popular accounts of Einstein's relativity theory.[1]

However, in the second half of the nineteenth century, particularly in Britain, the concept of the fourth dimension was well known, and many contemporary adult readers of Lewis Carroll's *Alice* books would have been familiar with it. It is not my intention to argue that Carroll himself was a hyperspace philosopher; it is important to note, as Henderson does, that his "exploration of mirror images and symmetry in *Through the Looking-Glass* of 1872, with their four-dimensional implications, stands as comment on contemporary English fascination with higher dimensions rather than a sign of his own belief in the idea" (Henderson, *Fourth Dimension* 22). It is highly unlikely that Carroll supported *n* dimensional and non-Euclidean geometries, as evinced by the conservative stance he took in his 1873 text, *Euclid and His Modern Rivals*, the title of which is somewhat misleading: Carroll did not even discuss the recent developments in geometry here. Rather, he attacked contemporary attempts to update—with its original axioms intact—Euclid's *Elements* as a standard geometry textbook. A conservative in mathematics, Carroll, as Daniel J. Cohen observes, "avoided the strange functions of symbolical algebra and four-dimensional mathematics" (173). However, this avoidance is not indicative of a lack of awareness of the new mathematics. Indeed, Helena M. Pycior convincingly makes the case that rather than totally avoiding these developments, "the *Alices* embodied the mathematician [Carroll's] misgivings about symbolical algebra, the major British contribution to mathematics of the first half of the nineteenth century" (149). I will go one step further in this essay, arguing that, through the nonsense logic of Wonderland and the Looking-Glass World and the creatures that inhabit them, Carroll highlights some of the pitfalls of new developments in symbolical algebra, as well as non-Euclidean and *n* dimensional geometries of the later nineteenth century. While, as Pycior argues, "the roots of [Carroll's] nonsense verse may also be in symbolical algebra, which stressed in mathematics structure over meaning" (149), I will illustrate how, in fact, Carroll demonstrates what he perceived to be the dangers of separating symbols from meaning in mathematics. An understanding of the discourse of hyperspace philosophy is crucial to this argument: the concept of the fourth dimension is, like the fantastic spaces and creatures of the *Alice* books, a fiction that owes its origin to the contemporary attempt to assign literal meaning to empty symbols and phrases. Thus, by examining the common roots of these fantastic spaces, we can gain a deeper understanding of not only the *Alice* books, but also the network of ideas and anxieties in which both Carroll's work and hyperspace philosophy play a role.

In examining the work of hyperspace philosophers such as Hinton alongside Carroll's *Alice* books, I wish to highlight the emphasis that each writer places on the hypostatization of language. With hypostatization, we see a figure of speech given concrete existence, an interpretative strategy deployed frequently by the fantastic creatures of Wonderland and the Looking-Glass World. Hypostatization, as Jean-Jacques Lecercle and other critics have noted, is a key characteristic of nonsense literature: "one of the constant comic devices of the genre is the literalisation of abstractions, set phrases or metaphors" (208). In calling attention to this emphasis on literalization, I will argue that the fantastic spaces of Wonderland and the Looking-Glass World, like the fourth dimension of space, are simulacra that owe their origin to the inversion of signified and signifier, or, using the language of Carroll's Duchess, of "sounds" and "sense." If, as American nonsense writer and civil engineer Gelett Burgess proposes, "nonsense is the fourth dimension of literature," then the bizarre linguistic logic of the inhabitants of the *Alice* books can be read as a critique of the new mathematics and the rationale that supports its quirky offspring, hyperspace philosophy.

That contemporary and even first-generation readers of the *Alice* books would have made the connection between hyperspace philosophy and Carroll's most famous stories is demonstrated by Samuel M. Barton's claim in a 1913 issue of *Scientific Monthly*: in *Through the Looking-Glass*, "Mr. Dodgson, himself a mathematician of no mean note, is poking fun at the fourth dimension students."[2] Similarly, in 1943, American mathematician R. S. Underwood complained that "intoxicated with his verbiage [the hyperspace philosopher] begins to see Alice-in-Wonderland 'four-space' on the horizon" (171). Underwood's essay risks becoming a tirade as he describes this verbal intoxication of hyperspace philosophers elsewhere as "the prostitution of words" (170). Ridiculing the few who, in 1943, still believe in the fourth dimension as a "transcendental space" rather than as an independent variable of measurement usually given as time, the misuse of language that Underwood identifies as underpinning a hyperspatial treatment of the fourth dimension is the same process foregrounded in the fantastic spaces and situations of the *Alice* books. In both cases, the amenability of these constructed spaces to multiple, and at times contradictory, interpretations contributes to their broad appeal in the nineteenth century, and to a growing sense of anxiety about the arbitrary nature of "reality." Reading Carroll in our time, Alan Lopez highlights "the complex negotiations between the madness of nonsense and the epistemic and ontological doubt grounded in the simulacrum" (102). As I will show in the following examples, through Alice's interactions with the creatures of Wonderland and the Looking-Glass World, Carroll demonstrates an anxiety concerning knowledge and origins, which, in part, stems from a perceived dissolution between symbols and meaning. Similarly, hyperspace philosophers such as Hinton, while viewing the concept of the fourth dimension as an opportunity for mind expansion, also cast doubt on the ability of the human consciousness to grasp anything with certainty.

My observation of the connection between nonsense writing and hyperspace philosophy is not a new one: as previously noted, Burgess made the same connection between nonsense literature and the fourth dimension. In the figure below, published as the frontispiece to his 1901 collection, *The Burgess Nonsense Book*, Burgess proclaims that "nonsense is the fourth dimension of literature." Though obviously comical in tone, this cartoon makes an important connection between these two offshoots of nineteenth-century literature and mathematics. The image depicts a schoolroom scene, with a mathematical symbol featured on the chalkboard. The symbol appears to denote "the square root of negative infinity." Here is a "meaningless"

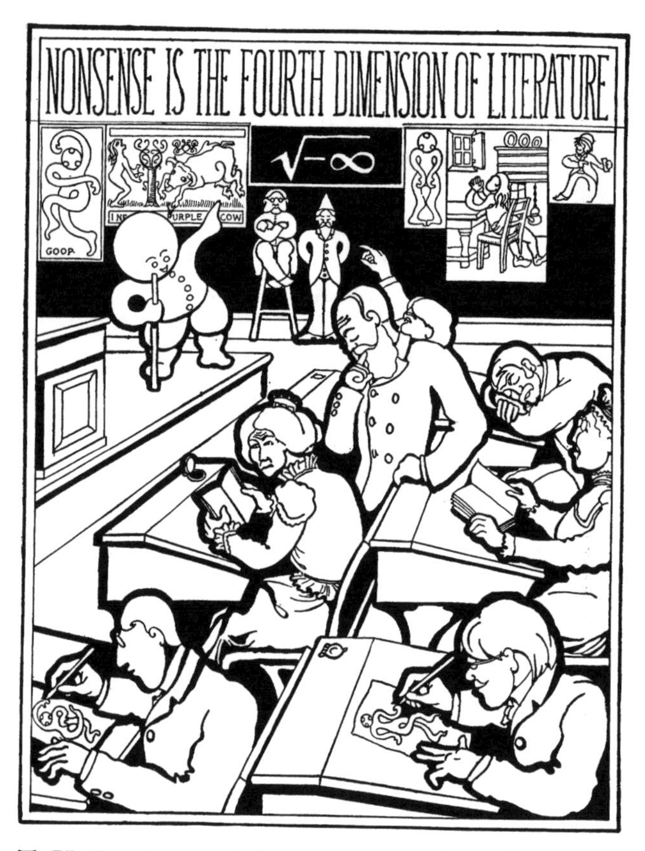

THE NONSENSE SCHOOL

expression: there is no "natural" number represented by this figure; it is an abstract symbol, with no correspondence to reality. It is no coincidence that the creator of this cartoon was also Hinton's friend and the editor of his work in the United States. In his earliest text on the fourth dimension, Hinton began his discussion with a similarly "meaningless" mathematical expression, building from it his version of a spatial conception of the fourth dimension. In this essay, titled "What Is the Fourth Dimension," Hinton explained:

> If there is a straight line before us two inches long, its length is expressed by the number 2. Suppose a square to be described on the line . . . this figure is expressed by the number 4, *i.e.*, 2 x 2 . . . generally written 2^2. . . . If on the same line a cube be constructed, the number of cubic inches in the figure so made is 8, *i.e.* 2 x 2 x 2 or 2^3. . . . The question naturally occurs, looking at these numbers, 2, 2^2, 2^3, by what figure shall we represent 2^4, or 2 x 2 x 2 x 2[?] (*Scientific Romances* 9–10)

Here Hinton is trying to take an algebraic symbol, 2^4, and make it correspond to a geometric, "real" object, just as 2^2 and 2^3 can be said to "represent" squares and cubes. Hinton, like other hyperspace philosophers of the nineteenth century, blurred the difference between symbolical algebra and its mathematical cousin, geometry. While the former treats of imaginary numbers and variables that need not be representative of anything visible in the physical world, Victorian geometry attempted to be more descriptive. In her study of Victorian geometry, Joan Richards explains this difference: "geometrical arguments are clearly more descriptive than analytical ones. To argue that a proof involving circles requires a conception of space is much easier than arguing that an analytical demonstration involving *a* and *b* requires an understanding of number" (39). The concept of the fourth dimension of space grew out of a slippage between the languages of these two forms of mathematics, a hypostatization of abstract symbols.

The potential for such slippage was present in the writings of Victorian geometers, as Richards shows in an example taken from an essay by the mathematician George Salmon, "On Some Points in the Theory of Elimination" (1866):

> The question now before us may be stated as the corresponding problem in space of *p* dimensions. But *we consider it as a purely algebraical question, apart from any geometrical considerations.*
>
> We shall however retain a little of the geometrical language, both

> because we can thus avoid circumlocutions, and also because we can more readily see how to apply to a system of *p* equations, processes analogous to those which we have employed in a system of three.[3]

In this passage, Salmon is specific that he is not referring to an actual space of "*p* dimensions"; rather, he is considering a purely formal problem. For him, the language of descriptive geometry is simply a matter of convenience. A few years later, however, in an address to the mathematics and physics section of the British Association in 1869, another prominent mathematician, Joseph J. Sylvester, actually made the jump from an abstract treatment of *n* dimensions to the suggestion of the "reality of transcendental space" of four or more dimensions.

Sylvester's support for the reality of higher spatial dimensions was, as Richards notes, "rather circuitous" (56). Rather than attempting to illustrate his own conception of four or more dimensions, he cited Arthur Cayley, "the Darwin of the English school of mathematics," as a key supporter (Sylvester 238). Additionally, in a footnote he mentioned William K. Clifford in conjunction with speculations about the fourth dimension, suggestively remarking:

> If an Aristotle or Descartes, or Kant assures me that he recognises God in the conscience, I accuse my own blindness if I fail to see him. If Gauss, Cayley, Riemann, Schalfi, Salmon, Clifford, Krönecker, [*sic*] have an inner assurance of the reality of transcendental space, I strive to bring my faculties of mental vision into accordance with theirs. (238)

Embedded within this gratuitous name-dropping is a circular sort of logic, a finessing of the absence of origin similar to that labeled "*Perpetum Moblie*" by Carroll in a letter to the *St. James Gazette* in 1882: "'That is to say, Mr. Pyke will first introduce Mr. Pluck, and then Mr. Pluck, being regularly introduced, will be qualified to introduce Mr. Pyke'" (*Diaries* 405). Mocking the formalities of parliamentary procedure, Carroll identified a perpetual oscillation obfuscating the absence of origin in line with Jean Baudrillard's theory of the simulacrum, which results in "the generation by models of a real without origin or reality: a hyperreal. The territory no longer precedes the map, nor survives it. Henceforth, it is the map that precedes the territory—*precession of simulacra*—it is the map that engenders the territory" (2). Like the dimensional analogy where 2^4 must correspond to a real object, the "perpetual motion" of introductions in Carroll's letter is an example of form preceding, and indeed engendering, "reality."

It is probable that Carroll was familiar with the dimensional analogy, as Alexander Taylor has argued. According to Taylor, it was "inevitable" that Carroll was aware of Fechner, who published his lighter mathematical writing under the pseudonym of "Dr. Mises":

> It was in any case probable that Dodgson-Carroll would hear of Fechner-Mises, but the presence of Max Müller at Christ Church [Oxford] made this inevitable. Professor Müller had been at school (1836–41) and University (1841–4) [with Fechner] in Leipzig before coming to Oxford. . . . [Müller] probably corresponded with Fechner and there were books by Fechner in his library. (89)

That Carroll was concerned with, or at least aware of, the dimensional analogy is further demonstrated by the fact that he owned a first-edition copy of Abbott's *Flatland*.[4] *Flatland* was published after the *Alice* books, and Carroll may have been interested in Abbott's book because his Flatlanders, being two-dimensional creatures born of the dimensional analogy, are products of the same interpretative impulse that rules the inhabitants of Wonderland and the Looking-Glass World. Writing of Abbott's geometrically shaped and named Flatlanders such as "A. Square," Mark McGurl observes:

> The inhabitants of *Flatland* exist as "characters" in two senses of that term, both as represented beings and as conventional symbols, somewhat as though the type beneath our eyes has detached itself from the pulp upon which it is pressed and come to life. It is a bizarre form of life, lived laterally, confined to the two-dimensional plane of the page. (57)

Like the four-dimensional space they analogically represent, Flatlanders are reified ink, symbolic—linguistic—notation brought to life through hypostatization. Much of the comedy and the anxiety embodied in the nonsense of the *Alice* books results from this form of literalization as well. Peter Alexander provides an example of Carroll's use of hypostatization for comedic effect in *Through the Looking-Glass* during the "Lion and the Unicorn" episode, when Alice claims she sees "nobody" on the road. The White King takes her literally, exclaiming: "'I only wish *I* had such eyes, . . . to be able to see Nobody! And at that distance, too'" (Alexander 563, italics in the original).

The White King, a Looking-Glass World creature, literally interprets

Alice's figure of speech, hypostatizing "nobody" into a proper noun, Nobody. The crossing over from the abstract to the concrete demonstrated here mimics the logic of hyperspace philosophy; creation of the spatial fourth dimension occurs by shifting from the language of symbolical algebra to descriptive geometry. Thus, in his complaint against the hyperspace philosopher's verbal intoxication, which causes one to see "Alice-in-Wonderland 'four-space,'" Underwood identified the common genesis of these Victorian fantastic spaces: Wonderland, the Looking-Glass World, and the fourth dimension are all alternative worlds that arise out of the hypostatization of abstract symbols, words, and phrases.

Asserting that the concept of the fourth dimension as hyperspace results from "straining for weird and meaningless conclusions which spring from the accidental implications of unfortunate technical terms" (171), Underwood demonstrates frustration with the hyperspace philosopher that is reminiscent of Alice's frequent, exasperated outbursts at the nonsensical logic of Wonderland and Looking-Glass World creatures. The interpretative activity of hyperspace philosophers such as Hinton corresponds to that of Carroll's fantastic creatures such as the White King. Indeed, that Carroll was fond of pointing to the pitfalls of mathematical misunderstanding is suggested by the example of the White King and Nobody cited above. Here we can observe an allusion to the potential for hypostatization embedded within the language of mathematicians, where the number zero, or "the null class," is treated as a "real" number, rather than a symbol denoting the absence of quantity.[5]

Peter Heath similarly observes the tendency toward reification and hypostatization demonstrated by Carroll's characters, noting that, at times, even Alice risks falling prey to the logic of nonsense. Citing her conversation with the Mad Hatter about time, Heath writes: "Alice is being seduced into the fallacy of reification—a common ailment of philosophers," by allowing herself to participate in a discussion about time as if it were a person who could be beaten, murdered, or made angry.[6] The literal interpretation of a figure of speech implies an insistence on the precise use of language as a tool for communication, on the intention "to say what one means." However, as Gabriele Schwab notes, the Wonderland and Looking-Glass World creatures' tendency toward literal interpretation is what causes most of the breakdowns in communication between themselves and Alice: "due to the nonsense-characters' fanatic insistence on literality, Alice increasingly loses the rhetorical securities of her own symbolic order" (163). Perhaps even more distressingly for Alice, her model of understanding is not threatened by those who are ignorant of the "superior" order of the upper-middle-class world she inhabits: the characters she encounters are well aware of the rules and regulations of Alice's order. It would be impossible for the inhabitants of Wonderland and the Looking-Glass World to insist on taking her literally at her word, if they did not possess at least some familiarity with Alice's linguistic model. As Jacqueline Flescher argues, "the backbone of nonsense must be a consciously regulated pattern" implying "a knowledge of the normal sequence of events" (128).

Thus it is nonsense's link to the "normal" paradigm that works to expose the arbitrariness of the norm, for the reader. Here, according to Lecercle, is where "radical nonsense emerges. . . . We now have [articulation] as the source of proliferation of potential meaning," rather than the clarification of one specific meaning (130). The proliferation of meaning threatens the stable order of Alice's above-ground world, just as the "nonsense" logic of hyperspace philosophy lends itself to multiple interpretations, threatening more traditional mathematicians such as Underwood. Returning briefly to the Burgess cartoon, we can see a schoolroom scene depicted with an instructor motioning to the symbol on the chalkboard, and the students reacting in various ways. Two students are, it appears, trying to draw an anthropomorphic representation of this symbol. Two others are reading texts. Another is sleeping, and one appears to be attempting to question the instructor. Thus one can engage with the "nonsense" of "the square root of negative infinity" in a number of ways. In order to embrace this proliferation of meaning, one has to be willing to "play the game" of the simulacrum and to accept that "sounds" can precede "sense," in which case it is the interpreter of the "Word" that possesses creative potency, rather than the speaker.

Lecercle illustrates Carroll's inversion of "sounds" and "sense" through the mouth of his hypocritical and nonsensical linguist, the Duchess of Wonderland. It is the Duchess who tells Alice to "take care of sense and the sounds will take care of themselves" (92). Here the Duchess appears to support a common-sense approach to language, where the speaker's intentional meaning is determined *before* he or she commences a speech act. However, the Duchess's own behavior subverts this "proverb." She is not consistent: her other "proverbs" appear to be completely arbitrary within the context of her conversation with Alice. Also, and more importantly, as Lecercle notes,

> Her "moral" is a parody of the proverb, "Take care of the pence and the pounds will take care of themselves." But in this case at least, it is not possible to say, as she does, that meaning is the origin of saying, for the origin of her idiosyncratic, falsely proverbial meaning is to be found in the saying of the original, conventional proverb. (123–4)

Therefore, while explicitly supporting the function of language as a logical activity that serves in the communication of meaning, the Duchess's own practice implies the exact opposite: articulation—written or spoken language—can and sometimes does precede intentional meaning. In such cases, the meaning is unfixed and thus open to multiple interpretations. Here is the reversal of the sense/sounds "moral," where "sounds" precede "sense" and, as a result, the "sense" is unfixed. This logic of the map preceding the territory has disturbing implications for conceptions of reality that are dependent on a monological epistemology founded in monotheism, as Gilles Deleuze implies: like the "I am that I am" of Yahweh, "the name saying its own sense can only be *nonsense*" (67, italics in the original).

Deleuze's remark also illustrates what was perhaps disturbing about the proliferation of meaning engendered by simulacra such as the spatial fourth dimension: the ability to imagine alternatives to the accepted order of the universe. Richards notes that in an 1844 address to the Cambridge Philosophical Society, the prominent philosopher and Trinity College master William Whewell "used the example of mathematics to establish the reality of necessary truth, and to demonstrate that human minds could grasp it" (29). A necessary truth, according to Whewell, is self-evident because it is impossible to even conceive of its contradiction (28). However, developments in non-Euclidean and *n* dimensional geometries, along with the rise of symbolical algebra, proposed multiple alternatives to previous mathematical certainties.

Of course, more is at stake here than the loss of mathematical certainty, as Richards observes: "Whewell's category of necessary truth was critically important for the assurance that man [*sic*] really could come to know his world. This assurance in turn supported his basically conservative outlook in which there were certain immutable truths about God" (29). By implication, a challenge to the "divine truths" of mathematics thus undermines a sense of reality that originates with, and is sustained by, an omnipotent speaker/creator. Epistemology is under threat here, as well: Kant had stated "that complete space . . . has three dimensions, and that space cannot have more is . . . apodictically certain" (40–1). Therefore, the theories of Hinton and other hyperspace philosophers offered a means of liberating the consciousness from "self-evident" limitations while simultaneously undercutting faith in the ability of the mind to accurately identify "self-evident" truths. Hinton was explicit about what he saw as the consciousness-expanding implications of hyperspace philosophy: in recognizing the possibility of the fourth dimension, he wrote, "the mind acquires a development of power, and in this use of ampler space as a mode of thought, a path is opened by using that very truth, which, when first stated by Kant, seemed to close the mind within such fast limits" (*New Era* 6–7).

Carroll's insight into the potentially threatening ontological implications are demonstrated in a more complicated inversion of "sounds" and "sense" during the Humpty Dumpty episode in *Through the Looking-Glass*. Humpty Dumpty, though he boasts of being "master" over words, does not have a static relationship with language. Lecercle observes the master/slave dialectic of Humpty Dumpty's "mastery" over words, drawing on a Nietzschean metaphor:

> Articulated language, like a bee, constructs a liveable world for the speaker, giving [him] an impression of control over the world of phenomena through [his] own control over language. It also, like a spider, captures and imprisons [him] in a network of constraints, thus enslaving [him], dictating [his] vision of the world. (154)

Articulated language—a nursery rhyme—brought to life, Humpty Dumpty is in a precarious position in Carroll's text. Although he may be "master" over the words he "employs," the course of his own life is predetermined by words that have their origin outside of the text of *Through the Looking-Glass*. Indeed, the originator of the Humpty Dumpty nursery rhyme—"Mother Goose"—is unknown. Thus, Humpty Dumpty's "liveable world" is constructed, determined, and eventually annihilated by the very language he boasts of controlling.

We are reminded of the precariousness of Humpty Dumpty's situation at the beginning of his encounter with Alice. Alice realizes that the egg shape she sees sitting on a wall is, in fact, Humpty Dumpty: "'It can't be any body else!' she said to herself. 'I'm as certain of it, as if his name were written all over his face!'" (218). Indeed, Humpty Dumpty's name, and thus his fate, is inscribed on his "person"; his name is descriptive of the unusual shape of his "body." The narrator informs us that his name "might have been written a hundred times, easily, on that enormous face" (218). After her identification of Humpty Dumpty, Alice immediately recognizes the fate that is implied by his identity and holds out her hands to catch him, "for she was at every moment expecting him to fall" (218). Provoked by this reminder of his own mortality, Humpty Dumpty—addressing a nearby tree—insults Alice. "Alice," the narrator informs us, "didn't know what to say to this: it wasn't at all like conversation" (219). Humpty Dumpty violates what Alice perceives to be the "rules" of polite conversation, and in an attempt to regain control, she begins chanting—"softly to herself"—from Humpty Dumpty's ur-text:

> *Humpty Dumpty sat on a wall:*
> *Humpty Dumpty had a great fall.*
> *All the King's horses and all the King's men*
> *Couldn't put Humpty Dumpty in his place again.* (219)

It is important to observe here not only Alice's aggressive play for control over the conversation, but also her recourse to the safety provided by the structure of the nursery rhyme; her nervous chanting allows her to assert control over herself, as well. This is the point where, according to Lopez, Humpty Dumpty's "heretofore given identity as 'real' [is] brought into question as perhaps nothing more than a rehearsed nursery rhyme" (112). Thus threatened, he returns fire: "'Don't stand chattering to yourself like that,' Humpty Dumpty said, looking at her for the first time, 'but tell me your name and your business'" (219). Humpty Dumpty retaliates by demanding that Alice state her name and her purpose, and thus constrain herself within the web of language as well.

There is a tendency in Carroll scholarship, as Michael Hancher observes, to conflate Humpty Dumpty with Carroll himself (49). However, I would argue that Humpty Dumpty is more accurately—and productively—read as a representative of the logic of the hyperspace philosopher. Like Lecercle, Hancher observes the inversion of what he calls "stipulative definition," the rule of language that designates the order of "sense" before "sounds" (49). Humpty Dumpty defines his terms only *after* he articulates to Alice:

> "There's glory for you!"
> "I don't know what you mean by 'glory'," Alice said.
> Humpty Dumpty smiled contemptuously. "Of course you don't—till I tell you. I meant 'there's a nice knock-down argument for you!'" (224)

This inversion of "sense" and "sounds" can be viewed as logical, Hancher argues, because Humpty Dumpty is—in Carroll's interpretation of him—a Looking-Glass World creature. However, I would argue that Humpty Dumpty's manipulation of language is not entirely the result of the simple mirror-image inversion of Hancher's stipulative definition. His very existence predetermined by the text of a nursery rhyme of ambiguous origin, and by the proper noun that denotes his name and his frame, Humpty Dumpty resembles the hyperspace philosopher who must carefully guard against the exposure of the hypostatization at the foundation of the concept of the spatial fourth dimension.

Hinton faces a similar concern with the unstable ontology of his four-dimensional space. While, as Ian Bell notes, some antipositivist, nineteenth-century scientists such as Ernst Mach managed to apply analogical reasoning in a way that "foreground[ed] its self-consciousness as an instrument, as a means of critical inquiry by virtue of this distance, this confessed removal into another lexical register," the movement from the language of symbolical algebra to descriptive geometry at the heart of the hyperspace philosophy of writers such as Hinton must remain precariously in the background (121). Although Hinton often foregrounds his reliance on analogical reasoning throughout his oeuvre, beneath this insistence on the similarity between the hyperspace of the fourth dimension and the observable space of the third dimension lurks the absence of any direct connection between the fourth and third dimensions.

While Hinton's hyperspace philosophy seeks to address the ways in which preexisting conceptions of space and language might limit the human mind in constructing and encountering "reality," at its heart lies a sense of anxiety concerning its own origin. The question that Hinton avoids asking constantly haunts the boundaries of his writing: is hyperspace philosophy in control of its own discourse, or is it being manipulated by the very language with which it expresses itself? The answer, for Carroll, it seems, would have been affirmative. If, as Cohen argues, Carroll "clung to the traditional idea that mathematics was a paradigm of simplicity and a conduit of absolute truth about the cosmos," then it is not difficult to imagine his negative reaction to *n* dimensional geometry and other developments in mathematics as threatening not only to the profession, but to the mind and spirit as well (173). Thus it seems likely that, as Pycior argues, his mediocrity as a mathematician was not due to his lack of awareness of new developments in the field: "[Carroll's] rejection and ridicule of symbolical algebra was well informed, but based on a conservative view of mathematics" (150). Rather, and somewhat paradoxically, though he was notably lacking in mathematical inspiration, Carroll's most creative inventions—Wonderland and the Looking-Glass World—were born, in part, of his conservative reaction to developments in his professional field.

The potential for disorder engendered by symbolic algebra and the new geometries was just as disturbing to Carroll as the nonsensical logic of Wonderland and the Looking-Glass World is to Alice. As Kathleen Blake observes, Alice—with her preoccupation with decorum and rules in game playing—fulfills the role of "adult" in most of her encounters with the inhabitants of Wonderland and the Looking-Glass World (80). Like Carroll, she plays the voice of tradition against the liberties that characters such as the Duchess, the Mad Hatter, and others take with the order of language and logic. The nonsense logic of the inhabitants of Carroll's fantastical spaces in the *Alice* books thus functions as a parody of the logic that engenders fantastical mathematical spaces such as the fourth dimension. Carroll's Alice clearly delivers the verdict on the logic of "sounds" before "sense" that I have identified as lying at the heart of hyperspace, the Looking-Glass World, and Wonderland (especially the courtroom scene). In this increasingly chaotic episode, upon hearing the King ask the jury for their verdict, the Red Queen interrupts: "No, no! . . . Sentence first—verdict afterwards." Outraged by this inversion of the judicial procedure, Alice "loudly" retorts: "stuff and nonsense! . . . The idea of having the sentence first!" (129). Burgess's cartoon is therefore a playful inversion of the stance that Carroll appears to support in the *Alice* books; the concept of the fourth dimension—or the logic of the new mathematics that allows the loophole for its creation—is "nonsense." However, as I have argued, perhaps what was most threatening about this "nonsense" was not its lack of meaning, but the proliferation of seemingly arbitrary fictions that it engendered. While this giddying multiplication of possible realities and spaces is appropriate for fantasy—or "dreaming," as in the *Alice* books—for Carroll and a number of his more conservative colleagues, it had no place interfering with the apodictic certainties of mathematics and theology.

NOTES

1. See Henderson, "Four-Dimensional."
2. Quoted in Henderson, *Fourth Dimension* 22. As Evelyn Fox Keller and others note, Carroll was, in fact, at best a mediocre mathematician: "His mathematical

work was dull, pedantic, and notably lacking the qualities we have come to identify with all creative activity, including mathematical creativity" (134). See also Heath 3.

3. Salmon, quoted in Richards 54, emphasis added. The essay originally appeared in an 1866 issue of the *Quarterly Journal of Pure and Applied Mathematics*. Salmon's choice of the variable p is arbitrary and interchangeable with n.
4. See Lovett 19. I am thankful to Mark Burstein for directing me to this source.
5. See Carroll, *Annotated Alice* 223.
6. Heath 69 n. 7. Heath attempts to distinguish this sort of literalization from the genre of nonsense writing, claiming that it should be classified under "absurdity," which he opposes to nonsense: "The difference between the two is that whereas [nonsense] neglects or defies the ordinary conventions of logic, linguistic usage, motive and behavior, [absurdity] makes all too much of them" (4). However, it seems contradictory to claim it is possible to "make all too much" of the "ordinary conventions" of language and logic, as such a strict adherence to literal interpretation removes one from the realm of the ordinary and conventional.

WORKS CITED

Abbott, Edwin Abbott. *Flatland: A Romance of Many Dimensions*. London: Seeley, 1884.

Alexander, Peter. "Logic and Humour in Lewis Carroll." *Proceedings of the Leeds Philosophical and Literary Society*, Literary and Historical Section 6.2 (1948–1952): 551–66.

Baudrillard, Jean. *Simulations*. Trans. Paul Foss, Paul Patton, and Philip Beitchman. Cambridge: MIT Press, 1983.

Bell, Ian F. A. "The Real and the Ethereal: Modernist Energies in Eliot and Pound." *From Energy to Information: Representation in Science and Technology, Art, and Literature*. Ed. Bruce Clarke and Linda Dalrymple Henderson. Stanford: Stanford University Press, 2002. 114–25.

Blake, Kathleen. *Play, Games, and Sport: The Literary Works of Lewis Carroll*. Ithaca: Cornell University Press, 1974.

Burgess, Gelett. *The Burgess Nonsense Book*. New York: Frederick A. Stokes, 1901.

Carroll, Lewis. *Alice's Adventures in Wonderland* and *Through the Looking-Glass*. *The Annotated Alice: The Definitive Edition*. Ed. Martin Gardner. London: Penguin, 2001.

———. *The Diaries of Lewis Carroll*. Ed. Roger Lancelyn Green. London: Cassell, 1953.

Cohen, Daniel J. *Equations from God: Pure Mathematics and Victorian Faith*. Baltimore: Johns Hopkins University Press, 2007.

Deleuze, Gilles. *The Logic of Sense*. Trans. Mark Lester with Charles Stivale. London: Athlone Press, 2001.

Fechner, Gustav Theodor. "Der Raum hat Vier Dimensionen." *Vier Paradoxa*. Leipzig: Voss, 1846.

Flescher, Jacqueline. "The Language of Nonsense in *Alice*." *Yale French Studies* 43 (1969): 128–44.
Hancher, Michael. "Humpty Dumpty and Verbal Meaning." *Journal of Aesthetics and Art Criticism* 40 (Fall 1981): 49–58.
Heath, Peter. *The Philosopher's Alice:* Alice's Adventures in Wonderland *and* Through the Looking-Glass. New York: St. Martin's Press, 1974.
Henderson, Linda Dalrymple. "Four-Dimensional Space or Space-Time? The Emergence of the Cubism-Relativity Myth in New York in the 1940s." *The Visual Mind II*. Ed. Michele Emmer. Cambridge: MIT Press, 2005. 349–57.
———. *The Fourth Dimension and Non-Euclidean Geometry in Modern Art.* Princeton: Princeton University Press, 1983.
Hinton, Charles Howard. *A New Era of Thought*. London: Swan Sonnenschein, 1888.
———. *Scientific Romances*. First and Second Series. 1884–1886. New York: Arno Press, 1976.
Kant, Immanuel. *Prolegomena to Any Future Metaphysics That Will Be Able to Present Itself as a Science*. Trans. Peter G. Lucas. Manchester: Manchester University Press, 1953.
Keller, Evelyn Fox. "Lewis Carroll: A Study of Mathematical Inhibition." *Journal of the American Psychoanalytic Association* 28.1 (1980): 133–60.
Lecercle, Jean-Jacques. *Philosophy of Nonsense: The Intuitions of Victorian Nonsense Literature*. London: Routledge, 1994.
Lopez, Alan. "Deleuze with Carroll: Schizophrenia and the Simulacrum and the Philosophy of Lewis Carroll's Nonsense." *Angelaki: Journal of the Theoretical Humanities* 9.3 (Dec. 2004): 101–20.
Lovett, Charles C. *Lewis Carroll among His Books: A Descriptive Catalogue of the Private Library of Charles L. Dodgson*. Jefferson, North Carolina: McFarland, 2005.
McGurl, Mark. *The Novel Art: Elevations of American Fiction after Henry James*. Princeton: Princeton University Press, 2001.
Pycior, Helena M. "At the Intersection of Mathematics and Humor: Lewis Carroll's *Alices* and Symbolical Algebra." *Victorian Studies* 23 (Autumn 1984): 149–70.
Richards, Joan L. *Mathematical Visions: The Pursuit of Geometry in Victorian England*. San Diego: Academic Press, 1988.
Schwab, Gabriele. "Nonsense and Metacommunication: Reflections on Lewis Carroll." *The Play of the Self*. Ed. Ronald Bogue and Mihai I. Spariosu. Albany: SUNY Press, 1994. 157–79.
Sylvester, Joseph J. "A Plea for the Mathematician." *Nature* 30 Dec. 1869: 237–9.
Taylor, Alexander L. *The White Knight: A Study of C. L. Dodgson*. Edinburgh: Oliver & Boyd, 1952.
Underwood, R. S. "Mysticism in Science." *Scientific Monthly* 56.2 (1943): 168–72.

Steve Hooley and
Cristopher Hollingsworth

Thoughts on Alice

An Interview with Rudy Rucker

S. H. Lewis Carroll's odd vision still appeals to new readers after all these years, but a great deal of his purpose was social satire, and many of his jokes and situations refer to current events long forgotten. Today his work is still prized for its imagination and humor, but the casual reader generally sees only the surface. Why is there a Lewis Carroll influence in your work, out of all the things you've read and internalized?

R. R. Like many people, I first read the *Alice* books before I was old enough to appreciate them. I had the clear sense that there were a lot of jokes and mental games that I wasn't getting. But I liked the books anyway for being so prickly, strange, and hyperactive. Over the years, I reread *Alice* many times; I had a nice boxed set of *Wonderland* and *Looking-Glass* with the Tenniel illustrations in color, Random House, 1946. More than sixty years later, I still have these copies sitting beside my desk.

When I was a young teenager, I came across Martin Gardner's *Annotated Alice*, and I loved finally finding out about all the little gimmicks and tricks that were embedded in the books. I was by then a regular reader of Gardner's "Mathematical Games" column in *Scientific American*, and he often related mathematical and logical puzzles to things found in Carroll's work.

I am especially drawn to the transreal or autobiographical elements of Carroll's oeuvre. I feel an affinity to the man; we're both soft-spoken, scribbling mathematicians with a wild sense of humor. I, too, am capable of spending hours talking to children and telling them tales. And I love how Carroll blends mathematics and logic with whimsy and madness.

The cultural referents to *Alice* that have affected me are not so much the primary British ones, but rather the secondary American ones. I saw the

1951 Disney version of *Alice* when it came out—I would have been five or six years old, and this was certainly one of the first feature-length cartoons (or feature-length movies of any kind) that I ever saw. I particularly liked the scenes when Alice was lost in the forest and encountered strange-looking creatures, such as a glasses-wearing pencil stub who walks on two legs. Just last month I finally got around to using that talking pencil stub as a character in a science fiction story, "Jack and the Aktuals." (He plays the role of a mathematician from a world of higher infinities.)

I was sent back to Carroll's work in 1966 by seeing a clip of the Disney cartoon as part of a psychedelic light show backing up Jefferson Airplane, who were playing a concert at Swarthmore College, where I was then a student. The clip was a loop showing Alice endlessly falling down the rabbit hole. I'd always longed to directly experience Alice's worlds, and for a brief time I imagined that mind-blowing drugs might be a way to get there.

This was a common notion of that time; it was certainly suggestive that Carroll had written of a hookah-smoking caterpillar sitting on a mushroom. In a way, psychedelicism is a form of orientalism. It's all about finding a way to get out of your straitlaced normal scene. In my own life, I found I didn't have the stamina for repeated doses of powerful psychedelics; instead I learned to get my kicks from imagination and math—just like Carroll.

S. H. An obvious parallel between your work and Carroll's is the way you send your protagonists searching for new worlds like in *The Hollow Earth*, the caves and tunnels in *White Light*, the higher dimensions of *Spaceland*, or sideways into mirrored brane worlds as in *Postsingular*—rather than always out into space.

R. R. Realistic space travel has never interested me as a theme, although I do get excited when I see giant pictures of Jupiter or even of Earth. But I don't like the groupthink that comes with large team missions; I prefer forms of alternate world travel that are accessible to quirky individuals. Another problem with real space travel is that it's so slow—unless of course you use some form of faster-than-light drive, like I do in my galaxy-spanning space epic, *Frek and the Elixir*. Of course, once you have FTL, it's really the same as magic doors to other worlds, like in *Master of Space and Time*.

Alice's looking glass is a wonderful paradigm for a door to another world, even better than the wardrobe in the Narnia books—although that's a pretty great image as well. The looking glass is like an Einstein-Rosen bridge, if you will. I love that when Alice pushes against the mirror, it's soft like taffy—and then she slowly pops through. There's kind of a birth thing going on there.

The Carrollian notion of changing one's size has interested me from my earliest years. It may well have been his work that first set me to thinking along these lines. I remember that as a very young boy, I had a variety of mind games I liked to play before going to sleep. One of them was imagining what I'd do if I could fly, and another was imagining what it would be like to shrink to a tiny size.

As well as *Alice*, another early influence on this front was the movie *The Incredible Shrinking Man*. My first novel, *Spacetime Donuts*, is, in some sense, *The Incredible Shrinking Man* written on a roller towel. That is, my characters shrink down so far that they reemerge on the same Earth that they shrank down into. The scale proves to be circular.

Georg Cantor's discovery of the transfinite levels of infinity only happened near the end of Carroll's life, but Carroll would have loved the transfinite, not to mention fractals. In some ways my novel *White Light* is a very Lewis Carroll book. We both like to turn the knob up to eleven.

In the mid-1980s I felt a little lost—I had just been fired from a somewhat Carrollian job as a professor of mathematics at a women's college—and I consoled myself by reading Carroll's diaries. Something that I found very encouraging was the fact that, at the end of 1863, the very year that he'd written *Alice in Wonderland*, he wrote in his diary that he'd accomplished nothing of any importance that year! You never know when you're doing your best work.

During this same period, I read Carroll's two books on logic, bound as one under the title *Symbolic Logic and The Game of Logic*. I describe some of his ideas in the "Logic" chapter of my nonfiction book *Mind Tools*. He made up these wonderfully mad syllogisms to illustrate modes of logical reasoning. The syllogisms are almost like haiku, where the restriction is that the three lines must represent a rigorously logical argument about three properties of things: if you accept the first two premises, you are logically obliged to grant the correctness of the third.

In 1985 I myself wrote a series of transreal Carrollian syllogisms, each illustrating a distinct mode of reasoning, and each of them crafted to express something about my personal life. I'll give four of them here, taken from pp. 203–4 of *Mind Tools*, each preceded by a sentence of explanation.

I was living in Lynchburg, Virginia, the hometown of evangelist Jerry Falwell.

> No beggar is honest;
> All evangelists are beggars.
> No evangelist is honest.

I had been dismissed from my teaching job due to faculty politics, even though I was in fact a popular teacher.

> No teachers are enthusiastic;
> You are enthusiastic.
> You are not a teacher.

Ronald Reagan was president.

> No president is a moron;
> Some illiterates are morons.
> Some illiterates are not president.

As always, I was terminally out of step with mass culture.

> Everything he likes is esoteric;
> No esoteric things are on TV.
> Nothing on TV is what he likes.

S. H. Alice, in Wonderland, is a rather passive observer and commenter. Rudy in Wonderlands is a different proposition. Your viewpoint characters pry and poke and taste, even without the "eat me" signs, and even while running from the devil. Do you feel this difference reflects a modern viewpoint or perhaps the difference in the characters' sex?

R. R. Over the years I've learned to make my characters more dynamic and active. Passive characters are a common weakness for beginning authors, perhaps because authors are often somewhat shy and retiring people. I goad myself to make my characters take charge and do things.

But I don't remember Alice as being all that passive. She's a somewhat willful little girl, and I think she kicks or breaks a few things in the stories. Carroll reports that the real-life Alice once said to her governess, "Nurse, let's pretend I'm a hungry hyena and you're a bone." I used to quote this to my own children, and we'd laugh and laugh.

By the way, another Carroll line that my kids and I loved was from "The Wasp in the Wig," an omitted chapter of *Through the Looking-Glass*: "And every time they see me, they shout and call me pig." What a wonderful man to write a thing like that in a children's book! I still like quoting that line in a surprised, abashed, elderly tone.

Back to your question, I'd almost say that Alice has been a role model for some of my women characters, such as Darla Starr in *Wetware* and her twin daughters, Yoke and Joke, in *Freeware*, not to mention Thuy Nguyen in the *Postsingular* series. I specifically remember one scene when the evil robots have implanted a zombie box on Darla's neck, and she's being forced to run through a long tunnel that goes from the human city beneath the surface of the moon to the robot-occupied zone.

> The corridor stretched on and on, mile after mile. With her legs numb and out of her control, Darla soon began to feel that she was falling down and down the light-striped hallway, endlessly down some evil rat's hole. *Rat*, thought Darla bleakly, I wonder if that's what they're taking me for, to get a rat [permanent robotic controller] in my skull. How ever will that feel? (*Wetware* 114)

S. H. Would it be correct to say that you intend your books as mind-expanding adventures à la *Flatland*, rather than as a social commentary like Carroll intended?

R. R. Indeed it's true that both these authors' work informs mine. And you open an interesting topic by trying to benchmark Carroll, Abbott, and me on the adventure vs. commentary axis.

But I would quibble a bit with two of the assumptions implicit in your question. First of all, it's not obvious that these modes are in fact opposed. Firstly, *Flatland* is very much a social commentary; the book lampoons sexism, prejudice against the handicapped, classism, and organized religion. Secondly, at least as I read the *Alice* books, they're focused upon logical sleight of hand, space warping, and word games rather than upon social issues.

This said, I'll grant that *Alice* has more social realism than does *Flatland*. The *Alice* books give us telling sketches, or at least caricatures, of types drawn from various strata of society. In this sense *Alice* has a richer feel than *Flatland*. Rather than having his characters be conceptual placeholders—like Abbott's High Priest—Carroll's characters are extremely detailed and idiosyncratic—think of the Red Queen.

I do to some extent identify with Abbott's A Square. He talks about higher dimensions all the time, and people think he's crazy. But A Square wasn't crazy, and neither am I. It's just that we see things more deeply than most people do. I think harder, and I have the tools of mathematics to help me dig.

In my fiction I try to achieve a synthesis of the two modes you describe—to have both the adventure and the social realism. On the one hand, I like to have a series of mind-boggling thought experiments and jeux d'esprit at the core of my tales. But at the same time, I like for my characters to be realistic and warty, like Bruegelian sketches from life.

My angle on satire tends to be oblique and nonstandard. Sometimes I depict characters who are so alienated, so entrenched in their rebellion, that they don't mention social issues at all. It's not so much that they're unaware of society's problems as that they've turned their backs on consensus reality. Their radicalism goes without saying. They're looking for a different path to the core. In this context, "No more second-hand God" is a relevant slogan.

S. H. There are a few events or characters in your work, for instance the elevator-operating shrimp and Mad Tea Party with Cantor, Hilbert, and Einstein in *White Light*, that seem intended to recall Carroll. Do you plan to put them in, or are they improvisations? ("Hmm, needs shrimp.")

R. R. I think that Carroll's images have permanently infested my mind, and that they pop out unexpectedly.

One Carroll bit that I've used a few times is his description of how the elixir in the "Drink Me" bottle tastes: "a sort of mixed flavour of cherry-tart, custard, pine-apple, roast turkey, toffy, and hot buttered toast." I give the addictive and empowering grolly fungus that kind of flavor in *Spaceland*, and I think merge in *Wetware* has that kind of smell. I believe I include red wine, roast turkey, and orange marmalade in this idealized flavor.

I know I have some characters like Tweedledum and Tweedledee in one of my novels, saying "Nohow" and "Contrariwise." I love that pair; they reduce logic to its barest minimum. And I love Humpty Dumpty talking about the words he uses coming by "for to get paid."

In my novel *Freeware* I have some tiny soft toy robots called Silly Putters, and they're modeled on the beasts in Carroll's "Jabberwocky" poem, which is presented and then analyzed in the course of *Through the Looking-Glass*.

Thus I wrote about a jubjub bird, a slithy tove, a mome rath, and a bandersnatch. The rath and the jubjub bird are always furiously fighting. That hyperactive Carroll thing. I laughed so much when I was writing about them.

And I couldn't resist giving the bandersnatch a penchant for lifting up girls' skirts. The unknowable nature of Carroll's sexuality adds a fillip of humanity to his work.

One thing I want to mention is Carroll's propensity for having objects that talk. There's a philosophical doctrine known as hylozoism that says everything is alive. I've always been attracted to this idea.

I drew very specifically on the Carrollian notion of talking objects near the end of my autobiographical novel, *The Secret of Life*. At the end of *Through the Looking-Glass*, Alice is at a dinner, and the ham on the table stands up, bows, and says something. I have very much the same thing happening at the end of *The Secret of Life*: "'Hello,' said the ham. 'I see you are on your fourth [magical] power. We weren't sure you'd be able to take it this far.' It spoke in a precise, hammy tenor" (242).

I find the end of *Through the Looking-Glass* very sad, if only because that's the end of Alice's wonderful adventures. I loved my world of *The Secret of Life* very much as well, and I was correspondingly sad when I finished writing about it.

I recently finished writing a novel that's called *Hylozoic*; it's about a near-future Earth in which all of our objects are alive. I probably wouldn't have reached the point of writing this book if I hadn't been weaned on Carroll. His animals talk, his furniture talks, his food talks. In a deep sense, this is a correct and reasonable way to see the world. Everything is alive. Everything talks.

C. H. In your 30 June 1999 *Salon* interview you talk about Margaret Wertheim's idea that single-point perspective gave human beings a "mental tool for thinking of space as an undivided unity," which in turn made it "possible to develop physics." You extend Wertheim's thought with this analogy: "Cyberspace is to Mental Space as Perspective is to Physical Space." What sort of space does Carroll's Wonderland establish, and what kind of unique mental operations and experiences does this space make possible?

R. R. Okay, if you adopt the Renaissance notion of visual perspective, it lets you bundle our physical space into a single compact image with a vanishing point. And if you say that your mental life resembles the Internet, then you have a unified cyberspace in which to arrange the world of ideas.

For Carroll, there's not a crisp distinction between the physical world and the mental world. Alice walks around in her dreams. So it's easy for things to change size, or for characters to hop great distances.

C. H. In the introduction to your short-story anthology, *Mad Professor,* you describe your fiction as having four qualities: thought experiments, power chords, gnarliness, and wit. It appears to me that you use Carroll's Wonderland not only as a source for power chord riffs, but also as a larger imaginative pattern—call it a myth. What is the Alice myth and what accounts for its success across cultures and media?

R. R. One point to make about Alice in the books is that she's never frightened; she takes all these odd things as a matter of course. She goes down the rabbit hole and begins falling several miles, and she's not sweating it at all, she's just chirping and talking to herself and looking around. This is, I would say, a myth of invulnerability, as in "The pure shall inherit the Earth."

Having invulnerable, unperturbed characters is a general stylistic trick that's useful in science fiction or fantasy. It can be boring to have your characters shriek, "Oh my God! I can't believe this! How can this be happening!" To my way of thinking, it's more amusing to simply have them accept the strangeness and deal with it.

Imperturbability is a common mythic pattern in fairy tales, and we might well say that the *Alice* stories are reality-based fairy tales. That is, strange things happen, but Alice is surrounded with the bric-a-brac of ordinary life, while things turn curiouser and curiouser. This again connects to the fact that the Wonderland tales are very much like waking dreams.

C. H. You define gnarl as a "process that is complex and unpredictable" in the context of prose style. Please explain more about literary gnarl, its relationship with Stephen Wolfram's thought, and your identification of William Burroughs as "master of the gnarl." Is Lewis Carroll another such master?

R. R. I've been under the influence of the philosopher of science Stephen Wolfram ever since I met him in Princeton in 1984. I'm very taken with his notion that our reality consists of lawlike processes that we might as well call computations.

The interesting point is that even if reality is a completely deterministic computational system, we can't predict or foresee what's going to happen. Why not? Because the reality-generating computations are so vast and complex that there's no shortcut way to summarize them. In essence, the fastest way to generate tomorrow is to let Earth's natural processes run on unmolested for another twenty-four hours. There aren't any shortcuts. Reality is incompressible.

When I wrote about this in my nonfiction tome *The Lifebox, the Seashell, and the Soul*, I made the point that a literary creation, too, can be both deterministic and unpredictable. How so? I am in some sense preprogrammed to create the kinds of stories that I do—but I'm unable to guess in advance the exact details of what I'll come up with.

It's like cooking. You have your list of ingredients and your recipe steps. But the exact taste and texture of the finished dish is something that only emerges during the cooking process.

Something I've always liked about William Burroughs is that he is very loose in his style; he'll switch into something completely unexpected without a word of apology. He lets the deep structure of his story percolate upward. And I think Carroll has some of this same freedom. He doesn't worry overly much about whether a particular scene fits in—he just goes with it. And, by going with it, he accesses some potentially deeper truths.

C. H. If culture is an organism and Carroll's *Alice* works are cultural genes, what does the *Alice* information undergird, direct, or enable?

R. R. As I said earlier, I think of the *Alice* tales as waking dreams. Carroll's work represents a turning point between traditional fairy tales and the scary-dream narratives of Kafka and Borges.

Animated cartoon films have done much to make waking dreams more plausible than before. But even in the context of cartoons, the reality shifts in the *Alice* tales remain radical and surprising.

The tendency in any commercial adaptation of *Alice* is often to water down the surrealism and to smooth out the ragged plot. Fortunately, the desktop computer revolution also makes it possible for dedicated artists to make very faithful films of *Alice*—and for this reason, the *Alice* stories continue to celebrate the gnarliness and unpredictability of the individual mind.

WORKS CITED

Abbott, Edwin A. *Flatland: A Romance of Many Dimensions*. 5th ed., rev. New York: Harper and Row, 1983.

Carroll, Lewis. *The Annotated Alice: The Definitive Edition*. Ed. Martin Gardner. New York: Norton, 2000.

———. *Mathematical Recreations of Lewis Carroll: Symbolic Logic and The Game of Logic, Both Books Bound as One*. New York: Dover, 1958.

The Incredible Shrinking Man. Dir. Jack Arnold. Universal International, 1957. Film.

Rucker, Rudy. "Finding God among the Aliens." Interview by Mark Dery. *Salon* 30 June 1999. Accessed 24 Jan. 2009.

———. *Freeware*. New York: Avon Books, 1997.

———. *Frek and the Elixir*. New York: Tor Books, 2004.

———. *The Hollow Earth*. New York: William Morrow, 1990.

———. *Hylozoic*. New York: Tor Books, 2009.

———. *The Lifebox, the Seashell, and the Soul: What Gnarly Computation Taught Me about Ultimate Reality, the Meaning of Life, and How to Be Happy*. New York: Basic Books, 2005.

———. *Mad Professor: The Uncollected Short Stories of Rudy Rucker*. Philadelphia: Running Press, 2006.

———. *Master of Space and Time*. New York: Bluejay Books, 1984.

———. *Mind Tools: The Five Levels of Mathematical Reality*. Boston: Houghton Mifflin, 1987.

———. *Postsingular*. New York: Tor Books, 2007.

———. *The Secret of Life*. New York: Bluejay Books, 1995.

———. *Spaceland*. New York: Tor Books, 2002.

———. *Spacetime Donuts*. New York: Ace Books, 1981.

———. *Wetware*. New York: Avon Books, 1987.

———. *White Light*. New York: Ace Books, 1980.

Carol Mavor

Alicious Objects

Believing in Six Impossible Things before Breakfast, or Reading *Alice* Nostologically

> Nostology: another word for gerontology (from Greek *nostos*, a return home, with reference to aging or second childhood + *-logy*)

As children, we find it impossible to believe that we will grow old. Unlike the White Queen, who brags, "Why, sometimes I've believed as many as six impossible things before breakfast,"[1] the child simply cannot believe the outrageous fact of impending old age. Alice, who is just seven in *Wonderland* and seven and a half in *Looking-Glass*, finds it impossible to believe that the White Queen is "one hundred and one, five months and a day" (Carroll, *Annotated* 199). For sure, this is because the White Queen reports her age with the preposterous specificity usually associated with the child, who often swaggers age in *both* years and halves, just as Alice boasts: "I'm seven and a half, exactly." And, undoubtedly, Alice would have to doubt the centenarian queen because few people live to be over one hundred. But somewhere in there is the fact that Alice, like all of us when we were children, cannot imagine herself as growing old.

Alice, like most children, finds it easy to believe in talking rabbits, talking legs of mutton, babies that turn into pigs, pebbles that turn into cakes, and her eventual queendom—"'Well, this *is* grand!' said Alice. 'I never expected I should be a Queen so soon'" (250). It is easier to believe in Wonderland and the Looking-Glass World than in growing old.

Like the remoteness of Alice's "poor little feet," after she opens up "like the largest telescope that ever was! Goodbye feet!"—gray hair for the mop-topped youth is "almost out of sight" (20). The future, not the past, is the child's foreign country. To be old, to the child, is to be a *boojum*.

Nevertheless, when Alice Liddell (the real Alice of Wonderland fame) reaches the age of eighteen, her face (as photographed by Carroll on 25 June 1870) betrays the emptiness of *The Snark*'s "Ocean Chart." It was the last sitting. Her eyes say it all: the approach of the mountains and the seas, the rivers and the trees, the countries and the cities and the elderflowers of old age.

While the *Alice* stories have long been understood, and rightly so, as an attachment to childhood, especially girlhood, what happens when we read Alice geriatrically? This essay reads the two *Alices* (both *Wonderland* and *Looking-Glass*), not as nostalgically yearning for childhood, but as nostologically yearning for agedness. Nostology's desire (so rarely acknowledged, so foreign to appreciation) is to live in the moment as an ancient, an elder, an antique, as if in the midst of a golden anniversary celebration, as if not governed by a ticking retirement watch, as if one did not know what day yesterday was or even what day today is, as if one were not a morning glory, but an evening primrose (already popped for the last time, withered and confused in its twilight time), as if one were an already bloomed night-blooming cereus flower.

I may have written a book entitled *Reading Boyishly*,[2] but time flies faster than looking-glass bread-and-butter-flies, who live on weak tea with cream. Today, I am advocating for reading not youthfully, but geriatrically. As self-proclaimed twin of Carroll's shawl-dropping, crooked, mussed old White Queen (I have given up on Alice); I now advocate for jam rules anew. I embrace the confusion. I do not resist. This nostological logic is articulated best by the White Queen herself:

> "The rule is, jam to-morrow and jam yesterday—but never jam *to-day*."
>
> "It *must* come sometimes to 'jam to-day,'" Alice objected.
>
> "No, it ca'n't," said the Queen. "It's jam every *other* day: to-day isn't any other day, you know."
>
> "I don't understand you," said Alice. "It's dreadfully confusing!"

If you are young, and reading this, live backwards.

> "Living backwards!" Alice repeated in great astonishment. "I never heard of such a thing!"
>
> "—but [said the White Queen] there's one great advantage in it, that one's memory works both ways."

> "I'm sure mine *only* works one way." Alice remarked. "I ca'n't remember things before they happen."
>
> "It's a poor sort of memory that only works backwards," the Queen remarked.
>
> "What sort of things do *you* remember best?" Alice ventured to ask.
>
> "Oh, things that happened the week after next," the Queen replied in a careless tone. "For instance, now," she went on, sticking a large piece of plaster on her finger as she spoke, "there's the King's Messenger. He's in prison now, being punished: and the trial doesn't even begin till next Wednesday: and of course the crime comes last of all."
>
> "Suppose he never commits the crime?" said Alice.
>
> "That would be all the better wouldn't it?" the Queen said, as she bound the plaster round her finger with a bit of ribbon. (196–7)

If you are old and reading this, then, to twist Freud's words from another context, "you are yourselves the problem."[3] Embrace yourselves.

Whether young or old, remember things *before* they happen.

If you prick your finger, be sure to scream, like the White Queen does, *before* you are pricked. As the likeable old gal herself comments: "What would be the good of having it all over again?"—when you have "done all the screaming already"? (198)

Like Carroll's camera, which revealed the world upside down and backward, like Carroll's glass negatives, which revealed black as white and white as black, what follows is a nostological look at Alice through aged, nearsighted eyes, plagued by cataracts, framed by objects, that *perfectly makes* no(stological) sense at all.

This is an essay on believing, only to forget, six things for starting obsolete and extinct, as if one were a living dodo remembering forward. My six objects, which all turn on helplessness, are as follows:

1. The pansy face of an *ars oblivionalis*
2. A mouthful of stones
3. A pullover with *two* neckholes
4. A house split in *two*
5. A scepter crowned by a dodo
6. A boat full of holes

Embracing helplessness,[4] this essay waxes *nostologically* about the White Queen, rather than *nostalgically* about Alice.

It wants to make growing old less shameful.

Object One: The Pansy Face of an *Ars Oblivionalis*

Both the young child and the elderly person are studies in forgetting, are figures empty of what went before.

When we are old, we forget, especially, the recent past. We are too old to remember. (*"You are old, Father William," the young man said, "And your hair has become very white . . ."* [49]).

When we are young, we only have the recent past. We are too young to remember.

Old people are babies in their second childhood. Babies are often understood as wise old men. (Consider the legend of Lao-tzu, the Tao-te-king, who "meditated for eighty years in the uterus of his mother: he was born an old man of eighty. Lao: old + tzu: child" [Barthes 155].) Even the very middle-aged Red Queen (who, like so many midlifers, gets nowhere while running in the same place) instructs Alice to treat the elderly White Queen like a child: "Pat her on the head, and see how pleased she'll be! . . . and sing her a soothing lullaby" (257).

As Carroll wrote, in regard to his development of the character of the White Queen:

> Lastly, the White Queen seemed, to my dreaming fancy, gentle, stupid, fat and pale; helpless as an infant; and with a slow, maundering, bewildered air about her just *suggesting* imbecility, but never quite passing into it; that would be, I think, fatal to any comic effect she might otherwise produce. There is a character strangely like her in Wilkie Collins's novel *No Name*: by two different converging paths we have somehow reached the same ideal, and Mrs. Wragge and the White Queen might have been twin-sisters. (Carroll, "Alice on the Stage" 296)

The small child and the geriatric have empty pansy faces.
Is it because they are thinking or because they are not?

"There's pansies, that's for thoughts." (*Hamlet* 4.5)

Pansy comes from the French *pensée* (a thought).

As the Red Queen says in "The Garden of Live Flowers": "Speak in French when you ca'n't think of the English for a thing" (166). That's a thought.

I remember the singing pansies in Walt Disney's rendition of *Alice in Wonderland.* (Because I was born of that time when fairy tales came to the child first, and possibly only, through celluloid, this is my first Alice memory.) These brightly colored pansy flowers, unforgettable to me, as if thinking about the etymology of their own name, persist: "You can learn a lot from the flowers."

The pansy face of an *ars oblivionalis*. Alice singing "All in the Golden Afternoon," from Walt Disney, *Alice in Wonderland*, 1951.

A pansy is but a bigger sibling to those tiny pansies known in English and German as forget-me-nots (*Vergißmeinnicht*).[5] A pansy is the flower of thought for forgetting.

In *Alice's Adventures Underground*, the original manuscript for *Alice's Adventures in Wonderland*, the Dodo (the very emblem of extinction, the animal forgotten) leads the way along the river "fringed with rushes and forget-me-nots"[6] toward a little cottage where Alice can dry off. This mostly forgotten part of the story does not appear in the final *Alice*.

If I may echo Umberto Eco, forgetting can only be accidental. In other words there can be no art of forgetting, as there can be an art of memory. An *Ars Oblivionalis*? "Forget it!" is Eco's answer (254).

Object Two: A Mouth Full of Stone

Proust and Carroll, in their own very different ways, were interested in stories of cakes that turn into stones.

For Proust, it was the crumbs of his famed madeleine-memory cake of his *In Search of Lost Time*, which resided within his body, only to resurface from a stumble upon uneven paving stones. ("The happiness which I had just felt [as a result of the uneven paving stones] was unquestionably the same as that which I had felt when I tasted the madeleine soaked in tea" [4.255–6].)

For Carroll, it was the inverse, a story of pebbles into cakes:

> the next moment a shower of little pebbles came rattling in at the window, and some of them hit her in the face. "I'll put a stop to this," she said to herself, and shouted out, "You'd better not do that again!" which produced another dead silence.
>
> Alice noticed with some surprise that the pebbles were all turning into little cakes as they lay on the floor, and a bright idea came into her head. "If I eat one of these cakes," she thought, "it's sure to make *some* change in my size; and as it ca'n't possibly make me larger, it must make me smaller, I suppose."
>
> So she swallowed one of the cakes, and was delighted to find that she began shrinking directly. (44)

Inversely, inside Carroll was a hard, insoluble, undigested crystal stone, which (did not shrink him but rather) starved him from growing up. As Virginia Woolf has written:

> [Inside Carroll there was an] untinted jelly [that] contained within it a perfectly hard crystal. It contained childhood. And this is very strange, for childhood normally fades slowly. . . . But it was not so much with Lewis Carroll. It lodged in him whole and entire. He would not disperse it. And therefore as he grew older, this impediment in the center of his being, this hard block of pure childhood, starved the mature man of nourishment.[7]

Carroll's "crystal" lodged inside him was his personal joy *and* his torture. Perhaps it was the cause of his famed stutter. Perhaps it also allowed the Oxford don to lose his stutter, to become at ease, in the presence of little girls. Medical lore claims that reading with marbles in your mouth, perhaps made of stone, as featured in Ann Hamilton's 1992 video *aleph*, will cure stuttering. Perhaps it was with stones in his mouth that Carroll first dreamed of pebbles turning into cakes, of stone into sugar.

A mouthful of stones, from Ann Hamilton, *aleph*, 1992.
Courtesy Ann Hamilton Studio.

And here, I begin to trip all over myself as I sort through a collection of stones that now include Ruskin's. Ruskin, the famous man of stones, was important to both Proust and Carroll.

Ruskin's writing, including *The Stones of Venice*, is uttered in the stones that built the foundation of much of *In Search of Lost Time*, a very, very long book that Proust would call his "novel Cathedral" (Leonard 52). Ruskin's actual name may be mostly obscured by the massive structure of the *Recherche*, but the stones are there, and will shimmer once found.

For Ruskin, stones, pebbles, jewels, and rocks were things to hold and collect, like art and little girls. As Marcia Pointon has pointed out ("John Ruskin's"), mineralogy was Ruskin's first love. Its language would infuse his descriptions in adult life of not only great cathedrals but also his worship of the body of the girl. Ruskin's crystalline child-self that grew up holding and collecting rocks, pebbles, and jewels[8] became an adult grammar of crystallography.

Ruskin loved stones that were very rare, as well as ordinary pebbles. Lecturing at the London Institute in 1876, Ruskin held out a little black pebble and recalled his meeting with the great geologist James Forbes, who was like a dark stone: "a man made of mountain flint in his inaccessibility and taciturnity" (Pointon, "These Fragments" 199). In Ruskin's hands, Forbes was very hard, fine-grained gray-black quartz, a metaphor for the solid, nearly impenetrable geological Time. With another black pebble, "one that used to decorate the chimney-piece of the children's playroom" in his aunt's house in Perth when he was just seven (the age of Alice herself), Ruskin waxed sentimental, becoming closer to the rock-collecting boy that he had been just a half century ago (Pointon, "John Ruskin's"). Time was near.

As Pointon points out, with two black pebbles, "Ruskin exposed the bond between two sorts of time: the human span of time evoked by the image of himself at age fifty-seven and his self at age seven, and the mineralogical span of time that forms the life of the pebble" ("These Fragments" 199–200). By *touching* endless (geological) Time and short-lived (personal) time, Ruskin *attempts* to impose order on the chaos of (White Queen) Time (Pointon, "John Ruskin's").

Carroll's library was full of Ruskin's books, including, of course, the three volumes of *The Stones of Venice* (Stern 19–20). Both Carroll and Ruskin found girls to love in the Liddell family. (For Carroll, it was Alice Liddell; for Ruskin, it was Edith Liddell.) In Wonderland, the "Drawling-master" who came once a week to teach "Drawling, Stretching, and Fainting in Coils" is a playful joke about Ruskin, who came once a week to the Liddell home to teach drawing, sketching, and painting in oils (Gardner 98 n. 18). But perhaps what links these two men curiously together is their coupling of stones and little girls.

When Carroll "was simply too happy for words, he would do as the Romans did and write in his diary: 'I mark this day with a white stone.' In so far as these Diaries cover his life (they have been shortened, and several volumes are lost), they show that Bachelor Dodgson was unspeakably happy on exactly 27 days. On 23 of these he had spent part or most of the day among the little girls to whom 'Lewis Carroll' was dedicated" ("White Stone Days").

Carroll turns young girls into (white) stone.

Likewise, Ruskin understands girls as stones. As if tampering with the Medusa story, Ruskin's girls, especially in his *The Ethics of Dust*, "are quite specifically seen in terms of the ancient and precious stones of the earth—as beautiful crystals, gems or jewels" (Robson 98).

Ruskin turns young girls into (precious) stone.

Both Ruskin and Carroll metamorphosized stones into girls: it was an acceptable way of eating them up.

Object Three: A Pullover with *Two* Neckholes

As adults, we often feel that our child self was another person or even that the child we once were has died. The contemporary French artist Christian Boltanski claims that it was the death of "Little Christian" that made space for his creative production: "I began to work as an artist when I began to be an adult, when I understood that my childhood was finished, and was dead. I think we all have somebody who is dead inside of us. A dead child. I remember the Little Christian that is dead inside me."[9]

Throughout *Alice* there is a continual theme of losing her (child) self or forgetting who she is. "'And now who am I? I *will* remember if I can! I'm determined to do it! . . . L, I *know* it begins with L!" says Alice, in the forest of forgetting (177). As a kind of twin to the White Queen, Alice is always in danger of losing herself, as if she were suffering from what would later be called Alzheimer's disease.

In 1901, when

> Auguste D(eter), 1850–1906, was first examined by Dr. Aloïs Alzheimer, he began with many queries. Auguste could answer many of the doctor's questions, but she did not remember when she got married and was documented as repeating the word "twin," seemingly without reason. When asked to write her name, she could only give her title. In the words of the study: "When she has to write 'Mrs. Auguste D.' she writes 'Mrs.,' and we must repeat the other words because she forgets them. The patient is not able to progress in writing and repeats, 'I have lost myself [*Ich habe mich verloren*].'" (Whitehouse 17)

To lose oneself strikes fear in all of us.

But what if we were not so afraid of forgetting? What if remembering the past was as fictional as remembering forward? What if we were less anxious about finding that dead child within and we just were, well, "Mrs. Wragge," as so affectionately rendered by Wilkie Collins? Would we fear forgetting so deeply? Would we fear old age so deeply? Maybe the primary right of the aged is the right to forget. "Forgetting one's misfortune is already half of happiness."[10]

Perhaps to sing along with the pansies and forget-me-nots is to forget. Perhaps to score Time with black pebbles is to forget. Perhaps to mark a day with a white stone is to forget. Perhaps Carroll (as inspired by Ruskin and Collins) is practicing an art of forgetting (*ars oblivionalis*). As Harald Weinrich has so astutely observed: "The verb 'forget' is composed of the verb 'get' and the prefix 'for.' The prefix converts the movement *toward* implicit in 'get' into a movement *away*, so that one might paraphrase the meaning of 'forget' as 'to get rid (of something)'" (1).

The stones of Carroll are washed with the waters of Lethe (the mythical river of forgetting). As the poet Stephanie Bolster writes of Carroll's white stones in a poem entitled "White Stone," these mythical pebbles of remembering are always already just out of our grasp: "It is a shining shape receding as we near it" (Bolster 19). Carroll's white stones are cousins to Alice's dream rushes as she floats down the Looking-Glass's Lethe: "What mattered it to her just then that the rushes had begun to fade, and to lose all of their scent and beauty, from the very moment that she picked them?" (204).

If our fear of old age is a fear of losing our memory, then might it not be better to dip memory in the oblivion of Lethe than to drown in our own tears?

No Name is essentially the long story of how Magdalen Vanstone, a rich, beautiful, happy young woman, suddenly loses her father and mother, only for it to be discovered that her seemingly perfect father was not legally married to her wonderful mother. (Early in life, Mr. Vanstone had been taken advantage of by a disreputable woman in America, whom he had married and who refused divorce.) After the death of her parents, Magdalen thereby loses her inheritance (to a wicked uncle) and her right to her own name (hence the novel's title). Magdalen then spends some five hundred pages trying to get back what is rightfully hers (her money and her name).

Her endlessly complex series of schemes, including disguising herself and taking on other identities, is aided by a likeable swindler (with parti-colored eyes) named Captain Wragge. But Magdalen, I would argue, experiences her tenderest connections in the novel with the always outrageous Mrs. Wragge.

Mrs. Wragge, who was extremely large, was nevertheless very meek and gentle. This "giantess of amber satin,"[11] with her "faded blue eyes" and pansy "moon-face" (163), is always frustrating the much smaller, compulsively neat Captain Wragge. Mrs. Wragge was "the crookedest woman" (163) that Captain Wragge had ever met.

The couple is a study in contrasts. Captain Wragge fears forgetting the tiniest morsels of information. He has to write everything down, in clear black and white, in one of his many, many ledgers or he will "go mad!" (163). Captain Wragge is driven mad by Mrs. Wragge. She even falls asleep crooked. As soon as her left heel is pulled up, the right one falls. Or she only wears one of her shoes, with the other simply left in another room. Her cap is awry. Her head is always buzzing. Captain Wragge has to shout at her constantly because if he speaks softly to her, she will drift.

Mrs. Wragge, like the White Queen, is always out of order, going everywhere and nowhere at once. Stuck on one book, *Treatise on the Art of Cookery*, she cannot get past the recipe for making an omelet with herbs: "mince small! How am I to mince small, when it's all mixed up and running?" (166).

Mrs. Wragge was terrible at not only cooking, but also sewing. In regard to her horrific Oriental Cashmere Robe, "half made, and half unpicked again" (374), which constantly screams "I won't fit," she remarks:

> I know I've got an awful big back—but that's no reason. Why should a gown be weeks on hand and then not meet behind you after all? It hangs over my Bosom like a sack—it does. Look here, ma'am, at the skirt. It won't come right. It draggles in front, and cocks up behind. It shows my heels—and, Lord knows, I get into scrapes enough about my heels, without showing them into the bargain! (376)

In *Through the Looking-Glass*, the White Queen turns into the knitting sheep that holds so many needles that she looks like a porcupine. One suspects that Mrs. Wragge may have been teaching her in the art of knitting. Nevertheless, Mrs. Wragge just might make a sweater perfect for Alice, who is "very fond of pretending to be two people" (18). It would be a duplicate of Rosemarie Trockell's *Schizoid Sweater*, with *two* neckholes to comfortably fit Alice and her twin: either the loveable Mrs. Wragge or the loveable White Queen.

Schizo-Pullover, 1988, wool, 60 x 66 cm, © Rosemarie Trockel, VG Bild-Kunst, Bonn 2009. Photo by Bernhard Schaub, Köln/Cologne. Courtesy Sprüthe Magers, Berlin/London.

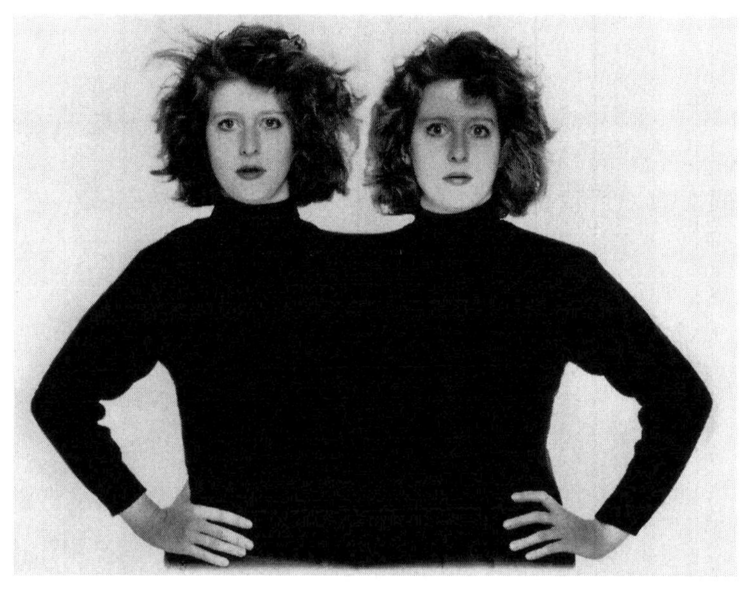

"*Schizo-Pullover* (worn)," 1988. © Rosemarie Trockel, VG Bild-Kunst, Bonn 2009. Photo by Bernhard Schaub, Köln/Cologne. Courtesy Sprüthe Magers, Berlin/London.

Object Four: A House Split in *Two*

Dementia: from Latin *de* = "apart, away" + *mens* = (genitive *mentis*) "mind"

Dementia is to become apart from the world, as exemplified in Gordon Matta-Clark's *Splitting* (1974). The White Queen, Mrs. Wragge, and Mrs. Auguste D. live in the crack, live in both halves.

Splitting is twin to *Schizoid Sweater.*

A house split in two. "Splitting," 1974. Photograph by Gordon Matta-Clark, San Francisco Museum of Modern Art. Courtesy Artists Rights Society, New York.

Object Five: A Scepter Crowned by a Dodo

Carroll's Dodo, its very name a play on the stuttering of Do-do-dodgson, is an obsolete beast that we cannot help loving and laughing at, at once. The Dodo is a queer creature: beyond reproduction, it is as helpless and useless as the thimble that it offers (back) to Alice as a prize after the caucus race:

> "But she must have a prize herself, you know," said the Mouse.

> “Of course,” the Dodo replied very gravely. “What else have you got in your pocket?” it went on, turning to Alice.
>
> “Only a thimble,” said Alice sadly.
>
> “Hand it over here,” said the Dodo.
>
> They all crowded round her once more, while the Dodo solemnly presented the thimble, saying “We beg your acceptance of this elegant thimble”; and, when it had finished this short speech, they all cheered. (32)

Not only is the Dodo a mirroring of Carroll’s own speech, the beast is a true repetition of his own queer nonreproduction. (Perhaps this is some of the reasoning behind Carroll’s blatant critique of Darwin in the form of a child’s fairy tale.[12]) The Dodo is Carroll’s own inner law: a birdly “ancient, masochistic adolescent” (Cixous 235). Carroll, who must have long known that he would not procreate, with his typical comic verve, always coupled by a melancholic patheticness, engenders the Dodo. Of note is the fact that Oxford held during Carroll’s time and still today holds the remains of one of the last dodos.

In Tenniel’s illustration (32), the Dodo is the only animal with hands, which makes him that much more human: one hand offers Alice the un-treasure of a thimble (perhaps this is the seed of J. M. Barrie’s figuring of a thimble as a kiss in *Peter Pan*) and the other hand clenches a cane. The cane, of course, comically emphasizes that the dodo could not fly (the reason for its extinction).

A cane is not far from Queen Alice’s scepter:

> *“To the Looking-Glass world it was Alice that said*
> *“‘I’ve a sceptre in hand, I’ve a crown on my head.*
> *Let the Looking-Glass creatures, whatever they be*
> *Come and dine with the Red Queen, the White Queen, and me!’”* (260)

A scepter is, perhaps, simply a gilded, treasured cane.

“Curiouser and curiouser” (20) is the fact that the emblem of London’s Royal College of Art is a scepter with the helpless dodo on one end (and in a complete inverse of this nonflying, extinct bird, we find a phoenix at the other end of the baton).

A scepter with a dodo is a *special* gilded, treasured cane for living and ruling nostologically.

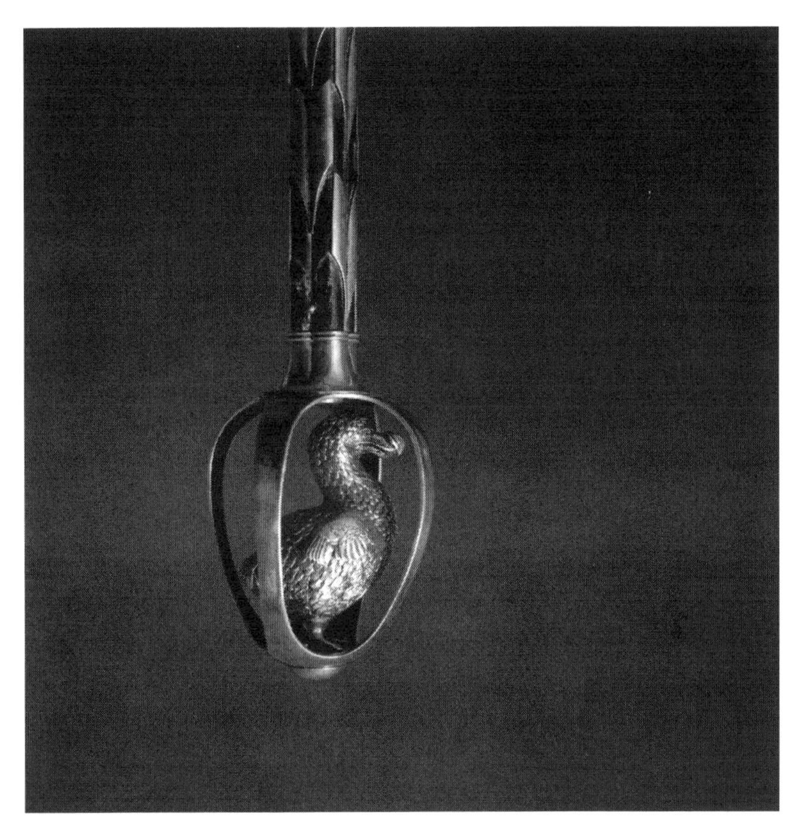

A scepter crowned by a dodo. "Dodo," 2007. Photograph by Olivier Richon. Courtesy of the artist.

Object Six: A Boat Full of Holes

> "Mrs. Wragge is not deaf," explained the captain. "She's only a little slow. Constitutionally torpid—if I may use the expression. . . . Shout at her—and her mind comes up to time. Speak to her—and she drifts miles away from you directly."
>
> —WILKIE COLLINS, *No Name*

Esther Teichmann's photograph *Mythologies I* (2008) features an older woman rowing on what looks to be an Alicious "golden afternoon." The image is painted over, as if to make the memory shimmer like an opal.[13] An older man lies in the boat too; he is resting his head on her lap. They are not remembering (their heads are not in the fateful state of "buzzing" that Mrs. Wragge complained of). They are peacefully "drifting," and Captain Wragge is not yelling.

The photograph was shot by Esther Teichmann: a girl-photographer[14] in a secluded swamp of dead trees in the Black Forest. It is the Alice story, told in a boat, long ago, retold nostologically.

A boat full of holes. "Mythologies I," 2008, hand-tinted C-type, 40 x 50 inches. Photograph by Esther Teichmann.

The picture was taken near the village edge of where the girl-photographer grew up in Germany. This landscape, in the valley of the Black Forest, is a surreal, Wonderland-Looking-Glass place. Almost subtropical, it has its own kind of Alicious magic, made not by Carroll's Thames upon which the fairy tale of *Alice's Adventures in Wonderland* was told all on a "golden afternoon" (7), but by the Rhine, which flows through the valley of this *different* forest of forgetting. Teichmann's Black Forest is twin to Alice's wood "where things have no names" (176) (not unlike Wilkie Collins's Magdalen, who eventually chooses to forcefully embrace her out-of-wedlock status as a girl with "no name"). The Black Forest, like Alice's woods and the woods of Hansel and Gretel and Little Red Riding Hood and so many other enchanted stories, is a fairy-tale forest: so rich it has inspired not only the great Romantic poets, but even a cake of cherries, kirsch, cream, and chocolate shavings.

This swamp of dead trees is a place that the girl-photographer returns to often. She has long wanted to capture its fantastical quality, pinning it down like a rare, iridescent butterfly. Her idea was to emphasize the castle-in-the-sky trait of this magical watery space by enhancing the scene with love. To the *mise en scène* she decided to add her parents, who are (to adapt lines from Carroll) "but old children, dear, / Who fret to find their bedtime near" (135).

The cast of three (the girl-photographer and her parents) drove to the swamp at five A.M. to get a picture in the low light of dawn, "beneath such dreamy weather . . . moving through a land / Of wonders wild and new" (7).

After setting up her photographic paraphernalia, the girl set her parents (let's call them "Alice" and "Charles") afloat in their boat inflated "with breath of bale" (136), gently pushing them out into the mirror of shallow water. But the "pleasance of our fairy tale" was soon fraught. The boat got caught on waterlogged trunks and branches. Full of tiny holes, the little boat (which had been found by the girl in the family's cellar of mostly useless treasures) was threatening to collapse. Helpless, it was in constant need of resuscitation.

As the girl was working on her last take, Charles started moaning and waving his hands frantically. He had a horrible leg cramp. He was trying to stand up in the boat to relieve his pain, but he could not get his footing in the always-on-the-verge-of-sinking boat. The girl-photographer was shocked and moved to see her father in such a state of helplessness in the helpless boat. Using a rope attached to the boat, the girl pulled Alice and Charles to the log she was standing on. Leaving Alice in the boat, she hoisted Charles out of the golden brown liquid. Holding onto his girl, the two limped to shore, camera, dinghy, and Alice left behind.

A few steps before land, Charles let go of his girl, thinking that his cramp had subsided, only to slip off the slimy, algae-covered land. Before the girl-photographer could blink her eyes, Charles's legs and torso disappeared into the unforeseen, bubbling quicksand: "Down, down, down" (14). Immediately, Charles grabbed onto the girl-photographer, still on her log of safety. With unprecedented strength, she dragged her father out, covered up to his neck in swamp treacle.

Charles stood shaking. He was sobbing, which shocked the girl-photographer. She pulled off his wet clothes, wrapping him in the towels that Alice had thoughtfully packed, somehow having remembered the tragedy before it happened.

"I weep for you," the Walrus said:
"I deeply sympathize."
With sobs and tears he sorted out
Those of the largest size
Holding his pocket-handkerchief
Before his streaming eyes. (187)

The girl-photographer sat Charles down on another dry log and turned to Alice, still on the always-about-ready-to-sink boat on the lake. (Alice had lost herself: she was laughing and picking dream rushes.) The girl-photographer did not yet notice the fringe of forget-me-nots (*Vergißmein-nicht*) that remained half hidden under the log upon which Charles sat.

NOTES

1. Lewis Carroll, *The Annotated Alice*, edited by Martin Gardner, 199. All further citations to *Alice's Adventures in Wonderland* and *Through the Looking-Glass* are from this same edition and will be parenthetically noted in the body of the text.
2. *Reading Boyishly: Roland Barthes, J. M. Barrie, Jacques Henri Lartigue, Marcel Proust, and D. W. Winnicott.*
3. I am referring, of course, to Freud's famous "Lecture on Femininity," in which he states: "Nor will you have escaped worrying over this problem—those of you who are men; those of you who are women this will not apply—you are yourselves the problem" (113).
4. In a recent lecture, Adam Phillips spoke on the value of helplessness, as something *not* to overcome, but as a state to sustain (without exploitation). Phillips makes this central point: helplessness is where we start from and helplessness is where we all end up. As Phillips comically remarks, paraphrasing D. W. Winnicott, even philosophers were once babies. Phillips's provocative work begs the question: "What if we grew into helplessness, rather than out of it?"
5. As Weinrich writes: "the little flower known as the forget-me-not (German *Vergißmeinnicht*; both forms derived from the Old French *ne m'oubliez mie*, botanically *myosotis*), which was often mentioned in the Middle Ages and has since become indispensable for lovers in many countries, and which is a reminder to be faithful that is at least as effective as its positive version, the pansy (derived from French *pensée*)" (3).
6. See Gardner in Carroll, *Annotated* 31 n. 2.
7. Woolf 48–49. Likewise, in the words of Marina Warner, "the enigma of Carroll is insoluble: how does the stiff, pendantic, Tory don, High Churchman and lacklustre lecturer in mathematics fit with the lightfooted, breezy, amiable, humourous inventor of stories, games, jokes, puzzles and treats?" (Warner 11).

8. See Robson on what she sees as Ruskin's child-self, which is gendered as feminine: "a crystalline girlish-self" (98).
9. Boltanski, as cited in "Studio." For a full discussion of the death of the child that once was, see my *Reading Boyishly* and *Pleasures Taken*.
10. Weinrich 15. On the political perils of forgetting and remembering, especially after Auschwitz, see Weinrich's chapter "Auschwitz and No Forgetting," 183–205.
11. Wilkie Collins, *No Name* 163. All further citations to *No Name* will be parenthetically noted in the body of the text.
12. William Empson, as quoted in Warner 14.
13. The painting over of the photograph, with its pink, blue, and green opalescent colors, gives the image a sixties, tripping, Jefferson Airplane, go-ask-Alice-when-she's-ten-feet-tall kind of look. But the look is also reminiscent of Carroll's painted-over photographs of nude girls, like the one of Evelyne Hatch (1879), painted over with its own surreal, Titianesque oils.
14. Teichmann is twenty-eight years old, hardly a girl, but this story is hardly true.

WORKS CITED

Barthes, Roland. *The Neutral: Lecture Course at the Collège de France (1977–78)*. Trans. Rosalind E. Krauss and Denis Hollier. New York: Columbia University Press, 2005.

Bolster, Stephanie. "White Stone." *White Stone: The Alice Poems*. Montreal: Véhicule Press, 2005. 19.

Boltanski, Christian. "Studio." *Tate Magazine* 2 (Nov.–Dec. 2002): n.p. Accessed 15 Dec. 2008.

Carroll, Lewis. "Alice on the Stage." *Alice's Adventures in Wonderland* and *Through the Looking-Glass and What Alice Found There*. Ed. Hugh Haughton. London: Penguin, 2003. 293–7.

———. *The Annotated Alice: The Definitive Edition*. Ed. Martin Gardner. New York: Norton, 2000.

Cixous, Hélène. "Introduction to Lewis Carroll's *Through the Looking-Glass* and *The Hunting of the Snark*." *New Literary History* 13.2 (1982): 231–51.

Collins, Wilkie. *No Name*. London: Penguin, 1994.

Eco, Umberto. "An *Ars Oblivionalis*? Forget It!" *PMLA* 103.3 (1988): 254–61.

Empson, William. "*Alice in Wonderland*: The Child as Swain." *Some Versions of Pastoral*. London: Hogarth Press, 1986. 251–94.

Freud, Sigmund. "Lecture on Femininity." *The Standard Edition of the Complete Psychological Works of Sigmund Freud*. Ed. James Strachey. London: Hogarth Press, 1964. 112–35.

Hamilton, Ann. *aleph*. VHS. Jane Hamilton Studio, 1992.

Leonard, Diane. "Ruskin and the Cathedral of Lost Souls." *The Cambridge Companion to Proust*. Ed. Richard Bales. Cambridge: Cambridge University Press, 2001. 42–58.

Mavor, Carol. *Pleasures Taken: Performances of Sexuality and Loss in Victorian Photographs*. Durham: Duke University Press, 1995.

———. *Reading Boyishly: Roland Barthes, J. M. Barrie, Jacques Henri Lartigue, Marcel Proust, and D. W. Winnicott*. Durham: Duke University Press, 2007.

Phillips, Adam. "Freud's Helplessness." Freud Museum Memorial Lecture, London. 26 Jun. 2008. Lecture.

Pointon, Marcia. "John Ruskin's Lapidary Loves." University of Manchester, Department of Art History and Visual Studies. 20 Feb. 2008. Lecture.

———. "'These Fragments I Have Shored against my Ruins.'" *The Story of Time*. Ed. Kristen Lippincott. London: Merrell Holberton, in association with the National Maritime Museum, 1999. 198–202.

Proust, Marcel. *À la recherche du temps perdu*. Ed. Jean-Yves Tadié. Vol. 4. Paris: Éditions Gallimard, 1988. In English: *Remembrance of Things Past*. Trans. C. K. Scott Moncrieff, Terence Kilmartin, and Andreas Mayor. Vol. 3. New York: Random House, 1981.

Robson, Catherine. *Men in Wonderland: The Lost Girlhood of the Victorian Gentleman*. Princeton: Princeton University Press, 2001.

Stern, Jeffrey. *Lewis Carroll Bibliophile*. Bedfordshire: White Stone Publishing (The Lewis Carroll Society), 1997.

Warner, Marina. "'Nonsense Is Rebellion': The Childsplay of Lewis Carroll." *Lewis Carroll*. Ed. Charlotte Byrne. Published in conjunction with the exhibition curated by Roger Taylor. London: British Council, 1998. 7–25.

Weinrich, Harald. *Lethe: The Art and Critique of Forgetting*. Trans. Steven Rendall. Ithaca: Cornell University Press, 2004.

"White Stone Days." Rev. of *The Diaries of Lewis Carroll*, ed. Roger Lancelyn Green. *Time Magazine* 29 March 1954. *Time.com*. Accessed 15 Dec. 2008.

Whitehouse, Peter J., et al., eds. *Concepts of Alzheimer Disease: Biological, Clinical, and Cultural Perspectives*. Baltimore: Johns Hopkins University Press, 1999.

Woolf, Virginia. "Lewis Carroll." *Aspects of Alice*. Ed. Robert Phillips. London: Victor Gollancz, 1972. 48–49.

Image

Cristopher Hollingsworth

Improvising Spaces

Victorian Photography, Carrollian Narrative, and Modern Collage

> However irregular and desultory his talk, there is method in the fragments.
> —SAMUEL TAYLOR COLERIDGE, *On Method*

Introduction

I wish to reconsider the role of photography in the genesis and cultural success of Lewis Carroll's *Alice's Adventures in Wonderland* and *Through the Looking-Glass and What Alice Found There.* This argument's goal, however, is not to produce a comprehensive rereading/explication of Carroll's classic Victorian texts; it is, rather, to better understand the relationship between Carroll's actual photographic practices and the unique mode of narration showcased in the *Alice* books. Because I approach Carroll's photography and creative writing as mutually informing products of the same specific context, there is tension between my ideas and the still-dominant direct-experience model of photographic influence that was first proposed by Helmut Gernsheim in 1949. This theory assumes what amounts to a one-to-one correspondence between the optical-chemical effects of early photography and operationally similar verbal structures. My research suggests, instead, that a fuller explanation of the relationship between photography and the *Alices*' rhetorical and narrative structures must be gleaned from the contextual patterns of Carroll's remarkably creative and socially complex life.

It is my argument that, instead of following the conventional plotting and moral cadence of narrative progress that mark other Anglo-American Victorian literary fairy tales, the *Alice* books assert a forward-looking improvisational mode of narration that Carroll perfected through entertaining child subjects and manipulating photographs. Viewed in this way, crucial aspects of the persistent and widening appeal and influence of Carroll's classic texts are attributable to the *way* they unfold through a largely unpredictable series of episodes and incidents. It is this aleatory motive (inflected by a specific social and material context) that anticipates and in some respects arguably undergirds the modernist exploration of mixed media, collage, and assemblage.[1]

The Direct-Experience Model of Photographic Influence

Serious consideration of photography's influence on Carroll's creative writing begins with Helmut Gernsheim's 1949 *Lewis Carroll, Photographer.*[2] Gernsheim, believing that the truest and, therefore, best photograph eschews obvious artifice and technical mediation, dislikes in principle the allegorical and the retouched or colored photographs so popular with the Victorians.[3] Gernsheim makes plain that mixtures of painting and photography compromise the expressive integrity of both arts and "are . . . abominations which destroy the photographic image" (32). From this perspective, Carroll's value and importance as a photographer are a function of his anticipating (Gernsheim's) modernist photographic taste (Nickel 12–7, 30–3).

To Gernsheim, photography affects Carroll's writing but not the other way around; and the effects of photography on Carroll's writing are limited to "allegori[es]" of direct sense experiences (Gernsheim 35). In his definitive 2002 essay "'All in the Golden Afternoon': The Photographs of Charles Lutwidge Dodgson," Roger Taylor follows Gernsheim's lead, elaborating what Friedrich A. Kittler might call a naïve "aesthetics of applied physiology" (Kittler 189). Carroll's relevant photographic experience is presented as a set of optical and chemical stimuli directly enabling specific sensory experiences (such as materialization, inversion, reversal, and changes in size) that cohere without cultural mediation, forming a powerful "conceptual framework" (Taylor 11).

Though it is likely that Carroll's imagination was to one degree or another quickened and shaped by his direct experience of photographic apparatus and processing, it is prudent to be cautious about any aesthetic theory founded on the assumptions that the eye transmits unmediated visual percepts that embody ideas and naturally cohere into a rationally intelligible system. Moreover, it does not necessarily follow that Carroll's view of the world through his camera and the stimulations of the darkroom are the sole or even primary sources of elemental aesthetic patterns like reversal and inversion. The topos of the antipodal world, for example, is an ancient and pervasive fixture of imaginative literature; for another, the trope of the looking-glass book/realm considerably predates the Victorian era.[4] For these reasons, it makes sense to me that the effects of photography on Carroll's imaginative writings cannot be restricted to a few visually explicable tropes, even when gathered under the rubric of a "conceptual framework."

Carroll's Picture Making in Its Social Context

Like many middle-class Victorians, Carroll found photography fascinating and diverting, a source of novel intellectual challenges and experiences that was at the same time a strategic tool for maintaining, strengthening, establishing, and documenting social relationships. The photographic process resulted in a socially flexible material artifact that meshed with a range of already established practices of familial and sentimental documentation, collection, and cataloging. Simultaneous with the governmental urge to put a face on criminality and anthropological projects of documenting the nineteenth-century European's idea of the human family, the domestic photograph was solidifying the Victorian family's image of itself, an image that could be organized, perfected, circulated, and compared with others. Generations before the middle-class domestic sphere was penetrated and complicated by radio, photography was changing the bourgeois family, offering it new social, educational, and entertainment experiences, teaching it how to be and behave in the machine's presence.

In middling as well as affluent Victorian homes, it was likely that photographic images were understood and enjoyed more broadly and variously than Gernsheim would approve: as sketches, colored to resemble paintings, assembled into albums for display, used to document important occasions and relationships, and as private and public visual totems of the beloved, the departed, and the celebrated. But even as the sociological machine of Victorian domesticity was shaping photographic practice—creating markets, patterns of consumption, and new artistic genres—photography was shaping Victorian society and its subjects, introducing into the domestic order that produced Lewis Carroll and made classics of his *Alice* books a different and modern aesthetic rhythm.[5] During the mid-1860s, Lady Mary Filmer also felt and sought to explore this rhythm.[6] According to Mary Warner Marien, Filmer "may have been the first artist to collage photographs, that is, to cut, arrange, and paste photographs on a surface so as to make a statement separate from the individual items included in the work" (160). Carroll's response to the experiential rhythm of Victorian photography was exactly contemporary and aesthetically related to Filmer's. Each artist felt the logic and possibilities of what we now call collage. Writing about collage as a historically located expressive mode, Katherine Hoffman tells us that it "may be seen as the quintessential twentieth-century art form with multiple layers and signposts pointing to a variety of forms and realities, and to the possibility or suggestion of countless new realities" (1). And what other pre-twentieth-century narrative better fits this definition than Carroll's *Alice* books?

Photomatter and Carrollian Narrative

I argue that Carroll's photographic and literary pursuits were mutually informing, building on and focusing his taste for and experience of working with mixed and variegated media. As is well known to Carroll's present-day admirers and commentators, as a youngster Carroll diverted himself and his siblings by making a series of illustrated family magazines comprising various brief comedic elements, including drawings, verse, and parodies such as the pretend Anglo-Saxon fragment that eventually became "Jabberwocky." In the boy we see the outlines of the man: already an adept imitator and confident wit, the precocious young Carroll showed a commitment to entertaining children (he was the oldest boy of eleven siblings) through an amalgam of visual and verbal invention and absurdity.[7] But more important for the coming invention of Wonderland is that as a youth Carroll was integrating bits of text and image via assemblage: experimenting with the heterogeneous substance, whimsically variable structure, and improvisational logic that inform Victorian bourgeois artifacts such as the scrapbook,[8] the commonplace book, popular illustrated periodicals like *Punch*, and photo albums.

Generations of critics have interpreted *Alice's Adventures* and *Looking-Glass* as versions of traditional literary genres, such as the fairy tale, pastoral, and quest.[9] In my view, however, even though Carroll's *Alices* suggest and may be said to play with conventional plotting, these stories are committed to a different narrative rhythm and motive. In a traditional story, the relationships between elements (and thus the elements themselves) are generally meaningful and dramatically logical: such a narrative serves laws of causation and continuity that in good Aristotelian fashion drive toward a satisfying conclusion. In the story "Cinderella," for example, which in its bourgeois formulation follows the plot of an unjustly displaced aristocrat who is properly restored, the heroine must lose her mother so that her father may remarry a cruel stepmother. This stepmother must be cruel so that Cinderella will be mistreated and, especially, so that she will be forbidden to attend the prince's ball. It is this unnatural and unjust prohibition that necessitates and authorizes the intervention of a magical donor figure—and so on with the rest of the links in this narrative chain. There are wonders here, such as a pumpkin turning into a carriage and back again, but each aspect of this tale, however fabulous and potentially diverting when viewed in isolation, strongly tends to serve the obvious plot.

There is some of this programmatic wonder making in the *Alices*, as when Alice learns to modify her height through nibbling on mushroom parts; but Carroll designed his stories exactly so that the reader's sense of dramatic causation and relations are generally uncertain and often beside the point. And in the absence of a firm plot, marvels begin to wander, becoming assertive, argumentative, and obscure and even inexplicable.[10] What makes Wonderland Carroll's and so supremely interesting and useful to us moderns and postmoderns is exactly that its contents and connections serve a unique narrative rhythm, a mode of narration that can only be titled "Carrollian."

As I have come to understand it, the unit or pulse of Carrollian narrative rhythm is most strongly present in the interstices and quasi-relations *between* elements and episodes, becoming sensible and enjoyable as a series of surprises arising from discontinuities, absurdities, and whimsies. Take for example the episodes of the pool of tears and the caucus race and their narrative relationship. It makes perfect narrative sense that giant Alice cries a pool of tears in which she, having shrunk considerably, later nearly drowns. But the agent of her shrinking is the Rabbit's fan, a marvelous object that is largely incidental to the plot and through which little or none of the energy of wish-fulfillment flows (Bloch 163). Nor, for that matter, is it dramatically necessary either that the pool should be full of animals or that Alice should later play a game with these animals. The caucus race's ostensible purpose is to dry Alice and her companions, and it does as much; but this racing/drying does not tightly participate within a greater narrative process. Depending on expectation and perspective, this episode's purpose may be one or more of the following: to enable a series of puns, to satirize political process, to evoke Victorian attitudes toward Darwinism, or to showcase a concrete poem. However, when *felt* as a moment of relative (but internally ambiguous) stasis between unpredictable slippages, the caucus race pleasingly contributes to the narrative's improvisational feel, functioning as one movement in a rhythm of narrative absurdity. It is here, at these moments of (non)articulation redolent with the (arbitrary) creative force of chance—where and when the reader fresh from one scene or situation, so to speak, casts a thread of expectation into the gulf of fortuity only to pull out an unexpected creature—that the causal relationship between Carrollian rhythm and the space of Wonderland becomes sensible. It seems, finally, that while we may momentarily wish the hookah-smoking Caterpillar to make sense or generally desire Alice to become a queen, in Wonderland and the Looking-Glass World our fantasy drive is reduced to an appetite for the diverting surprise of the next pun, absurdity, or puzzling marvel.

Given the generative overlap between Carroll's photographic practice and his experiments with narrative, the observations of the Dada photomontage artist Hannah Höch are appropriate and illuminating. In particular, her concept of "photomatter" (what I take to mean the intrinsically heterogeneous and variegated "image surface" generated by the manipulation of photographic images) strongly suggests a causal relationship between photography and the Carrollian aesthetic, a linkage that highlights in an explanatory fashion Carroll's nascent modernity (and, more recently, postmodernity):

> The peculiar characteristics of photography and its approaches have opened up a new and immensely fantastic field for a creative human being: a new, magical territory, for the discovery of which freedom is the first prerequisite. But not a lack of discipline, however. Even these newly discovered possibilities remain subject to the laws of form and color in creating an integral image surface. Whenever we want to force this "photomatter" to yield new forms, we must be prepared for a journey of discovery, we must start without any preconceptions; most of all, we must be open to the beauties of fortuity. Here more than anywhere else, these beauties, wandering and extravagant, obligingly enrich our fantasy. (Höch 220)

One of photography's primary creative powers, according to Höch, is that of "yield[ing] new forms." And the source of this form creation is exactly what we have already marked as being central to Carrollian narrative: the representation and exploitation of chance through improvisation: the "wandering and extravagant" "beauties of fortuity." As Roland Barthes reminds us in *Camera Lucida*, the photograph is material proof that something or someone existed at a particular moment in time (4–7). Yet photographs are also physical evidence of profound technological mediation. Thus, because the practice of manipulating photographic images amounts to a manipulation of discrete bits of machine-made reality, the resulting artifacts powerfully and simultaneously assert fact and artifice, ontological stability and crisis. As I will make clearer below, Carroll's last pre-*Alice* photography text, the 1860 short story "A Photographer's Day Out," indicates that his understanding of chance was a sovereign factor in the photographic process, a potentiality for aesthetic failure as well as novelty.

Part of a history of machine-involved image making (Armstrong 8), photography stimulated and shaped the consciousness of individual bourgeois Victorians and, more broadly, Victorian society as well. According to Nancy Armstrong, it was during the Victorian period that a "differential system" of "transparent and reproducible images" came to supplant earlier modes of representational authority, contributing to what in Victorian fiction writing she calls the "pictorial turn." Anticipated by the same novelistic techniques that it would soon undergird, this system of images, Armstrong states, "became basic psychological equipment" for the Victorian middle classes, the consumers of realist novels as well as Carroll's children's books (3–5). In the course of interpreting *Alice's Adventures* and *Looking-Glass*, Armstrong goes so far as to link Carrollian narrative with consumer behavior and subjectivity and to causally relate the activity of "playing with images" and Victorian identity (222–31). Perhaps, then, photomatter was as central to the undermining of Victorian certainties and the quickening and shaping of their replacements as were scientific discoveries such as the discovery of deep geological time and evolutionary theory.

When writing *Alice's Adventures*, Carroll did not seem entirely aware of his story's profound formal originality.[11] By 1889, however, Carroll publicly considers that his *Alices* represent an "original [narrative] line" or "pattern" (Preface 257). Equally significant are his unambiguous statements of 1887 to the effect that chance and not design was the source of *Alice's Adventures*: "I distinctly remember, now as I write, how, in a desperate attempt to strike out some new line of fairy-lore, I had sent my heroine straight down a rabbit hole, to begin with, without the least idea what was to happen afterwards" ("Alice on the Stage" 280). In her recollections of Carroll, Alice Liddell Hargreaves clarifies the crucial linkages between photography, Carroll's peculiar way of storytelling, and the *Alice* books. Carroll's narrative making appears to have been stimulated through the "fortuity" of "interruption":

> We used to go to his rooms in the Old Library, leaving the Deanery by the back door, escorted by our nurse. When we got there, we used to

> sit on the big sofa on each side of him, while he told us stories, illustrating them by pencil or ink drawings as he went along. When we were thoroughly happy and amused at his stories, he used to pose us, and expose the plates before the right mood had passed. He seemed to have an endless store of these fantastical tales, which he made up as he told them, drawing busily on a large sheet of paper all the time. They were not always entirely new. Sometimes they were new versions of old stories: sometimes they started on the old basis, but grew into new tales owing to the frequent interruptions which opened up fresh and undreamed-of possibilities. In this way the stories, slowly enunciated in his quiet voice with its curious stutter, were perfected. (Hargreaves 274–5)

Hargreaves clearly links a specific photographic situation and practice with the fortuitous genesis, variegated substance, and improvisational structure of Carrollian narrative. Carroll's stories "grew" and, indeed, were "perfected" through "the frequent interruptions which opened up fresh and undreamed-of possibilities"—stories that served as essential tools in Carroll's photographic process.

Hargreaves's recollections highlight the importance of a photographic context for understanding not just *Alice's Adventures* but Carroll's unique style of creativity, a complex social performance intimately coordinated with photographic apparatus, process, and image. From the start of his photographic experiences Carroll was hardly what we would now call an amateur photographer. We know that after taking receipt of his Ottewill camera on 1 May 1856, and at first with the help of his cousin, Reginald Southey, Carroll set out to learn the wet-plate process and the rudiments of technique. But knowledge of practical chemistry and optics and the aesthetics of shot composition constitute only part of the "black art" as it was understood and tirelessly practiced by Carroll, Victorian and member of an educated, respectable, and well-connected class. The purpose of the sort of photography that well-to-do Victorians welcomed into their homes was not the production of modernist art images. Carroll and his contemporaries gave meaning to, used, and enjoyed the photograph by putting it into what for them was proper and appreciative circulation within an established and rule-bound but nonetheless dynamically changing social economy.

Much more so than our sort of family and leisure picture taking, domestic Victorian photography was a performance: a highly social practice that Carroll obviously relished. From 1857 to 1862, while teaching at Christ Church, fulfilling his family and social obligations, and growing as a writer, Carroll "added the better part of seven hundred new photographs to his inventory" (Taylor 24). By Edward Wakeling's reckoning, during Carroll's twenty-four years and two months practicing the art, he made about 2,700 images (240). This means that Carroll was taking an average of nine or ten pictures a month, of which, according to my calculations, approximately 86 percent were portrait images of some type. Even in these days of fast and reliable film, automatic winders, and digital-image technology, it is impressive for an amateur photographer to average eight skilled to remarkable portrait images a month over a quarter century. But when one considers the temperamental collodion process that Carroll used for his pictures—the precise steps needed to prepare the glass plates, the dependence upon natural light, an exposure time sometimes so lengthy that subjects had to pose and remain still, and the tricky chemistry of developing and fixing the image—2,322 unique portrait images requiring hundreds of separate sittings borders on the miraculous. To this somewhat distant and yet adored oldest brother and uncle, academician, eccentric, and confirmed bachelor, the circumstances of child portraiture above all other photographic situations promised a controlled and coordinated and yet extemporaneous performance that constellated and made useful his skills of avuncular cajolery, verbal wit and play, storytelling, and sketching. This circumstance, the complexities of which Carroll treated as photomatter, is the source of the *Alices'* rhythm and contemporary feel—a situation that, significantly, depended upon the deployment and mediation of a special order of machine.

Photomatter and the Enrichment of Fantasy

Close analysis of Carroll's creative writing involving photography indicates that even though he was smitten with photography from the start, his initiation into the photographic situation and hence his mastery of the aesthetics of photomatter took time. As Carroll became increasingly experienced behind the lens, his manner of representing the camera and the photographic situation changed. Perhaps recapitulating a larger cultural movement involving the machine's integration into the bourgeois domestic sphere, Carroll begins with an image of the machine as external to the self (psychologically neutral and aesthetically inferior). Over time, however, Carroll's verbal treatments of photography work toward the machine's psychosocial embedment, a process marked by the disappearance of the physical camera and a notable increase in original formal experimentation, particularly involving techniques of collage and improvisation. The apogee of the curve I am charting is the structure of *Alice's Adventures*; from which *Looking-Glass*, by dint of its more formulaic nature, is a slight but telling falling off. Carroll himself seemed to realize that he had exhausted something special through writing the *Alice* books. In 1874, based on a fairy story he had published in 1867, Carroll attempted a second original pattern in children's literature (Preface 257). Whereas the Alice pattern is distinguished by an improvisational narrative that begins with the whim of sending Alice down a rabbit hole with no preconceived reason or path, the pattern of *Sylvie and Bruno* is an equally peculiar but ultimately less original and satisfying amalgam of "acceptable nonsense for children [and] some of the graver thoughts of life" (260).

Near the start of Carroll's journey to modern Wonderland is his 1855 sketch "Photography Extraordinary." In this text Carroll, uninterested in accurately representing the details of the photographic process, uses the concept of "development" to lampoon schools of literary style. Yet the several ways Carroll characterizes the photographic medium in "Photography" are worth closer attention. The first—combining the stance of the aesthete, the satirist's suspicion of newfangled gadgetry, and elements of the then commonplace idea of the clunky, utilitarian, and aesthetically irrelevant machine—treats photography as an instrumentalist and inferior imitation of writing, a means of "reduc[ing] the art of novel-writing to the merest mechanical labor" (1109). Carroll has represented photography according to an old technological pattern, as a mechanism external to and thus hardly relevant to the self. But the sketch also signals Carroll's genuine interest in the photographic medium, gesturing toward the hybrid nature of a new order of machines and the experiences they enable: the "mesmeric rapport established between the mind of the patient and the [camera's] object glass" (1110).

After Carroll obtained his first camera in mid-May 1856, he began his photographic experiments predictably enough: landscape studies, family pictures, and portraits. But "by 1857 another kind of vision was taking shape. . . . [Carroll was taking pictures] which involved costumes, role-playing, and greater attention to staging" (Nickel 16). Indeed, "Hiawatha's Photographing," written in 1857, suggests that Carroll, now an avid practitioner of the "black art," conceives of photography as inherently theatrical: involving dressing up, posing, posturing, and its own sort of drama.[12] Both "Photography

Extraordinary" and "Hiawatha" are evidence that photography stimulated Carroll's literary talent, but the latter also shows that the nature of this stimulation has changed. The satirical focus of "Hiawatha"—as well as the source of its dramatic structure—is the photographic situation itself, which Carroll represents as a series of "picture[s that] failed" (35), either because a subject moved or the likeness captured was deemed unacceptable. The poem's closing episode has the photographer "tumbl[ing] all the tribe together" (103) for a family portrait. In light of the distinctive narrative structure of the *Alice* books, it is revealingly appropriate that Hiawatha "did at last obtain a picture / where the faces all succeeded" through "happy chance" (105–7) and not design. But this Hogarthian "perfect likeness" reveals too much. Anticipating the *Alices'* many scenes of social absurdity, the entire family "unrestrainedly abused" their portrait "as the worst and ugliest picture" (108–11). Subjected to the family's "angry, loud, discordant voices" that remind the speaker of dogs "howl[ing]" and cats "wail[ing]," Hiawatha loses his "politeness and patience" (121–6). Like Alice, who becomes exasperated while on the stand during the Knave's trial—"Who cares for you? . . . You're nothing but a pack of cards!" (97)—Hiawatha tires of these "most unpleasant people" (117). He leaves them quickly and with a piece of his mind (127–34).

"A Photographer's Day Out," a short story written in 1860, is Carroll's last pre-*Alice* photography text. As with "Hiawatha," "Day Out" is a series of increasingly slapstick situations. However, where the first piece ends with the photographer abruptly packing up his equipment and leaving a boorish family with a too-revealing portrait and strong words, the second concludes with lawbreaking and mayhem: trespass, property damage, and fighting. Not only is the content of "Day Out" wilder than Carroll's preceding photo-satires, it contains even more specific anticipations of the *Alices*. For instance, the protagonist's friend uses the term "uglify" ("Day Out" 979), which in a slightly different guise shows up in the Mock Turtle's description of his formal schooling as one branch of submarine arithmetic, "uglification" (*Alice's Adventures* 76). More important, however, is Carroll's use of the photographer's diary (organized by picture and sitting number) as an experimental structure: this is an episodic sequence/logic that makes chance the ground of immediate experience and places fortuity at the center of narration. Because such a narrative structure may contain nearly anything without subjecting it to clear—which is to say, conventional—dramatic necessity, its potentials and pleasures are similar to those I have located in the *Alice* books: variety and inventiveness of incident and, borrowing a metaphor from Walter de la Mare, discontinuous movement from one "translucent bead of fantasy" to the next (58).

Perhaps the most interesting moment of "Day Out" is when Tubbs describes the negative of landscape he has just shot, hoping to impress Amelia, his friend's sister (who at this very moment is at her house with another suitor):

> Eagerly, tremblingly, I covered my head with the hood, and commenced the development. Trees rather misty—well! the wind had blown them about a little; *that* wouldn't show much—the farmer? well, *he* had walked on a yard or two, and I should be sorry to state how many arms and legs he appeared with—never mind! call him a spider, a centipede, anything—the cow? I must, however, reluctantly confess that the cow had three heads, and though such an animal may be curious, it is *not* picturesque. (984–5)

Tubbs, unsuccessful at love and mimetic photography, speaks of the unintended products of photography, the meeting of machine and the vagaries of the world—the "misty" trees, the multilimbed and spiderish farmer and his triple-headed cow—as defects: at best the cow might be regarded as "curious." But the energetic detailing of these defects suggests something else: that to Carroll they are new ways of seeing, moments when the machine shapes life into unexpected violations and forms. Anticipations of Wonderland waiting for its Queen: vaporous trees, a human centipede, a prosaic cow ironically alluding to mighty Cerberus. Such uneven and curious blendings, combinations, and visually involved allusions are figures in a new rhetoric of experience and expression, one of modernity's elemental structures devoted to and endlessly generating the "beauties of fortuity."

Framed thus, the oddly loose and repetitive and yet fecund structure of Carroll's world-famous children's stories share the motive and success of what Carroll set out to achieve over the summer of 1875. During these several months he "devoted himself to organizing and numbering the whole of his [considerable] photographic inventory" (Taylor 67), including his "albums, first begun in 1856" (66), the year he took up the then difficult and stylishly new art of photography. In Carroll's eyes, Cohen writes, "his photographic albums were his special art treasure" (Cohen 295). According to Taylor's exhaustive analysis of Carroll's photographic albums, the ones he "named his 'A' sequence . . . were his show albums and intended for general circulation" (Taylor 66). The photographs in these albums, which were intended to "reflect the range and variety of" his skills, are arranged not chronologically or thematically but so that, as in the *Alices*, "the viewer encounters something new and fresh with each turn of the page" (67). This manner of inventiveness involving photographs returns us to the implications of Höch's discussion of photomatter. In its many varieties image technology and its mechanical kin have "opened up a new and immensely fantastic field" of human expression, experience, and social practice, thereby enabling an unparalleled explosion of new forms—as well as new formal and social experiments.

Alice has become a culture hero and her story a modern myth. It is therefore fitting and I think reassuring that "freedom is the first prerequisite" of any who wishes to explore, inhabit, and enjoy this "new, magical territory" that rises at the margin of the present and future. To begin this "journey of discovery," Höch wisely suggests, "we must start without any preconceptions." Like Alice pursuing the White Rabbit, "we must be open to the beauties of fortuity."

NOTES

1. For a sampling of established arguments concerning Carroll's structural and thematic anticipations of modernity, see Dusinberre, Holquist, and the essays by Henkle, Rackin, and Stern collected in Guiliano.
2. All quotations are from the revised edition of 1969—the body of which, Gernsheim assures us, bears only a "few minor [factual] alterations" from the 1949 original (v).
3. See Henisch and Henisch 93–116 for a discussion of the practices and techniques of "overpainting" photographs.
4. For a solid treatment of the English nonsense tradition, see Malcolm. Reichertz investigates the convention of the world turned upside down and the genre of the looking-glass book. Also essential to consider is the influence of *Punch* magazine on Carroll's ludic style and Tenniel's inestimable visual contributions to the published *Alices*. And finally, as Taylor himself notes, there is the influence of Thomas Hood to consider, whose "comic drawings, prose, and poetry . . . [offer] many interesting precedents for the interpretation of Dodgson's literary and artistic output" (Taylor 114 n. 39).
5. The phrase "rhythm of narrative expectation" seeks to formalize as a term of literary analysis the implications of T. S. Eliot's observation, paraphrased by Kenner, that "in the twentieth century . . . the internal combustion engine altered people's perception of rhythm" (Kenner 9). Particular artistic works feature (amplify, modify, and artistically exploit) such technologically involved changes in rhythm. Marcel Duchamp's *Nude Descending a Staircase #2*, for

instance, challenges traditional expectations of the painted nude by representing the more abstract spatial-temporal rhythm of the photographic motion study.

6. I was introduced to the rich implications of Lady Filmer's use of photographs through the work of Patrizia Di Bello. Dore Ashton was kind enough to make me a list of essential texts on the subject of collage.
7. Heath accurately classifies Carroll as an absurdist, not a nonsense writer. However, Heath is wrong to limit Carroll's absurdity to the philosophical. In itself philosophical absurdity, the distortion of reason through overextension or gross amplification cannot easily function as more than a trope. It is Carroll's *narrative* absurdity—his abuse of storytelling conventions and expectations—that makes possible his unique narrative structure. See also Empson (292–3), who situates Carroll's absurdity within a psycho-rhetorical context.
8. Milner observes that the family magazines of Carroll's youth, such as *The Rectory Umbrella* and *Mischmasch*, were constructed according to a "scrap-book idea" (xi). Taylor suggests that "these childish efforts reveal an early interest in combining narrative structure and pictorial expression, something to which he would return with photography" (Taylor 11).
9. See Demurova for a treatment of the *Alices* and the fairy-tale genre. Propp's *Morphology* is the classic analysis of the fairy tale's episodic structure. Empson's is the best-known view of *Alice's Adventures* as a "version of pastoral." See Rackin for an influential opinion of the *Alices* as modern versions of the quest.
10. Eisenstein penetratingly connects Carroll's method with Kandinsky's definitively modernist and widely influential *"attempts to divorce all formal elements from all content elements"* (Eisenstein 117, italics in the original).
11. See Carroll's 10 June 1864 letter to Tom Taylor (*Selected Letters* 19). At this moment Carroll is aware that his story has a few characteristics that distinguish it from other "fairy-tale[s]": it lacks fairies and does not reveal its dream frame until the end. At the same time, however, the way that Carroll writes about choosing a title suggests that he does not yet grasp his narrative's uniqueness.
12. Groth sees "Hiawatha" as evidence that Carroll participated in an elite "critical backlash" against the "accessible commercial photographic studios" and their production of "a new gestural repertoire of poses and theatrical backdrops" that Carroll and his fellow aesthetes found tasteless (Groth 205).

WORKS CITED

Armstrong, Nancy. *Fiction in the Age of Photography: The Legacy of British Realism.* Cambridge: Harvard University Press, 1999.

Barthes, Roland. *Camera Lucida.* Trans. Richard Howard. New York: Hill and Wang, 1981.

Bloch, Ernst. "The Fairy Tale Moves on Its Own in Time." Trans. Jack Zipes and Frank Mecklenburg. *The Utopian Function of Art and Literature: Selected Essays.* Ernst Bloch. Ed. Jack Zipes. Cambridge: MIT Press, 1993. 163–6.

Carroll, Lewis. *Alice's Adventures in Wonderland* and *Through the Looking-Glass*

and What Alice Found There. Alice in Wonderland. Ed. Donald J. Gray. 2nd ed. New York: Norton, 1992. 1–209.
——. *The Complete Illustrated Lewis Carroll*. Ware: Wordsworth, 1998.
——. Excerpts from "*Alice* on the Stage." *Alice in Wonderland*. Ed. Donald J. Gray. 2nd ed. New York: Norton, 1992. 280–2.
——. "Hiawatha's Photographing." Carroll, *The Complete Illustrated Lewis Carroll* 768–72.
——. "A Photographer's Day Out." Carroll, *The Complete Illustrated Lewis Carroll* 979–85.
——. "Photography Extraordinary." Carroll, *The Complete Illustrated Lewis Carroll* 1109–13.
——. Preface. *Sylvie and Bruno*. Carroll, *The Complete Illustrated Lewis Carroll* 255–63.
——. *The Selected Letters of Lewis Carroll*. Ed. Morton N. Cohen. London: Papermac, 1996.
Cohen, Morton N. *Lewis Carroll: A Biography*. London: Papermac, 1995.
Coleridge, Samuel Taylor. "On Method." *The Portable Coleridge*. Ed. I. A. Richards. New York: Viking Press, 1961.
de la Mare, Walter. "On the *Alice* Books." Phillips, *Aspects of Alice* 57–65.
Demurova, Nina. "Toward a Definition of *Alice*'s Genre: The Folktale and Fairy-Tale Connections." Guiliano 75–88.
Di Bello, Patrizia. "Between Picasso and Lady Filmer: Sentimentality, Photography, and The History of Collage." Visual Cultures Forum. Twentieth Century and the Victorians Conference. Trinity and All Saints College, Leeds, UK. 12 July 2005. Lecture.
Duchamp, Marcel. *Nude Descending a Staircase #2*. 1912. Oil on canvas. Louise and Walter Arensberg Collection. Philadelphia Museum of Art.
Dusinberre, Juliet. *Alice to the Lighthouse: Children's Books and Radical Experiments in Art*. New York: St. Martin's Press, 1987.
Eisenstein, Sergei. *The Film Sense*. Trans. and ed. Jay Leyda. New York: Harvest, 1970.
Empson, William. "*Alice in Wonderland*: The Child as Swain." *Some Versions of Pastoral*. London: Hogarth Press, 1986. 253–94.
Gernsheim, Helmut. *Lewis Carroll, Photographer*. Rev. ed. New York: Dover, 1969.
——. *The Origins of Photography*. New York: Thames and Hudson, 1982.
Groth, Helen. "Literary Nostalgia and Early Victorian Photographic Discourse." *Nineteenth-Century Contexts* 25 (2003): 199–217.
Guiliano, Edward, ed. *Lewis Carroll, a Celebration: Essays on the Occasion of the 150th Anniversary of the Birth of Charles Lutwidge Dodgson*. New York: Potter, 1982.
Hargreaves, Alice Liddell. "Alice's Recollections of Carrollian Days." *Alice in Wonderland*. Ed. Donald J. Gray. 2nd ed. New York: Norton, 1992. 273–8.
Heath, Peter. "The Philosopher's *Alice*." *Modern Critical Views: Lewis Carroll*. Ed. Harold Bloom. New York: Chelsea House, 1987. 45–52.

Henisch, Heinz K., and Bridget A. Henisch. *The Photographic Experience 1839–1914: Images and Attitudes*. University Park: Pennsylvania State University Press, 1994.
Henkle, Roger B. "Carroll's Narratives Underground: 'Modernism' and Form." Guiliano 89–100.
Höch, Hannah. "A Few Words on Photomontage." Trans. Jitka Salaguarda. *Cut with the Kitchen Knife: The Weimar Photomontages of Hannah Höch*. Maud Lavin. New Haven: Yale University Press, 1993. 219–20.
Hoffman, Katherine. "Collage in the Twentieth Century: An Overview." *Collage: Critical Views*. Ed. Katherine Hoffman. Ann Arbor: UMI Research Press, 1989. 1–37.
Holquist, Michael. "What Is a Boojum? Nonsense and Modernism." *Alice in Wonderland*. Ed. Donald J. Gray. 2nd ed. New York: Norton, 1992. 388–98.
Kenner, Hugh. *The Mechanic Muse*. New York: Oxford University Press, 1987.
Kittler, Friedrich A. *Discourse Networks, 1800/1900*. Trans. Michael Metteer. Stanford: Stanford University Press, 1990.
Malcolm, Noel. *The Origins of English Nonsense*. London: Fontana Press, 1977.
Marien, Mary Warner. *Photography: A Cultural History*. New York: Harry N. Abrams, 2002.
Milner, Florence. Foreword. *The Rectory Umbrella* and *Mischmasch*. Lewis Carroll. New York: Dover, 1971. v–xii.
Nickel, Douglas R. *Dreaming in Pictures: The Photography of Lewis Carroll*. New Haven: Yale University Press, 2002.
Phillips, Robert, ed. *Aspects of Alice: Lewis Carroll's Dreamchild as Seen through the Critics' Looking-Glasses, 1865–1971*. New York: Vanguard Press, 1971.
Propp, Vladimir. *Morphology of the Folktale*. Trans. Laurence Scott. Austin: University of Texas Press, 1968.
Rackin, Donald. "Blessed Rage: Lewis Carroll and the Modern Quest for Order." Guiliano 15–25.
Reichertz, Ronald. *The Making of the Alice Books: Lewis Carroll's Uses of Earlier Children's Literature*. Montreal: McGill-Queen's University Press, 1997.
Stern, Jeffrey. "Lewis Carroll the Surrealist." Guiliano 132–53.
Taylor, Roger. "'All in the Golden Afternoon': The Photographs of Charles Lutwidge Dodgson." *Lewis Carroll, Photographer: The Princeton University Library Albums*. Roger Taylor and Edward Wakeling. Princeton: Princeton University Press, 2002. 1–120.
Wakeling, Edward. "Register of All Known Photographs by Charles Lutwidge Dodgson." *Lewis Carroll, Photographer: The Princeton University Library Albums*. Roger Taylor and Edward Wakeling. Princeton: Princeton University Press, 2002. 240–75.

Stephen Monteiro

Lovely Gardens and Dark Rooms

Alice, the Queen, and the Spaces of Photography

When Lewis Carroll wrote *Alice's Adventures Under Ground* as a Christmas gift for Alice Liddell in 1864, he closed his illustrated manuscript with a drawing of the recipient who had inspired the tale two years earlier. The fictional Alice reached the imaginary space of the narrative only after this historical Alice had undertaken the competing "adventure," as she termed it (Liddell 6), of posing before Carroll's camera on several occasions. Carroll based his drawing on one of these photographs, taken in July 1860 in the deanery garden of Christ Church, Oxford, where he was a mathematics lecturer. Unsatisfied with the results (he later called his illustrations "horrid"; Carroll, *Letters* 608), he covered over the sketch with the photograph before delivering his gift.[1]

The physical overlap of manuscript and photograph as a prominent aspect of what would evolve into *Alice's Adventures in Wonderland* suggests an attendant conceptual overlap of two realms of representation that were equally dear to Carroll—the literary and the photographic. The photograph pasted into the written text echoes the mutability of identity and space that ripples through *Alice's Adventures.* Being both the source of the drawing and its eventual replacement, it is just one link in a chain of representations of Alice. Furthermore, the photograph does not signify a return to reality—by 1864 Alice Liddell was no longer the little eight-year-old girl seen in this image—but, rather, the existence of a rival fantasy. Photograph and manuscript present competing spaces of narrative potential, both available to fantasy yet derived from recognizable traces of reality intersecting in the persona of Alice.

The terms of photography's production and consumption permeate Carroll's Wonderland, not only as they concerned his prolific activity as a dedicated amateur photographer with artistic aspirations, but also as they involved the mid-nineteenth-century flood of small, mass-produced *carte-de-visite* portraits generated by commercial studios for an insatiable British public. These conflicting spheres of photography cast their shadows on the spaces and actions of the story.

As surrealist photographer Brassaï noted in an early essay on Carroll's photography, "A great affinity . . . links his universe full of trap doors, mirror play and changes in size, with that of the photo. First and foremost, he was at home in the unreal space of the camera" (111).[2] From the opening entry hall with its small, cameralike doorways to the gallery of characters stuffed into the courtroom like a bulging parlor photo album, photography's shadow also encompasses the fluctuations in Alice's "developing" body and personality as well as the flat, playing-card-sized royal court, not to mention the remarkable figure of the Cheshire Cat, whose emerging and lingering apparition recalls the vicissitudes of prints in darkroom baths.

Wonderland's space opposes the relatively private world of Carroll as a photographer employing fantasy (and sometimes elaborate scenarios) in depicting a universe of shifting identities centered on Alice Liddell and other children against the highly standardized, quasi-industrial professional production of *carte-de-visite* portraiture. The *carte-de-visite* photograph transformed photography into a public spectacle and popular currency that tended to blur social distinctions by reducing sitters to a severely limited range of settings and poses. By comparing these divergent mid-nineteenth-century photographic practices with the characters and circumstances of Wonderland, one finds ways in which *Alice's Adventures* reflects the potential meanings and consequences of these differing approaches in the construction of self and the evolution of the social sphere in British society.

Alice at the Door

Carroll bought his first camera in 1856, at twenty-four years of age and only a month after creating his pseudonym from his actual name, Charles Lutwidge Dodgson. In the years that followed, this shy Oxford scholar avidly photographed family, friends, and acquaintances—especially children—in prints as large as 20 × 25 centimeters (8 × 10 inches) that he arranged in albums for himself and to share with potential sitters. Parallel to these activities, Carroll also collected the cardboard-mounted, 9 × 5 1/2 centimeter (3 1/2 × 2 1/4 inch) *carte-de-visite* portraits of admired celebrities and

Lewis Carroll, "The Beggar-Maid," a portrait of Alice Liddell, albumen print, 16.3 x 10.9 centimeters (6 7/16 x 4 5/16 inches), 1858. The Metropolitan Museum of Art, Gilman Collection, Gift of the Howard Gilman Foundation, 2005. Image © Metropolitan Museum of Art.

the royal family. He regularly solicited such portraits from the numerous children he befriended in the wake of the success of his *Alice* books. "'I'm a whale at' photographs," he enthused to Anne Isabella Thackeray in 1872, when writing to request photographs of her little cousins (Carroll, *Letters* 170–1). Indeed, by the time he gave up taking photographs in 1880, Carroll had created nearly three thousand images and amassed many more, filling dozens of albums (Taylor and Wakeling 123, 126).

The birth of Wonderland in the early 1860s lies at the junction of Carroll's most productive years as a photographer and a period of unprecedented growth in commercial portrait photography. Although professional portraits had been available since the first daguerreotype studios opened in Britain in 1841, the daguerreotype's limitations as a direct, unique image produced on a silver-coated copper plate meant significant costs and the impossibility of mass circulation. The wet collodion process, invented in Britain in 1851 and the basis of *carte-de-visite* portraiture, produced a glass negative that rivaled the minute detail of the daguerreotype but offered the possibility of virtually unlimited paper-based prints.

By 1860, wet collodion photography had triggered a significant drop in costs and a sharp rise in the production and circulation of portraits as photography became affordable to an astonishingly broad segment of society. It is estimated that between 64 and 72 million *carte-de-visite* photographs were sold annually in Britain at their peak in popularity, both in personal commissions of private citizens and store-bought portraits of well-known Victorian personalities. Images of the queen sold especially well, with 3 to 4 million examples changing hands between 1860 and 1862.[3]

In the 1860s, any portrait photograph was still considered a relatively unmediated, precise representation of the person before the camera, despite its divergence from physical reality as a reduced, two-dimensional, monochromatic depiction. Even a discerning critic like Elizabeth Eastlake, who in 1857 published a highly regarded essay exploring the complexities of photography and its societal role, described photography as "the sworn witness of everything presented to [its] view." "What indeed are nine-tenths of those facial maps we called photographic portraits," she contended, "but accurate landmarks and measurements for loving eyes and memories to deck with beauty and animate with expression, in perfect certainty, that the ground-plan is founded upon fact?" (65). Nevertheless, the most straightforward portrait still bore the ambiguity of representing the physical existence of the depicted person while revising the terms of that presence by the reduction, compression, and multiplication of depicted space.

John Ruskin, who claimed he was introduced to photography by Alice Liddell's father, Christ Church dean Henry George Liddell, offered another perspective on photography's unusual properties, musing that early photographs of Venice looked "as if a magician had reduced the reality to be carried away into an enchanted land" (341). Carroll embraced this difference between photography and reality, evoking a greater imaginary space contingent on the real in resisting the medium's reputation as a transparent means of visual evidence and endowing the photograph with competing elements of fantasy. Producing a singular hybrid, this imaginary space lay at the intersection of the child sitter's psyche and environment.

In his photographs of Alice Liddell and other children, Carroll regularly coordinated conventional social spaces, like the studio, garden, or house, with unusual costumes, props, and poses to evoke the inaccessible, fluid spaces of the childhood imagination. In "The Elopement" (1862), for example, eleven-year-old Alice Jane Donkin steps tentatively out of her upper-story bedroom window onto a dangling rope ladder, dressed in a cape and holding her sack of belongings tightly in hand as her eyes fix on the space below. The composition recalls Alice's brave claim while falling down the rabbit hole that henceforth she wouldn't complain "even if I fell off the top of the house" (*Wonderland* 8). In the circa 1858 portrait of Kathleen Tidy, a little girl is nestled in a tree, ensnared by a tangle of branches that nearly obscure her face. The 1865 photograph of Mary Hunt Millais, entitled "The Waking," shows a barefoot girl of five in a white nightdress, sitting on the floor, leaning into a corner.

Carroll photographed Alice, Lorina, and Edith Liddell on at least seven occasions from 1856 to 1860, though the earliest surviving prints date from 1857 (Taylor and Wakeling 241–51). In those images, Alice appears variously as a beggar in rags, a Chinese girl with a paper parasol, a smiling girl in her Sunday best, and a flower-crowned Queen of the May. She feigns sleep in one image, sits astride her seesaw in another, and opens her mouth to eat cherries in a third.

One corner of the deanery garden was a favorite setting for Carroll, and in a pair of portraits of Alice taken on a single day in 1858, the girl inhabits the same physical space but embodies very different psychological conditions and personas. In one, she dons a bright cotton dress with billowing sleeves, white socks, and shiny leather shoes. She smiles demurely, standing straight in a wooden planter like a freshly blossomed flower, her hands at her sides. In the other photograph, entitled "The Beggar-Maid," she leans against the garden wall in torn muslin rags that slip off her shoulder. The smile is gone, replaced by a wary frown. Her left hand rests in a fist on her hip as her right hand is cupped for a coin and her now bare feet reach beyond the planter's edge. Although it is the same girl, in the same location, these divergent narratives discourage reading a unified identity across the pair. Recalling the narrator's description of the Wonderland Alice as a "curious child . . . very fond of pretending to be two people" (*Wonderland* 12), these images move from one Alice to the next, suggesting the "true" Alice is only to be found somewhere between them.

The complexities of space in Carroll's photography, where the elasticity of subjectivity vies with the sitter's irreducible physical presence, reverberate in

Wonderland. Like the divergent, even contradictory, portraits of Alice Liddell, Wonderland's Alice constantly shrinks and expands during the story, losing control of body and identity. "How puzzling all these changes are!" she cries at the pigeon (*Wonderland* 43). "I know who I was when I got up this morning, but I think I must have changed several times since then," she reports to the Caterpillar. "I can't explain *myself*, I'm afraid, Sir, . . . because I'm not myself, you see" (*Wonderland* 35). As the protagonist measures the "new" Alice against the "old" Alice, she is tangled in a confusion similar to that evoked by the photographs, whereby her essential physicality negotiates shifting representations.

Douglas Nickel draws a comparison between the "general theme [of] the otherworldly" in Carroll's photography's and the "alternate realities" of Carroll's best writing (45). In fact, the narrative space created in Carroll's photographs was complemented at the time of its making by storytelling around the camera and darkroom. "He told us stories, illustrating them by pencil or ink drawings as he went along," Alice later said of the sittings. "When we were thoroughly happy and amused at his stories, he used to pose us, and expose the plates before the right mood had passed. He seemed to have an endless store of these fantastical tales" (Liddell 5–6).

Carroll produced at least twenty-seven images of the Liddell children before he recounted Alice's underground adventures, and it is conceivable that portions of that tale may have originated from the banter of these sessions. From a practical standpoint, such stories were also a way of sustaining a child's interest in the act of photography since, before Kodak introduced roll film and mail-order processing in the late 1880s, creating a photograph was a laborious affair requiring considerable skill. The wet collodion process in particular required that each glass negative be coated with its photosensitive solution immediately before use and developed quickly after exposure, before the solution dried (Cohen, *Reflections* 18–20). All work had to be done on the spot, whether in the studio or in the field, making photography as much a trap as an escape.

Carroll evokes the environment of photographic production early in his construction of Wonderland when Alice, shortly after falling down the rabbit hole, reaches a long hall where she discovers "a low curtain she had not noticed before, and behind it . . . a little door about fifteen inches high" (*Wonderland* 9–10). Only slightly larger than the camera Carroll would have used for his photographs, Alice's discovery suggests the back of such an apparatus, with a curtain to cover the photographer's head and the sliding plate holder that blocks the camera's viewfinder. His description continues, suggesting a lens body when "Alice opened the door and found that it led into a small passage, not much larger than a rat-hole" (10). Then, in an action that must recall the thrill of looking through the camera to see the uncanny, shimmering image of the world made small on the viewfinder's ground glass,[4] Alice peered through the door and "looked along the passage into the loveliest garden you ever saw" (10). The power of this brief incident forges Alice's principal desire—not to return home, but to attain that magical garden, like crossing through the camera's lens.[5]

Just as the world Alice occupies *before* the door in Wonderland offers her as much enchantment, in the end, as that distant garden she reaches later in the narrative, the environment Carroll created around his camera was as captivating for the Liddell girls as any Oxford garden seen through his ground glass. "Much more exciting than being photographed was being allowed to go into the dark room," Alice admitted, since "we felt that any adventure might happen there" (Liddell 6). Moreover, the darkroom promised "the additional excitement of seeing what we look like in a photograph" (5). As Carroll normally developed only his negatives before 1868 and entrusted any subsequent printing to professional firms (Taylor and Wakeling 93), what Alice and the others would "look like" in these darkroom images was a startlingly surreal, ghostly representation in reversed tones. Like the upside-down world of Wonderland or the lateral reversal of the Looking-Glass House in Carroll's sequel volume, *Through the Looking-Glass*, his darkroom offered a glimpse of selfhood at odds with everyday reality.

If these negatives represented Alice, but differed radically from her self-image with their additional details of pose, attitude, costume, and lighting, then could "she" be someone else entirely? As the developing baths conjured her spectral image, the link between chemical interventions and new perceptions of self anticipated the fictional Alice's peculiar habit of drinking bottles of unknown potions to induce physical changes. Additionally, any mistake in the development process risked the destruction of her fragile image, just as Wonderland's Alice notes that her eating and drinking strange things risks "my going out altogether, like a candle" (*Wonderland* 12).

The Queen and Her Pack

It is only at the moment when Alice masters the chemical changes that alter her appearance—in this instance, nibbling carefully at a piece of mushroom to shrink her body to fit the garden door—that she enters the social spaces of the Queen and her court that mark the second half of the story. She shrinks to "about a foot high" (61), or slightly larger than the size of Carroll's largest photographs, to enter the cameralike door. Once through the door's passage, however, she immediately discovers that the inhabitants of this beautiful new environment are two-dimensional and shaped like playing cards. After encountering the five, two, and seven of spades hastily painting a rosebush, Alice witnesses a procession of the King and Queen of Hearts, along with the rest of the royal family and their court, observing that their bodies are "oblong and flat" (63).

"Why, they're only a pack of cards, after all," Alice tells herself, "I needn't be afraid of them!" (63). Although possibly a veiled expression of Carroll's own ambivalence toward the *carte-de-visite*, even if that remark went unnoticed it is easy to imagine that the playing-card Queen brought her real-life *carte-de-visite* counterpart to mind for many nineteenth-century readers.

John Mayall, "Her Majesty," a portrait of Queen Victoria, hand-colored albumen print on cardboard mount, 10.5 x 6.1 centimeters (4 1/8 x 2 3/8 inches), 1861.

By the mid-1860s, millions of the small, cardboard-backed portraits of Queen Victoria circulated throughout Britain and the world. Indeed, Queen Victoria championed the *carte-de-visite* not only by posing at leading studios, but by avidly assembling dozens of *carte-de-visite* albums with the help of her husband, Prince Albert, who himself was an early advocate of photography's many applications. Eleanor Stanley, one of Victoria's ladies-in-waiting, wrote in 1860 that "I have been writing to all the fine ladies in London for their and their husbands' photographs for the Queen," before lamenting that "I believe the Queen could be bought and sold, for a photograph" (Gernsheim and Gernsheim 261).

The precariousness of selfhood in Wonderland reflects not only Carroll's personal photographic vision but also implies a potential instability facing Victorian culture with the public's increasing reliance on commercial photographic portraiture in the assertion of personal identity. Depicting everyone from the queen to celebrities to middle-class merchants and their families, these photographs facilitated social mobility, opening new territories for the representation of self within the changing social fabric. "The *carte* was so potent because it was a thinking of the self through things," explains John Plunkett. "It was part of an individual's construction of themselves in relation to a wider collective identity" (55). Commercial portraiture offered the illusion of asserting one's uniqueness while restricting the sitter to a narrow repertoire of poses and settings, essentially reducing the subject to the combination of stereotype and conflation that haunts the characters of Wonderland. Jean Sagne calls the result so many "attempts to escape the anonymity of the crowd, ultimately only to return to it" (Frizot et al. 11).[6]

In 1860, the same year Carroll made the photograph of Alice Liddell that appears in the original manuscript of *Alice's Adventures*, prominent London photographer John Jabez Edwin Mayall published his *Royal Album*, the first commercially available set of *carte-de-visite* photographs of the royal family. "In one sense the publication of the portraits was a tacit acknowledgement on the part of the Queen that the public could invade her privacy through the agency of photography," remark Frances Dimond and Roger Taylor in *Crown and Camera*, a study of photography and the royal family (20). "From the *carte-de-visite*, we learn the astounding fact that kings and queens are in dress and features exactly like other people," explained a journalist for *All the Year Round* in 1863 (Plunkett 71). That reaction is echoed in similar but far stronger terms when Alice exclaims that she "needn't be afraid of them" (*Wonderland* 63).

An immediate marketing success (even Carroll bought a set [Taylor and Wakeling 25]), *Royal Album*'s fourteen portraits were followed by the production and sale of photographs of other celebrities. These were often displayed in stationers' windows, creating a street-side spectacle of characters to rival Wonderland's garden procession. "Wherever in our fashionable streets we see a crowd congregated before a shop window," remarked the journalist Andrew Wynter in 1862, "there for certain a like number of notabilities are staring back at the crowd in the shape of *cartes de visite*" (Wynter, "Cartes," *Living Age* 673). Paying little mind to social distinctions, these displays might unite the portraits of the prime minister, a boxer, the queen, an opera singer, a member of Parliament, and a serial killer under the public's gaze in the same standard format, and sometimes posed in identical studio settings. These juxtapositions became a common source of public amusement and derision as such images eventually landed in private parlor albums, side by side with the owner's family and friends, to create an unprecedented iconographic overlap of social circles and a compression of social space. As a critic warned in the *Reader* at the peak of the *carte-de-visite* format's popularity, "the poorest carries his three inches of cardboard; and the richest can claim no more" (Plunkett 69).

Like the rest of society, Lewis Carroll was fascinated by the *carte-de-visite* photograph. Not only did he buy those representing the royal family, he collected those of child actors and dearly treasured the portraits received from his "child-friends" (Carroll, *Letters* 170). Although most of his photographs were produced in larger sizes, after 1871 he occasionally printed portraits in *carte-de-visite* format in deference to his sitters' wishes and even licensed negatives of his more famous subjects (like Alfred, Lord Tennyson and Dante Gabriel Rossetti) to *carte-de-visite* publishing houses (Cohen, *Reflections* 132).

Carroll recognized the potential harm of the *carte-de-visite*, however, in its influence on one's lifestyle and sense of self. "Three inches is such a wretched height to be," protests Alice to the Caterpillar (60), and Carroll appears to have shared the opinion, severely restricting the distribution of *carte-de-visite* portraits of himself (Carroll, *Letters* 266–8). He systematically refused requests for his portrait (little girl admirers being the occasional exception), fearing the circulation of his image in albums would adversely affect his life. "I have always refused applications for photographs or autographs, as my features and my handwriting belong to me as a private individual," he pointedly explained in 1883. "I often beg even my own private friends, who possess one or the other, *not* to put them into albums where strangers can see them" (Carroll, *Letters* 446).

Sagne notes that "exchanging *cartes* works as a means of integration. It places the individual on the social scene, inserts him into its structure"[7] (Frizot et al. 13); and Carroll anticipated concerns raised by this type of integration: namely, that the gift or sale of one's photograph to another amounted to the transfer of control over one's privacy and, perhaps, identity. While he easily hid behind his pseudonym in letters and books, his photograph's "faithful" likeness would merge the public Carroll with the private Dodgson, an inevitable and intractable confusion of identity that Carroll found intolerable. That unease extended to his photographs of Alice Liddell. When he published a facsimile of the *Alice* manuscript in 1885, he insisted that the inserted photograph of Alice (and thus the drawing it concealed) be excluded from the reproduction, demonstrating his desire to separate the identity of the girl from the character, even as his work deliberately challenged the possibility of making such distinctions (Carroll, *Letters* 561).

Carroll's wariness of "strangers" seeing his face in albums underlines the increasingly central role that the parlor album played in portraiture's circulation at that time. In fact, the photographic album had developed commercially only with the rise of the *carte-de-visite*. Unlike the scrapbooks and sketch albums in which Carroll carefully organized and affixed the photographs he produced, mass-produced *carte-de-visite* albums contained slotted pages. This design permitted, and even encouraged, the regular rearrangement of the photographs inside to conform to changes within the family and greater society. "The album at the same time served as an illustrated book of genealogy and expressed a form of hero-worship," explains Helmut Gernsheim (*Lewis Carroll* 8), as it interposed portraits of family and friends with the day's famous personalities. The major studios' dual commerce in portraits of celebrities and private clients allowed for an unprecedented iconographic mixing of classes and circles as these images found their way into many a parlor. Noted one contemporary critic, "These handy little records of old familiar faces stand in the same relation to the grand portraits that grace the National Gallery and the drawing room that small change does to gold or paper money. They are the democracy of portraiture" (Wynter, "Cartes," *British*, 12 Mar. 1869, 125).

The potential iconic power of the queen and her family was ultimately dissipated by the copresence of her subjects in thousands of very similar images. Once royalty began posing for commercial studios, any middle-class citizen could retrace their steps simply by engaging the same photographers at the modest price of a guinea for a dozen prints (Gernsheim, *Rise of Pho-*

tography 198). When the Prince of Wales posed leaning over a writing desk in Mayall's studio, for example, other clients were given the same opportunity. As a result, one could be recorded examining one's papers at a desk used by the future king of England, effectively collapsing social hierarchies onto the same spatial and visual coordinates.

From these contemporary circumstances, one could reinterpret Wonderland's garden and concluding trial scenes as an amusing cautionary tale of the destabilizing effect the spread of such photographic portraits could have on perceptions of self and social hierarchy. Allan Sekula has claimed that photographic portraits of the period placed subjects within a social hierarchy by representing a "*private* moment of sentimental individuation . . . shadowed by two other more *public* looks; a look up, at one's 'betters,' and a look down, at one's 'inferiors'" (347). In the space of these Wonderland scenes, where the King and Queen are jostled and importuned by knaves,

John Mayall, "H. R. H. The Prince of Wales," albumen print on cardboard mount, 10.3 x 6.3 centimeters (4 1/16 x 2 1/2 inches), circa 1863.

John Mayall, portrait of unidentified sitter, albumen print on cardboard mount, 10.3 x 6.2 centimeters (4 1/16 x 2 7/16 inches), circa 1863.

soldiers, hatters, gardeners, and duchesses (not to mention a wide assortment of animals), up and down are hardly distinguishable.

The courtroom, normally a symbol of society's structure and order, becomes a site of social restructuring in a way recalling the *carte-de-visite* album. "Birds and beasts as well as the whole pack of cards" (*Wonderland* 86) are crowded nearly on top of each other, straining the social (and natural) order. When Alice tips over the jury box, the King warns her that the trial cannot proceed until she reinserts "all the jurymen . . . back in their proper places—*all*" (*Wonderland* 93) as though they were *carte-de-visite* portraits slipped from their slotted pages. The King himself, doubling as a judge, confounds social distinctions in appearing both as sovereign and civil servant, much as Queen Victoria did in her competing portraits in regalia and ordinary dress. Wearing his crown over his judge's wig, "he did not look at all comfortable, and it was certainly not becoming," the narrator explains (*Wonderland* 86). Even more unsettling, perhaps, "important" and "unimportant" become interchangeable terms during his proceedings (*Wonderland* 93), a development that constantly shifts priority much in the way that an album's flexible layout might.

In the evolving social environment reflected in commercial portraits, a viewer's recognition of celebrities and famous studio settings in an album became imperative for the host to insinuate himself successfully into differing social contexts via these images. In a comparison of Wonderland's events with parlor games, Kathleen Blake observes a similar activity for Alice during the trial. "[Alice] is pleased with herself for being able to identify all the figures at the trial," Blake notes, while the jurors "are afraid of forgetting their own name" (128). Similar moments of recognition and confusion were yoked exercises in the album, as social identity was continually updated.

It is only Alice's renewed, forceful dismissal of those around her as "nothing but a pack of cards," coupled with her growth to "full size," that finally halts these events through triggering the violent revolt of the cards. In response to Alice reasserting her physical difference from these flat representations and rejecting their hierarchical mischief, the little cards rise up and assault Alice, swarming about as she swats them and screams "half of fright and half of anger" (*Wonderland* 97). This battle between body and image interrupts the fantasy space and the hold of its photographic allusions, as Alice abruptly finds herself back where she started, above ground, while those lively cards are reduced to "dead" leaves falling on her face (*Wonderland* 97–8). Nevertheless, even after this restoration, Alice's earlier plaintive question, "But if I'm not the same . . . Who in the world am I?" (*Wonderland* 15) endures like the darkened impression of a developed negative. The question could apply just as well to the transformations produced through the proliferation and circulation of commercial photographic portraits across social spheres as it could to a little girl who posed alternately in her best dress and beggar's rags. As explored in Carroll's work, such competing photographic spaces—the private and public, the amateur and commercial—offered as much room for ambiguity for their Victorian audiences as the world down the rabbit hole.

NOTES

1. The manuscript is housed in the British Library, but the drawing was only discovered when the photograph was removed in 1977.

2. "Une grande affinité reliait . . . [Carroll's] . . . univers plein de chausse-trappes, de jeux de miroir, de changements de taille, avec celui de la photo. D'emblée il fut chez lui dans l'espace irréel de la chambre noire." Unless noted otherwise, all translations from the French are mine.
3. Wynter, "Cartes," *British*, 12 Mar. 1869 (126) and 25 Mar. 1869 (149).
4. The image on the ground glass would be upside down. That Alice sees this world as right side up may only confirm that it is already an upside-down world. For an examination of Wonderland as an "antipodean location," see Reichertz 35–6.
5. Of course, *Through the Looking-Glass* also begins with a powerful moment suggestive of photography when Alice's passage into a laterally inverted mirror world mimics the photographic negative's reorganization of reality.
6. "Répétition sans fin des mêmes poncifs, mêmes postures dignes, effet de lassitude de ces visages, *tentatives de sortir de l'anonymat de la foule pour finalement y revenir.*"
7. "L'échange des cartes joue comme facteur d'intégration. Il place l'individu sur la scène sociale, l'implique dans sa structure."

WORKS CITED

Blake, Kathleen. *Play, Games, and Sport: The Literary Works of Lewis Carroll.* Ithaca: Cornell University Press, 1974.

Brassaï [Gyula Halász]. "Lewis Carroll photographe ou L'Autre côté du miroir." *Lewis Carroll.* Ed. Henri Parisot. Paris: L'Herne, 1987.

Carroll, Lewis. *Alice's Adventures in Wonderland. Alice in Wonderland.* Ed. Donald J. Gray. 2nd ed. New York: Norton, 1992. 1–99.

———. *Alice's Adventures Under Ground: A Facsimile of the Original Lewis Carroll Manuscript.* Ann Arbor: University Microfilms, 1964.

———. *The Complete Works of Lewis Carroll.* New York: Modern Library, 1970.

———. *The Letters of Lewis Carroll.* Ed. Morton N. Cohen. 2 vols. London: Macmillan, 1979.

Cohen, Morton N. *Reflections in a Looking Glass.* New York: Aperture, 1999.

Dimond, Frances, and Roger Taylor. *Crown and Camera: The Royal Family and Photography, 1842–1910.* New York: Viking, 1987.

Eastlake, Elizabeth. "Photography." *Classic Essays on Photography.* Ed. Alan Trachtenberg. New Haven: Leete's Island Books, 1980.

Frizot, Michel, Serge July, Christian Phéline, and Jean Sagne. *Identités: de Disdéri au photomaton.* Paris: Centre national de la photographie, 1985.

Gernsheim, Helmut. *Lewis Carroll, Photographer.* London: Max Parrish, 1949.

———. *The Rise of Photography: 1850–1880, The Age of Collodion.* New York: Thames and Hudson, 1988.

Gernsheim, Helmut, and Alison Gernsheim. *Queen Victoria: A Biography in Word and Picture.* London: Longmans, 1959.

Liddell, Alice. "Alice's Recollections of Carrollian Days as Told to her Son, Caryl Hargreaves." *Cornhill Magazine* 73.433 (1932): 1–12.

Nickel, Douglas R. *Dreaming in Pictures: The Photography of Lewis Carroll*. New Haven: San Francisco Museum of Art/Yale University Press, 2002.
Plunkett, John. "Celebrity and Community: The Poetics of the *Carte-de-visite*." *Journal of Victorian Culture* 8.1 (2003): 55–79.
Reichertz, Ronald. *The Making of the Alice Books: Lewis Carroll's Uses of Earlier Children's Literature*. Montreal: McGill-Queen's University Press, 1997.
Ruskin, John. *Præterita: The Autobiography of John Ruskin*. Oxford: Oxford University Press, 1949.
Sekula, Allan. "The Body and the Archive." *The Contest of Meaning*. Ed. Richard Bolton. Cambridge: MIT Press, 1989.
Taylor, Roger, and Edward Wakeling. *Lewis Carroll, Photographer: The Princeton University Library Albums*. Princeton: Princeton University Press, 2002.
Wynter, Andrew. "Cartes de Visite." *British Journal of Photography* 12 Mar. 1869: 125–6.
——. "Cartes de Visite." *British Journal of Photography* 25 Mar. 1869: 148–50.
——. "Cartes de Visite." *The Living Age* 22 Mar. 1862: 673–6.

Franz Meier

Photographic Wonderland

Intermediality and Identity in Lewis Carroll's *Alice* Books

Photography and the Construction of Identities

Philosophers and theorists like Nietzsche, Cassirer, and McLuhan have repeatedly stated that human beings live in a world of symbols and that our "theoretical means of thinking are basically fictional in origin" (Klook and Spahr 57).[1] Writing in general (Neil Postman) and the novel in particular (Ian Watt) have in this sense often been seen in close connection with the development of the modern individual. Fictional texts offer a field of experience in which the reader may explore "virtual" models of identity and thus construct or reconstruct his or her own. This is particularly true for children and adolescents (and therefore fairy tales have always played an important role in their development); but it is also true for adults—especially if we consider identity as performative rather than essential in nature.

Visual art is another important medium[2] for the construction of identities. The early-modern discovery of the one-point perspective has often been connected with a new concept of individualism, sharply in contrast to the medieval worldview. With respect to the more recent past, the development of photography in the mid-nineteenth century probably marks the most decisive shift in paradigms of perception[3] and thus the "mediation" of identities—particularly as "nineteenth-century aesthetic theory frequently makes the eye the predominant organ of truth" (Christ and Jordan xix–xx). Walter Benjamin, in his famous essay "The Work of Art in the Age of Mechanical Reproduction," considers the technical reproduction of visual images in general both cause and symptom of a new experience of the world within a modern mass society (Benjamin, "Kunstwerk" 356–7, 374–6); and Roland Barthes even talks of an "anthropological revolution" (Barthes,

"Rhetoric" 44) when describing this interaction[4] between photography and changing patterns of perception.

Both theorists also make out a specific difference, which to me seems a decisive one, between the photographic and the painterly image. What Benjamin describes as the "magic value" of a photograph[5] and Barthes as its "punctum"[6] finds its common denominator in its supposed documentary character, in its "facticity." And here we can see its paradigmatic role for the construction of individual identity. The photographic portrait, contrary to the literary character and even to the portrait painting, seems to be a "double" rather than a fictional image. Because it is not "made" in the traditional sense of artistic creation, but "brought forth" by "an apparatus . . . which masquerade[s] as a transparent and incorporeal intermediary between observer and world" (Crary 136), it "assume[s] . . . representational authority" and seems to be a "transparent record of the truth" (Christ and Jordan xxv) and thus an objective offprint of the real self.[7] In the last instance, of course, this "transparency . . . [is] . . . illusory" (xxv), a myth—and not only because most photographers carefully select and arrange what they depict (xxv–xxvi). Like the mirror that plays such an important role in Jacques Lacan's theory of identity,[8] *every* photograph necessarily distorts its object, and therefore (in the case of a portrait) also disrupts the notion of the "real" self it seems to re-present.[9] The photographic portrait is one's "other" *and* one's "double" and thus "uncanny" in the Freudian sense.[10] For that very reason it is highly charged with problems of personal identity, which it simultaneously helps to construct and threatens to deconstruct.

Identity and Photographic Space in the *Alice* Books

Manifest and Latent Intermediality

Given that Lewis Carroll was a multifaceted personality himself, that he was interested in little children at an age where they are heavily occupied in forming their identities, that he wrote for such children, and that he made such a child the protagonist of his two most famous novels, it comes as no surprise that identity is an ubiquitous concern in the *Alice* books[11]—and that it has become so in Carroll scholarship as well. Feminists and psychologists in particular have seen Alice as a prototypical case of female identity formation;[12] but the relationship between identity and media (photography in particular) still needs to be fully addressed. Manifest aspects of intermediality in the *Alice* books, especially the genesis and function of Tenniel's illustrations, have of course been investigated early on (e.g., Hancher, Kelly, Lull); but critics seem to quietly accept that despite so many other all-pervading text-image relationships,[13] photography, the medium that, according to Gernsheim (Introduction 11), was Carroll's "main interest in life," should be totally absent from these texts. I have only been able to find very passing mention of this connection in two essays, one by Gordon and Guiliano, the other by Roger Taylor.[14]

Indeed, photography is never *explicitly* mentioned in the *Alice* books[15]—which is surprising, as "both of [them] were written during the period of Lewis Carroll's photographic activity" and the publication of *Alice's Adventures* immediately follows the photographer's "most important period" of 1863 and 1864 (Gernsheim, *Carroll, Photographer* 15). This discrepancy, however, I would argue, is only a superficial one; because once we stop searching for "explicit" references to photography and switch our attention to "implicit" intermedial connections,[16] we are bound to find an intricate subtext referring to photography on a metaphorical level. What is more, this metaphoric subtext creates a "photographic space" within Wonderland and the Looking-Glass World that is intricately related to surprisingly modern experiences of life and questions of identity. Three thematic fields in particular seem to me to contain clusters of metaphoric meaning related to photography and identity in these books. These are the themes of Space and Size, Mirrors and Doubles, and finally Time and Change.[17]

Space and Size

If in its nineteenth-century context photography did, as media theorists suggest, change and reflect people's (altered) perception of the world, the aspect that must have been affected most fundamentally was that of space. Every photograph, in a way we may no longer be aware of today, necessarily distorts "natural" space as it is perceived in everyday experience, not only through its limitation by a frame and its black and white[18] two-dimensionality, but also through spherical effects of the lenses, which cause, among other things, bending of lines, enlarging of foregrounds, or limitation of the depth of focus. Photography, it is true, *in a way* made space subject to objective control: scientists documented and measured space in photographs. But on the other hand, precisely *because* photography was considered an objective, scientific medium for the documentation of reality, it defamiliarized space, made it strange, inconsistent, and unpredictable. For example, micro- or telescopic photographs questioned accustomed spatial perception and revealed aspects of reality hitherto unrealized.

Alice experiences a similar defamiliarization of perception in Wonderland and behind the looking glass. Spatial relationships and size in particular become highly unreliable, relative, and prone to sudden changes—sometimes drug-induced and intentional,[19] sometimes not. Even while falling down the rabbit hole, Alice wonders about latitude and longitude (13); and her desired visit to the Wonderland garden crucially depends on her shrinking to proportions that allow her to enter a tiny door behind a curtain. The required size, we learn early on in the first chapter, was "ten inches" (17) or less (24)—an interesting size, considering that the format of Carroll's first and largest photographic camera, bought in 1856, was exactly 8 × 10 inches.[20] The size of the rosewood box itself (which was of course equipped with a darkening "curtain") was very likely then to have been exactly the "fifteen inches" (15) of the door through which Alice desperately tries to pass. Alice's Wonderland existence in the room with the little door may thus be read as living in a photographic box, or more abstractly speaking, in photographic space. (And the White Rabbit with his gloves and ever-ready pocket watch could allude to the photographer leading the way.[21]) It follows that her new size is that of a photographic plate and her immediate perspective—looking through the door of a hall at a faraway garden—recalls the view through a photographic lens. It also follows that whenever she grows again,[22] she gets into severe difficulties—as in the Rabbit's house in chapter 4 of *Alice's Adventures*, where she seriously threatens to burst. Tenniel's illustration for this scene (as well as Carroll's original drawing) foregrounds this spatial limitation of a frame or box.[23]

The finiteness of photographic space manifests itself in a more qualitative way as well: through lack of the third dimension. This feature, of course, links photographs to other printed visual media, including picture books like the *Alice* books themselves—and, for that matter, playing cards (*Alice's Adventures* chap. 8, 11, and 12), which play such a crucial role in the first of them.[24] Tenniel's illustration of the commanding Queen of Hearts in chapter 8 of *Alice's Adventures* (86) does a particularly good job, I think, in conveying, within a two-dimensional medium, this difference between two- and three-dimensionality, by giving the playing-card characters less perspective and "depth" than Alice and the rest of the picture. When Alice, therefore, having grown to her "natural" size again, finally denies

Alice in the White Rabbit's house. Illustration by John Tenniel.

the logic of "photographic" Wonderland and snappishly confronts its despotic "flat" characters with their ontological status, saying, "You're nothing but a pack of cards!" (129),[25] she could almost be saying, "You're nothing but photographs!"[26]

Mirrors and Doubles

If fragmentation and metamorphoses of bodies, and particularly distortions of sizes, figure prominently in *Alice's Adventures*, inversion[27] and duplication seem to be the master tropes of *Through the Looking-Glass*.[28] Considering the prominent framing device of the mirror (which, in contrast to photography, is explicitly mentioned in the text), it might therefore at first seem more appropriate to talk of a "mirror space" rather than a "photographic space" with respect to the second of the *Alice* books. There are, however, obvious ways in which a camera is similar to a mirror so that the latter can be seen as one more aspect of photographic space as well. Among these similarities are the stunning likeness of the depicted scene or person, the limitation of visible space, and the reversal of the image—which in the camera is upside down in addition to the left-right reversal in a mirror.[29] Carroll and Tenniel, of course, draw on such mirroring effects throughout both *Alice* books but, not surprisingly, especially in *Through the Looking-Glass*. Not only the "entrance scene" but several other episodes are dominated by optical reversal. The famous "Jabberwocky" poem, found in a "Looking-glass book" in chapter 1, is perhaps the most obvious example. It is even printed in mirror writing (154).[30]

In chapter 4, we encounter two other characters strongly connected to the mirror metaphor—and to photography: Tweedledum and Tweedledee. What makes them typical looking-glass characters from the first is their status as twins or doubles (indicated also in their names) and their simultaneous antagonism toward each other—a paradoxical structure reflected in their equal fondness of the words "ditto" *and* "contrariwise." But not only do they hug and fight each other, they both seem to come right from a photograph and to partake in some of the medium's intricacies. At the very beginning of the chapter, in addition to their astounding similarity, two aspects of their appearance that are also well known in photographic prints are explicitly pointed out: (a) Alice cannot see the depicted persons' backs and (b) "they stood so still that she quite forgot they were alive" (189).[31] The photographic potential of the two characters is further enhanced, I think, when we look at Tenniel's illustration accompanying this scene, in which they look exactly as if posing for—or, rather, *in*—a photograph.

Time and Change

As my photographic reading of Tweedledum and Tweedledee indicates, the new medium of photography challenged not only the traditional sense of space, but also that of time (and, as a consequence, movement). Even though in the mid-Victorian era the usual exposure time for a picture was still counted in seconds,[32] photographs were clearly seen as "freezing" time and "capturing" a moment. Once the picture was developed[33] and fixed, the result appeared as a fragment of past reality, caught "like a specimen in amber" (Nickel 66) and rescued from the pitiless transitoriness of time.

In the *Alice* books (and particularly in the second of them), just as in photographs, time is no longer a one-directional vector measured by mechanical clocks. Time stands still, as in the Mad Hatter's tea party (75–7), or runs backward, as in the Looking-Glass World, where memory works both ways and movement is really not possible. Thus, the Red Queen remembers best the "things that happened the week after next" (206), and in her country "it takes all the running *you* can do, to keep in the same place" (174). In such a world the watch-equipped rabbit, always in a hurry to keep an appointment, and the train conductor, whose "time is worth a thousand pounds a minute" (178), seem like odd relics from the utilitarian and materialist reality of Victorian capitalism. Photography—as well as the "photographic" Wonderland in the *Alice* books—offers an antidote to the all-pervading acceleration of life in this society: against the one-directional, mechanical time of pocket watches, clocks, and train schedules, but also against growing up and aging, the individual experiences of linear time that Carroll experienced in the lives of his child friends—and his own.[34] Crammed into the picture frame of the rabbit house in *Alice's Adventures*, Alice muses that "at least there's no more room to grow up any more here" (40); and, "That'll be a comfort, one way—never to be an old woman" (40). Later, as Alice steps through the mirror into the Looking-Glass World, the back of the clock beneath it on the mantelpiece "ha[s] got the face of a little old man and grin[s] at her" (150). In Tenniel's illustration, this personification of time has none of the violent features of ancient Chronos or the Grim Reaper; it resembles, instead, a circus clown. Time on the other side of the mirror, like in a photograph, loses its frightening aspects. Identity in "photographic" Wonderland is not threatened by change and development, by age or death.

But then, even in real life, time does not only *threaten* identity; it paradoxically also *establishes* it, because in addition to its "horizontal" dimension, our relation to others at a given time, identity also has a "vertical" one, that is, the continuity of the self in time. In other words, a person's identity is to a considerable extent his or her past. This "vertical" identity, however, is a precarious concept, all the more so in a modern society of increasing acceleration and mobility, in which nobody stays the same for very long. "It's no use going back to yesterday," says Alice, "because I was a different person then" (109).[35] In our typical personal development, we make sense of this unsettling insight and construct a continuous self out of these changing sets of personality with the help of two faculties, both again connected to time: memory and narration. We remember our past selves, thereby convincing ourselves of our existence in the present; and we connect these selves through a story line, a plot (sometimes called biography) that serves to harmonize our otherwise fragmented past identities (but paradoxically also makes obvious identity's variability in time).

The potential functions of photography and literature in this process seem obvious enough. As we all know from our holiday snapshots, photography is the medium of preserved memories (although it seems debatable whether the photograph supports or rather produces memory). Victorians in general were obsessed with time and memory, and by midcentury the photographic album was a staple item in middle-class drawing rooms. Moreover, the new medium even became part of the period's elaborate cult of burial practices and mourning customs (Jalland 289–90). For Carroll, also, the preservation of memories may have been an important motivation to devote himself to the new medium. It opened up the possibility to "freeze," to arrest his little child friends' unwelcome development; and it perhaps enabled him through identification with these eternally young sitters to forget, even suppress, his own fears of "growing up," aging, and dying (the paradox again being that the very process of "freezing" a person's development actually *is* a kind of "death"). In the words of Carol Mavor: "For Carroll, the photograph of the little girl served as a fetish simultaneously to ward off death and to express Carroll's anxiety about the nearness of his own 'bedtime'" (Mavor 35).

In sharp contrast to photography, the textual medium is inseparably bound to linear, one-directional temporality, and so is the narrative genre in particular. (A story has to progress in time; a character in a story has to grow older—if ever so little.) In the *Alice* books, Carroll does his best to limit time's workings to a minimum, attempting, even, to counteract it by introducing an extradiegetic "frame" narrative, with a story time of perhaps half an hour, in which the protagonist falls asleep and soon wakes up again. He also gives the intradiegetic narrative a highly episodic structure, thus counteracting a long-term development of plot; and he even partly reverses story time within the logic of the Looking-Glass World. And yet, the *Alice* books still are texts, narrations—and as such they are bound to linear time. In order to further diminish their one-directional temporality, Carroll therefore had to introduce elements of a nontemporal (or at least nonlinear) medium into his work.

As a first step in that direction, he famously added the illustrations (first his own, then those by Tenniel), which interrupt the temporal flow of the text and make the books a highly complex intermedial enterprise.[36] But he did not stop there and further introduced elements of the newly available medium of photography as a counterforce to check the text's inherent temporality. As I have tried to show, he created, within the narrative text, a metaphoric subtext, a photographic space, with continual thematic references to a medium that transcends one-directional time and—what is more—simultaneously foregrounds those questions of identity so vitally important for him, for Alice, and for future readers of the *Alice* books.[37]

NOTES

1. Unless otherwise noted, all translations from the German are mine.
2. My use of "medium" in the context of this chapter largely follows that of Wolf (165). He takes "medium" to mean "not just a technically or materially defined channel of information transference (like writing, print, radio, TV, etc.), but a conventionally distinct cognitive frame of reference, which is defined firstly by a specific (e.g., symbolic or iconic) use of a semiotic system (language, image)—or a combination of such systems—as a means of transportation for cultural contents, and only secondly by its technical channels of communication."
3. For a stimulating challenge of this widespread position, see Crary, who claims that the decisive change as regards concepts of vision and the observer took place before the "invention" of photography around 1839 (17). This "systemic shift, which was well under way by 1820" (5), is basically one from a clear separation of object and observer—as manifested in the camera obscura—in the seventeenth and eighteenth centuries to a blurring of these categories and a dominant awareness of the physiological basis of perception (and thus the subjective and constructive character of "reality")—as illustrated by the stereoscope—in the early decades of the nineteenth century. Due to his historical focus, Crary gives only passing mention to the medium of photography; but where he

does so, he insists that despite some ostensible continuities with the earlier paradigm of "realistic" vision (13, 31n, 133), the new medium has to be considered "within a social, cultural, and scientific milieu where there had already been a profound break with the conditions of vision" (27; see also 4n, 13n, 133–6). As concerns my argument here, Crary's position does at best, I think, relativize my claim for the importance of photography after the popularization of the medium in the 1850s. For this later phase in the history of perception, at least, I would rather side with Christ and Jordan, who, in the introduction to their valuable collection of essays, hold against Crary's "subjective model" that "the photograph, the binocular telescope, and microscope seem to tell a different story, in which optical inventions extend our powers of objective observation" (xxii). As Christ and Jordan rightly claim (xxii), more research has to be done if the question of "objective" or "subjective" vision in Victorian times (or particular phases thereof) is to be decided. Most likely, however, the result will be a dialectical solution as also suggested by Christ and Jordan: "Neither an exclusively subjective nor an exclusively objective model provides a sufficient explanation for the Victorian idea of visual perception. Rather, the Victorians were interested in the conflict, even the competition, between objective and subjective paradigms for perception. The ideas that most powerfully engaged their imagination were those such as perspectivism or impressionism that could simultaneously accommodate a uniquely subjective point of view and an objective model of how perception occurs" (xxiii). For a similar position with regard to the Victorians' attitude toward photographs, see Nickel's remarks quoted in note 7 below.

4. Neither Benjamin nor Barthes, of course, argues for a simple "technological determinism" (Crary 8, 31)—and neither do I claim such a causal relationship between medium and discourse myself.
5. See Benjamin, "Geschichte" 302n: "The most exact technical device can invest its products with a magic value, which for us a painted picture can no longer possess. In spite of the photographer's virtuosity and the model's calculated pose, the spectator nevertheless feels the unpredictable drive to search in such a picture for the tiny spark of chance, here and now, which has, as it were, singed the picture's being."
6. Barthes, in *Camera Lucida* (27), defines the *punctum* as "sting, speck, cut, little hole—and also a cast of the dice. A photograph's *punctum* is that accident which pricks me (but also bruises me, is poignant to me)."
7. Nickel (32–44) convincingly argues that the preference for "realism" or "objectivity" in (Carroll's) photographs is to some extent a modernist bias (particularly furthered by Gernsheim, *Carroll, Photographer* 32n), whereas indeed this use of the medium existed harmoniously side by side with another, imaginative and fictional-allegorical one in Victorian times in general and in Carroll's photographic work in particular (see, for example, his many costume photographs). Nevertheless, and without implying any aesthetic judgment, I would argue that the mere awareness of the technical means

of its production endowed photography *as a medium* with a special air of documentary "facticity" even for Victorians and even in the most allegorical of their photographs. Nickel himself, of course, goes no further than to state that "audiences in Dodgson's day could accept the *simultaneity* of the objective and the subjective in a photograph" (41, emphasis added), that they were able to relish in it the "*simultaneity* of the real and the ideal" (39, 55, emphasis added)—a position that perfectly fits Christ and Jordan's argument concerning Victorian concepts of vision in general, as quoted in note 3 above.

8. In his theory of the "*stade du miroir*" Lacan famously claims that the little child gains an idea of its (body's) oneness by identifying with its "imaginary" ideal in a mirror. Lacan's crucial point, however, is that the mirror image is always reversed, that is, distorted, as well as distanced—and thus "wrong" in several respects. Our first recognition of ourselves in the mirror is thus already a misrecognition/*méconnaissance* and our sense of identity based on a "lie" from the very start.
9. Nevertheless, "the very claims that the photographer could make for the transparency of representation . . . increased his power to mythologize the elements he presented" (Christ and Jordan xxvi).
10. Freud's definition of the "uncanny" combines familiar/*heimlich* with its well-known but suppressed and thus unconscious opposite. One of the incarnations of the uncanny, according to Freud (257–61), is the double, which threatens the subject's identity and is thus often seen as an omen of its annihilation.
11. "Who am I?" (24, 186), "Who are *you*?" (49), "*What* are you?" (57), and "Who is this?" (85) are recurring questions throughout both texts. In addition to that, there are several instances in which Alice wonders about her name (179, 185, 269).
12. See Little and the articles in chapters 7–8 of Phillips (279–416).
13. The importance of text-image relations is already announced in the first paragraph of *Alice in Wonderland* with Alice's rhetorical question "and what is the use of a book . . . without pictures?" (11). But apart from illustrations we also find a "pattern poem" (35), mirror writing (154), and graphic typography (178).
14. Gordon and Guiliano, in an introductory paragraph, interpret Haigha and Hatta in *Looking-Glass* as the "positive," "developed" from the "negative" Hare and Hatter in *Wonderland* (1); and in a later passage, on the "serially picaresque" structure of the *Alice* books, they speculate whether "Carroll may in fact have thought photographically" (15). They also suggest that Carroll's photograph of Ethel and Lilian Brodie "prefigures" *Wonderland*'s opening scene and propose that the book itself then "commences as a revolution against a text" (16). Taylor ("Occupation" 32n), on the other hand, in a short paragraph (32–3) muses on inversions, distortions, and metamorphoses in photography and finally simply remarks that "to the imagination of the man who was to write *Alice's Adventures in Wonderland* and *Through the Looking-Glass and What Alice Found There*, this must have been infinitely appealing" (33).

15. There are mentions of other optical instruments, however, such as the telescope (16, 20, 179), the microscope (179), the opera glass (179), and, of course, the mirror.
16. See the concepts of "*(implizite) intermediale Systemreferenz*" (Intermedial Systems Reference) in Wolf (174–5, 178); or Rajewsky's "*(simulierende) Systemerwähnung (qua Transposition)*" ([simulating] Systems Reference [qua transposition]; 94–113, 115, 157). Rajewsky's typology of intermedial relations is largely based on interactions between textual and filmic narratives, however, and is therefore rather limited in its applicability. Besides, she seems to insist on the necessity of clear intermedial "markers" and a presupposed authorial intentionality—two implications I do not deem necessary to discuss.
17. There are of course others, whose investigation I shall have to dispense with for reasons of space and time, one of them being the field of chemistry, to which I shall occasionally refer in the notes.
18. The question of color vs. black and white would be another field of photographic metaphor worth analyzing in more detail. Carroll, though reportedly not a friend of retouching in portrait photography, nevertheless sometimes improved his own prints and had some of them colored by an artist friend. A similar duty, of course, is performed by the gardeners in "The Queen's Croquet-Ground," who paint its white roses red (82–3; see also Gernsheim, *Carroll, Photographer* 32). The two kittens, one black, one white, in *Through the Looking-Glass*, could be another motif related to that question.
19. The first of several chemically induced metamorphoses (hitherto mainly seen as an argument for Alice as an "Acid Head"; see Fensch, "Lewis Carroll" and *Alice in Acidland*) happens when Alice drinks from the strange bottle with the label "drink me" attached to it (16–7). There is some potential for photographic metaphor here, as well: because of the wet collodion process prevalent at the time, which meant immediate developing of the still wet photographic plate, photographers were equipped with "a chest full of bottles" (Gernsheim, *Carroll, Photographer* 24) of poisonous fluids that, later in the darkroom, made the sitter magically reappear on a glass plate—changed in appearance, shrunk, and finally reversed again on a cardboard print.
20. See Gernsheim, *Carroll, Photographer* 26n. Without reference to Gernsheim's dates, Taylor gives "61/2 × 81/2 in." as the largest plate size of the Ottewill camera Carroll purchased in 1856 ("Golden Afternoon" 27).
21. Taking a photograph at the middle of the nineteenth century was a complicated process; it had to do more with chemistry than with optics and was not by accident called the "black art" because of the blackening silver that left its long-lasting blotches on the photographer's clothes and hands (Gernsheim, *Carroll, Photographer* 26; Gordon and Guiliano 3). Photographers therefore often wore gloves in public to conceal their blackened hands. (So, by the way, did Carroll all year round [Baatz 31].) They also, of course, carried pocket watches to measure the precise time of exposure.

22. As Alice puts it in the first of these instances: "Now I'm opening out like the largest telescope that ever was!" (Carroll 20).
23. It is therefore significant that the format of Tenniel's picture here roughly equals the usual ratio of sides in Victorian photographic plates. Space, incidentally, seems to be limited in the early scene of *Through the Looking-Glass* as well, in which Alice cannot get away from the house and into the garden (Carroll 164–5).
24. The gardeners in "The Queen's Croquet-Ground," for example, are described as "oblong and flat" (84), and the Knave in the courtroom scene is characterized as "being made entirely of cardboard" (128).
25. During the Knave's trial, the giant Alice, after knocking over the jury box of creatures, accidentally places the lizard back into his "box" "head downwards" (123).
26. Incidentally, the Queen's ubiquitous brutal sadistic threat "Off with [his/]her head!" (86 and elsewhere) might allude to the accidental photographic decapitation of a subject through inattentive framing. Carroll makes this threat explicit in his "mock Old English" story "The Ladye's History" of 1858 (Cohen 245–6; Gernsheim, *Carroll, Photographer* 46). In a much later letter to Xie Kitchin of February 1880, he asks her "not to grow any taller—if you can help it," or else she might not fit on his photographs anymore; and he adds a little sketch in which she is shown with half her head and feet "cut off" by the frame of the picture (sketch and quote in Hinde 105).
27. On "inversion themes" in Carroll's literature and life, see Gardner's long note 5 in *Annotated Alice* (Carroll 147–51).
28. There are, of course, instances of doubling and mirroring in *Alice's Adventures* as well. For example, Alice talks to herself and is characterized as a "child [who] was very fond of pretending to be two people" (18).
29. Although we know that there was a distortion mirror among the technical gadgets that Carroll collected in his chambers for the entertainment of children, a mirror, unlike a photographic camera, does not usually distort one's natural size. And yet, there is some change of proportions involved in the Looking-Glass World as well; only now it is no longer Alice but the looking-glass characters, particularly the chess pieces, that do the growing and shrinking. Thus Alice can easily lift the Queen (and King) out of the cinders of the fireplace upon the table in chapter 1; but when Alice meets her again in the "Garden of Live Flowers" (chapter 2), the Queen has "grown a good deal" and was "half a head taller than Alice herself" (169)—a size she will keep until the end of the book, when "she had suddenly dwindled down to the size of a little doll" (279) again.
30. Later on, this famous "nonsense poem" becomes the object of linguistic/philosophical analysis by Humpty Dumpty, whose very name has a duplicate structure, and whose language philosophy deals with (or, rather, ostentatiously ignores) the problem of representation so pronouncedly addressed by mirrors and photographs. One of his main strategies of decoding the "Jabberwocky" poem, furthermore, is to untangle its "portmanteau words" (225), in which "there are two meanings packed up into one word" (225). Given that Victorian

portmanteaux were often built like "oyster-shell suitcases," we might detect another "mirror-structure" in this concept as well.

31. Contrary to a real person, a photographic portrait is limited to the single perspective of the photographic lens at the time of exposure. In everyday experience, chains of signs such as the names on Tweedledum's and Tweedledee's collars would, even with only slight movement of the object *or* the spectator, complete themselves in the mind of the viewer. The photograph's view, however, is forever limited to the one perspective given at the moment of exposure, which in this case lets Alice see only the endings "DUM" and "DEE" (189).
32. Occasional photographs of street scenes with clearly distinguishable persons or vehicles were made as early as 1859 (Schnelle-Schneyder 56–59, 64), but actual "snapshots" were practically impossible for average photographers before the 1880s (Gautrand; Frizot).
33. A possible parallel to the chemical process of picture development can be seen in the strange gradual materialization, smile first, of the Cheshire Cat (90). Alice Liddell later in her life recalled that "much more exciting than being photographed was being allowed to go into the dark room, and watch him [Carroll] develop the large glass plates. What could be more thrilling than to see the negative gradually take shape, as he gently rocked it to and fro in the acid bath? Besides, the dark room was so mysterious, and we felt that any adventures might happen then!" (qtd. in Cohen 164; see also Gernsheim, *Carroll, Photographer* 23). Seeing a Cheshire cat gradually take shape, smile first, and then disappear again in reverse order might be just such an adventure that became imaginable in the darkroom's "mysterious" atmosphere.
34. "The physical model for Alice wandering through Wonderland is Alice Liddell; the spiritual and psychological Alice is Charles [Dodgson] himself," writes Cohen (195); and Guiliano calls him "a man preoccupied with time and death" ("Adventures" 540).
35. For the "developmental" aspect of the *Alice* books, see particularly chapters 4 and 5 in Rackin.
36. Just *how* important this aspect was to him can be detected from the fact that he eliminated a whole chapter, "The Wasp in a Wig," for lack of a fitting drawing.
37. A sense of how strongly Carroll must have felt about this emerges from a look at the last page of his original manuscript *Alice's Adventures Under Ground*. Here Alice's sister dreams (in another dream within a dream) of Alice as a grown woman. But, typical for Carroll, the life of this grown woman, like that of her author, is largely dominated by childhood: taking a part in other children's worlds and, last but not least, recollecting her own childhood, "remembering her own child-life, and the happy summer days." The last act in the book is again an act of memory. Underneath these last words of the book Carroll originally placed a drawing of Alice Liddell (according to Gardner in *Annotated Alice* 132 n. 10, not discovered until 1977), which concluded the series of illustrations he

integrated throughout the manuscript. Later on, however, he "pasted over [this drawing] a trimmed portrait photograph" of Alice (Cohen 128), thus for once physically introducing the medium that he otherwise more subtly related to the narratives and to their theme of threatened identity.

WORKS CITED

Baatz, Willfried. 50 *Klassiker: Photographen von Louis Daguerre bis Nobuyoshi Araki*. Hildesheim: Gerstenberg, 2003.

Barthes, Roland. *Camera Lucida: Reflections on Photography*. Trans. Richard Howard. London: Vintage, 2000. Originally published as *La chambre claire: note sur la photographie* (1980).

———. "Rhetoric of the Image." *Image – Music – Text*. Trans. Stephen Heath. New York: Hill and Wang, 1978. 32–51. Originally published as "Rhétorique de l'image" (1964).

Benjamin, Walter. "Das Kunstwerk im Zeitalter seiner technischen Reproduzierbarkeit." [1936/1939]. *Medienästhetische Schriften*. Ed. Detlev Schöttker. Frankfurt: Suhrkamp, 2002. 351–83.

———. "Kleine Geschichte der Photographie" [1931]. *Medienästhetische Schriften*. Ed. Detlev Schöttker. Frankfurt: Suhrkamp, 2002. 300–16.

Carroll, Lewis. *Alice's Adventures in Wonderland* and *Through the Looking-Glass*. *The Annotated Alice: The Definitive Edition*. Ed. Martin Gardner. London: Penguin, 2001.

Christ, Carol T., and John O. Jordan. Introduction. *Victorian Literature and the Victorian Visual Imagination*. Ed. Carol T. Christ and John O. Jordan. Berkeley: University of California Press, 1995. xix–xxix.

Cohen, Morton N. *Lewis Carroll: A Biography*. New York: Random House, 1995.

Crary, Jonathan. *Techniques of the Observer: On Vision and Modernity in the Nineteenth Century*. Cambridge: MIT Press, 1992.

Fensch, Thomas. *Alice in Acidland*. New York: A. S. Barnes, 1970.

———. "Lewis Carroll—The First Acid Head." *Story: The Yearbook of Discovery*. New York: Four Winds, 1969. 253–6.

Freud, Sigmund. "Das Unheimliche" [1919]. *Studienausgabe*. Vol. 9. Ed. Alexander Mitscherlich et al. Frankfurt: Fischer, 1994. 191–270.

Frizot, Michel. "Geschwindigkeit in der Fotografie: Bewegung und Dauer." *Neue Geschichte der Fotografie*. Ed. Michel Frizot. Cologne: Könemann, 1998. 243–57.

Gautrand, Jean-Claude. "Spontanes Fotografieren: Schnappschüsse und Momentaufnahmen." *Neue Geschichte der Fotografie*. Ed. Michel Frizot. Cologne: Könemann, 1998. 233–41.

Gernsheim, Helmut. Introduction. *Lewis Carroll: Victorian Photographer*. Milan: Franco Maria Ricci, 1980. 7–11.

———. *Lewis Carroll, Photographer*. Rev. ed. New York: Dover, 1969.

Gordon, Jan B., and Edward Guiliano. "From Victorian Textbook to Ready-Made: Lewis Carroll and the Black Art." *Soaring with the Dodo: Essays on Lewis*

Carroll's Life and Art. Ed. James R. Kincaid and Edward Guiliano. Special issue of *English Language Notes* 20 (1982/1983): 1–25.
Guiliano, Edward. "Lewis Carroll's Adventures in Cameraland." *AB Bookman Weekly* 69.4 (1982): 523–48.
——, ed. *Lewis Carroll, a Celebration: Essays on the Occasion of the 150th Anniversary of the Birth of Charles Lutwidge Dodgson*. New York: Potter, 1982.
Hancher, Michael. "*Punch* and *Alice*: Through Tenniel's Looking-Glass." Guiliano, *Lewis Carroll, a Celebration* 26–49.
Hinde, Thomas. *Lewis Carroll: Looking Glass Letters*. London: Collins & Brown, 1991.
Jalland, Pat. *Death in the Victorian Family*. Oxford: Oxford University Press, 2000.
Kelly, Richard. "'If You Don't Know What a Gryphon Is': Text and Illustration in *Alice's Adventures in Wonderland*." Guiliano, *Lewis Carroll, a Celebration* 62–74.
Klook, Daniela, and Angela Spahr. *Medientheorien: Eine Einführung*. Rev. ed. Munich: Fink, 2000.
Lacan, Jacques. "The Mirror Stage as Formative Function of the *I* as Revealed in Psychoanalytic Experience." *Écrits: A Selection*. Trans. Alan Sheridan. London: Routledge, 2002. 1–8.
Little, Judith. "Liberated Alice: Dodgson's Female Hero as Domestic Rebel." *Women's Studies* 3 (1975/1976): 195–207.
Lull, Janis. "The Appliances of Art: The Carroll-Tenniel Collaboration in *Through the Looking-Glass*." Guiliano, *Lewis Carroll, a Celebration* 101–11.
Mavor, Carol. "Dream Rushes: Lewis Carroll's Photographs of Little Girls." *Pleasures Taken: Performances of Sexuality and Loss in Victorian Photographs*. Durham: Duke University Press, 1995. 7–42.
Nickel, Douglas R. *Dreaming in Pictures: The Photography of Lewis Carroll*. New Haven: Yale University Press, 2002.
Phillips, Robert, ed. *Aspects of Alice: Lewis Carroll's Dreamchild as Seen through the Critics' Looking-Glasses, 1865–1971*. New York: Vanguard Press, 1971.
Rackin, Donald. Alice's Adventures in Wonderland *and* Through the Looking Glass: *Nonsense, Sense, and Meaning*. New York: Twayne, 1991.
Rajewsky, Irina O. *Intermedialität*. Tübingen: Francke, 2002.
Schnelle-Schneyder, Marlene. *Photographie und Wahrnehmung am Beispiel der Bewegungsdarstellung im 19. Jahrhundert*. Marburg: Jonas, 1990.
Taylor, Roger. "'All in the Golden Afternoon': The Photographs of Charles Lutwidge Dodgson." *Lewis Carroll, Photographer: The Princeton University Library Albums*. Roger Taylor and Edward Wakeling. Princeton: Princeton University Press, 2002. 1–120.
——. "'Some Other Occupation': Lewis Carroll and Photography." *Lewis Carroll*. Ed. Charlotte Byrne. London: British Council, 1998. 26–38.
Wolf, Werner. "Intermedialität: Ein weites Feld und eine Herausforderung für die Literaturwissenschaft." *Literaturwissenschaft: intermedial – interdisziplinär*. Ed. Herbert Foltinek and Christoph Leitgeb. Wien: Österreichische Akademie der Wissenschaften, 2002. 163–92.

Mou-Lan Wong

Generations of Re-generation

Re-creating Wonderland through Text, Illustrations, and the Reader's Hands

> Whatever the process is of one's experience of *Alice's Adventures in Wonderland* [and] *Through the Looking-Glass* . . . the sensation is neither that of rereading nor of reading as though for the first time.
> —HAROLD BLOOM, introduction to *Lewis Carroll: Modern Critical Views*

Whenever we read the *Alice* books, the implication of Humpty Dumpty's famous phrase "which is to be master" lurks recurrently between the lines of Lewis Carroll's stimulating nonsense. Do readers have sovereignty over these stories, blithely and efficiently extracting from Carroll's language its meanings and wonders? Or do these illustrated texts subtly dictate to the reader, actively involving him or her in the creation and experience of Wonderland? There are, of course, no simple answers to questions like these, especially since the subtending issue involves the thorny category of the reader's experience. Certainly the pronounced range and striking variety of Carroll criticism strongly suggest that any interpretation of the *Alices* is more a subjective than an objective exercise. In fact, the *Alice* books are so difficult to define (much less to master) that scholars do not even agree whether or not they belong to children's literature. While studies on Victorian children's literature almost always include a discussion of the *Alice* books, Peter Heath, in *The Philosopher's Alice*, finds that "of all those who read them, it is the children especially who have the smallest chance of understanding what they are about" (3). Roger Lancelyn Green sides with Heath and believes that "*Alice* has moved up in the literary scale and been accepted as a classic for the adult" (32). Walter de la Mare suggests a kind of middle ground, claiming that "even though there are other delights in them which only many years' experience of life can fully reveal, it is the child that is left in us who tastes the sweetest honey and laves its imagination in the clearest waters to be found in the *Alices*" (65). De la Mare's sentiments are echoed by Virginia Woolf when she argues that "Carroll has shown us the world upside down as a child sees it, and has made us laugh as children laugh"; thus "the two *Alices* are not books for children; they are the only books in which we become children" (71). To W. H. Auden, however, the books do not just make us desire to be children, but, more specifically, we desire to become Alice, who is "an adequate symbol for what every human being should try to be like" (5).

Not everyone agrees with Auden's universal Alice, but there is a clear critical consensus that the *Alice* books demonstrate an adaptability that contributes to their status as timeless classics. For instance, Robert Phillips perceives that "Carroll's Alice may prove to be the hardiest perennial of them all" (xix), and F. J. Harvey Darton argues that, unlike *The Water Babies*, which is a fine "museum piece, the *Alices* will never be put in a museum, because they will neither die nor grow out of fashion" (263). In the preface to a collection of essays celebrating the 150th anniversary of Charles Lutwidge Dodgson's birth, Edward Guiliano claims that the "*Alice* books are classics, and like all great works of literature they repay the readers with fresh insights and aesthetic rewards" (vii). However, unlike other "great works of literature," many of the "insights" and "rewards" of the *Alice* books intimately involve particular drawings that are precisely rendered and exactly placed. John Tenniel's *Alice* images are in fact so integral to the books that critics like Edward Hodnett find them to "have permanently fused with the dream-tales, which have become one classic, endlessly enchanting to generation after generation of readers, young and old, wandering in the Alicean field" (195).

Roger Simpson, in his book on John Tenniel, asserting that because analyses of the *Alices* "invariably say far more about the commentators and their times than they do about their source," claims that it is "a pointless task to attempt any longer to speculate about the 'meaning' of . . . [these] . . . books" (143). Given that over a fourth of Simpson's volume is dedicated to the visual examination of *Alice* illustrations, his use of the word "speculate" strikes me as genuinely Carrollian rather than inconsistent. In my view, the point of the *Alice* books, books filled with both pictures and conversations, is to cause readers to "speculate," both mentally and visually, the Wonderland that Carroll and Tenniel collaboratively produced. Indeed, understanding Carroll's play on various levels of seeing and reading is a vital step, not only toward fully appreciating Wonderland's structure, but also toward explaining its prevailing success and influence across a wide range of disciplines.[1]

Aesthetically, Tenniel's illustrations are exclusively Victorian in their execution and production. According to Hugh Haughton, Tenniel's "graphic idiom . . . is as pedantically referential as an exhibition catalogue of Victorian social types, settings, furniture and costume—just like Carroll's own" (xliii). Simpson, agreeing with Haughton, finds that the illustrations in *Alice* and Carroll's narratives are "archetypal products" of their own period (143). In fact, Simpson believes that the *Alice* books are "far from being ahead of their time" and are "purely backward-looking, summarizing the century's two dominant streams of popular art"—namely, "gothic horror and satire" (144). If both Carroll's and Tenniel's work does not escape from the Victorian framework, why do the *Alice* books still appeal to modern readers and scholars? In his *Philosophy of Nonsense*, Jean-Jacques Lecercle observes that "even the best Victorian novels need, on the part of the reader, some adaptation of the Victorian frame of mind," yet "nonsense, that arch-Victorian genre, is hardly affected by the changes, . . . it easily bursts out of the Victorian frame of mind and seems directly to address ours" (223–4). There is no doubt that Carroll's unique literary genius has greatly contributed to the *Alices'* longevity. However, critics have generally failed to recognize the acute power of spatial perception abundantly demonstrated by Carroll's attention to the subjects and layout of Tenniel's illustrations. Indeed, the *Alices* are marked by a studied and dynamic cooperation of printed text and illustration, a characteristic that helps explain why Haughton, even while clinging to his belief that the *Alice* books are essentially Victorian, finds them to "have gone on to generate new meanings with every generation of readers" and notes that as the "countless subsequent interpretations, translations and adaptations show, Alice's adventures continue and are 'to be continued'" (lx).

One of the factors contributing to the *Alice* books' transgenerational freshness is encoded in the physical layout of text and illustrations. Yet for this encoding to exist, the prerequisite premise is that Carroll had indeed carefully planned the content and the placement of Tenniel's illustrations. Although most of Carroll's correspondence with Tenniel was destroyed, there exist, fortunately, surviving documents that support this view. In the Christ Church archives in Oxford, two manuscript charts handwritten by Carroll detail the page placements, sizes, and conditions of each illustration in the two *Alice* books. The disciplined documentation fits the meticulous character of a person who constantly organized his life by recording and organizing thousands of letters and photographs with lists and tables.[2] In the preface to *Sylvie and Bruno*, Carroll mentions his insertion of what he calls "padding" into the text in order to manage the placement of the illustrations. He confesses that "in order to bring a picture into its proper place, it has been necessary to eke out a page with two or three extra lines: but I can honestly say I have put in no more than I was absolutely compelled to do" (xi). When it comes to the placement of the illustrations, it is interesting to see that Carroll makes significant allowances by altering the shape of the text to "fit" its illustrations. A surviving letter from Tenniel also demonstrates how Carroll yielded to several textual changes suggested by Tenniel, in particular, the suppression of an entire episode.[3] In order to unravel some of the discrepancies surrounding critical views on the *Alice* books, it is useful to attend to how Carroll assembles layers of visual and verbal interplay around the imagery of hands. The importance of hands to the *Alice* books is signaled by their imposition on most Wonderland and Looking-Glass World characters, despite their original anatomy. Not only does Tenniel add hands to chess pieces and playing cards, he imposes hands in addition to the wings on the Dodo (*Alice* 35). In several of the illustrations the gestures of hands denote a sense of orality. For instance, when the Mad Hatter sings his distorted version of "The Star," his hands are depicted in accordance to a singing pose (103); when the Queen of Hearts orders Alice's beheading, she points at Alice with an extended right arm while barking, "Off with her head!" (117);[4] and when the King of Hearts discovered the tarts beneath him, he gestures toward them when he utters, "Why, there they are!" (186). In *Through the Looking-Glass*, soon after Alice enters the Looking-Glass World, she finds herself to be invisible and gigantic in comparison to the chess pieces around her. When she sees the White King trying to write in his memorandum, Alice cannot help reaching out her hand and grabbing the end of the King's pencil. The King complains to the Queen as "it writes all manner of things I don't intend—," and the Queen concurs, "That's not a memorandum of *your* feelings!" In fact, what Alice writes through the King's hand is what the reader actually sees in Tenniel's accompanying illustration on the same page: "*The White Knight is sliding down the poker*" (20).

The image of Alice's giant hand is first shown by Tenniel in *Alice in Wonderland* after she becomes trapped in the White Rabbit's house by growing to an enormous size. This inset illustration, with the text encompassing it on three sides, is the kind of illustration that, to Michael Hancher, allows a seamless, uninterrupted spatial flow of the narrative, while benefiting from the visual synchronized effects of text and illustration (120–7).[5] The page depicts Alice's hand reaching down to frighten the White Rabbit, who breaks the cucumber frame, while the matching text alongside runs from top to

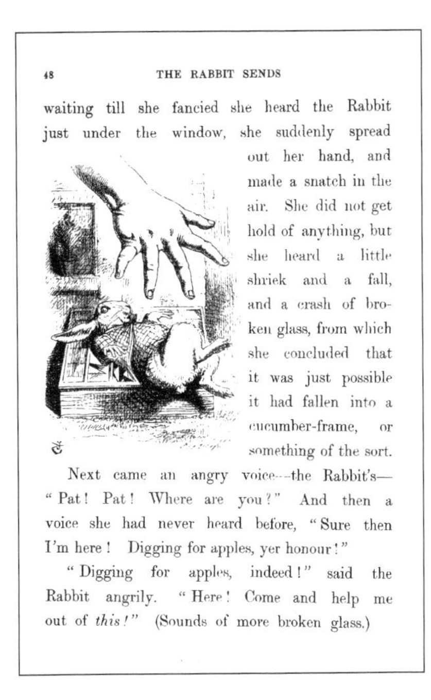

48 THE RABBIT SENDS

waiting till she fancied she heard the Rabbit just under the window, she suddenly spread out her hand, and made a snatch in the air. She did not get hold of anything, but she heard a little shriek and a fall, and a crash of broken glass, from which she concluded that it was just possible it had fallen into a cucumber-frame, or something of the sort.

Next came an angry voice—the Rabbit's—"Pat! Pat! Where are you?" And then a voice she had never heard before, "Sure then I'm here! Digging for apples, yer honour!"

"Digging for apples, indeed!" said the Rabbit angrily. "Here! Come and help me out of *this!*" (Sounds of more broken glass.)

Alice's giant hand over the White Rabbit. Illustration by John Tenniel, in *Alice*, p. 48. Reproduced with permission of the Bodleian Library, University of Oxford.

bottom: "she suddenly spread out her hand, and made a snatch in the air. She did not get hold of anything, but she heard a little shriek and a fall, and a crash of broken glass, from which she concluded that it was just possible it had fallen into a cucumber-frame, or something of the sort" (*Alice* 48).

Not only does the narrative correspond closely with the illustration, the spatial orientation of the illustration and the word placement of the narrative are carefully coordinated to match each other. At the top of the illustration we see Alice's open hand, which is described in the text beside it: "she . . . spread out her hand." In Tenniel's illustration, the White Rabbit, appearing beneath Alice's hand, crashes onto a cucumber frame. In the narrative, the White Rabbit is represented verbally by the second "it" located immediately above the words "cucumber-frame." The proximity of the words representing their corresponding parts of the illustration seems too carefully contrived to allow for mere coincidence. The illustration fits nicely beside the text so that even if one tries to read the narrative without looking directly at the illustration, the image lingers so enticingly within the peripheral vision that it seems to be effortlessly incorporated into the reading process.

In his discussion of synchronicity, Hancher simply finds that the illustration seems to act as a parallel visual narrative alongside the text.[6] However, the conspicuous "synchronized" nature of text and illustration is just the basic element of play on the visual and verbal in the *Alice* books. Upon close inspection, text and illustration do not correspond as immaculately as Hancher believes. In fact, this particular illustration should be divided into two halves by the space between Alice's hand and the White Rabbit/cucumber frame. As it stands, the illustration yokes together two distinct moments in the narrative: one when Alice spreads her giant hand and the other when the White Rabbit falls into the cucumber frame. According to the narrative, since it is only after Alice snatches at the White Rabbit that it falls and crashes into the frame, Alice's widespread hand looming above the White Rabbit is actually asynchronous. Yet through the proximate placement of the words to their counterparts in the illustration, Carroll persuades his readers that the illustration is a continuous visual narrative comparable to the text. The actual snatch of the hand is not visualized except in the reader's mind's eye, which animates the out-stretching fingers of Alice's giant hand in the illustration according to the verbal text. Another level of verbal-visual play lies in the reenactment of the sound of the breaking glass. The fact that Alice is trapped inside the room and unable to see the events depicted by the reader is mirrored by the fact that the reader is deaf to the crashing of the glass heard by Alice. Through the visual accessibility of the illustration, the sound of glass breaking echoes back from the illustration via a rereading of the text, and reinforces Alice's speculation that a cucumber frame is broken. In addition to the placement of Tenniel's illustrations, Carroll also plays with the visual elements of the printed word to enhance the visual and verbal exchange in the *Alice* books. In a letter to his publisher in 1868, four years before the publication of the sequel to *Alice's Adventures in Wonderland*, Carroll was already planning the use of printing the words in reverse:

> Have you any means, or can you find any for printing a page or two, in the next volume of *Alice*, in *reverse*? . . . If no better way can be found, I suppose there would be no great difficulty in printing it on paper, then transferring it, before the ink dries, to wood, and then cutting and electrotyping as a picture. (Cohen and Gandolfo 59)

In his reply, Macmillan assures Carroll that this kind of printing is expensive but possible, and the affirmation resulted in a verse of "Jabberwocky" in mirror writing. The employment of mirror writing in *Through the Looking-Glass* is obviously appropriate since the book plays on different inversions and reversals associated with the mirror. In *Through the Looking-Glass*, the significance of the mirror writing is enhanced owing to Carroll's layout of the book so that in this instance it replaces the illustrations. When Alice first examines the poem "Jabberwocky," it remains illegible until she sets it next to a mirror. The layout of page 21 in *Through the Looking-Glass* indicates that the body of text between the two reflections of "Jabberwocky" actually functions as a visually deciphering looking glass. The word "Looking-glass" is capitalized throughout the book, but with its placement in the middle of the passage, Carroll is alerting the reader to the refracting nature of text in his "Looking-glass book." Furthermore, by visually differentiating his narrative and the poem, which is in italics and indented, Carroll employs the words in his text as a verbal looking glass that alters the visual outlook of the two variations of the "Jabberwocky" verse that appear before and after the primary narrative. Considering that the first verse was reproduced in a method mainly reserved for illustrations, the text not only interacts but also actually transforms the visualization of the verse-image and reconfigures it as acceptable verbal text.

Although mirror writing does not appear in *Alice's Adventures*, like *Through the Looking-Glass* the story is similarly disrupted and enriched by the narrator's interpolated comments. Most of these interpolations correspond to Alice's thoughts, such as when, in chapter 3, the narrator mentions the child hero's "idea" of the Mouse's "long and . . . sad tale," thereby accenting the elaborate tail/tale pun that culminates in a typographically constituted tail-shaped image. Two other such interpolations, however, directly refer to Tenniel illustrations: first, an instruction to the reader, "(If you don't know what a Gryphon is, look at the picture)" (138); second, another instruction to the reader, this time referring to the King wearing a crown on top of his judicial wig, "(look at the frontispiece if you want to know how he did it)" (163). Through these textual references to visual representations, Carroll's narrator orchestrates exactly where and when the reader should make a specific Tenniel drawing (each itself a sort of looking glass) part of his or her reading experience.

In this light the motive and critical value of Carroll's interpolations are together revealed: far more than gestures upon which Tenniel's pictures are hung, these moments actively work to (con)fuse visual and verbal representations *via the reader's experience*, a strategy seeking to eliminate the barrier between "reality" and the imaginative spaces that Carroll's masterpieces engender. It is therefore telling that these moments of "verbal visualization" need not refer to a graphic illustration. An excellent example of verbal visualization occurs during the trial of the Knave of Hearts, when a guinea pig suddenly

> cheered, and was immediately suppressed by the officers of the court. (As that is rather a hard word, I will just explain to you how it was done. They had a large canvass bag, which tied up at the mouth with strings: into this they slipped the guinea-pig, head first, and then sat upon it.)
>
> "I am glad I've seen that done," thought Alice. "I've so often read in the newspapers, at the end of trials, 'There was some attempt at applause, which was immediately suppressed by the officers of the court,' and I never understood what it meant till now." (172)

The interplay between the different threads of narrative is key to our discussion of the verbal and the visual, as Carroll plays on what Alice "sees" and what she "reads." The main narrative relates what happens to the guinea pig with the words "immediately suppressed by the officers of the court," which is supposedly what Alice sees. However, rather than reporting Alice's mental experience, here the parenthetical interpolation reverses its role, giving a detailed account of the event that Alice actually "sees," as she claims immediately afterward. She then reapplies the words "immediately suppressed by the officers of the court" to what she "reads" in newspapers. If indeed Alice "sees" the process of the "suppression" of the guinea pig, she should not be aware of the words "immediately suppressed by the officers of the court." Here Alice usurps the place of the reader of her own story as she herself "reads" the words in the narrative, of which she is a part, so that she both "reads" and "sees" the events of the narrative. Carroll's deliberate misapplication of the verbs "see" and "read" is disguised behind his nonsense definition of the word "suppressed," so that the reader, like the *Times* reviewer, might overlook the significance of the visual and verbal interplay and dismiss it as just "an excellent piece of nonsense" (5) without understanding where the excellence lies.[7] The placement of Tenniel's double-paged illustrations similarly displays Carroll's interest in the expressivity of connections between reading and seeing. One of the most striking effects of text-illustration co-ordination can be found in *Through the Looking-Glass* as Alice is entering the Looking-Glass World.

LOOKING-GLASS HOUSE. 11

there. And certainly the glass *was* beginning to melt away, just like a bright silvery mist.

In another moment Alice was through the

12 LOOKING-GLASS HOUSE.

glass, and had jumped lightly down into the Looking-glass room. The very first thing she did was to look whether there was a fire in the

Alice passing through the looking glass. Illustrations by John Tenniel, in *Looking-Glass* pp. 11–12. Reproduced with permission of the Bodleian Library, University of Oxford.

On page 11, Alice is seen with her head next to the looking glass, and on the next page, on the same leaf, appears an illustration with Alice on the other side of the looking glass. As Hancher points out, "The leaf, in effect, is the glass," and even Tenniel's monogram found next to the fireplace is "thoughtfully reversed . . . so that in the second illustration it is seen as if through the leaf" (130). Not only is the movement of Alice physically portrayed by the turning of the page, but the text beneath both pictures also reflects this passage. On page 11, the narrative ends with "In another moment Alice was through the"; it continues with the word "glass" beneath the illustration on the next page. As a consequence of the reader's eyes moving across these two pages, the reader's understanding also travels, but imaginatively, with Alice "through the glass." Owing to limitations of space I cannot offer an extended phenomenological analysis of this moment that coordinates printed text, two graphic illustrations, and the specific reader's involvement/response.

Thus the following sketch will have to suffice. Alice's movement is visually reinforced along with the narrative in three ways: first, in the layout of the text; second, in the placement of the illustration; and third, in the corporeal structure of the book itself. The coordinated precision of narrative, text, and illustration opens a new dimension in the actual structure of the book, a personal dimension that relies on the reader's action. With its visual inversions and reversals as well as by bestowing smiling faces on inanimate objects, the second illustration entices the reader to see Alice from the other side of the glass, that is, in the Looking-Glass World. Furthermore, by incorporating the mechanics of a book through its uncanny placing of the two illustrations, Carroll generates a visual phenomenon that necessitates a physical action or re-action from the reader. In fact, Carroll designs the illustrations so that the reader is propelled through his or her own action into Carroll's nonsense world. In other words, the reader's personal space corresponds with, overlaps, and superimposes itself onto the Wonderland framework orchestrated by Carroll and Tenniel.

Normally, in the act of reading, the most dramatic and noticeable physical movement is the act of page turning. When absorbed in reading, our minds and eyes are constantly working and turning; but these actions, undergirded by habit, are not ordinarily registered at the forefront of experience. In relation to the rest of the body, the hands holding the book and periodically turning the pages are usually what break the silence.[8] Although most readers are accustomed to this interruption in the reading process, there nevertheless exists the interval required to turn a page, a minor but inherently disruptive event that Carroll exploits. These optical illusions—the pair of illustrations and the deliberate break in the phrase "the glass"—placed by Carroll ensure, at the pivotal moment when Alice enters the mirror, that the reader follows her seamlessly into the Looking-Glass World verbally, visually, and physically.

Carroll's employment of the mechanics of the page as a medium for the interaction of text, reader, and illustrations can be traced back to *Alice's Adventures*, when Alice encounters the mysterious Cheshire Cat for the second time. As Alice converses with the Cat, it whimsically disappears and reappears on top of a tree. Being unaccustomed to conversing with someone she can't see, Alice complains to the Cat, "I wish you wouldn't keep appearing and vanishing so suddenly: you make one quite giddy" (93). Unlike the illustrations of Alice entering the looking glass in figure 2, which are placed on two sides of the same leaf, the pictures of the disappearing Cheshire Cat are both placed on the recto side of overlapping leaves. This results in the first image being placed on top of the other so that when the reader turns the page, the Cheshire Cat, who is visually present in the first page, disappears from the same location, thus reinforcing the process of vanishing described in the book: "It vanished quite slowly, beginning with the end of the tail and ending with the grin, which remained some time after the rest of it had gone" (93). The reader is able to flip the page back and forth and enjoy the optical illusion of making the Cat disappear and reappear. In *The Nursery Alice*, the same design and layout for this pair of illustrations is implemented, but Carroll tells his readers to attempt a different kind of optical trick: "If you turn up the corner of this leaf, you'll have Alice looking at the Grin: and she doesn't look a bit more frightened than when she was looking at the Cat, *does* she?" (36). The answer to his rhetorical question is undoubtedly affirmative, not only because Alice remains the same as on the previous page, but because Alice's facial features are not actually depicted to inform the reader whether she is frightened or not. Carroll's comment in *The Nursery Alice* actually points out a third level of optical exchange, that between the text and its illustrations. What is most interesting is not that the Cheshire

PIG AND PEPPER. 91

"Well then," the Cat went on, "you see a dog growls when it's angry, and wags its tail when it's pleased. Now *I* growl when I'm pleased, and wag my tail when I'm angry. Therefore I'm mad."

"*I* call it purring, not growling," said Alice.

"Call it what you like," said the Cat. "Do you play croquet with the Queen to-day?"

PIG AND PEPPER. 93

at least not so mad as it was in March." As she said this, she looked up, and there was the Cat again, sitting on a branch of a tree.

"Did you say pig, or fig?" said the Cat.

"I said pig," replied Alice; "and I wish you wouldn't keep appearing and vanishing so suddenly: you make one quite giddy."

"All right," said the Cat; and this time it vanished quite slowly, beginning with the end of the tail, and ending with the grin, which remained some time after the rest of it had gone.

Alice and the Cheshire Cat. Illustrations by John Tenniel, in *Alice*, pp. 91 and 93. Reproduced with permission of the Bodleian Library, University of Oxford.

Cat is in the process of disappearing in the second illustration, but that Alice has vanished completely. Her original position in the first illustration is now covered with text; thus, Alice is overwritten by words.

Visually, in fact, it is Alice who disappears and reappears from illustration to illustration. This turns Alice's complaint about the Cheshire Cat making her "giddy" into a complaint that us readers of Carroll are justified in making. Furthermore, considering the fact that Alice's remark about this "giddiness" cuts across the space her image occupied on the previous page, it is an appropriate annotation for the Dodgson-Tenniel collaboration, which creates verbal-optical illusions through juxtaposing interlocking yet interchangeable illustrations and words.

The third and final instance of the page-turning mechanism in the *Alice* books occurs in *Through the Looking-Glass*, at the end of Alice's feast with the Queens, when Alice can no longer bear the ridiculousness of being prevented from eating by the Red Queen. Alice grabs hold of the Red Queen and shakes her into a kitten. At the same time, Alice manages to shake herself back into reality. Unlike previously discussed pairs of illustrations, the two corresponding illustrations of the Red Queen and the kitten are placed on facing pages with no other accompanying text. Their text is arranged by Carroll to occupy a leaf of the book between the two full-page illustrations. The illustrations are placed on the opposing pages with the Red Queen on the verso (page 214) and the kitten on the recto (page 217), while their texts, sandwiched between the two illustrations, are respectively located on pages 215 and 216.

Comparing Alice's entrance and exit, Isabelle Niéres notices that Alice's return from the Looking-Glass World is asymmetrical because the image of the kitten is superimposed on the Queen rather than being a reflection (207). To Niéres, in order for Alice's exit to be symmetrical, Tenniel's illustration of the kitten should be engraved in reverse. What Niéres does not realize is that the orientation of the pages depicting Alice entering the Looking-Glass World is the reverse of those treating her exit. In the former locus, the book is laid out so that two pages of text sandwich the two illustrations of Alice penetrating the looking glass. In the latter, however, the two complementary illustrations encompass a unit of the text: in this arrangement, as Alice escapes from the realm of mirroring madness, the usual way of reading the *Alice* books is altered. This arrangement reconfigures the leaf of the book between the two illustrations in figure 4 as yet another mirror that Alice travels through. As Alice finally wakes from her dream, Carroll is

CHAPTER X.

SHAKING.

SHE took her off the table as she spoke, and shook her backwards and forwards with all her might.

The Red Queen made no resistance whatever; only her face grew very small, and her eyes got large and green: and still, as Alice went on shaking her, she kept on growing shorter——and fatter——and softer——and rounder——and——

CHAPTER XI.

WAKING.

——and it really *was* a kitten, after all.

Shaking the Red Queen into Dinah. Illustrations by John Tenniel, in *Looking-Glass*, pp. 214–17. Reproduced with permission of the Bodleian Library, University of Oxford.

deliberately suggesting that Tenniel's illustrations relinquish their function as visual looking glasses in a dream world. Like the textual mirror between the two verses of "Jabberwocky," here the leaf of text becomes a "mirror" of disillusionment that allows both the character Alice and her reader to see the kitten without further optical distortions. Richard Kelly notes a comparable kind of disillusionment at the end of *Alice's Adventures*, when Alice is about to leave the chaos of Wonderland. Kelly finds that in Tenniel's illustration, the cards and the animals are depicted normally without personification; even the White Rabbit, who remains in his jacket throughout the book, is undressed and thus "dehumanized" (65).

The process of visual-verbal interplay is reinforced by how Carroll reprioritizes text and illustrations. On page 216, the whole of chapter 11 comprises a title and one fragment of a sentence that accompanies the illustration it faces. Here the text is reduced to the status of caption, a subtext, and Tenniel's drawings are elevated to primary status. Moreover, a close examination of the illustrations depicting Alice's hands suggests another level of visual-verbal interplay. Although the kitten is a central figure of the illustration on page 217, Alice's (relatively) giant hands are at least as noticeable and even more important, as it is the hands, and not the kitten, that have agency.

This image of Alice's hands clutching the kitten recalls the earlier picture of Alice's giant hand snatching at the White Rabbit. Through the reading and rereading of the breaking of the cucumber frame in both the narrative and the proximate illustration, it is the reader who re-creates an interactive aesthetic experience through an individual perspective. The mental process of visual and verbal reenactment is reflected and redirected in the physical action of the reader in Carroll's application of page-turning illustration pairs in the *Alice* books. Thus, the hands clutching the Red Queen and then the kitten visually emulate the reader's hands holding the *Alice* book—hands that are present and active in the reader's peripheral vision throughout the reading process. The situation of a small amount of written text between two large illustrations encourages the reader, when turning the page, to notice that his or her hand at some level is similar to Alice's: large, powerful, and actively involved in the movement from one world to another. This small unit of text inserted between the two illustrations forces the reader to bring his or her own enormous hand across the visual plane, which simultaneously contains both illustrations at the precise moment when the page is turned. I would go so far as to argue that in this moment, effectually, three pairs of hands appear in the reader's vision, with his or her own being the most prominent. This designed moment of visual synonymy between the reader's hands and Alice's hands indicates that, far from subordinating his text to Tenniel's illustrations, Carroll is paying tribute to the hands that help him in the creation of the Looking-Glass World. From this perspective—one that foregrounds the cooperation of the reader's body and the physical artifact of the book—they are also the hands that open up the space of Wonderland alongside the invisible hands of both Tenniel and Dodgson.

NOTES

1. Nina Demurova, in her attempt to define a genre to suit the *Alice* books, finds that "philosophers, logicians, mathematicians, physicists, psychologists, folklorists, politicians, as well as literary critics and armchair readers, all find material for thought and interpretations in the *Alices*" (86).
2. Cohen observes that Carroll "was an indefatigable record keeper. His diary, letter register, photograph register . . . are only tips of the iceberg" (*Biography* 290).
3. In an 1870 letter to Carroll, Tenniel wrote: "I think that when the *jump* occurs in the Railway scene you might very well make Alice lay hold of the goat's *beard* as being the object nearest to her hand—instead of the old lady's hair. . . . Don't think me brutal, but I am bound to say that the '*wasp*' chapter doesn't interest me in the least, & I can't see my way to a picture. If you want to shorten the book, I can't help thinking—with all submission—that *there* is your opportunity" (*Wasp in a Wig* 16). Dodgson complied with both of Tenniel's suggestions regarding *Through the Looking-Glass*.
4. In fact, Carroll referred to this particular illustration as "off with her head" when arranging it for publication (Williams 197; Hancher 121). Such a label suggests that Carroll planned and developed certain illustrations according to specific verbal qualities.
5. In his comprehensive study of Tenniel's *Alice* illustrations, Michael Hancher focuses on how the 1866 original edition text and illustrations are "significantly juxtapose[d] on the page" so that "the narrative moments of text and illustrations are visually synchronized" (120).
6. Thus, according to Hancher, this "synchronicity" seems to be the sole reason why the "unusually complementary relationship of Tenniel's illustrations to Carroll's text . . . cannot be fully appreciated in casually laid-out editions" (120).
7. Not realizing that *Alice's Adventures* is a coachievement of Carroll and Tenniel, the anonymous author of "Christmas Books," a review essay in the 26 December 1865 issue of *The Times*, only mentions Carroll in a subordinate clause after lines of praise and admiration for Tenniel's "extraordinary grace" in his production of the illustrations (5).
8. In the Victorian period, books were sometimes read aloud in the drawing room as a form of entertainment. In effect, owing to the disadvantage of being unable to see the illustrations, the audience would naturally experience a lesser degree of intimacy with the physical book. However, the reader, who actually hears his or her own words while viewing the images, might have an even more integral

experience of the verbal and the visual. Moreover, it should be noted that Carroll was an accomplished amateur photographer, and records in his diaries putting on magic lantern shows with narratives and songs to entertain an audience—all suggesting that his interest in and expertise with the multimedia experience was not limited to the specific interplay of printed word and image (*Diaries* 2.127, 3.7).

WORKS CITED

Auden, W. H. "Today's 'Wonder-World' Needs Alice." *New York Times Magazine* 1 July 1962: 5.

Bloom, Harold, ed. *Lewis Carroll: Modern Critical Views.* New York: Chelsea House, 1987.

Carroll, Lewis. *Alice's Adventures in Wonderland.* London: Macmillan, 1866.

——. *Lewis Carroll's Diaries.* Ed. Edward Wakeling. Vols. 1–9. Luton: Lewis Carroll Society, 1993–2005.

——. *The Nursery Alice.* London: Macmillan, 1890.

——. *Sylvie and Bruno.* London: Macmillan, 1889.

——. *Through the Looking-Glass and What Alice Found There.* London: Macmillan, 1872.

——. *The Wasp in a Wig.* Ed. Martin Gardner. London: Macmillan, 1977.

"Christmas Books." *The Times* 26 Dec. 1865: 4–5.

Cohen, Morton N. *Lewis Carroll: A Biography.* London: Macmillan, 1995.

——, and Anita Gandolfo, eds. *Lewis Carroll and the House of Macmillan.* C. L. Dodgson. Cambridge: Cambridge University Press, 1987.

Darton, F. J. Harvey. *Children's Books in England: Five Centuries of Social Life.* London: Cambridge University Press, 1932.

de la Mare, Walter. *Lewis Carroll.* London: Faber & Faber, 1932.

Demurova, Nina. "Toward a Definition of *Alice*'s Genre: The Folktale and Fairy-Tale Connections." Guiliano 75–88.

Green, Roger Lancelyn. "Alice." *Lewis Carroll.* London: Bodley Head, 1960. Rpt. in Phillips 13–38.

Guiliano, Edward. *Lewis Carroll, a Celebration.* New York: Potter, 1982.

Hancher, Michael. *The Tenniel Illustrations to the "Alice" Books.* Columbus: Ohio State University Press, 1985.

Haughton, Hugh. Introduction. *Alice's Adventures in Wonderland* and *Through the Looking-Glass.* Lewis Carroll. London: Penguin, 1998. ix–lxv.

Heath, Peter. *The Philosopher's Alice.* London: Academy Editions, 1974.

Hodnett, Edward. *Image and Text: Studies in the Illustrations of English Literature.* London: Scolar, 1982.

Kelly, Richard. "'If You Don't Know What a Gryphon Is': Text and Illustration in *Alice's Adventures in Wonderland.*" Guiliano 62–74.

Lecercle, Jean-Jacques. *Philosophy of Nonsense: The Intuitions of Victorian Nonsense Literature.* London: Routledge, 1994.

Niéres, Isabelle. "Tenniel: The Logic behind His Interpretation of the Alice Books." *Semiotics and Linguistics in Alice's Worlds*. Ed. Rachel Fordyce and Carla Marello. Research in Text Theory 19. Berlin: Walter de Gruyter, 1994. 194–208.

Phillips, Robert S, ed. *Aspects of Alice: Lewis Carroll's Dreamchild as Seen through the Critics' Looking-Glasses, 1865–1971*. London: Gollancz, 1972.

Simpson, Roger. *Sir John Tenniel: Aspects of His Work*. Rutherford, NJ: Fairleigh Dickinson University Press, 1994.

Williams, Sidney H., Falconer Madan, and Roger L. Green. *The Lewis Carroll Handbook*. Rev. ed. London: Oxford University Press, 1962.

Woolf, Virginia. *The Moment: And Other Essays*. London: Hogarth, 1947.

Culture

Anne Witchard

Chinoiserie Wonderlands of the Fin de Siècle

Twinkletoes in Chinatown

> Anarchy, the political celebration of play and of nostalgic paedophilia, seeks to blow up the wholly illegitimate world of the adult and build in its place the free kingdom of the good child.
>
> —JAMES R. KINCAID, *Child-Loving*

In 1916, the publication of a collection of stories set in London's Chinese Quarter in Limehouse brought their author instant notoriety. Thomas Burke's *Limehouse Nights: Tales of Chinatown* was banned by the circulating libraries while according to literary gossip, "the possibility of securing a conviction was being seriously discussed at headquarters" (Gawsworth 8–9). The *Times Literary Supplement* of 28 September 1916 protested that in place of "the steady, equalised light" which the author "should have thrown on that pestiferous spot off the West India Dock Road, he has been content . . . with flashes of limelight and fireworks" (464). What so appalled the establishment was Burke's *misappropriation* of London's dockside underworld. Britain was at war, and relations between Chinese men and white girls in the East End had become an issue of national concern. Sensational stories in the press fostered anxiety about the exploits of Limehouse Chinese who preyed upon the giddy susceptibilities of a certain "type" of girl to "oriental" vice. While Sax Rohmer's *Fu Manchu* stories reinforced the myth of a criminal conspiracy of Chinese-run dope and gambling consortiums, Thomas Burke's Limehouse fictions upset patriotic orthodoxies by conjuring an orientalized Wonderland of the capital's East End. In the Chinatown streets of Limehouse Causeway and Pennyfields, the scents of spices and opiates, "cinnamon and acconite, betel and bhang," hang in the air (Burke, *Limehouse* 156). Men "dark or lemon-faced," wearing "the raiment of pantomime" (Burke, *Wind* 20), are mesmerized by little girls with "curl-clad faces" who exult in the "blatant life . . . the glamour, the diamond dusks" of the East End streets (Burke, *Limehouse* 184, 154). Burke's investment in the Chinatown scenario as a site of hybridity and transgression reveals an agenda far more complex than just a timely reflection of current press preoccupation. A close examination of the orientalist paradigm that encompasses both a fascination with slum life beyond law and order, where racial borders are not "properly" maintained, and the extant cult of the little girl, throws into focus for us overlooked connections between the carefully staged tableaux of Lewis Carroll's "orientalist" photography and the topsy-turvy Wonderland of his *Alice* books.

While reviewers registered Burke's Limehouse stories on a sliding scale of shock value, "some too terrible for thought, some cheaply startling" (Seldes 66), the erotic focus on the prepubescent slum girl is an aspect of their content that went quite unremarked. In the title story, "The Chink and the Child," "that strangely provocative something about the toss of the head and the hang of the little blue skirt as it coyly kissed her knee . . . smote Cheng. Straight to his heart it went . . . and night after night he would dream of a pale, lily-lovely child" (17–8). *Limehouse Nights* departed from current convention in its portrayal of Chinese men who are, "if not exactly heroic, then often admirable characters" (Parssinen 119), yet it would seem that Burke's anomalous sympathy for "the Chinaman"[1] is predicated upon an identification with his supposed vulnerability to the charms of little girls:

> Tai Ling was a queer bird. Not immoral for, to be immoral, you must first subscribe to some conventional morality. Tai Ling did not. He was just non-moral. . . . He was in love with life, and song, and wine, and warmth, and the beauty of little girls . . . by our standards a complete rogue yet the most joyous I have ever known. (38)

Western perceptions of oriental amorality have long encouraged imaginative evocations of Chinese Otherness as spaces of "mythopoetic transgression" (Stallybrass and White 24). Margins are signifiers of all that the centers deny or repress, and Chinatown operates for Burke in the same way as did the eighteenth-century chinoiserie dream of Far Cathay, a place of wish fulfillment, its aura of mystery and danger inspiring imaginary flights of desire as well as fear. The bizarre land to the east, where every European value was turned topsy-turvy, offered a mirror reversal of the "proper" way of being by reminding of the artificiality of cultural constructs. The influence of chinoiserie pervades Western culture, but its most marked impact in the nineteenth century was on the stage. After the translation into English of

Antoine Galland's *Les mille et une nuits* (*Thousand and One Nights*), which included *Aladdin and His Wonderful Lamp*, the China of *Aladdin* quickly became a staple of the theater and pantomime. Pantomime humor allows the questioning of orthodox social structures; it exposes sententiousness and pomposity by reversing the expected order of things. The topsy-turvy world of *Aladdin* gave the Victorians a space of distortion and "anti-representational exuberance" (Porter 182). The topsy-turvy would find its ultimate literary incarnation in Lewis Carroll's Wonderland, where Alice's adventures consist of a series of cultural confrontations. Her conversation with the languid Caterpillar, coiled on top of a psychotropic mushroom and smoking a hookah, grounds Wonderland's origins in oriental strangeness: "the tautological turn that their conversation takes demonstrates, not that the caterpillar is incorrigibly illogical, but rather that he refuses to be comprehended by Alice's categories of meaning" (Bivona 151).

Carroll was an enthusiastic pantomime goer (provided there was no coarseness). He especially delighted in the transformation scenes and the masses of stage children of whom "two or three thousand . . . [were] annually engaged in London for the Christmas entertainments" (Wagner 34). John Ruskin, a fellow proponent of the cult of the little girl, gives an idea of Victorian obeisance to pantomime's panorama of girlhood in his description of the 1867 production of *Ali Baba and the Forty Thieves*:

> The forty thieves were girls. The forty thieves had forty companions who were girls. The forty thieves and their forty companions were in some way mixed up with about four hundred and forty fairies, who were girls. There was an Oxford and Cambridge boat-race, in which the Oxford and Cambridge men were girls. There was a transformation scene, with a forest, in which the flowers were girls, and a chandelier, in which the lamps were girls, and a great rainbow, which was all of girls. (Ruskin 20)

The staging of orientalized Otherworlds in the Victorian theater indulged an erotic sensibility that thrilled to the proximity of fairy-girlhood. As the genre reached its spectacular peak, pantomime traditionalists were to complain of "optical dazzle," yet Ruskin's concern was declining moral standards thanks to the prevalence of orientalized themes.

> Presently after this, came on the forty thieves, who, as I told you, were girls; and there being no thieving to be presently done, and time hang-

> ing heavy on their hands, arms, and legs, the forty thief-girls proceeded to light forty cigars. Whereupon the British public gave them a round of applause. Whereupon I fell a-thinking; and saw little more of the piece, except as an ugly and disturbing dream. (Ruskin 21)

Underlying Ruskin's indictment of the audience's applause is a horrified fascination. The intensity of his reaction to the spectacle of baby ballerinas, cross-dressed as Eastern robber-bandits and toting cigars, demonstrates the ambiguity in the spectacle of innocent infant flesh that ceaselessly suggested its opposite, the oriental scenario providing a visual manifestation of the contrast between purity and vice.

In 1912, the theater critic W. R. Titterton observed that there are "two ways of magic," first, the fairyland that enchants with the mysterious "aerial motion" of filmily draped fairies, and second, "our splendid old English way with fairy-land—to show it as a continuation of the Mile End Road (eastwards)" (Titterton 231). Here Titterton precisely captures the imagination of Ruskin's and Carroll's time, in thrall to pantomimes that combined the gauzy magic of the fairy with the sexual frisson of the *Arabian Nights* oriental. Most significantly, Titterton associates this pantomime fairyland with the mystique of an orientalized East End, which he describes as a place of "magic and queer costumes as a matter of course" (Titterton 177). Here, down the Mile End Road, lay the dramatic potential of "the foreign quarters" of the turn-of-the-century metropolis. While London's thoroughfares were still "free from the reek of petrol," districts were "emphatically themselves," as Thomas Burke would write nostalgically of these prewar years: "when the foreign quarters *were* foreign . . . East was East and West was West" (Burke, *London* 8–9). In his fictional accounts of Limehouse, Burke employed the highly theatricalized and eroticized imagery that, from the mid-nineteenth century, mapped the orient onto the East End: there in Limehouse "was the blue moon of the Orient. There, for the bold, were the sharp knives, and there, for those who would patiently seek, was the lamp of young Aladdin. I think Gina must have found it" (Burke, *Limehouse* 156). This indeed suggests "limelight and fireworks," a "transformation scene" of the slum, conjuring the topsy-turvy world of the pantomime fairy and the *Arabian Nights* in a scenario that animates those strange dualities captured by Lewis Carroll in his photographs of Lorina and Alice Liddell, Xie Kitchin, Helen Saunders, Daisy Whiteside, Rose Laurie, and Ethel Hatch, costumed as Chinese merchants.

Chinese Transformations

Carroll, "a splendid theatre-goer" (Terry 357), consistently used props to compose his photographs and acquired a cupboard full of theatrical costumes.[2] Many of his pictures taken in the 1870s show the influence of the pantomime trend for staged tableaux. Victorian sexual fantasies of oriental possibility were fed by girls arrayed as "Eastern beauties": "Tartar maidens in amber silk and furs, girls from Cochin China in creamy robes and feathered headdresses, Lapps in white furs, Japanese in embroidered purple, girls from China in terracotta and gold robes" (Wilson 184).[3] Carroll's biographer, Morton Cohen, notes his predilection for dressing his sitters in "dramatic finery": costumes included those of Denmark, Greece, and Turkey, and, he adds, "from time to time a young female poses as a 'Chinaman'" (Cohen, *Lewis Carroll: A Biography* 164). Some significance is intimated here, but Cohen does not take it further. Roger Taylor's essay "All in the Golden Afternoon," in *Lewis Carroll, Photographer*, notes but fails to quantify the particular success of Carroll's "best-known" pictures: the diptych of opposing images taken in 1873 of nine-year-old Xie Kitchin dressed up as a Chinese tea merchant, "On Duty" and "Off Duty." Taylor speculates that Carroll

> clearly went to some trouble to locate six authentic-looking tea chests as well as a full Chinese outfit, complete with shoes and hat of the correct size to fit Xie. What prompted the photos remains a mystery, but more than likely it was a theatrical or literary reference that now eludes us. (97)

On Sunday evening of 13 July, Carroll wrote to Xie Kitchin's mother that he was hoping to do "a really good 'Chinese Merchant,'" telling her, "I'll see about tea-chests in the morning, so if I'm not in when she comes, I hope she'll wait" (Cohen, *Lewis Carroll and the Kitchins* 8). Carroll had begun negotiating plans for the picture some days previously. Although by the 1870s tea was being sold in packets, grocers mostly sold loose tea straight from the chest.[4] Tea traders often wrote to their agents in Canton to insist that the tea remain in its original Chinese crates or chests. The picturesque chests were imported in thousands, and once on display in British shops, the Chinese characters "that in China had served the practical purpose of identifying the kind of tea became exotic hieroglyphs that signified China itself" (Haddad, ch. 3, para. 57). Victorians based their fanciful visions of China on the willow-pattern world of chinoiserie porcelain and a tea chest; a genuine artifact from China was "something that provided them with a material link

"Xie Kitchin as 'Chinaman': 'On Duty.'" Gersheim Collection, Harry Ransom Humanities Research Center, University of Texas at Austin.

to a distant and enchanting land" (Haddad, ch. 3, para. 56). John Haddad cites children's books that instructed young readers to examine tea chests for information on China. Three examples are as follows: In D. P. Kidder's *The Chinese; or, Conversations on the Country and People of China* (1846), a character acknowledges: "When I see Chinese figures on tea-chests, they have almost always fans or umbrellas in their hands; and then there are sure to be two or three temples at no great distance" (Haddad, ch. 3, para. 60). *Peter Piper's Tales about China* (n.d.) advised: "You may form a good idea of the manner in which the Chinese dress upon ordinary occasions, by noticing the figures which they delineate upon their . . . tea-chests" (Haddad, ch. 3, para. 60). The narrator of *People and Customs in Different Countries* (1837) described the crates as "all marked over with strange looking characters" that are as comprehensible to the Chinese as "A, B, C" are to "our people" (Haddad, ch. 3, para. 60).

Though locating the "authentic-looking tea chests" would have presented Carroll with little problem, persuading Mrs. Kitchin to release Xie from her governess proved rather more. He had written to her four days previously (9 July 1873): "If, however, the Chinese dress comes, there will be no use in your talking about Miss Donkin—come she must! And if Miss D. won't give way, then lessons ought—anything rather than miss the Chinese Merchant!" (Cohen, *Lewis Carroll and the Kitchins* 6). Carroll's implication that "the Chinese dress" was to be delivered is used as an argument for urgency and raises questions.

Taylor's suggestion that Carroll "clearly went to some trouble to locate . . . a full Chinese outfit, complete with shoes and hat of the correct size to fit Xie" overlooks the fact that he had used the costume on at least two occasions before. "Lorina and Alice Liddell in Chinese Dress" was taken in the Deanery Garden in spring 1860, over a decade earlier. In this picture, a large Chinese parasol provides the narrative link, and the "transformation scene" is completed by the inscription of the girls' names underneath the picture in mock Chinese characters. Just as it would be for Xie, the costume happens to be a perfect fit for eleven-year-old Lorina, while Alice (b. 1852), smaller in

"Xie Kitchin as 'Chinaman': 'Off Duty.'" Gersheim Collection, Harry Ransom Humanities Research Center, University of Texas at Austin.

"Lorina and Alice Liddell in Chinese Dress." Morris L. Parrish Collection, Department of Rare Books and Special Collections, Princeton University Library.

an identical costume, curls up on a chair. Another picture taken on this day was perhaps intended as a companion piece. A wistful Lorina stands alone, leaning on the closed parasol. The contrasting situations between the two pictures, the open and closed parasol, the solitary, unguarded pose of the second picture, anticipate the later studies of Xie Kitchin, "On Duty" and "Off Duty." These photographs develop this scenario that points to other, playful ways of being, far from the social proprieties of well-to-do Victorian little-girlhood with its restrictive regime of manners, blackboards, and buttoned boots. Again the pictorial narrative counters an attentive pose with one of provocative indolence, while the discarded Manchu pom-pom hat and slippers and disheveled tea chests suggest an aftermath of which the disconcertingly phallic positions of the fan are suggestive.

On 5 June 1871, Carroll photographed nine-year-old Julia Frances Arnold in the Chinese costume, and she wore it again two years later (16 July 1873), just two days after the session with Xie. A week later (23 July 1873), Helen Standen wears the costume. Some historians have suggested that the Chinese costumes were borrowed from Oxford's Asmolean museum. If this was the case, it was a very regular borrowing and one that in the end was not returned. After Carroll died, the contents of his dressing-up box were acquired by the Art and Antique Agency, 41 High St., Oxford, which advertised them in its catalog as "FANCY DRESS Used by LEWIS CARROLL's Child Friends." Among the items listed is "Chinese Mandarin's Robe—Thick blue cotton with black and white pattern, 12s 6d." Potential buyers are directed here to the "On Duty" photograph of Xie Kitchin in *Strand Magazine*, April 1898 (Stern 92).

Perhaps, then, Carroll fabricated the "arrival" of "the Chinese dress" as a ploy, a means of obtaining Xie's mother's cooperation. In 1888, the fourteen-year-old Isa Bowman visited Carroll in Oxford. He wrote an account, "Isa's Visit to Oxford," describing her "looking at a lot of dresses . . . kept in a cupboard, to dress up children in, when they came to be photographed. Some of the dresses had been used in Pantomimes at Drury Lane . . . some had been very magnificent once, but were getting old and shabby" (Foulkes 136). The catalog of the Art and Antique Agency lists other Chinese costumes: "Large Chinese Robe Mauve llama trimmed with white braid, 17s 6d / Small white Llama Robe – Short wide sleeves, 5s." We can link these to other "Chinaman" pictures. In July 1875, Carroll was in London staying at the home of the Pre-Raphaelite artist Henry Holiday, where he set up a makeshift studio and took a series of theatrically composed pictures, two of them "Chinese."[5] In the first, entitled "A Chinese Bazaar" (10 July 1875), Daisy Whiteside poses as a merchant, dressed in the braid-trimmed Chinese robe and the signature pom-pom hat. She stands, her hand resting on a tall Chinese vase placed on top of an inlaid lacquer box. The inscription in Carroll's idiosyncratic violet ink reads "Me givee you good piecey bargain." Three days later (13 July 1875), fifteen-year-old Rose Lawrie, wearing the same costume, sits cross-legged next to the same props for a picture entitled "The Heathen Chinee." The reference is to a poem by the American author Bret Harte, "Plain Language from Truthful James" (1870), widely known as "The Heathen Chinee." Harte, who had written short stories satirizing discrimination against Chinese immigrants, regretted the sensational popularity of this poem. The poem's tone is ironic; the narrator, who has been trying to cheat a Chinese man out of his wages, finds that the member of the "inferior race" is running a confidence game of his own. Most readers, however, could not see the narrator's hypocrisy as Harte intended. The poem's refrain became a popular expression of anti-Chinese sentiment. "Which I wish to remark, / And my language is plain / That for ways that are dark / And for tricks that are vain, / The heathen Chinee is peculiar" (1–5, 55–9). For our purposes it is interesting to note that it is not the best-known lines with which Carroll captions his photograph, but those that describe Ah Sin's smile as "child-like" (24): "Which we had a small game, / And Ah-Sin took a hand: / It was euchre the same / He did not understand; / But he smiled as he sat by the table / A smile that was child-like and bland" (19–24). Douglas R. Nickel points out how Carroll utilized the "capacity of tableau photography to articulate gender roles, especially by reversing them" (60). Carroll's captions draw attention to the narrative conflation of "the Chinaman" and the child. In a blurring of gender and ethnicity, Carroll's make-believe Chinatown child gives access to the erotic social world of the urban poor, the exoticized orient, and a terrain of childhood agency.

What is latent in Carroll's pictures would become manifest in *Limehouse Nights*. Carroll owned a special print of "Off Duty" where the metonymic suggestion of the tea chests has been completed by the watercolor embellishment of a "Chinese" scene. Now the barefoot Xie lounges on a flagstoned bund, with a fleet of junks serving as a backdrop to the piled-up tea chests. There is an uncanny similarity between Carroll's watercolored print of Xie and the cover illustration of Burke's pseudonymous *Song Book of Quong Lee*, in which a Chinese seaman, leaning on a pile of tea chests on a pagoda-lined bund, gazes across the water at London's Limehouse riverside. Foucault's explanation of the heretopic space illuminates these conjunctions: "The heterotopia is capable of juxtaposing in a single real place several spaces, several sites that are in themselves incompatible" (Foucault 24). The sailors who plied cargoes of tea from China brought with them the suggestion of strangely garbed juvenile sing-song girls and Flower Boats (floating brothels). The youthful "fiddle strumming harlots" of China's ports were said to engage in peculiar "ceremonials . . . like the burning of joss sticks to *Cheng Neung*, the Fox-elf and patron saint of whores" and to remove only their silk pajama pants while "each whitened face set in a halo of gilded framework and red pom-poms, rarely altered a muscle during the whole performance" (Hugill 57). Hugill's description conjures the theatricality that mobilized a colonial chinoiserie erotics, a scopophilic conflation that is perhaps nowhere else so vividly exemplified as by Carroll's photographs of little girls dressed as Chinamen.

Carroll's special print of "Xie Kitchin as 'Chinaman': 'Off Duty.'" Hand water-colored on albumen print. Gersheim Collection, Harry Ransom Humanities Research Center, University of Texas at Austin.

Burke's London Chinatown stories would exploit the fantasy of cultural difference inherent in the confluence of a Pekin Street or an Amoy Place, suggesting transgressive possibilities: "You will observe that he [Cheng] claimed her, but had not asked himself whether she was of an age for love. . . . It may be that he forgot that he was in London and not Tuan-tsen" (*Limehouse* 23). By normalizing socially dangerous situations, *Limehouse Nights* operates in a looking-glass space, according to Foucault "absolutely real" and "absolutely unreal" (24). The Chinese Limehouse accords with Foucault's conception of a heterotopia, a place that has "the curious property of being in relation with all other sites, but in such a way as to suspect, neutralise, or invert the set of relations that they happen to designate, mirror, or reflect" (24). For Foucault, the heterotopia is a geographical site of contrast where social meaning is incommensurate with the body of society, its incongruous Otherness established in relation to difference. Like a utopia, it holds up a mirror to society, but unlike a utopia it corresponds to a real place on the map. China as a land of topsy-turvy, remote and fantastic, served traditionally in this way as a mirror in which to scrutinize the cultural disquietudes of the West. Heterotopia are spaces of alternate ordering "that marks them out as Other and allows them to be seen as an alternative way of doing things" (Hetherington viii). Their qualities are not intrinsic but representative, a conjunction of social meaning offering alternatives. Keith Hetherington points out that the use to which "Otherness is put as a mode of (dis)ordering . . . is the most significant aspect of heterotopia" (Hetherington 51).

In *Limehouse Nights*, the most English of institutions are undermined. Young Cockney girls eat chow mein with chopsticks in the local cafés, blithely gamble their housekeeping money at Fan Tan and Puck-a-Pu, burn joss sticks in their bedrooms, and painstakingly prepare opium pipes in the corner pub. In "The Chink and the Child," Burke explores the sexual opportunity afforded by the topsy-turvy. Cheng rescues little Lucy, who has run away from a violent father only to be taken by some prostitutes to a Limehouse opium den: "From what horrors he saved her that night cannot be told, for her ways were too audaciously childish to hold her long from harm in such a place" (*Limehouse* 21). Lucy is transformed by Cheng's ministrations, "dressed up" in Chinese robes, "formless masses of blue and gold, magical things of silk," and her bruises anointed from "a vessel that was surely Aladdin's lamp" (25).

She is now his "White Blossom . . . Twelve years old!" Cheng's ecstatic articulation of her tender years is echoed as "the clock above the Millwall Docks shot twelve crashing notes across the night" (24). The child "seemed the living interpretation of a Chinese lyric. And she was his; her sweet self and her prattle, and her birdlike ways were all his own. Oh beautifully they loved. For two days he held her. Soft caresses from his yellow hands and long, devout kisses were all their demonstrations" (26).

Alice on the Stage

The Victorian and Edwardian fantasists, such as Lewis Carroll, Edward Lear, and J. M. Barrie, "needed a child as muse" to trigger the invention of their Wonderlands (Wullschläger 5). Thomas Burke's muse was the music-hall ingenue Elise Craven. On 30 December 1908, *The Tatler* pronounced Miss

Craven's debut in *Pinkie and the Fairies* at His Majesty's Theatre "an unusual success" (339). Burke composed a poem, "Elise Craven, Dancing," an ode to a little ballerina whose performance holds spellbound a rough and raucous music-hall crowd: "It is but Infant Joy she takes / And melody in glistening flakes / From her delighted limbs she shakes / Little Twinkletoes!" (*Pavements* 20–21, lines 12–16). In his evocation of the dancer as Infant Joy, Burke alludes to William Blake's vision of the child. The Romantic conception of childhood radiance became debased by the Victorian insistence upon childhood innocence, the "pure child" becoming highly sentimentalized and "a symbol of what one might term secular expiation" (Coveney 56). Burke's poem exemplifies this in its grasping for a Blakean conception of innocence, and he would go on to develop the poem's scenario in the *Limehouse Nights* story "Gina of the Chinatown: A Reminiscence." Gina Brentano at thirteen has "started as a gay fifth-rate vaudevillian," a little dancer who knowingly treasures her East End home for its oriental theatricality: "She was a mandarin's daughter in Pennyfields. She was a sailor's wife in the Isle of Dogs. In the West India Dock Road she was a South Sea princess, decked with barbaric jewels and very terrible knives" (155).

A succession of long-running stage productions testifies to the continuing popularity of theatrical chinoiserie in the opening years of the twentieth century. There was *A Trip To Chinatown* (1898), *San Toy* (1899), *A Chinese Honeymoon* (1901), *The New Aladdin* (1906), *See See* (1906), and *Kismet* (1911), shows that presented a mirror reversal of the "proper" way of being, the trend reaching its apotheosis with the wartime hit *Chu Chin Chow* (1914). Burke's presentation of Limehouse draws on those concepts of Chineseness that found expression in the staged orientalisms of Victorian and Edwardian theater. What I want to trace here, however, is a less obvious theatrical debt that his Chinatown fiction owes to the influence of the 1886 stage adaptation of Lewis Carroll's *Alice's Adventures in Wonderland*, with its crucial presentation of a child heroine as "protagonist in an alternative world" (Crozier 215).

The cult of the child on the stage really took off with the emergence of child-based dramas in which little girls with speaking parts exerted a benevolent influence on the adults around them. These "established as something of a stereotype the idea of the child whose inherent virtue enables her to elevate those around her not by what she does but by what she is" (Crozier 173). Middle-class cultural reticence about sex, which encouraged the submerging of physical desire into a spiritual ideal, found an outlet in this enormously popular theatrical child. The innocent child, especially in the slum, functioned as "a means of emotional absolution from guilt in a society in which natural instinct was an unmentionable vice, and in which the religious means for expiation of guilt were decreasingly sought" (Coveney 302). We recognize her then in Burke's Chinatown girls: Marigold is "lovely and brave and bright" (Burke, *Limehouse* 36); Gina, "gentle-and-brave-and-gay" (151), scatters "laughter and love and kindness around Poplar, Shadwell, Limehouse and Blackwall" (184). Burke is as convinced as any Victorian sentimentalist of the redemptive qualities of the girl child working magical transformations on her drab surroundings. His first novel, *Twinkletoes: A Tale of Chinatown* (1917), would allow him to elaborate further upon his besetting preoccupation.

In December 1886, Henry Savile Clarke's production of *Alice in Wonderland* opened at the Prince of Wales Theatre. It was the year following W. T. Stead's exposé of child prostitution in the *Pall Mall Gazette*, regarding which a distraught Lewis Carroll had appealed to the prime minister for an injunction. Arguing that the debate itself was more likely to corrupt young women than the doubtful existence of the offenses, Carroll's stance was to plead for censorship on behalf of "our pure maidens, whose souls are being saddened, if not defiled, by the nauseous literature that is thus thrust upon them" (Robson 182).[6] Carroll had given Savile Clarke permission to adapt *Alice* for the theater on the sole condition that "neither in the libretto nor in any of the stage business, shall any coarseness, or anything suggestive of coarseness, be admitted. This piece ought to be an Operetta . . . and not a Pantomime" (Lovett 37). Because the production was constrained by Carroll's nervous strictures for decorum, it failed to interpret his surreal sense of Wonderland. A sleeping Alice was surrounded by a chorus of fairies who sang a song of enchantment lulling her "to the dream-world of Wonderland" (Lovett 52). Brian Crozier notes the importance of the production, however, in that here "the fairy world was isolated from the pantomime and its attendant vulgarity," thus instigating a firm association between childhood and fairyland that had not been "as apparent in dramatisations of fairy themes before" (Crozier 228). After *Alice* the theatrical focus of interest in children widened from melodrama, "sentimental, often domestic, and always naturalistic" (Crozier 215), to include fantasy worlds. It was a revolution in representational terms, the vital significance of which centered on the role of the child as protagonist. Henceforth, theatrical fairylands appropriated the ideal condition of childhood, a world devoid of responsibility, and the sparkling child star, denizen of this marvelous place, was the ideal being. A revival of *Alice* in 1898 and again in 1900 prompted an upsurge of interest in children on the stage, offering a surfeit of leading roles for child actresses in musical fairy plays such as Charles Kingsley's *The Water Babies* (1902), Frances Hodgson Burnett's *A Little Un-fairy Princess* (1902), Barrie's *The Little White Bird* (1902), and stories adapted from Hans Christian Andersen and the brothers Grimm. Meanwhile, young actresses still had an essential role in popular melodrama. The actress in the role of ragged urchin or vulnerable waif was the pivotal figure around which fantasies of innocence and endangered purity might feverishly spin. A particularly successful and influential production was *Blue-Bell in Fairyland* (1901), its winning formula a timely combination of pantomime fairy, frolicsome musical comedy, and maudlin slum melodrama. Ellaline Terris had received excellent reviews for her "brightness and animation" in *Alice in Wonderland* (1900), and now critics warmed to her heart-winning "unaffected charm" as Blue-Bell, a London girl from the slums, a vivacious flower seller who gets transported to fairyland (*Daily Telegraph*). After this, the slum girl was less frequently a figure of pathos than a high-spirited ragamuffin, enjoying an enviable freedom of the streets. It was a dream of just such infant autonomy, denied to the respectable classes, that prompted the Wonderlands and Neverlands, the oriental bowers of dimly recalled *Arabian Nights*, of late Victorian and Edwardian fantasy.

Twinkletoes

By the end of the Edwardian era, the cult of the little girl was no longer sustainable in quite the same way, but Burke was as prurient and obsessive in his affections as any High Victorian. The anarchic Wonderlands, fairy grottoes, and arcadian idylls of nineteenth-century fantasy were rooted in an age of absolute values and class certainties, in a certain idea of childhood, and in intellectual securities untainted by cynicism. They were also shaped by social and sexual repressions. Victorian morality created the presexual girl child as the epitome of innocent beauty, awakening longing without itself demanding sexual satisfaction. With the new century the juvenile delinquent took her place. The middle-class norm of dependent adolescence began to be extended to social groups that had never before had that conception of youth, and the slum districts were invaded by child savers. The Children's Act of 1908 banned the sale of tobacco to children under sixteen and entry to taverns by children under fourteen. Twinkletoes breaks all these laws with merry impunity: She "poured herself out a small Bass [beer]—her customary breakfast. She paused for a moment at the door to finish her third cigarette, tossing back the crowding curls, a petulant leg kicking idly at nothing. Then with a thrill of dainty frock she skipped into Shantung Place" (Burke, *Twinkletoes* 87–8). Even as civil liberties were being increasingly curtailed, Burke wove his stories around the alien enclaves of the metropolis, romanticizing remote regions of outlaw encampment. Yet while adolescent autonomy is harnessed as a symbol of class antagonism, it fails to mask desire.

Burke's fetishistic imaginings of girlhood in Chinatown fix the vision of the erotic child just as Carroll's photographs did. A description of the mantelshelf and walls of the cottage in Shantung Place, "decorated with framed and unframed photographs of Twinkletoes" (116), provide a litany of her adorable versatility:

> Wherever you looked you saw her: Twinkletoes as a toddler; Twinkletoes in silk coat and lace hat; Twinkletoes in her indoor frock and pinafore, reading; Twinkletoes in furs; Twinkletoes buried in brown velvet; Twinkletoes robed only in a towel; Twinkletoes as a pantomime fairy; Twinkletoes in an early Victorian ballet; Twinkletoes as Maud Allan; Twinkletoes in white silk and Scotch kilt; Twinkletoes as a winter spirit, as a summer spirit, as the voice of Spring, her slim body swathed only in ropes of roses. (*Twinkletoes* 116)

Kincaid explains that the photograph gives permanent access to the *idea* of the child. It is "an end in itself, an erotic world on its own" (227). Lindsay Smith recognizes Lewis Carroll's formulation of desire assuming a "visible enactment of cultural difference across the intricately clothed body of the little girl as object for the photographic lens" and notes that he "rehearses in photographs fantasies of racial, cultural and sexual difference through the visual intricacies of costume dramas and child masquerade," intricacies that both for Carroll and for Burke were underwritten by contemporary issues of "children's rights and age-of-consent legislation as negotiated in various cultural spaces" (Smith 97). Chinoiserie Wonderlands on the stage, in the photographic frame, and in fiction are spaces where normal constraints are turned topsy-turvy, breaking their social function for the pleasure of affording some kind of reciprocity with the child. Burke's Limehouse girl is the product of notions of childhood purity, yet she has consensual sex with "Yellow men." She is the clichéd sunny waif exposed to the "horrors" of the slum, but at the same time, in a spirit of heady defiance, the "horrors" are embraced and debunked. Like Wonderland, the Chinese Limehouse is full of risk; it has "danger everywhere but no consequence" (Kincaid 290).

NOTES

1. During the period encompassed by this study, the terms "Chinaman" and "Chinamen" were used when speaking about the Chinese. Today both words are offensive to Chinese people and those of Chinese descent. My own usage is contextualized within the framework of this essay.
2. Years afterward, one of his child friends, Ethel Arnold, described the treasures of Carroll's rooms, dolls, toys, puzzles, and "all sorts of fancy dress (of which he kept an almost inexhaustible stock in the great cupboard)" (*Atlantic Monthly*, Jan. 1929, cited in Foulkes 13).
3. Jacqueline Rose sees the figure of the child star at the close of the century as a skillful recombination of the late Victorian components of the pantomime procession. The "sexual, pictorial, and spectacular combination of ideal purity and handsome flesh" is reworked for the spectator in the image of "fairy, purity and flesh" (98). See Foulkes 54–55 for the influence of the pantomime on *Alice's Adventures in Wonderland*.
4. At this point 90 percent of tea drunk in Britain was imported from China.
5. See Nickel for a discussion of theatricality as a hallmark of Victorian visual culture, especially in Pre-Raphaelite painting. Another influence more than likely was John Thompson's *Illustrations of China and Its People* (1872). Following the publication of these photographs, Thompson set out "armed with note-book and camera to explore 'the highways and the byways' of London, the back streets and courts where the struggle for life is none the less bitter and intense, because less observed" (preface). *Street Life in London* (1877) is an example of the pictorial convention of social exploration that conflated oriental peoples with London's poor.
6. Robson cites from Carroll's letter of 22 July 1885 to *St. James' Gazette*.

WORKS CITED

Bivona, Daniel. "Alice the Child-Imperialist and the Games of Wonderland." *Nineteenth-Century Literature* 41.2 (1986): 143–71.

Burke, Thomas. *Essays of Today and Yesterday*. London: Harrap, 1928.

——. *Limehouse Nights: Tales of Chinatown*. London: Grant Richards, 1916. Reprint, London: Daily Express Fiction Library, n.d.

——. *London in My Time*. London: Rich & Cowan, 1934.

——. *Out and About: A Notebook of London in War-Time*. London: Allen & Unwin, 1919.

———. *Pavements and Pastures: A Book of Songs*. London: privately printed, 1912.
———. *The Pleasantries of Old Quong*. London: Constable, 1931. Republished as *A Tea-Shop in Limehouse*. Boston: Little, Brown, 1931.
———. *The Song Book of Quong Lee of Limehouse*. London: Allen & Unwin, 1920.
———. *Twinkletoes: A Tale of Chinatown*. London: Readers Library, 1917.
———. *Verses*. London: Privately printed, 1910.
———. *The Wind and the Rain: A Book of Confessions*. London: Thornton Butterworth, 1924.
Cohen, Morton N. *Lewis Carroll: A Biography*. London: Macmillan, 1995.
———, ed. *Lewis Carroll and the Kitchins*. New York: Lewis Carroll Society of North America, 1980.
Coveney, Peter. *The Image of Childhood*. London: Peregrine Books, 1967.
Crozier, Brian. "Notions of Childhood in London Theatre, 1880–1905." Diss. Cambridge University, 1981.
Daily Telegraph. Rev. of *Blue-Bell in Fairyland*. 19 Dec. 1901: 4.
Foucault, Michel. "Of Other Spaces." *Diacritics* 16.1 (1986): 22–27.
Foulkes, Richard. *Lewis Carroll and the Victorian Stage: Theatricals in a Quiet Life*. Aldershot: Ashgate, 2005.
Gawsworth, John, ed. Foreword. *The Best Stories of Thomas Burke*. London: Phoenix House, 1950.
Haddad, John. *The Romance of China: Excursions to China in U.S. Culture 1776–1876*. Project Gutenberg e-book. Accessed 25 July 2008. http://www.gutenberg-e.org/haj01/frames/fhajack.html.
Hetherington, Keith. *The Badlands of Modernity: Heterotopia and Social Ordering*. London: Routledge, 1997.
Hugill, Stan. *Sailortown*. London: Routledge & Kegan Paul, 1967.
Kidder, D. P., ed. *The Chinese; or, Conversations on the Country and People of China*. Department of Rare Books, Library of Congress. New York: G. Lane and C. B. Tippet, 1846.
Kincaid, James R. *Child-Loving: The Erotic Child and Victorian Culture*. New York: Routledge, 1992.
Lovett, Charles C. *Alice on Stage: A History of the Early Theatrical Productions of Alice in Wonderland*. Westport: Meckler, 1990.
Nickel, Douglas R. *Dreaming in Pictures: The Photography of Lewis Carroll*. New Haven: Yale University Press, 2002.
Parssinen, Terry M. *Secret Passions, Secret Remedies: Narcotic Drugs in British Society 1820–1930*. Manchester: Manchester University Press, 1983.
People and Customs in Different Countries. Uncle Oliver's Books for Children. Auburn: Oliphant and Skinner, 1837.
Peter Piper's Tales about China. Albany: R. H. Pease, n.d.
Porter, David. *Ideographia: The Chinese Cipher in Early Modern Europe*. Palo Alto: Stanford University Press, 2001.
Robson, Catherine. *Men in Wonderland: The Lost Girlhood of the Victorian Gentleman*. Princeton: Princeton University Press, 2001.

Ruskin, John. "The Corruption of Modern Pleasure—(Covent Garden Pantomime)." *Time and Tide by Weare and Tyne: Twenty-five Letters to a Working Man of Sunderland on the Laws of Work*. London: Everyman's Library, J. M. Dent & Sons, 1867.

Seldes, Gilbert. "Rediscovery and Romance." *Dial* 19 July 1917: 66.

Smith, Lindsay. *The Politics of Focus: Women, Children and Nineteenth-Century Photography*. Manchester: Manchester University Press, 1998.

Stallybrass, Peter, and Allon White. *The Politics and Poetics of Transgression*. London: Methuen, 1986.

Stern, Jeffrey. *Lewis Carroll, Bibliophile*. London: White Stone Publishing, 1997.

The Tatler. 30 Dec. 1908.

Taylor, Roger. "'All in the Golden Afternoon': The Photograph's of Charles Lutwidge Dodgson." *Lewis Carroll, Photographer: The Princeton University Library Albums*. Roger Taylor and Edward Wakeling. Princeton: Princeton University Press, 2002. 1–120.

Terry, Ellen. *The Story of My Life*. London: Hutchinson, 1908.

Thompson, John. *Illustrations of China and Its People: A Series of Photographs with Letterpress Descriptive of the Places and People Represented*. London: Sampson Low, Marston, Low and Searle, 1873.

——, and Adolphe Smith. *Street Life in London*. London: Sampson Low, Marston, Searle and Rivington, 1877.

Times Literary Supplement. Rev. of *Limehouse Nights* by Thomas Burke. 28 Sept. 1916: 464.

Titterton, W. R. *From Theatre to Music Hall*. London: Stephen Swift, 1912.

Wagner, Leopold. *The Pantomimes and All About Them: Their Origin, History, Preparation and Exponents*. London: J. Heywood, 1881.

Wilson, A. E. *Edwardian Theatre*. London: Arthur Baker, 1951.

Wullschläger, Jackie. *Inventing Wonderland: The Lives and Fantasies of Lewis Carroll, Edward Lear, J. M. Barrie, Kenneth Grahame and A. A. Milne*. London: Methuen, 1995.

Helen Pilinovsky

Body as Wonderland

Alice's Graphic Iteration in *Lost Girls*

"With Proper Assistance, You Might Have Left Off at 7."

In point of fact, Alice Liddell couldn't have left off at 7, no matter how many critics have projected that desire for her arrested development onto her fictionalizing[1] friend Lewis Carroll. Alice, the fictional Alice, most certainly didn't, continuing down over the course of 145 (and a half, give or take) years. Robert Graves famously refers to Alice as "that prime heroine of our nation"; but while Alice may have started her life as a British schoolgirl, it is impossible to deny that her appeal has broadened. Today, one may encounter Alice in many forms, for Alice is a more broadly based creature than many other literary characters, not dependent upon the vision of one creator alone. This is due in part to the extended life cycle afforded to a character who is in the public domain and present in numerous iterations, and partially to the process of creation that brought her about. Fundamentally, Alice exists within a Wonderland of our own construction, an ever-shifting locale that reflects social concerns and the kinds of growth *we* feel she should experience: from the whimsy of a world based in nursery rhymes, to a sexualized landscape that must be navigated with care.

Looking at a chronological listing of the most popular images of Alice, it is undeniable that she's been maturing with the passage of the years: the once innocent child heroine is now commonly depicted as a physically mature young woman, and the Wonderland that surrounds her is more commonly employed as a place of experience than as a place of innocence. As Alice's persona has changed, so, too, has her perspective, resulting in a concurrent shift to Wonderland. The question that faces the contemporary readers who confront her multiple revisionings is, why? What do these changes say about the character, and what do they say about *us*? I would argue that

Alice's maturation is based in an uneasy fascination with the circumstances surrounding the composition of her original story and the myth of her relationship with Lewis Carroll, and that in many retellings Alice is aged in order to excuse that interest. It is abhorrent to apply that rationale to any one individual, but in a culture whose "Alice industry" has extended beyond the traditional representation of a seven-year-old heroine to an equally common nubile iteration, whose trade goods consist of more broadly salable lingerie than of commemorative tea sets, the assessment is hard to deny.[2]

Retellings of Carroll's *Alice* stories follow three primary paths: those that continue Alice's original adventures in their Victorian setting,[3] those that update her still childish situation into more contemporary circumstances, and those that diverge from their surroundings to focus on *her* maturation. This last type is an interesting and even natural outgrowth from the narrative arcs of her origin stories in *Alice's Adventures in Wonderland* and *Through the Looking-Glass*, but the points of termination in such stories are fascinating in what they reveal about modern attitudes toward the heroine's journey. In one of the *Alice* story's more interesting revisionings, Alan Moore and Melinda Gebbie's *Lost Girls*, the character Alice is a worldly-wise devotee of debauchery who utilizes her trauma as a looking glass, reflecting upon the nature of childhood and fantasy and, thus, herself. This examination addresses that trajectory and its current culmination in *Lost Girls*: it will engage in textual analysis to a limited extent, but the primary focus will be on the social factors that cause the texts to be situated as they are. Parodic representations of Alice are nothing new: consider the 1976 movie *Alice in Wonderland* (sometimes subtitled "A Musical Porno"), the popular dark video game adaptation *Alice* presented by American McGee, or the various comic book retellings that have sprung up in recent years. However, Moore and Gebbie's approach to the issue of Alice stands on the shoulders of giants because it uses the observations and intimations of previous interpretations to directly address the taboo issue that is central to the cultural fixation with *Alice*: the circumstances surrounding its composition.

Inspired by an unusual friendship and an afternoon's storytelling, the Victorian *Alice* story's origins are convoluted: the tales began interactively, being composed off-the-cuff by Charles Lutwidge Dodgson, better known as Lewis Carroll, while he played with the children of an Oxford dean, Henry Liddell. His favorite of these children, Alice Pleasance Liddell, was both the inspiration for and first recipient of the book that bears her name. In the prefatory poem beginning *Alice's Adventures in Wonderland*, we see an idealized version of their idyllic composition, occurring "all in the golden afternoon" (xxvii), with the sun setting at dusk foreshadowing but not concretizing the end of their adventures. In marked contrast, the poem concluding *Through the Looking-Glass* anagrams her name with the first letter of each line and contains the evocative verse, "Still she haunts me, phantomwise, / Alice moving under skies / Never seen by waking eyes" (240, lines 10–12), seemingly referencing their famous, mysterious split. As A. S. Byatt notes, "Much of what has been written about Charles Lutwidge Dodgson, alias Lewis Carroll, and his relations with the original Alice, has made it harder, not easier, to remember the nature and significance of [her first reading of *Alice*]" (xi). While this is certainly true, it cannot and should not be neglected. The myths, rumors, and realities of Carroll's relationship with Alice Liddell have colored the reading and retelling of *Alice* significantly. Karoline Leach has explored the various potential fallacies surrounding the relationship between Lewis Carroll and Alice Liddell in detail: she presents the myth quite lyrically, writing, "Alice the child was the love of his life and the passion of his tragically deviant soul, and for a brief while she gave him happiness. But then, goes the story, things got out of hand" (163). Leach's theories about the reality that counters the myth are fascinating but beside the point for our purposes: as matters stand, it is the "Carroll Myth" that influences the presentation of Alice in popular culture. The text and subtext of the Carroll Myth together grow more explicit in revisionings such as *Lost Girls*, creating a kind of palimpsest of influence and comprehension. That palimpsest is layered, first, in the actual text and, second, in the interplay between the text and the biographical and pseudobiographical projections of critics and readers over the years. The third layer grows out of the interplay between the first two, producing works as diverse as Katie Roiphe's novel *Still She Haunts Me*, which posits a Carroll-Liddell affair; Peabody's collection of short narratives titled *Alice Redux*, which presents everything from the idea of an adult Lorina undergoing therapy for her childhood with Sigmund Freud in "Lilith in Wunderland" to "Alice's Agency," a story centered on the idea of three girls named Alice, Wendy, and Dorothy coming together in their travels (and travails); and, perhaps most unique of all, Moore and Gebbie's *Lost Girls*. The relationship between Alice Liddell and Lewis Carroll may complicate the reading of the original *Alice* in a problematic fashion, but the complications that arise from that reading are the very ones that give us our numerous retellings and revisionings: to read them without keeping that in mind is to cripple our own understanding of them.

In 1865 Dodgson published *Alice's Adventures* under the name Lewis Carroll, with *Through the Looking-Glass* following in 1872. Rather than being grounded in fairy stories as so many other works of the period were, the *Alice* books were founded in traditional English nursery rhymes. Although Carroll himself referred to it as a "fairy-tale," in a letter he specified that it contained "*no* fairies" before considering titles such as *Alice among the Elves* and *Alice among the Goblins*. Indeed, it very well may be that Carroll selected the title *Alice's Adventures in Wonderland* exactly because the story contains no fairies and markedly diverges from the commonplace fairy-tale structure (Carroll, *Letters* 65). Jack Zipes remarks that Carroll's writing was part of a trajectory on the part of Victorian fantasists who were on a "quest for a new fairy-tale form [that] stemmed from a psychological rejection and rebellion against the 'norms' of English society," and that "Carroll made one of the most radical statements on behalf of the fairy tale and the child's perspective by conceiving of a fantastic plot with no ostensible moral purpose" (xx, xxii). Additionally, he served the fledgling genre of the fantasy well with his creation of a self-contained fantastic universe that did not depend on any preexisting literary template.[4]

Carroll's Wonderland set the stage for much of the generic work that would follow, giving us a template of the fantastic as a reflection of the inner landscape of the psyche (although to later authors we owe a debt for the creation of fantastic worlds that can touch upon and influence our own in fashions other than the purely personal, as in the "dreaming" of Carroll and George MacDonald). John Clute acknowledges the *Alice* books as crosshatch fantasy, "tales where thresholds are sharply demarcated; in tales of this sort, though contiguities may exist, there will be little intermixing of realities between worlds" (237). Alice's dream world is presented to us as possessing the potential to affect her larger reality in its last lines, when her sister ponders the probability that Alice will "keep, through all her riper years, the simple and loving heart of her childhood; and how she would gather about her other little children, and make *their* eyes bright and eager with many a strange tale, perhaps even with the dream of Wonderland" (109). However, some critics reject the notion that the figure of Alice would ever work to promulgate the fantasy. According to James R. Kincaid, "Alice has no simplicity to maintain or regain . . . she will not even, in a vulgar and pathetic idea we could not keep ourselves from adding, use the story to bring other children to us, others with bright and eager eyes. She could never tell the story. She didn't get it" (*Child-Loving* 294). In Kincaid's eyes,

Alice's adventures, exciting as they are, will not affect or contaminate anyone other than herself within her self-contained universe. Kincaid views Alice as being an unchildlike child and, as such, almost antithetical to the nature of the fantasy, unlikely to disseminate its lessons in the wider world. This is potentially true, certainly, depending upon how one interprets Wonderland's role in her life: is it a necessary stopping point on the journey through maturation where she can perform a crucial transition, or is it a potential and rejected endpoint? Kincaid would appear to believe the latter, reading Alice as a figure who receives but rejects an offer of playful magic in favor of dull and unimaginative responsibility. However, this is an understanding predicated on specific interpretive strategies that depend more on social than generic criticism. The fantasy in question in Kincaid's reading is that of the erotic child, rather than the fantasy produced through recognized literary conventions. It is a crucial distinction. Clearly, the fantasy of *Alice* has thrived as well, although not as a Victorian child-lover would have desired or predicted. In an interesting kind of synecdoche, fictional Alice has preceded cultural Alice by growing up—perhaps in keeping with Kincaid's observations concerning her fundamentally unchildlike nature. But the importance of *Wonderland* to Alice, the importance of *fantasy* to Alice—to deny either is to negate her very existence. And to reserve fantasy for children (and appropriately childlike children, at that) alone is untenable. At the time of the *Alice* books' creation, the adult fantasy was a contradiction in terms; today, that audience is assumed, and the prefix "adult" holds an entirely different connotation. And yet, somehow, both are still eminently applicable to Alice, and specifically to her recent depiction in *Lost Girls*, for reasons that are certainly hinted at within the original text.

Critics admire *Alice's Adventures* as the first piece of children's fiction with no specific moral ax to grind, making much of its anarchic nature; however, critics also note the tale's peculiarly antifemale views. U. C. Knoepflmacher observes that, "for Carroll, power always involves the gender distinctions on which society insists" (172). This traditional hierarchy is somewhat skewed in the world of Alice, where men are nonentities, and adult women are powerful, malevolent, and illogical—unlike Alice herself, who is exempt of these qualities by dint of her age. Certainly Carroll, with his comments concerning the wisdom of "leav[ing] off at 7" and his inexplicably, unreasonably hostile maternal figures, evinces a modicum of distaste for mature femininity. In his attitude toward the virtues of girlhood, critics note an interesting element of transposition. As Auerbach and Knoepflmacher put it, the most admired authors of Victorian fantasy—Carroll foremost among them—were men who glorified the state of childhood in their tales of imaginary lands where their characters could avoid the pressures of adulthood. In contrast, "most Victorian women . . . envied adults rather than children. . . . If they were good, they never grew up" (1). Auerbach and Knoepflmacher illustrate quite neatly the disparate expectations of the genders as writers as opposed to characters, but do a disservice to Alice: it is clear that Alice eventually does grow up, both in Carroll's world and in our own.

The story of Alice can be read as a story of maturation that resents its necessity. As Knoepflmacher puts it, "Carroll knows that Alice must repudiate his desire to linger forever in a mid-summer dream world in which time can stand still. At the same time, however, by prolonging the attempt to detain his heroine . . . he also rebels against that inevitability" (167–8). Truly, Carroll strenuously resists maturation in *Alice's Adventures*, as when Alice, motivated by the most classic of childhood reasons, unfairness, at long last rebels against the rules of Wonderland embodied in the concept of "sentence first, verdict afterwards" (107). Her rebellion, which results in her expulsion from Wonderland, is enforced by her vehement denial of illogic (a sentiment that contains the seed of eventual adulthood) when she denies the spurious authority of the Red Queen and King, crying out, just before she awakes, "You're nothing but a pack of cards!" Similarly, however wistfully, Carroll acknowledges Alice's ongoing maturation in *Through the Looking-Glass*, when Alice makes it across the chessboard kingdom, mastering all matter of whimsy, only to finally exert her own authority against the disorder that surrounds her when she shakes the (new and improved) Red Queen back into a kitten. In Wonderland, Alice explores the boundaries of her dream world but ultimately fails to exert her own authority; in the Looking-Glass World, Alice possesses a concrete purpose, which she fulfills. She becomes a queen and imposes on her surroundings her own sense of order. This conclusion gestures toward Alice's eventual adulthood and even, possibly, toward her acquisition of the characteristics that Carroll so abhorred. It is a resolution that reflects the Victorian ambiguity toward childhood, maturity, and, most certainly, their crossroads, sexuality.

Kincaid has written extensively about the sexualization of children in Victorian culture and in contemporary life. In *Child-Loving*, he observes that Carroll used his readers' awareness of the terrible story of inevitable maturation as

> an ominous background against which to develop [his] much more alluring plots. Alice [is] asked to decide about growing up, to mold [her] life . . . around this decision. These are crisis stories, like those crisis-of-vocation or of-faith plots so loved by the Victorians. The question raised . . . is, "Will you agree to grow up?" Alice seems to find the prospect so untroubling she recognizes no dilemma at all. (278)

Kincaid is writing, however, from a position of sympathy for the child-lover that necessitates our alliance with adult readers who possess a marked investment in the continued existence of child as child. He does not, necessarily, speak on behalf of the author with this assessment, as it is difficult to deny the occasionally threatening nature of both Wonderland and the Looking-Glass World. Kincaid reads both arenas as wholly positive, nurturing spaces where children can remain children, whimsical and free: he says, "Alice rushes by . . . rapidly, hardly noticing the landscape and the lovers she is leaving behind" (278). In his reading, many if not all of the figures Alice encounters in these spaces are affectionate if not adoring, in the older sense of the word. However, this optimistic reading is predicated on a worldview that privileges the adult respondent rather than the child character. Her inevitable maturation is presented as ingratitude, if not outright betrayal of an unspoken pact. Kincaid reads Carroll's veiled suggestion that "she might very well have left off growing altogether at seven—'with proper assistance'" not as a "grim suggestion that Alice could have arranged for her own execution," but rather "literally and dearly, as offering a whole world of help to Alice in remaining a child" (278). This is an interesting interpretation, but it omits acknowledgment of the point in the cohesive story in which the *observation*, not the offer, is made. Such assistance wasn't made available in Wonderland, and in the Looking-Glass World, it comes too late. The past tense is imperative, in multiple senses. In many ways, his analysis seems more suitable for the later readings of *Alice*, where Wonderland is redefined in keeping with the expansion of our collective psyche.

Considering the general Victorian fascination with the cult of the child, it's hardly surprising that its "prime heroine" was arrested at the age of seven. Considering our contemporary fascination with a "youth culture" that orbits around the image of a somewhat more mature young woman (for whom, typically, the verb "arrested" holds a different meaning), it's equally unsurprising that *our* Alices differ in degree and in kind from their distinguished predecessor. The more interesting question is why they resemble her as closely as they do.

Alice, created a hundred years before most of the other classic figures of children's literature, starts off with one key advantage: she's in the public domain. In the hundred years since her copyright expired, she has passed from being a specific character to being a near archetype: images of Alice appear in every medium. Carolyn Sigler has speculated that the "*Alice* books' enduring power and appeal may very well lie in the fact that, like dreams, they *can* mean whatever readers *need* them to mean" (xiv). The clearly discernable aging process that Alice displays over the course of her 145 years would seem to indicate that at least some portion of the population *needs* Alice to grow up, culminating with the mature Alices of today. Various iterations proceed along a trajectory depicting a heroine who shoots along the path of her life from Carroll's own innocent seven-year-old, based on Alice Liddell herself, to John Tenniel's only slightly older version, modeled on the similarly aged Mary Babcock, to Arthur Rackham's more adolescent depiction of 1907 and the similarly styled, still dominant Disney version of 1951, into the even older versions featured in works such as *The Oz/Wonderland Chronicles* and *Return to Wonderland*, to stop at a point that can only be described as "nubile." One work that coincides with the shift in interest from innocence to experience during the sexual revolution aptly demonstrates the manner in which Alice ages: the 1976 film *Alice in Wonderland* (subtitled *An X-Rated Musical Comedy*) was put into rapid production when producer Bill Osco realized that Carroll's manuscript was in the public domain, allowing him to make explicit that which was originally implicit (or, indeed, absent). Spurred by an encounter with an importunate suitor, this Alice enters *her* Wonderland after retreating to the original *Alice's Adventures* as a bastion of simplicity; however, falling asleep, the version that she finds in her psyche bears only a superficial resemblance to the original. Reversing the polarity of the original Victorian narrative, the 1976 *Alice* rejects the notion of a glorified childhood. This twentieth-century Wonderland conveys that maturity—physical, sexual, and emotional maturity—can be magical, and that there's little to fear from the inevitability of growing up. Capturing the zeitgeist of the times, *Alice in Wonderland: An X-Rated Musical Comedy* was booked in the same theaters as *Star Wars*, apparently grossing in excess of $90 million worldwide. Roger Ebert observes that "the camera suggests that the most amazing things are happening just offscreen" (Ebert 1). It is, in fact, Wonderland rather than Alice that is the star of this movie: its success, coupled with its unorthodox interpretation of Wonderland, suggests that Alice's sexualization at the time was not regarded as a deviation from the accepted interpretation so much as an updating of its norms and attitudes.

Lost Girls performs a similar function in its explicitly sexual treatment of the events of the *Alice* books, but it goes beyond Carroll's universe to postulate what happened next. Sigler's observation that the "shift from imitating the Alice books to merely referring to details of the Alice mythos, of course, not only reflects changes in literary culture but larger social and cultural changes as well" is apt here (xvii). While the incorporation of adult mores into a children's story may seem an inexplicable split upon its surface—from children's classic (even with slightly older representations of our heroine) to pornography depicting Wonderland as a delightfully corrupting influence—the issues that Moore and Gebbie explore in their interpretation in turn explain away at least some of the cognitive dissonance. They trace the trajectory of Alice's journey to its (un?)natural conclusion in *Lost Girls* to present an Alice who has most certainly grown up, and who, perhaps, was in actuality quite mature all along.

Let us return to Byatt's observations concerning Lewis Carroll: that while "Carroll invented the least sentimental, most real child character in children's literature . . . his own extratextual comments, and even more the intense biographical interest in his relationships with his little-girl 'child-friends' makes it . . . difficult to respond to Alice as she is in her own worlds" (xiii). Almost inevitably, references to Alice refer back to this relationship, coloring the reader's response to the text: almost inevitably, "the obscure psychology of a man who went to the seaside to meet little girls with a pocket full of safety pins in case they needed them to pin their dresses up to paddle" intrudes upon the fundamental story (xiii). Even the editor of *The Letters of Lewis Carroll* felt it necessary to warn readers that "the *dramatis personae* of this collection differ as a group in one respect from the recipients of other people's letters: so many of them are little girls and their mothers" (Cohen, in Carroll, *Letters* xx). Carroll's fondness for and interaction with little girls is undeniable, but the nature of those interactions, and what motivated them, is still a mystery—one that apparently demands exploration for many critics. Byatt acknowledges the

> many analyses of these preoccupations, some attempting to defend the innocence of the Victorian passion for naked innocents, some darkly analyzing Carroll's hypothetical sexual preferences, some concentrat-

> ing on Carroll as that not uncommon figure, the Victorian adult who would have preferred to have remained a child. (xiv)

However, she brushes these analyses away as being contradictory and insoluble, as well as, in her eyes, inapplicable, choosing never to return to them. I would argue, however, that it is the mystery at the heart of the composition of *Alice* concerning the precise nature of the relationship between Carrol and little girls that has shaped a pervasive cultural conceptualization of Alice, that has kept her name a watchword of modern culture, and that has captured and kept the attention of a period possessed of wholly different concerns. In my mind this mystery is an aspect of what Leach called the Carroll Myth, rather than a conclusion based on incontrovertible historical fact. Indeed, it is the possibility of premature maturation that fascinates modern audiences in a fashion that is both obscure and disturbing: in a culture that sexualizes little girls and infantilizes grown women to the extent that ours does, Alice's story and its backstory together exert a magnetic pull. Kincaid addresses the nature of that attraction on a cultural level in his *Erotic Innocence: The Culture of Child Molesting*. He argues that our cultural fascination with narratives of abuse is predicated on a prurient interest that is permitted by our strong disapproval. He grounds his argument in the Victorian conceptualization of "childhood," and in

> the Romantic heritage of "the child and its body" and our current reckless expenditure of this dangerous nineteenth-century inheritance. These stories seemed sweet and beneficent to Wordsworth, Dickens, and Beatrix Potter; but they have soured over time. It's not so much that they became silly and sentimental, though they may have, but that they took a turn into nightmare. These are nightmares we deal with pathologically: through disavowal, projection, and displacement. (7)

Applying Kincaid's logic on a micro rather than a macro level, we find a compelling argument for Alice's appeal, as well as for the alterations—although we are left in the dark as to where that turn into nightmare occurred. Kincaid argues that a prurient interest in child sexuality has been present from the inception of the conceptualization of childhood. I to allow for maintain that this interest functioned as an undercurrent in a period when if women conformed they remained eternal children (to paraphrase Auerbach and Knoepflmacher), and that the peculiarly overlapping quality of our perception of the two classes of being, children and women, intensified sharply with the realization that women, too, could grow up. But how? And into what? As it is certainly true that "our culture has enthusiastically sexualized the child while denying just as enthusiastically that it was doing any such thing," strategies have been enacted to extend that ambiguous denial even into Wonderland, to encourage our heroine's maturation to a new and contemporarily acceptable level of maturity, including sexual maturity, while maintaining the attractive myth of innocence as innocence willingly despoiled (*Erotic Innocence* 13). Bluntly phrased, society has aged Alice to excuse its attraction to her and to her circumstances, and Moore and Gebbie address the text and subtext of Alice's appeal quite graphically. Pornographically? You decide.

No mistake can be made: *Lost Girls* is most indubitably pornographic in nature, and *not* intended for children, despite its source material, and despite its comic-book format.[5] Its Alice is a paradox of conflicting motivations and decisions, and its apparent Wonderland is quite different from the localization of the straight-line translation of Carroll's fantastic region, which we find in an explicit drawing of Alice's debauchery. When we see an image of Alice in the company of a millinery-loving lunatic serving tea (2.17.7), we automatically transpose its details onto the Mad Hatter of the original *Alice's Adventures*—despite the fact that the *Lost Girls* version features nudity, depravity, and a version of the Cheshire Cat that puns visually upon crude slang for a certain portion of the female anatomy. (Moore and Gebbie use the cognitive dissonance between what we expect to see and what is really depicted to underscore the eventual epiphany that the site of this tea party is in no way a Wonderland, Carrollian or otherwise.) A richer understanding of Moore and Gebbie's Wonderland, however, is not so easily had. Will Brooker posits that the aristocratic sexagenarian Alice of Moore's text "presumably holds the same relationship with Alice Hargreaves as Tenniel's blonde did with the young Alice Liddell: half-sisters with some similarities of personality despite the difference in appearance" (156). I would disagree, and say that this Alice bears no relation whatsoever to Alice Hargreaves—but she does bear a definite connection to the Alice of Carroll's original text, not as a half-sister, but as a descendent, legitimate or illegitimate. So, too, is Wonderland: it does not exist in a 1:1 ratio with its inspiration, but goes off beyond it, and a bit to one side. Moore and Gebbie's Wonderland is a state of mind as much as anything else: it is a space that allows, not for nonsense, but rather for freedom from nonsensical social restrictions concerning sex, society, and, most of all, personal autonomy. In this light, the use of the trappings of Wonderland is a deception, a literary red herring: it is only when we, as readers, succumb to the belief that Carroll's Wonderland is a place of perversion and debauchery alone, that Moore and Gebbie reveal its true equivalent in the realm of *Lost Girls*, the space created by story. Gebbie's beautiful Art Nouveau–influenced imagery and Alan Moore's poignant observations about the nature of childhood, sexuality, and the transformation from innocence to experience (two states not necessarily opposed in the world of the story) elevate this artifact above erotica, into a category all its own, even though Moore insists upon the blunt label of pornography, saying that "erotica is material relating to love . . . what we wanted to talk about was sex" (Wolk 22). And talk about sex they do, although not exclusively: in between bouts of erotic activity, the events that led them to the positions they hold (literally and figuratively) are explored. In Neil Gaiman's words: "It is one of the tropes of pure pornography that events are without consequence. No babies, no STDs, no trauma, no memories best left unexamined. *Lost Girls* parts company from pure porn in precisely that place: it's all about consequences, not to mention war, music, love, lust, repression and memory." One of the most interesting metaconsequences that Moore addresses is the way our image of Alice has been warped.

In *Lost Girls* three women meet in a hotel and share their stories: Dottie Gale, Wendy Potter, and Lady Alice Fairchild. As their stories are revealed, it becomes clear that these are three familiar characters: Dottie (aka Dorothy Gale), Wendy Potter (née Darling), and Lady Alice Fairchild (strongly implied to be our very own, never surnamed, Carrollian Alice). And in the events that follow, Alice is clearly the instigator, leading them, as she says in the first pages of the tale, to be "queens together" (1.6.3).

The story begins with our three heroines meeting at a decadent vacation spot in Austria, the Hotel Himmelgarten, which caters to sybarites who are considerably above the common breed of pleasure seekers. Encountering one another, the three women quickly realize that they have more in common than their taste for adventure: after Alice takes it upon herself to seduce Dorothy with the aid of a little opium, the drug relaxes their mutual inhibitions further than they'd dreamed. As Dorothy describes an early sexual fantasy/experience that took place in a field of poppies, Alice experiences a vision that hearkens back to her own youthful peccadilloes: a hookah-smoking figure located, not atop a mushroom, but rather between the folds of Dorothy's labia. The two part ways, shaken, but reconvene to discuss their experiences and their attitudes, soon to be joined by a third, Wendy. As José Alaniz puts it, "*Lost Girls*, in its opening gambit, makes the linkage between storytelling, desire, and the polymorphous sex act itself a central theme" (273). Their sharing is physical as well as psychological, in keeping with the nature of the collection, but the observations that arise in their discussions are especially relevant to any discussion of how and why the heroines of children's literature have been sexualized.

When our heroines first begin to share, Alice says, "Desire's a strange land one discovers as a child, where nothing makes the slightest sense" (1.6.3). This statement is true of all the characters from children's literature whose behavior has been subjected to Freudian analysis, true of all figures who mature alongside their readers in society, and certainly true of the respective protagonists of *Lost Girls*. Dorothy is primarily concerned with the power that sexuality grants her, the power that the desires of others give to her. Of her encounter with the Cowardly Lion, she says, "I made him scared: I made him tame; heck, I even made him brave" (2.18.5). Wendy has been ashamed of her adolescent explorations with a gang of youths led by a free-spirited Peter since they took place, feeling simultaneously empowered by her experiences and somewhat distressed by their implications and their possible repercussions. And Alice? Alice is the most damaged by her experiences and at the same time the one who has risen farthest above them.

Alice's story begins at fourteen, as, Narcissus-like, she admires her reflection in a pool. In a nod to the original Alice, before falling asleep, Moore's Alice speaks of her sister sitting beside her, reading "improving books, dull things with neither pictures nor conversation" (1.9.4). Moore adopts a classic fairy-tale narrative strategy of displacing blame for masculine wrongdoing onto a female "villain" when he has his Alice say, "In some ways, it was her fault, what occurred" (1.9.5): a friend of her father's by the name of Bunny (a White Rabbit to start her down her path who, coincidentally, matches Carroll's general description) molests her. Alice disassociates and imagines that it is her reflection in the sitting-room mirror that/who is with her, in a continuation of her narcissistic pool-gazing and an allusion to the events of *Through the Looking-Glass*. As we see the same looking glass being unpacked for Alice at the beginning of her sojourn at the Himmelgarten Hotel, we realize that the narrative that Moore delineates here is far longer than Carroll's representation (1.1.5).

This is an Alice still lost in her own reflection, having yet to face the necessary transition into self-awareness and maturity. Reflecting on her pool-gazing experience, Alice says, "I was thoroughly infatuated with myself; this underwater girl amidst the blonde and drifting weed, her face was mine, yet now and then a queer, deep fish would shimmer through it, just as if some dreadful thought had crossed her mind" (1.9.2). And later, as Alice reflects on her rape and disassociation, we read,

> I fell or floated down a hole inside myself, and at its far end all I could see was Mother's mirror. . . . I fell, and from the hole's far end she fell towards me, half bare, hair like wild rape, white lace petals opening about her skinny legs. . . . The mirror-glass was melting into silver, boiling into mist, and I reached out and felt the young muscle in her shoulder, in her neck, the child-silk at her nape. (1.9.5)

Literally embodying self-blame, Alice's reflection becomes her abuser, and Alice becomes thoroughly displaced through and from her trauma. Alice later says, "I no longer felt like me . . . I had not substance. I was the reflection. From beyond the mirror-pane the real me gazed out, lost . . . I have been there ever since" (1.9.8). This is an interesting deviation from Kincaid's reading of the original *Alice*:

> The child functions as a mirror for us, certainly, but it is a complex mirror yielding oblique, distanced views of desirable otherness. If the child should grow up, it would become not a trick mirror but a cheap dime-store reflector, providing nothing in the way of obliquity and nothing for desire. (*Child-Loving* 278)

Alice's reflection serves to become both her distorted, abusive reflection and her original, preserved self: *that* child retains obliquity but seems, in turn, nonreflective of the corruption that our grown-up Alice willingly explores. Like an inversion of the picture of Dorian Gray, the reflection retains the nature of the original, even as the original seeks dissipation—an interesting image of a mirrored double, and an interesting commentary on the nature of the doubled self.

Hearing tales of Dorothy's exploits later in the book, Wendy asks, "It is like magic, isn't it, the time before we're properly grown up? It's all so shadowy and wild." To this, Alice retorts, "What utter bosh. It all sounds rather healthy and outdoors to me, not shadowy at all" (2.14.8). Alice is still lost in that world of reflected denial, but it's a world of denial inhabited by many. Alaniz praises *Lost Girls* by saying,

> The perversion of . . . [our heroine's seminal experiences are] . . . in the end merely an unveiling, an unstripping of the sexual subtext behind

> so much children's literature . . . the child (-like) heroine's journey is driven by her desire to know, to see, to yield up the truth about her mysterious but alluring circumstances, her desired object, and, ultimately, of her own body. Children's literature, from *The Wizard of Oz* to *Peter Pan* to *Alice in Wonderland*, is merely the house-of-mirrors estrangement of a burgeoning, frightening sexuality. (276)

This observation meshes nicely with Wendy's naïveté but does a serious injustice to children's literature, simplifying it into a single-layered narrative: the truth lies somewhere between Wendy's and Alice's interpretations, between the adamant proponents of the fantasy (in all senses of the word) of the child, such as Kincaid's, and Alaniz's belief that it's all so painfully clear. The truth lies, I believe, in the malleable adaptability of Wonderland.

Moore first hints at the reasons behind Alice's leanings, saying, "I can say with some certainty that my experience had left me with a great fear and distrust of men. . . . I confess that all my feverish imaginings were soft and skirted: reassuring as the image in my looking-glass," and then exaggerates them (2.16.2). After seducing the majority of the "flowers . . . in [her] own dear little garden"[6] at boarding school (Alice notes that all of her friends are named for flowers: Lily, Rose, Pansy, Daisy), Alice fixates upon Miss Regent, soon to become Mrs. Redman, our substitute for the Red Queen. Alice joins Regent's household as her "assistant," participating in a deepening spiral of perversion, and for once, in Moore's sex-positive text, this term is applicable: Alice engages in nonconsensual sex with a variety of partners, all female, while under the influence of narcotics, blaming them for the loosening of her moral boundaries. These partners reflect the characters of Carroll's tale, but nearly all of them are transformed into women. The cross-dressing Sapphic host of a hemp-laced tea party is described as never removing her Ascot hat "even when in flagrante." Two enormous women who finish one another's sentences (2.17.7), Tweedle-like, toy mercilessly with Alice; and Alice's final descent into madness occurs during an encounter with the text's "Caterpillar," an impotent doctor with a grublike penis who trades opium for exhibitionism. Here the Wonderland of *Lost Girls* is presented as a place of nightmare, corruption, and debauchery, holding as little lessoning as its inspiration, but considerably less in the way of wonder. Yet, though this space of sexual experience descends from and refers to Carroll's Wonderland, it is not *Lost Girls'* Wonderland. This space is to be found in the Hotel Himmelgarten.

Although Alice is a ready conscript to the field of passion, saying, "Every-

Garden of Live Flowers from *Lost Girls* © Alan Moore and Melinda Gebbie. Reprinted with permission. www.topshelfcomix.com.

thing was sliding into that unreal domain beyond the mirror where my earliest sexual experience had stranded me, a world wherein the most outlandish of things were possible, bounded by nothing save the logic of desire," at the beginning of her sojourn, further events illustrate that the unchecked logic of desire is not to be trusted (2.17.5). It is even as Alice is interfered with by women that she "truly beg[ins] to lose [her] mind," realizing that she is a willing participant in the cycle of abuse:

> Everything was complicated. They were excited by violating a youngster. I liked being their victim, but I also shared their sadistic pleasure: I'd made the little oyster-girls suck me. Enjoyed their discomfort, their

> unwillingness. Years earlier, a pink, flustered man had shoved me down a moral rabbit-hole. Now, as a drug-addicted lesbian prostitute, I realized I was still falling. (3.26.7)

Only when her two counterparts regress her to her childhood in a role-playing scenario where the mature woman becomes once more a helpless girl does Alice achieve "understanding": she recounts how her degradation came to its climax when she transposes her blaming of her sister for her molestation with the corruption that she herself is administering to young Lily, the daughter of the submissive Mrs. White; as Lily pleasures her, she says, "Something inside me broke like glass" (3.29.5). She wakes the Red King from his stupor with a screamed confession, committing Mrs. Redman and herself to asylums, and herself, at least, to a period of honest reflection: she says, "All my life, I've assumed I pursued women, but . . . perhaps I was just running away from men? Certainly, women weren't always kinder or more gentle" (3.17.7). Alice continues her lifestyle after she is released from the asylum, but after the introspection offered by her games at the Himmelgarten Hotel, she demonstrates her growth by speculating about the possibility of a liaison with the "feminine" M. Rougeur. When asked if she doesn't prefer women, Alice replies, "Frankly, anything seems possible now. Who knows? We could take turns being the lady." Wendy responds, "Alice is right: I feel full of possibilities again, like when I was young. As if my imagination can wander where it likes" (3.30.2–3). Alice seals her redemption by abandoning the mirror that had held her trauma: "beautiful and imaginative things can be destroyed," she says, "beauty and imagination cannot. They blossom, even in wartime . . . my looking-glass, I once thought part of me was stuck inside it, but not now. We've rescued her. Now it's just a beloved old thing" (3.30.3). And off into the night our heroines flee, just before the advancing forces of war readily smash the mirror and all that it implies, suggesting that as one cycle ends, another begins.

For in conjunction with our heroine's introspections, we have witnessed the opening gambit in a chess game of gargantuan proportions. Our heroines have shared their revelations on the verge of war, their greatest sharing coming at the cusp of the Archduke's parade of 1914. The tale's events occur during the last days of the Belle Époque, concurrent with the last days of peace in Europe and featuring scenes of blissful orgies interspersed with Franz Ferdinand's assassination.

Who Dreamed It? from *Lost Girls* © Alan Moore and Melinda Gebbie. Reprinted with permission. www.topshelfcomix.com.

> And the spell was broken, just like that. As we came to ourselves we noticed how cold it had grown, a winter breath insinuated in the grass that paled the flowers and slowed the hearts of dragonflies. . . . Something had changed. A certain inclination of the light, a shift of pressure in the air. Without the burning armour of our lust, I'm sure we all felt naked then. Three goose-fleshed women in a wood, suddenly awkward, unsure of their grace, abandoned by desire. . . . Something quite glorious was finished with for good. (2.20.7)

Although the characters have been physical adults for many years, only now, with their traumas resolved, are they truly grown: the cessation of their prolonged childhoods marks the end of Europe's innocence. This, truly, is the equivalent to Carroll's Wonderland, and not the self-conscious rescripting of the details and personalities of *Alice*'s landscape. This, truly, is the boundary line between innocence and maturity. As Alaniz observes,

> a passion for narrative infects the characters almost as much as their lust for more common pleasures: Lady Fairchild writes porn novels, the hotel owner keeps a vast library of erotica, even Wendy's bore of a husband Harold secretly consumes over-the top pornography. . . . At the Himmelgarten, everyone, even the prudes, craves stories. (274)

Alaniz frames this observation with a Foucauldian analysis of sexuality, locating the appeal and success of the story within its unveiling of sexual strategies, claiming that "the series' most porno/erotic aspect is its narrative strategy" (274). This is a valid assertion, but I would extend its implications to strategies of growth via wonder, in a gambit that is perhaps even more basic to fantasy than to pornography.

Although *Lost Girls* suggests that when they leave the safe boundaries of the Himmelgarten Hotel our heroines will carry back into the world the

Snicker-Snack from *Lost Girls* © Alan Moore and Melinda Gebbie. Reprinted with permission. www.topshelfcomix.com.

atmosphere of freedom and lessons they have learned, the subtext of war and circumstance implies otherwise. Reality can be rejected only temporarily; its intrusion is as inevitable as the earlier texts' intrusion of maturity. Thus, Wonderland is still represented as a liminal space of transition and transformation, rather than as a viable final destination, even when its borders occupy the physical space of our own world. Despite Kincaid's arguments about the pleasant fantasy of remaining in stasis, both Carroll and Moore present Wonderland as a journey, not a destination. And Alice is still represented as the one who will carry its message out beyond those borders to disseminate it to the world at large via her own adult actions and choices. Even though the form of Moore's message is somewhat different from that of Carroll's, the functions of both messages are identical. Moore defines maturity as acceptance, Carroll as autonomy; yet both advocate maturity's necessity, a principle implying that personal progress does not necessarily negate any contextualizing societal cycle.

Several of Moore's observations and implications are problematic and even initially offensive. It is, for example, intensely difficult to reconcile his presentation of Alice's orientation toward women as being exclusively the outgrowth of her molestation, and her broadening of preferences late in life to include men as a sign of healing. Even more so, some of Moore's examples of sexual freedom straddle the border between asserting the right to free speech in sexual matters and apologizing for pedophilia. At one point, discussing the text of a lovingly illustrated incest fantasy (a pastiche of the work of Pierre Louÿs illustrated in the style of the Marquis von Bayros), we read a character's hesitant description of it as "an exciting story, but the children doing things . . . ," only to be rebuffed with the argument that these children "are only real in this delightful book" (3.22.3). A character asks the age of the characters, to be further put off with the explanation: "It is quite monstrous . . . except that they are fictions, as old as the pages they appear upon, no less, no more. Fiction and fact: only madmen and magistrates cannot discriminate between them" (3.22.3). Both scenarios are more complex than they appear, however, and enable Moore to engage with contradiction as well as levels of metanarrative. M. Rougeur claims that "pornographies are the enchanted parklands where the most secret and vulnerable of all our many selves can safely play" (3.22.8). This, too, can be seen as a kind of a revisioning of Wonderland, but a fundamentally shallow one that reduces the true freedom attained by Moore's central characters to a case of reader response. It works in a cyclical, self-referential, tautological fashion to justify the existence of the story, but it does not by any means do justice to the story. The Wonderland of *Lost Girls* does not lie purely in its prurient aspect.

Given the preponderance in the original *Alices* of what Knoepflmacher terms "male figures . . . fragile and ineffectual," coupled with hostile, irrational female characters, it is intriguing, upon deeper analysis, that the roles of all of those characters are usurped by women (195). The shift in gender decries Carroll's original commentary of one-sided opposition and victimization: it levels the playing field and creates a narrative in which all of the characters are clearly delineated as being or, rather, *thinking* themselves to be autonomous, Alice herself most of all. The reflections that she has sought are abusers and victims alike, mirroring what she interprets as her own complicity in her abuse, playing out both roles: this simplification removes the element of authorial self-insertion and (ironically enough, in a work of pornography) the male gaze. Brooker argues that "Moore's series can be seen as an interesting example of contemporary fiction that taps into the reading of Carroll and his children's stories as 'dark' and laden with hidden, adult perversions, but he projects those elements onto the figure of his heroine" (157–8). Brooker's assessment focuses on volume 1 alone, but it follows a pattern that is mitigated only by the conclusion of the series, where Alice's redemption consists of her acceptance of her own actions and desires. For the purpose of the narrative, it is an interesting effect: even in the conclusion, when Alice states her intention to pursue M. Rougeur, it is a far cry from the return to innocence normally signified by an unconventional female succumbing to a heteronormative relationship. Rather, finally, it signals her acceptance of herself and her desires, wherever they may take her.

The issue of literary pornography that verges on being pedophiliac is somewhat more complex: the example that Moore uses is pornography with no redeeming features or observations, true to the nature of Edwardian smut in every regard. And yet, simply by incorporating it into the story arc of *Lost Girls*, which *is* an important commentary upon the downside of glorified innocence, he justifies his overall position: to deny the possibility of fantasy at any stage is to taint it at every stage. Alaniz argues that

> Moore and Gebbie's project figures not so much as a perversion of innocent stories which children have blithely enjoyed for generations, but [as] a mission to unmask the veiled product of an institutionalized incitement to discourse on sex masquerading as literature for kids (by grown men). The authors of *Lost Girls* take on the task, so long the

> purview of critics, to reveal the children's stories as the true perversions, thereby stripping away their symbolic and metaphorical evasions, to shed light on the unabashed sexual substructure of those texts. (276)

I would argue that Alaniz overstates the case somewhat, and in doing so, does a significant disservice to the nature and function of children's literature. However, his observation concerning the validity of the broadened borders and bettered understandings that Moore and Gebbie provide includes the original texts in its purview, particularly insofar as we address the perceptions of contemporary readers. Alaniz implicates the original texts while excusing their revisions: this can and should probably be read as deliberate provocation, but it does not advance the cause of broadened fantastic borders any more than the inverse would. Removed from the social arguments of cause and effect, and limited to the metanarrative of *Lost Girls*, Moore makes an interesting case for intellectual freedom, and presents an even more interesting answer as to what happens when we let our characters grow up and experience all that life has to offer, including sex: we grow up alongside them, losing our pleasant illusions of projected innocence. This argument is implicit rather than explicit: it almost follows a kind of tautological logic. When we read about the sexual exploits of our favorite childhood characters, and witness their pain and confusion over having been kept in stasis, we recognize in them the hypocrisy of a system that will condemn the acknowledgment of the roots of their stories, even while salivating over their implications and making them explicit in their common social signifiers.

Does it justify the inclusion of immature characters in explicit pornography? To my mind, it does not. But it raises a series of fascinating questions about the nature of the collective attraction to Alice. The shift in representation from girl to woman reflects a concurrent shift in the focus of our cultural fascination from the innocence represented by the child to the potential of maturing youth. In Mary Louise Ennis's view, "Today's Alice, a bit wiser than Carroll's, is a postmodern empowered heroine in control of Wonderlands of her own (feminist) design" (12). I would say that today's Alice is as perplexed as her Victorian analog by the contradictions of the adult world—it's the nature of adulthood that has changed, not the girl. In reflecting upon Alice, we find ourselves reflected by ourselves. The views of the critic and the reader say much more about them and their society than they ever could about Alice. And as *Lost Girls* eloquently demonstrates, while that reflection may on occasion be tremendously disturbing, that's no reason not to confront it.

NOTES

1. Used purely in opposition to biographizing.
2. It is the lower-intensity, more broadly scaled manifestation of an observation made by Brooker concerning the propensity of some pedophiliac organizations to reference Carroll in their titles: he acknowledges that while we might "baulk" at the connection between Carroll's "coy" portrait nudes and explicit pornography featuring children, "we cannot ignore the fact that some people clearly believe the two have something in common" (53).
3. Please see Sigler for a comprehensive overview of Alice-inspired works ranging into the 1920s. Sigler says that an Alice-derived work contains "an Alice-like protagonist or protagonists, male and/or female, who is typically polite, articulate, and assertive; a clear transition from the 'real' waking world to a fantasy dream world through which the protagonist journeys; rapid shifts in identity, appearance, and locations; an episodic structure often centering on encounters with nonhuman fantasy characters and/or characters based on nursery rhymes or other popular children's texts, including Alice herself; nonsense language and interpolated nonsense verse, verse-parodies, or songs; an awakening or return to the 'real' world, which is generally portrayed as domestic (a literal return home); and, usually, a clear acknowledgement of indebtedness to Carroll through a dedication, apology, mock-denial of influence, or other textual or extratextual reference" (xvii). Although Sigler is talking about early twentieth-century retellings aimed at a child audience, interestingly, *Lost Girls* fits the bill on every count except for the "domestic" return home.
4. The self-contained fantasy universes of Carroll and later authors such as William Morris (who performed much the same function for adult fantasy that Carroll did for children's fantasy) are very different from predecessors of the shared-universe type: contrast their works with, for example, the fairy tale proper, where preexisting knowledge of how things work in fairy tales can be used as a kind of authorial shorthand. *Alice* is self-contained in the sense that it does not depend on any other fantasy universe to provide its structure.
5. This series of intersecting factors has caused much speculation about possible legal issues for publisher Top Shelf and various shops carrying the collection.
6. Figure 1 underscores the subtlety with which Moore and Gebbie interpolate the mores of sexuality into Carroll's story: using the chivalric language offhandedly, they reference the anthropomorphized blooms of *Through the Looking-Glass*, but recontextualize them in a more "romantic" light. This Alice, hands in her pockets, looks as restrained as her true Victorian predecessor (and more so), but the playful, smirking sprites who reach out to her offer considerably more in the way of temptation. Truly a Garden of Earthly Delights.

WORKS CITED

Alaniz, José. "Speaking the 'Truth' of Sex: Moore and Gebbie's *Lost Girls*." *Alan Moore: Portrait of an Extraordinary Gentleman*. Ed. Smoky Man and Gary Spencer Millidge. Leigh-on-Sea: Abiogenesis Press, 2003.

Auerbach, Nina, and U. C. Knoepflmacher, eds. *Forbidden Journey: Fairy Tales and Fantasies by Victorian Women Writers*. Chicago: University of Chicago Press, 1992.

Brooker, Will. *Alice's Adventures: Lewis Carroll in Popular Culture*. New York: Continuum Books, 2004.

Byatt, A. S. Introduction. *Alice in Wonderland* and *Through the Looking-Glass*. New York: Modern Library, 2002. xi–xxi.

Carroll, Lewis. *Alice in Wonderland* and *Through the Looking-Glass*. New York: Random House, 2002.

——. *The Letters of Lewis Carroll*. Vol. 1, *ca. 1837–1885*. Ed. Morton N. Cohen. New York: Oxford University Press, 1979.

Clute, John, ed. *The Encyclopedia of Fantasy*. New York: St. Martin's Griffin, 1999.

Ebert, Roger. "Alice in Wonderland (X)." Rev. of *Alice in Wonderland*, dir. Bud Townsend. *Chicago Sun-Times* 24 Nov. 1976. Accessed 26 July 2008. Rogerebert.com. http://rogerebert.suntimes.com/apps/pbcs.dll/article?AID=/19761124/REVIEWS/611240301/1023.

Ennis, Mary Louise. "Alice in Wonderland." *The Oxford Companion to Fairy Tales*. Ed. Jack Zipes. Oxford: Oxford University Press, 2000. 10–12.

Gaiman, Neil. Rev. of *Lost Girls*, by Alan Moore and Melinda Gebbie. *Publishers Weekly* 19 June 2006. Accessed 9 Aug. 2008. http://www.publishersweekly.com/article/CA6344082.html.

Kincaid, James R. *Child-Loving: The Erotic Child and Victorian Culture*. New York: Routledge, 1994.

——. *Erotic Innocence: The Culture of Child Molesting*. Durham: Duke University Press, 1998.

Knoepflmacher, U. C. "Expanding Alice: From Underground to Wonderland." *Ventures into Childland: Victorians, Fairy Tales, and Femininity*. Chicago: University of Chicago Press, 1998. 150–91.

Leach, Karoline. *In the Shadow of the Dreamchild: A New Understanding of Lewis Carroll*. London: Peter Owen, 1999.

Moore, Alan, and Melinda Gebbie. *Lost Girls*. Vols. 1–3. Atlanta/Portland: Top Shelf Productions, 2006.

Peabody, Richard, ed. *Alice Redux: New Stories of Alice, Lewis, and Wonderland*. Arlington, VA: Paycock Press, 2005.

Roiphe, Katie. *Still She Haunts Me*. New York: Dell, 2002.

Sigler, Carolyn, ed. *Alternative Alices: Visions and Revisions of Lewis Carroll's* Alice *Books*. Lexington: University Press of Kentucky, 1997.

Wolk, Douglass. "Alan Moore's Literary Pornography." *Publishers Weekly: Comics Week* 2 May 2006. Accessed 21 Mar. 2009. http://www.publishersweekly.com/article/CA6330239.html.

Zipes, Jack, ed. *Victorian Fairy Tales: The Revolt of the Fairies and Elves*. New York: Routledge, 1987.

Sean Somers

Arisu in Harajuku

Yagawa Sumiko's Wonderland as Translation, Theory, and Performance

In Japanese, the title of Lewis Carroll's *Alice's Adventures in Wonderland* is frequently translated as the marvelously ambiguous phrase *Fushigi no kuni no Arisu*. In this context, the word *fushigi* may suggest a variety of atmospheric sensations, including wonder, but also mystery, strangeness, bewilderment, or fear.[1] Moreover, this phrase may be translated back into English as Mysterious Country's Alice, a formulation that suggests that the *fushigi* terrain claims and reorients a person. As a domain for realizing *fushigi*, Wonderland entices the Japanese reader with an alternative experience, a unique space that enchants and beguiles. This "mysterious country," however, also has the power of possession as well as reformation: the *fushigi* world transforms *Arisu*, Alice, within its ambient enigma. For over a hundred years, Wonderland's linguistic and metaphysical peculiarities have inspired Japanese translators, playwrights, and animators. With considerable variation in their styles and approaches, Japanese authors have redesigned and resituated Wonderland according to differing interpretations of *fushigi* as a sensibility of wonder as well as mystery.

There have been over two dozen versions of *Fushigi no kuni no Arisu*, beginning with abbreviated children's versions in the late nineteenth century and, most recently, with Kinoshita Sakura's comic book rendition (Gentô-sha komikkusu, 2007). Those who have taken up the unique translational challenges that Carroll poses include Yanase Naoki, a renowned Joyce scholar who has produced the only complete version of *Finnegans Wake* in Japanese. However, of the many editions available, perhaps the most influential is Yagawa Sumiko's.[2] She is admired for her linguistic dexterity, but even more for her philosophically sophisticated idea of Wonderland as a space that contravenes the normative social expectations of Japanese society. In Yagawa's view, *fushigi no kuni* enables a countercultural mode that liberates the imagination from routine prescriptions. As she details in her noteworthy essay "Usagi-ana to shôjo" (The Rabbit Hole and the Girl, 1994), more than inviting a passive experience from the reader, Wonderland stimulates the interpenetration of textual and social spaces. This idea of Wonderland has influenced a Japanese subculture of neo-Victorian enthusiasts known as the *Gosu-Rori* (also *Goshi-Rori*, Gothic Lolita). Experimenting with her concepts, the *Gosu-Rori* have removed *Arisu* from a translated text, resituating her as the locus of a shared communal performance. In this coupling of Carroll's text and Japanese subcultural context, socially marginalized individuals use Wonderland as a stage for performing a specific subcultural identity. And when it emerges refashioned through *fushigi*, identity becomes an empowering statement of the fantastic.

Yagawa argues that Carroll's Wonderland defines an alternative realm for aesthetic enactment, one that favors unconventional forms of expression. One can reshape a new sense of self through the persona of *Arisu*. *Fushigi no kuni no Arisu* should not be read, then, only as entertainment or a storybook fantasy, but should be understood as a framework through which one acquires a fresh capacity to evaluate interpersonal relationships within society as a whole. *Arisu*, who is the agent of *fushigi*, challenges a reader's programmed behavior through the mysterious influences of Wonderland. In this way, Yagawa conceives of *Arisu* as an assertion of *fushigi* that functions as defiance. The *Gosu-Rori* subculture of Japan, as will be discussed below, put Yagawa's theories into practice through their impersonations of *Arisu*. They seek an invocation of Wonderland amid the quotidian aspects of Tokyo. For them, *becoming Arisu* in the everyday means to overturn restrictions that have suppressed or abused the individual personality. As Yagawa specifically maintains, actualizing the *Arisu* alternative through Wonderland is particularly meaningful for at-risk Japanese youths, who experience isolation, ennui, and maladjustment in their prescribed social roles. *Arisu*, to them, represents a personality shift from depression into wonder. Wonderland acts as a therapeutic site for psychological healing, through transformative identity performances in which *fushigi* acts as the mechanism of awakening.

Yagawa thus provides a theoretical assessment of Carroll's work as expressing alternative spaces for identity and identification. John Xiros Cooper makes a similar point about Carroll's works: they are "sites of resistance to the assimilative strategies of the adult, visited with varying degrees of violence on childhood" (150). Wonderland's aesthetics challenge those pretenses of the mainstream and their discourses of the manipulative and restrictive. Yagawa believes that those who are on the social margins, particularly adolescents and young adults who feel disenfranchised from mainstream Japan, can use Wonderland for creatively rebellious purposes. In a society inundated with imagery from *Hello Kitty* mobile phone straps and other tokens of plastic prettiness, Yagawa seeks a more complex understanding of what constitutes the lovely or the grotesque. She sees in Wonderland an ethos with deeper meanings than the cartoonish depictions of *moe* (Japanese slang: fascination) or *kawaii* (cuteness). As the *Gosu-Rori* demonstrate, following Yagawa, to become *Arisu* entails a performative subversion of internalized duties and generic behaviors, ones delineated by glass ceiling career limitations, scholastic pressures, or family expectations.

Although Yagawa's version of Carroll is perhaps the most prominent of its kind in contemporary Japanese literature, behind this translation is a century of tradition, which Kusumoto Kimie treats in his book-length study, *Hon'yaku no kuni no Arisu: Ruisu Kyaroru hon'yakushi, hon'yakuron* (Translating Alice's World: Lewis Carroll, a History and Critique of the Versions). Japanese translators have paid more attention to Carroll than to almost any other British author. Their methods and intentions, however, vary considerably. Indeed, the earliest attempts from the late nineteenth century can scarcely be called translations at all. They are, instead, bedtime reading directed toward very young children. Examples of this style appeared in such children's periodicals as *Shonen sekai* (A Boy's World 1895) and *Shôjo sekai* (A Girl's World 1899). These works reproduce imagery and plot elements from Carroll's original, although thoroughly reworked to suit Japanese tastes. They also stray considerably from finer aspects of the original plot.

One interesting aspect of these forerunning efforts is the extent to which they recast the Victorian cultural milieu into something more identifiably Japanese. In so doing, they may be said to investigate the ways in which Alice becomes *Arisu*, as she becomes recast according to Japanese cultural registers. For example, changing Alice's name to *Ai-chan* or *Miyo-chan* was commonplace. In fact, the foreign-sounding name *Arisu* did not become standard until the 1920s. Also, early illustrators gave *Ai-chan* Asian features and dressed her in the *kimono* or *yukata*, clothing indicative of Japanese adolescence. Although a number of translations continued to appear throughout the Taishô era (1912–1925), many of these continued to follow this derivative storybook format: heavily abridged, and highly improvisational in storyline.

Kusuyama Masao's *Fushigi no kuni* (1920) represents an attempt to render the original English word for word. However, his work, like the efforts of his less faithful predecessors, emphasizes a hybridized *Arisu*, a figure who retains Western properties augmented with elements that suggest Japaneseness. Translators like Yagawa followed these preliminary models, experimenting with how Alice/*Arisu* might be configured as an interracial identity.

For the next forty years, Wonderland—in part because it was conceived as a lexical space—was largely a matter for academics. But in the 1960s the avant-garde playwright Betsuyaku Minoru (1937–) proposed a new version of Carroll's signature space, interpreting Wonderland's dramaturgical atmosphere as a stage domain for fantastical (*fushigi-na*) theater. He thus anticipates Yagawa's theoretical formulation of Wonderland as countercultural performance. Betsuyaku's play *Fushigi no kuni no Arisu* dramatizes Wonderland as the contravening aesthetic for a new form of antiestablishment theater, within the broader movement of *gikyoku* (contemporary drama) in Japan. Premiering in the late 1960s and deeply concerned with social issues of that time, his *Fushigi no kuni no Arisu* depicts Wonderland as an operative space for interrogating normative society.

Betsuyaku's staging of the *fushigi no kuni* has little of the ornate decor found in Carroll. Act 1 begins with a bare stage, a choir chanting in the background, slowly intensifying in volume. The director's notes stipulate that their opening verses must be delivered *sôgon ongaku* (solemnly sung). Their choral dialogue is written in *katakana*, the syllabary generally reserved for representing foreign words.[3] Thus, in a conflation of English sentences and Japanese accents, they intone: "*Ai amu Arisu! Yuu aa notto Arisu! Ai amu Arisu! Yu aa notto Arisu!*" They then reassert this same point, but in Japanese: "*O-ira wa Arisu! O-mae-san wa chigau!*" (7). The action then shifts to a revised portrait of Carroll's Victorian culture, complete with shoeshiners and gravediggers, mingling in strange locations that suggest Japanese cities mixed with Dickensian decay. The character *Arisu* frequently speaks in a kind of formal Japanese almost majestic in syntax and diction, which clashes jarringly with the rough vocabulary of the world around her. *Fushigi no kuni no Arisu*'s vanishing identity theme, introduced by the opening lines, climaxes in the nightmarish final act, when she is forced by an invisible bureaucracy to undergo a hysterectomy. *Arisu* is first displaced, then exposed, and finally mutilated; but she continuously fights to recover her womb and self, hoping to birth authentic identities who will go on to defeat the homogeneous state. Betsuyaku's Wonderland is a redacted version of

Carroll's, an intersection of imaginative text, public drama, and social revolt that the playwright uses to critique a variety of concerns, from reproductive rights to the American military presence in Okinawa. In this way, Betsuyaku theorizes Wonderland as a portal to insubordination, an alternative world alive with countercultural power.

Although Yagawa Sumiko's translation of *Alice's Adventures in Wonderland* appeared relatively recently (1994), in Japan her version is highly regarded and widely read. Not only a respected translator, Yagawa is exceptionally noteworthy for her unique exposition of Wonderland as a contrary space in which individual sensibilities become disoriented and reframed. Yagawa articulates these theories of *Arisu* and her use of Wonderland as counternormative space in the essay "Usagi-ana to shôjo" (The Rabbit Hole and the Girl), which accompanies her translation. Where earlier translators discuss the technical issues of translating Carroll, Yagawa takes an entirely different strategy: she lays out an emotional manifesto that treats Wonderland as an instrument and space for therapeutic revolt.

The essay begins with an odd rhetorical question familiarly addressed to the reader: "*Anata wa honmono no usagi ni atta koto ga arimasu ka?*" (Have you ever met a real rabbit?; 176). A real rabbit, she tells us, is *yasei* (wild), not domesticated and dependent on a hand that feeds it—not caged and controlled (176). This is the same punitive situation that *Arisu* has to endure: her *nichijô-sekai* (mundane world; 177) entails the subjugation of her personality through social enforcement. Dreary hierarchies, prescriptive etiquette, and oppressive routines all act to contain her female adolescence. However, this banality of girlhood, trapped in a repetitive daylight world, is allayed through the authenticity of wildness, the energy that leads one down the rabbit hole. To emphasize this hole's importance in opening up the space of Wonderland, Yagawa selects several existentially charged words in asserting its unique power: the *usagi-ana* (rabbit hole) is a *hashiwatashi*, a bridge between two realms of being: the hegemonic and the imaginative (177). A descent through this passage involves a transformative *tsûkagirei* (rite of passage; 180). Such phrases develop Yagawa's conception of Wonderland as a destabilized domain, one that must be accessed before resistant strategies for the *honmono* (authentic) self can be actualized.

Arisu, the *shôjo* (girl), follows the *honmono no usagi* (the real rabbit) "down, down, down" the *ana* (hole; 177). This descent acts as a psychological catalyst that begins the process of negotiating the disconcerting novelties of Wonderland. Here the routine and mundane do not apply, and time and identity are free to drift: this is the realm of *fushigi*, of wonder and mystery. *Fushigi no Arisu* (Alice in wonderment) evokes performances and perceptions that are precluded by everyday *nichijô* (standards). This *fushigi* magic, Yagawa maintains, should not be dismissed as daydreaming or escapism. As her essay addresses forms of trauma among adolescents, Yagawa directs her concerns explicitly to contemporary at-risk youths in Japan who feel ashamed for being somehow unique or different, having not measured up to conventional ideals. *Fushigi*, the wonder of this new land, recontextualizes the negative emotional effects of the past into therapeutic experiences of creativity within Wonderland. In this domain, those who were formally isolated and alone find new connections and expressions to engage in a rediscovery of the *honmono* (authentic) person.

To establish a curative feeling of companionship, Yagawa makes frequent use of the informal pronoun *anata* (you) to position the reader in a face-to-face encounter with *Arisu* as a shared confidant. Yagawa states clearly that she reads *Alice's Adventures* as a haunted text, one overshadowed by a moody spirit of loneliness that is part of Alice's personal history. Yagawa's lexical choices and translational colorings reinforce a disconcerting ambience. This atmosphere, however, does not arise from Wonderland itself. Rather, the forlorn feelings are the residue of mundane social pressures—which is why, according to Yagawa, lonely, desperate individuals readily identify with *Arisu* (181). The *nichijô-sekai* (everyday world), rather than the *fushigi no kuni* (Wonderland), is responsible for *Arisu*'s confusion about herself and her own authentic purpose (180). Negotiating Wonderland means to overcome this stigma, to use *fushigi* as the alchemy of metamorphosis.

To further guide her readers into an identification with *Arisu*, Yagawa frequently uses the term *tomo no Arisu* (friend of Alice) to posit the paradigm of how to achieve interpersonal relationships with others who identify with the *fushigi* rather than the *nichijô*. What the orthodox masses judge as strange or unconventional is, in fact, wondrous, full of marvels and curiosities, and should be shared. *Arisu* reinvents her social situations through experiencing the wonders of Wonderland. Such a process reverses former impressions of being isolated and rejected. *Arisu*, therefore, offers an example that empowers the lonely and isolated (*kodoku*), leading them into a space that offers more flexible forms of acceptance: "*Shôjo Arisu towa sono yôna kodoku-na sonzai no daimeishi de ari*" (Youthful Alice has the capacity to befriend those of isolated existences; 181). Throughout her essay Yagawa argues that the personage of *Arisu* models a performative capability, particularly to

Japanese readers. More than just metaphorically sympathizing with *Arisu*, such readers can actively achieve a psychological state that embodies, or manifests, the philosophical temperament of *fushigi*, which has the power to redefine selfhood. *Arisu* is thus more than a literary character. *Arisu* is, in fact, an actualizing power, a superior identity with which one may align oneself. Through such an alliance, each individual can heal the childhood traumas of his or her own inner Alice, traumas such as loneliness and social maladjustment. By becoming connected with *Arisu*, one can network with other *Arisu*. Yagawa envisions, through the ideal of *tomo no Arisu* (friend of Alice), an alternative form of socialization within Japanese society. *Arisu*, as the explorer of Wonderland, begins as text, something read. But *becoming Arisu* means to expand the reader's experience into a performance of therapeutic transformation. Becoming *Arisu*, in a personalized form, means to refine oneself imaginatively through *Arisu*, so as to meet other *Arisu*. The *fushigi* sensibility of Wonderland thus enables a surmounting of seclusion, repression, and depression. In becoming friends with *Arisu*—and then *becoming Arisu*—new relationships will be forged, former inhibitions will be abandoned, and a novel reflexivity for evaluating relationships with self and others becomes available.

Yagawa has in mind many contemporary predicaments facing young Japanese, particularly an increase in suicides among the young. Yagawa's translation, published in the middle of the 1990s, arrived during a time of intense economic malaise in Japan that among several factors involved the collapse of financial systems, plunging property values, and the devaluation of the mechanical industries that had once propelled the market economy. The younger generation, especially, realized that they did not have the prospect of employment security. Also of concern to Yagawa is the pressure that Japanese society exerts on students through the school system, fostering a homogeneous environment that encourages distrust of the unorthodox. As the proverb says, *Deru kui wa utareru* (The nail that sticks up gets hammered down). Yagawa confronts these predicaments facing her readers, notably depressed teenagers, who are in truly terrible situations on the edges of society. For example, Yagawa addresses the victims of the widespread rise in *ijime* (bullying) throughout Japan. Increasingly frustrated, many students, unable to find acceptance or sympathy from other pupils or teachers, have gone so far as to leave school altogether (*tôkô-kyohi*). The sad development of *jisatsu sâkuru* (suicide circles), networks formed for the sole purpose of group suicide, adds urgency to the need to directly address troubled young people.

The extensive media attention given to this phenomenon culminated in the macabre horror film *Jisatsu sâkuru* (2002), whose title exploits the name for this disturbing trend. Yagawa, opposed to a generation's despair, passionately calls for those in difficult situations to not feel trampled, to not consider ending their own lives. As Betsuyaku had done previously, Yagawa points to Wonderland as an alternative, a format for questioning authority and its assessments. For Yagawa, Wonderland can lead to a restoration of faith in life, by suggesting new means for evaluating one's own self-consciousness and its negotiations with the world. In Wonderland, emotional awareness replaces emotional regulation.

Yagawa maintains that the psychological feeling of *fushigi* should be turned into physical performance, and her theories present themselves as a sociological commitment to at-risk youths. Identifying with *Arisu* through reading is one thing; but, in practice, how does one become a friend of *Arisu*? How does one become psychologically like *Arisu*, and thereby unleash repressed feelings? How are dormant imaginings awakened by Wonderland, the subterranean space of the *fushigi*? Yagawa does not offer specific instructions in this regard; but her impassioned defense of the *Arisu* mentality has been realized within Harajuku subcultures, that district of Tokyo known for social gatherings celebrating the outlandish, valuing costumed exhibitions and other expressions of the outré. In particular, the performative sensibility of *Arisu* within the *Gosu-Rori* closely enacts the kind of theoretical *Arisu*-as-resistance that Yagawa articulated. Their debt to the *fushigi* atmosphere of her translation, as well as its theoretical formulations, is widely acknowledged within their subcultural scene.

The blending of Carrollian imagery with Japanese pop culture can be documented back to the 1980s. *Akogare*—a broad term for idolized pop singers known for sentimental, girlish stage presences—frequently employed Wonderland imagery in their performances. Matsuda Seiko, a memorable example, capitalized on popular feminine trends by adopting the voice of adolescent, wistful lyricism. Her stage persona, underlined by starched ribbons and lace, sometimes featured onstage accompaniment by Red Queens and other Wonderland characters. Contemporary in feeling but resplendent in anachronistic significance, Matsuda tapped into a long-standing fascination for *meruhen* (märchen) realized through visions of old-fashioned quaintness suggesting European fairy tales. And the *manga* illustrator Ikeda Riyoko, using a similar style that also recalls the European baroque, gained enormous popularity through drawings that glorify and idealize the court society of prerevolutionary France. Examples include *Berusaiyu no bara* (The Rose of Versailles) and *Orufeusu no mado* (Orpheus's Window). Ikeda had an appealing ability to mimic Western costume and social intrigue pitched with a Japanese accent. Likewise, more recently, ethereal pop bands such as the Alice-motivated Malice Mizer fuse a Gothic-rococo persona with baroque orchestral patterns.

Emerging, in part, from these trends are the *Gosu-Rori*, whose identities are an underexamined subject and more frequently a topic for sensational travel shows that claim to expose the freaky oddities that are modern Japan.[4] Although *Gosu-Rori* defies summary definitions, this label can be broadly understood as the Japanese subculture in which women, and some men, dress in fashions derivative of Victorian children's attire, particularly as based on John Tenniel's illustrations of Carroll's *Alice* books. As their magazines assert, Alice is unquestionably the patron ideal to be emulated by the movement.[5] The *Gosu-Rori* act out their claims to alterity through an Alice-themed lifestyle, favoring settings and accessories that enhance the visibility of Wonderland as the locus of their countercultural collectivity. British-themed tearooms, parasols, petticoats, pinafores, and other items recreate Victorian models. Harajuku, a district in Tokyo known for its cutting-edge fashion, is their central meeting area. As neo-*Arisu*, the *Gosu-Rori*, through clothing, paraphernalia, and visual performance, invoke the space of Wonderland as the presence of an alternatively aesthetic imagination, one that contrasts with the urban landscape of contemporary Japan and its homogeneity.

The birth of the *Gosu-Rori* subculture coincided directly with the publication of Yagawa's translation in the 1990s. Their inspiration is profoundly Carrollian in influence, and through their artistic networks they act out Yagawa's theory of *becoming Arisu*. Wonderland, to them, allows for that recovered space in which one finds free expression through subversive modes of dress and other identifications that actualize and proclaim the *fushigi*. Imitating Alice disrupts or transcends the anonymity of their *nichijô-sekai* (everyday world), uniform patterns determined by governing institutions: schools, corporate offices, and so forth. The *Gosu-Rori* spectacle of Wonderland—as demonstrated through modes of costumed contravention and role play—makes visible the psychological shift of becoming *Arisu*. Through *Arisu*, the mundane becomes reclaimed through stylistic intervention. Wonderland acts as a code name for a sensibility of the *fushigi* and its atmospheric space.

The *Gosu-Rori*, operating through a persona fashioned on *Arisu*, are doing more than imitating illustrations. They design, with like-minded individuals, a self-governing network devoted to acceptance and self-empowerment.

Using Wonderland to critique social assumptions as to what is pretty, ugly, or normal was one of Yagawa's goals as a translator. Her version of *Fushigi no kuni no Arisu* frequently refers to the act of *misekakezan* (the calculation of appearances). This term, her neologism, describes those procedures that label one as ugly, as well as demanding a particular kind of repentance through *omekashi* (to make or become pretty in a trendy way). *Misekake* can mean to fashion a facade or pretense. Yagawa combines *kakezan* (arithmetic) with *miseru* (to show) in an ingenious coinage that foregrounds the computational construction of beauty. In this way of judging, ugliness, or its counterpart beauty, results from calculated assessment and group consensus rather than intuition or personal expression. Ugliness or beauty, therefore, asserts a result supposedly reached through objective evaluations. But Wonderland space resists such regulatory presumptions, restoring a more subjective sense of what is beautiful. In this regard, *fushigi*, through its power of Gothic alterity, upsets the beautiful/ugly binary upon which *misekakezan* relies. The strange adolescent actually manages to move outside the normal definitions of the beautiful or the weird. And, on this principle, the *Gosu-Rori* enthusiasts find in Carroll a release from the prescriptive discomfort of judgmental society. Yagawa's *Arisu* exemplifies how to reject the above-world standards, and how to seek instead reframed experiences that will not be so readily assessed and rejected by the mainstream.

The *Gosu-Rori* affiliation with Yagawa's version of Carroll is readily apparent in the periodicals and essays produced by this subculture. Yagawa's translations are the most cited, most preferred, and most esteemed. Glossy magazines such as *Goshikku & rorîta baiburu* (Gothic & Lolita Bible) acknowledge their affinity for Carroll by way of Yagawa.[6] Their behavior, after all, puts Yagawa's theory into practice: physically embodying through self-illustration the images and themes that Wonderland represents. This self-actualizing role play of the *Gosu-Rori* enacts a countercultural mutiny and overturns normative models of behavior. Although their attire and behavior may seem stereotypically feminine, their mode of fashion is undeniably outrageous and challenging, particularly in opposition to prescriptive roles such as OL (office lady) or *yamato nadeshiko* (old-fashioned Japanese girlhood). Moreover, gender norms are in fact frequently broken in their circles, as cross-dressing is explored and accepted. Participants are accepted for whatever gender image they choose to present: male, female, or variations that unbalance such distinctions.

A case in point is the androgynous Takemoto Novara, the most widely publicized spokesman for the *Gosu-Rori*. He emphasizes the transformative capability of the subculture in his novels and articles.[7] In his view, this movement enacts the freedom of *fushigi* as proclaimed within Carroll's world: Wonderland space becomes therapeutically helpful because personalized interpretations of its themes allow new perspectives. One can do more than just *read Arisu*, but *invoke Arisu*, embracing the space of the fantastic within contemporary social geography. Takemoto describes how the love of Carroll's classic book can lead one to networks of like-minded people and the camaraderie and acceptance that unites them. Many followers of Carroll identify closely with the *fushigi*, even though this makes them appear weird or ridiculous to mainstream society. Rather than feeling shame, through actualizing *Arisu* in the personality, marginalized youth can reclaim *fushigi* and rediscover innocence and wonder in the world.[8]

Yagawa's Wonderland is, therefore, distinct from the many *anime* and *manga* versions of *Fushigi no kuni no Arisu* that are also popular in Japan. Yagawa's hands-on approach to becoming *Arisu* in the everyday is very different from the kinds of virtual versions of *Arisu* as depicted in digital media. Konaka Chiaki is a leading example from among more than a dozen *Arisu*-inspired authors and directors of *manga* and *anime*.[9] He specializes in *Arisu* as an apparition of Victorian fantasy interfaced with futuristic technologies. As a symbol of the human encountering unknown digital worlds, Konaka's cyborg-like *Arisu* represents the condition of crossing the boundary between the physical and the cybernetic.[10] His complex *anime* series *Serial Experiments Lain*, first broadcast on TV Tokyo in 1998, explores the permeability of such divisions between flesh and circuit. One of this program's main characters is a postmodern *Arisu* wearing a black frock who roams a matrix network of cybernetic realities that are contiguous with the city of Yokohama. Konaka's *Arisu* has become interconnected with the *Wonderland of Wired*, a vast computer matrix that assimilates mortal existence into UNIX code.[11] Another example of a digital *Arisu* is found in the comic book *Alice in Cyberland* (Glam, 1997), which depicts gang warfare between rival factions in an electronic reality of neon and superheroes. Alice appears on the scene as a *shôjo* soldier taking on criminal technology.[12] In their content and purpose, these examples, which loosely renarrativize Alice according to the technological, have more in common with the themes of science-fiction *anime* in general, rather than relating to Carroll specifically.

Such films, television programs, and comic books emphasize the virtual *Arisu* over the tactile, the kind of digitized feminine that Susan Napier documents. These techno-*Arisu* tend to be favored by masculine-oriented *otaku* audiences, interested in a virtual fantasy of girlhood.[13] Conversely, the *Gosu-Rori*, as inspired by Yagawa, are driven not only to *visualize* the *fushigi* but to *become* the *fushigi*: the psychological and corporeal immersion of oneself into *Arisu*. This identity is achieved through tangible integration with *Arisu*, as an identity performance, aligning oneself with a visible subculture. Wonderland is not a remote, digital screen, but a subspace within commonplace materiality. To emphasize the importance of this immersing of selfhood into the *fushigi*, as a means of overcoming a poor self-image, Yagawa writes, "*Soredewa dôzo anata mo semete goissho ni atatakai manazashi o shôjo kara sorasazu kodoku-na michiyuki o saigo made mimamotte yatte kudasai masuyôni*" (All of you, at least, together can give a favorable gaze upon this girl [Alice]. Don't let your attention drift from her. Please care for her as she walks her lonely path; 181).

The one walking the lonely path is, of course, the Japanese reader becoming *Arisu*, a process modeled by Kaneko Kuniyoshi's illustrations accompanying Yagawa's translation, which depict the hybridity of an Alice turned into *Arisu*. In his sketches, which echo as well as revise Tenniel's, Kaneko minimizes background details, conveying feelings of incompleteness and vagueness. The sparse settings seem mysterious, but not entirely otherworldly. And while *Arisu*'s eyes are drawn in a significantly angular fashion, suggesting Asian features, because faces are rendered minimally, the viewer is invited to add personal details. Through suggesting Victorian scenes as well as Japanese environs, and representing Alice/*Arisu* as an interracial figure, Kaneko's illustrations provide Japanese-specific models for imitation.

Today, in the district of Harajuku, Wonderland is a password into environments where the fairy tale of Wonderland and costumed role playing are promoted. For example, several Wonderland-themed tea shops offer the *Gosu-Rori* a Wonderland ambience: plush chairs, a dozen different variations of Earl Grey tea, and plum puddings named after characters from Carroll's novel. Cafés such as Tearoom Alice and Café de Alice in Tokyo clearly announce their Wonderland proclivities. These *fushigi no kuni no kissa* (Wonderland teahouses), which welcome props and fancy dress, are a completely different environment from the notorious *meido* café, where voyeuristic men ogle compliant hostess-maids who submit to them as to returning house masters. In contrast, the patrons of the *Arisu* tea shops are primarily female, or sometimes men in women's clothes, as is the style of Takemoto. Costumes are encouraged, if not expected, for both staff and patrons. Services never include the forms of mild erotica entirely prominent in the *meido* café. Indeed, such activities would be entirely inappropriate, as they do not represent the mood of the *Gosu-Rori*. They place emphasis, instead, on attaining a propriety of cordial acceptance, as well as a protective sense of comfort and well-being. Nothing should interfere with, nor harm, their genteel eccentricity. Customers are free to enjoy their leisure time in quiet, knowing that they are in like-minded company and will not be bullied or gawked at.

These cozy teahouses of Tokyo are a few of many examples of how Wonderland, reconfigured as a subcultural space, has expanded into the Japanese urban landscape. Wonderland-themed restaurants also operate according to a fantasy-friendly etiquette that ensures an authentic, supportive ambience for their patrons. Harajuku is pocketed with rabbit-hole boutiques that offer Alice-embossed apparel and Victorian clothes, books, patterns for costumes, and other accessories. The networks of Wonderland participants thrive in situations such as these, wherein their alternative modes of identity performance will be enhanced and encouraged. Through such imaginative engineering, their Wonderlands find a home and family in *fushigi*-enhanced scenarios.

Yagawa argues that it is exactly this sort of interaction that is essential to understanding the contemporary Japanese meaning of Wonderland. In order for the dislocated *Arisu* of Japan to surmount their feelings of seclusion and low self-esteem, they need to relate to others who understand and share their experiences. But Yagawa never claims that such a transition from the passively marginal to the assertively social comes easily. Indeed, she notes that the confusion and nonsense of Carroll's Wonderland results, in part, from *Arisu*'s unhappy childhood experiences above ground. In this view, Carroll's text highlights the emotional experience of alienated children, externalizing their social phobias and the difficulties of interpersonal connections. *Arisu* must overcome the suppression of her personal expressiveness: "*Komyunikêshon mo naritatanai hentekorin-na mono bakari*" (Communication doesn't become something peculiar only; 180). Communication involves recognizing one's problems. Thus, the apparent illogic of Wonderland must be understood as an extension of *Arisu*'s own socially distressed psyche, an inherited condition applicable to Victorian England as well as contemporary Japan.

Yagawa depicts the inhibitory prescripts of Japanese society by mocking their rules embedded in language practices. Through Carroll's characters, Yagawa satirizes the contrived discourse of business Japanese as used in the corporate world. For example, she presents a Dodo who rattles on in a sanctimonious Tokyo dialect. Using Wonderland as her medium, Yagawa lampoons many different normative conventions, rebuking the hypocrisy of their supposedly proper behavior, their formalities in communication, and their intrinsic hierarchies. Yagawa's Eaglet cannot, in fact, tolerate such forms of rehearsed rhetoric. To him, artificial politeness masks the hidden processes of linguistic constraint and control. Exasperated, he screams out against them in a heavily idiomatic, and semantically innovative, phrase: "*Chinpunkanpun wa yametekure*" (Gibberish! Just stop!; 40). In rejecting what constitutes formulaic conversation, Yagawa points out that authentic communication requires one to shift away from dependencies on routine, superficial discourse. *Fushigi* exposes those patterns. Its atmosphere, which at first seemed nonsensical, can now result in empowered articulation.

Fushigi is thus a philosophy and program of psychological and social resistance. And though the *Gosu-Rori* version of Wonderland may appear quaintly trivial or nostalgic to some, through Yagawa's eyes anyone who seeks Arisu is earnestly and courageously engaged. This is so because Yagawa's understanding of Wonderland arises from, and is connected to, tensions, traumas, and other difficult social realities in contemporary Japan. Many of the *Arisu* of the *Gosu-Rori* take long subway rides from the suburbs to Harajuku. Their *normal* selves exist in acres of cramped quarters and monochrome concrete, where privacy is often unavailable. Their interpersonal lives are often horrible: they are frequently victims of *ijime* (bullying), having been marked out as social outcasts. These *Arisu* typically do not enjoy the more acceptable forms of activity for their age group, such as sports, or those *traditional* Japanese arts, such as after-school tea ceremony clubs. In opposition to these normative practices, their *Arisu* attire, paraded publicly, declares the *fushigi* before the crowds of the metropolis, and the institutions and expectations they represent. By enacting these Wonderland identities in the social sphere of the everyday, members of this subculture reject uniformity through a literary theatricality. Dedicated time and effort is required to sew and design *Arisu* clothing and to make Wonderland props; but these efforts, in a tactile way, coincide with deeply personal work in healing psychological damage.

Yagawa composed her translation as a response to the dilemma of depression and alienation in segments of Japanese society. To become *Arisu* means to operate according to the spirit of *fushigi* as it redefines the ways in which one may negotiate the complex terrain of Japanese identity. Yagawa's essay details specifically how disaffected personalities can find in *fushigi* a tactic for rejecting oppressive codes. From theory to performance, Yagawa's design of a therapeutic revolt has become a subculture of dramatic self-examination. *Arisu* leads the *Gosu-Rori* down the rabbit hole and into a countercultural subspace that contravenes generic versions of Japan. The *Gosu-Rori* versions of *Arisu* are fashioned into forms of rebellion, which may be inserted directly into the public view of a regimented society. What may otherwise appear hallucinatory or outlandish about Wonderland is actually emboldening for its participants.

Carroll's novel has become all the more compelling due to these Japanese contexts. The Harajuku spectacle of the *Gosu-Rori*'s performance within their *fushigi no kuni* continues to expand, psychologically endowing its participants with a recovered sense of the fantastic. In this way, Yagawa's theory of counternormative Wonderland has become translated into sociological reality, through engaged and engaging subcultural interventions.

NOTES

1. Japanese names are given in the traditional format: family name first. All translations are my own.
2. Yagawa Sumiko (1931–2002) found much recognition for her translations of Western classics, including works from Louisa May Alcott, Johanna Spyri, and the Grimm brothers. An English translation of Yagawa's retelling of the *mukashibanashi* (folktale) *Tsuru nyôbô* (*The Crane Wife*) has recently been published. Her last book, which examined the life and works of Anaïs Nin, was titled *Anaisu Nin no shôjo jidai* (The Girlhood of Anaïs Nin). Sadly, Yagawa committed suicide on 29 May 2002—the day before the publication of this final book.
3. Yagawa, to emphasize the interculturality of *Arisu*, sometimes presents Alice/*Arisu* through a typified form of exaggerated *gaijin* (foreigner) style speech. On occasion, Yagawa's *Arisu* speaks Japanese through *katakana* for an entire sentence, even though absolutely proper Japanese words are being said. As

katakana is the alphabet primarily employed to accommodate loanwords, Alice's foreignness and exotic qualities are hyperbolized. These hybridized convergences of cultural identifiers can be found occasionally in Japanese writing, in texts such as Betsuyaku's, as well as *Doraemon* comics, or Tachibana Sotô's novels.

4. Too frequently, television programs, travel articles, and newspapers represent *Gosu-Rori* performance as psychosexual fetishism, rarely examining the personal histories of those involved. In this way, mainstream media propagate stereotypes of Japan as an inscrutable world of bizarre people, with the *Gosu-Rori* presenting a virulent pedophilia and submissive infantilism particular to that nation. See Parker for an informative exception. Contributors to *Gosu-Rori* forums, such as magazines and blogs, express great offense at any such sexual sensationalizing.
5. For a visual sense of *Gosu-Rori* style, see the following Web sites. These two are operated by premier clothing retailers (although many *Gosu-Rori* prefer to design their own fashions): http://www.victorianmaiden.com and http://www.angelicpretty.com. And this one belongs to an *Alice in Wonderland* costume café in Ginza: http://www.diamond-dining.com/alice/.
6. See, in particular, volume 18 for an extensive assessment of *Fushigi no kuni no Arisu*.
7. Takemoto's novel *Shimotsuma monogatari* (2002), known misleadingly in English as *Kamikaze Girls*, became a best seller in Japan, as well as a popular movie, highly regarded for its blunt depiction of marginalized Japanese youths living in parochial towns. Some of Takemoto's many essays on *Gosu-Rori* philosophy, including thoughts on gender, etiquette, social stigmas, and fashion, can be found in English translations: http://www.curiosityvalentine.com/archive.html. Recently arrested for cannabis possession (September 2007), a serious crime in Japan, his subcultural visibility and following have together rapidly declined.
8. In the early twentieth century, notions of the *daraku jogakusei* (degenerate schoolgirl) circulated with popularity, exacerbating nationalist concerns for a decline in the younger generation's morals. Melanie Czarnecki and Inoue Mariko have documented the operation of this theme in Japanese print culture, particularly in the works of Hiratsuka Raichô. Similarly, media depictions of the *Gosu-Rori* now repeat this *daraku* rhetoric of moral panic: the *Gosu-Rori*, with their oddball apparel and bizarre behavior, are symptomatic of some broader vice in young Japanese women. Yagawa notes that the status quo will often interpret rebellion as degeneration, refusing to acknowledge the deeper issues of disaffection.
9. For a detailed study of Konaka's depictions of "virtual femininity," as derived in part from *Alice in Wonderland*, see Margherita Long.
10. *Fushigi no kuni no Miyuki-chan* (Kadokawa-shoten, 1995) is the illustrated story of Miyuki, an Alice-like surrogate who crosses over into a variety of parallel worlds, including one that is a conflation of an English Wonderland with a realm

known as Mah Jong Land. Chess pieces battle it out in mass conflict with mah jong tiles. Sexual content, including mild sadomasochism, is highlighted in such texts, which tend to be preferred by *otaku*. Such works are never reviewed by *Gosu-Rori* journals and magazines.

11. Other examples include *Kagihime monogatari: eikyû Alice rondo* (The Key-Princess's Story: Endless Alice Rondo; Trinet Entertainment, 2006) and *Mahô shôjo tai Arisu* (Alice's Witchling Coven; Studio 40, 2004). Both stories depict Alice as endowed with supernatural powers.
12. Murakami Takashi, a contemporary painter, created a thematic series of sketches, sculptures, and paintings centered on the theme *DOB's Adventures in Wonderland* (1999). DOB is a childish cyborg, cute in his pixilated colors, and a prototype of the *otaku*, someone who dabbles in fantasy, imagination, and erotica. The Carrollian informs Murakami's exhibit indirectly, and DOB demonstrates how Wonderland acts as a freely conceptualized notion of fantasy, one that suggests futuristic trends in Japanese art.
13. A contrast must be drawn between the *otaku* environment of the *meido kissa* (maid café) or *meido* café and the Alice tearooms of *Gosu-Rori*, as these two spaces are frequently conflated in Western media. As the name *meido kissa* implies, these establishments feature young women wearing uniforms stereotypical of Victorian maids, who act out a pantomime of servitude for their exclusively male patrons. This is a form of titillating playacting, in which men are the lords of the manor, and the maids curtsy and respond to their every whim. No attempt is made on the part of the viewer to assume a fantastic role himself; he keeps the clothing and other generic trappings of his routine social identity, along with the dominant status and prestige that it entails. The uniformed maids denote quintessential feminine subservience and concession to a temporary, erotic fantasy. Japanese newspapers—see Saho, for example—have frequently investigated such locations. In fact, concern is growing that many of these establishments are becoming fronts for soft-core prostitution where South Asian migrant workers are exploited.

WORKS CITED

Betsuyaku Minoru. *Fushigi no kuni no Arisu*. Tokyo: San'ichi shobô, 1970.

Carroll, Lewis. *Fushigi no kuni no Arisu*. Trans. Yagawa Sumiko. Tokyo: Shinchôsha, 1994.

———. *Fushigi no kuni no Arisu*. Trans. Yanase Naoki. Tokyo: Chikuma bunko, 1988.

Cooper, John Xiros. *Modernism and the Culture of Market Society*. Cambridge: Cambridge University Press, 2004.

Czarnecki, Melanie. "Bad Girls from Good Families: The Degenerate Meiji Schoolgirl." *Bad Girls of Japan: Historical and Contemporary Models of Transgressing Women*. Ed. Jan Bardsley and Laura Miller. New York: Palgrave, 2005. 49–64.

Goshikku & rorîta baiburu. Vols. 1–28. Tokyo: Indekkusu MOOK, 2000–2008.
Inoue Mariko. "Kiyokata's Asasuzu: The Emergence of the *Jogakusei* Image." *Monumenta Nipponica* 51 (Winter 1996): 431–60.
Kusumoto Kimie. *Hon'yaku no kuni no Arisu: Ruisu Kyaroru hon'yakushi, hon'yakuron.* Tokyo: Michitani, 2001.
Kusuyama Masao. *Fushigi no kuni. Sekai shônen bungaku meisakushû.* Vol. 9. Tokyo: Katei yomimono kankô-kai, 1920.
Long, Margherita. "Malice@Doll: Konaka, Specularization, and the Virtual Feminine." *Mechademia* 2 (Fall 2007). Accessed 25 Jul. 2008. http://www.complitforlang.ucr.edu/people/faculty/long/malice@doll.pdf.
Napier, Susan. "Vampires, Psychic Girls, Flying Women, and Sailor Scouts: Four Faces of the Young Female in Japanese Popular Culture." *The Worlds of Japanese Popular Culture.* Ed. D. P. Martinez. Cambridge: Cambridge University Press, 1998. 91–109.
Parker, Ginny. "The Little Girl Look Is Big in Japan Now." *Wall Street Journal* 17 Sept. 2004: A1.
Saho Yôko. "'*Moe*': *Rikaido akihabara nami?*" *Yomiuri shinbun* 23 June 2006: 5.
Yagawa Sumiko. "Usagi-ana to shôjo." *Fushigi no kuni no Arisu.* Lewis Carroll. Trans. Yagawa Sumiko. Tokyo: Shinchôsha, 1994. 176–81.

Contributors

Rachel Falconer is Professor of Modern and Contemporary Literature at the University of Sheffield. Widely published on twentieth-century literature, including Primo Levi and Salman Rushdie, Falconer is the author of *Hell in Contemporary Literature: Western Descent Narratives since 1945* (2005). An authority on works that are enjoyed and found meaningful by both children and adults, she most recently published *The Crossover Novel: Contemporary Children's Fiction and Its Adult Readership* (2008).

Cristopher Hollingsworth is Associate Professor of English at the University of South Alabama. He is the author of *Poetics of the Hive: The Insect Metaphor in Literature* (2001) and more recently an article demonstrating Lewis Carroll's influence on H. G. Wells's science fiction. He is currently writing a book on Wonderland and the twentieth century.

Steve Hooley works in the library at Georgia Southern University. He was born in the summer of 1954 and lives in Statesboro, Georgia, with his wife and son. As a lifelong reader of science fiction and fantasy, he has a huge number of books cluttering his house. He is a long-time attendee of the International Association for the Fantastic in the Arts (IAFA) conferences.

Karoline Leach is the author of *In the Shadow of the Dreamchild: The Myth and Reality of Lewis Carroll*, which helped to begin the current debate on the nature of Carroll's biography.

Carol Mavor is Professor of Art History and Visual Studies at the University of Manchester. Mavor is the author of three books: *Reading Boyishly: Roland Barthes, J. M. Barrie, Jacques Henri Lartigue, Marcel Proust, and D. W. Winnicott* (2007); *Becoming: The Photographs of Clementina, Viscountess Hawarden* (1999); and *Pleasures Taken: Performances of Sexuality and Loss in Victorian Photographs* (1995). Her work has been widely acknowledged and reviewed in publications in the United States and the United Kingdom, including the *Times Literary Supplement*, the *Los Angeles Times*, and the

Village Voice. Currently, she is finishing a novel entitled *FULL*, a book entitled *Black and Blue* (on Roland Barthes, Chris Marker, Alain Resnais, and Marguerite Duras), and a series of short essays on the color blue entitled *Blue Thoughts*.

Franz Meier currently holds the Chair of English Literature and Culture at the University of Braunschweig. His publications include *Die frühe Ding-Lyrik William Carlos Williams: Genese und Poetologie* (William Carlos Williams's Early Poetry of Things: Development and Poetics; 1991) and *Sexualität und Tod: Eine Themenverknüpfung in der englischen Schauer- und Sensationsliteratur und ihrem soziokulturellen Kontext, 1764–1897* (Sexuality and Death: A Combination of Themes in English Gothic and Sensation Fiction and Its Sociocultural Context, 1764–1897; 2002), as well as a number of articles on Gothic fiction, Victorian culture, Oscar Wilde, James Joyce, and (post)modern English and American poetry. His recent research is focused on the fields of gender studies, popular culture, and intermediality (text/image relationships).

Stephen Monteiro is an assistant professor at the American University of Paris, where he teaches visual culture and media. He received a PhD in art history and aesthetics from the University of Paris, Panthéon-Sorbonne, in 2007 and has written on photography, cinema, and contemporary art for numerous publications.

Helen Pilinovsky recently received her PhD in English and comparative literature from Columbia University, where she worked on issues of translation and genre formation in the realm of the fairy tale. Her dissertation is titled *Fantastic Emigres: Translation and Acculturation of the Fairy Tale in a Literary Diaspora*. She is now an assistant professor at California State University, San Bernardino. Her reviews have appeared in *Marvels & Tales: Journal of Fairy Tale Studies* and the *New York Review of Science Fiction*, and she has been published at the *Endicott Studio for the Mythic Arts*, in *Realms of Fantasy* magazine, and in a selection of academic journals. She has guest-edited issues of the *Journal of the Fantastic in the Arts* and *Extrapolations*, and she is the academic editor of *Cabinet des Fées*. Her interests include fairy tales, folklore, and the fantastic, as well as teaching, arguing literary theory, and silversmithing.

Christine Roth is Associate Professor of English at the University of Wisconsin, Oshkosh. She has written several essays on Barrie and Carroll, including the recent "Babes in Boyland: J. M. Barrie and the Edwardian Girl," which appears in *J. M. Barrie's Peter Pan In and Out of Time: A Children's*

Classic at 100 (2006). She is currently completing a book on cult of the little girl narratives in late Victorian England.

Rudy Rucker is a writer and a mathematician who worked for twenty years as a Silicon Valley computer science professor. He is regarded as a contemporary master of science fiction and received the Philip K. Dick award twice. His thirty published books include both novels and nonfiction books. Rucker's most recent pair of novels depict a near-future Earth in which every object becomes conscious. The first, *Postsingular,* appeared in fall 2007 and is also available for free download on the Web. The second, *Hylozoic,* appeared in 2009. His Alice-like adventures, *Mathematicians in Love* and *Spaceland,* are available in paperback. See his Web site for more information: http://www.rudyrucker.com.

Sean Somers is a Lecturer in the English Department at the University of British Columbia. His dissertation, now revised into a monograph under consideration, examined literary networks between Ireland and Japan in the early twentieth century. He has published, or has forthcoming, several articles that study various intersections of literary cultures between Japan and Europe, as well as translations of contemporary Japanese poetry.

Elizabeth Throesch is a Lecturer in English Literature at Leeds St. John University. She is currently working on a book-length study of the work of Charles Howard Hinton and the impact of hyperspace philosophy on a number of writers and thinkers at the turn of the century.

Anne Witchard is a Lecturer at the University of Westminster. Her book, *Thomas Burke's Dark Chinoiserie: Limehouse Nights and the Queer Spell of Chinatown,* is forthcoming.

Mou-Lan Wong is a DPhil candidate in English language and literature at St. Anne's College, Oxford. He is currently completing his dissertation on the nonsense works of Edward Lear and Charles Lutwidge Dodgson.

Index